W9-CZW-587

SHADOW MUSIC

SHADOW MUSIC

A Novel

JULIE GARWOOD

**Doubleday Large Print
Home Library Edition**

BALLANTINE BOOKS NEW YORK

Published in the United States by Ballantine Books, an imprint of The Random House Publishing Group, a division of Random House, Inc., New York.

BALLANTINE and colophon are registered trademarks of Random House, Inc.

ISBN 978-0-7394-9138-6

Printed in the United States of America on acid-free paper

**This Large Print Book carries the
Seal of Approval of N.A.V.H.**

To
Kendra Elyse Garwood
for all the joy and love you've added
to our family.
You are a treasure.

The wicked flee when no man pursueth: but the righteous are bold as a lion.

PROVERBS 28:1

Prologue

ONCE UPON A TIME IN THE YEAR OF THE VIOLENT storms that tore in from the sea, the first horde of warriors from a distant land came across our mountains and onto our shores. With steel weapons strapped to their chests and burnished armor glistening like shards of glass in the midday sun, they marched in pairs for as far as the eye could see. They did not ask permission nor care that they trespassed. Nay, they were on a quest, and nothing would get in their way. Crossing our fair land, they took our horses and our food, trampled our crops, used our women, and killed many of our fine men. They left destruction in their wake . . . all in the name of God.

They called themselves Crusaders. They fervently believed that their mission was holy and good because they had been told so by the pope, who blessed them and commanded them to journey to the other side of the world. They were to vanquish the infidels and force them to embrace their God and their religion. If the heathens refused, the soldiers were to kill them with their holy and blessed swords.

The pass through our mountains was the only route that would take the Crusaders forward on their quest, so they marched across it in legions, and once they reached the harbor on the other side of the mountains, they stole our ships to sail across the sea toward their destination.

Our small country was then called Monchanceux. We were ruled by our uncle, the benevolent King Grenier. He was a man who loved his homeland and wanted to protect it. We were not a rich country, but we were content. We had enough. When the invading horde stole from us, our king was enraged, but he did not allow anger to guide his hand. Because he was such a clever ruler, King Grenier came upon a solution.

He would make the next group of invaders pay a toll to cross over the mountain. Since the pass was so narrow, it could easily be defended. Our soldiers were conditioned to the cold and the snow and the bitter night winds. They could protect the ridge for months at a time, and winter fast approached.

The leader of these righteous invaders was outraged at the notion of paying for anything. He and his men were on a holy mission. He threatened to kill every soul in Monchanceux, including women and children, if he and his men were denied passage. Were King Grenier and his subjects in the good graces of the church, or were they heathens standing in the way of the Lord's work? The answer would determine their fate.

It was at that very moment that our good and wise king embraced religion. He told the leader of the army that he and all his subjects were just as holy, and he would prove it beyond any doubt.

He called forth the people of Monchanceux and addressed them from the balcony of the palace. The leader of the crusading army stood behind him.

"From this day forward our country will be

called St. Biel in honor of my family's patron saint. He is the protector of the innocent," King Grenier announced. "We will build statues of St. Biel and paint his image on the doors to our cathedral so that anyone who comes to our shores will know of his goodness, and we will send tribute to the pope to show our sincerity and our humility. The toll I collect will pay for this tribute."

The leader of the traveling throng found himself in a predicament. If he refused to pay the toll—in gold, of course, for the king would accept nothing less—then wouldn't he be refusing to allow the king to give tribute to the pope? And if the pope got wind that the Crusader had refused, what would the pontiff do? Excommunicate him? Execute him?

After a long night of contemplation and a good deal of ranting and raving, the military leader decided to pay the toll. It was a momentous occasion, for a precedent was set, and from that moment on, every Crusader desiring passage through our lands paid the toll without question.

Our king was true to his word. He had the gold melted down and made into coins, and upon each one was the image of St. Biel, a halo above his head.

The royal treasury had to be expanded to make room for all the gold coins, and a ship was prepared for the voyage to deliver the offering to the Holy Father. One day huge, heavy crates were loaded into the ship's cargo hold, and a crowd of citizens gathered at the harbor to watch the vessel depart for Rome. Shortly after that historic day, rumors began to spread. No one could verify that he had actually seen the gold or could estimate how much was sent. Several ambassadors claimed that only a pittance reached the pope. The talk of our king's vast fortune swelled and then receded like the tide lapping at our shores.

Eventually a quicker route to the Holy Land was discovered, and the Crusaders no longer tramped through our country. We were grateful for the solitude.

We were not, however, left in peace. Every few years someone arrived looking for the now-legendary gold. A baron from England came, for his king had heard the rumor, but after our ruler allowed him to make a thorough search of the palace and the grounds, the baron told him that he would return to England with the news: there was no treasure to be found. Because King

Grenier had been so hospitable, the baron warned him that Prince John of England was considering invading St. Biel. John, the baron explained, wanted to rule the world and was impatiently waiting to take over England's crown. The baron had no doubt that St. Biel would soon become yet another possession of England.

The invasion came one year later. Once St. Biel officially belonged to England, the search for the hidden gold resumed. Witnesses swore there was no rock left unturned.

If there had ever been a treasure, it had vanished.

SHADOW MUSIC

ONE

WELLINGSHIRE, ENGLAND

PRINCESS GABRIELLE WAS BARELY SIX YEARS OLD when she was summoned to her mother's deathbed. Escorting her was her faithful guard, two soldiers on either side, their gait slow so she could keep up with them as they solemnly made their way down the long corridor. The only sound was their boots clicking against the cold stone floor.

Gabrielle had been called to her mother's deathbed so many times she'd lost count.

As she walked, she kept her head bowed, staring intently at the shiny rock she'd found. Mother was going to love it. It was black with a tiny white streak zigzagging all around it.

One side was as smooth as her mother's hand when she stroked the side of Gabrielle's face. The rock's other side was as rough as her papa's whiskers.

Every day at sunset Gabrielle brought her mother a different treasure. Two days ago she'd captured a butterfly. It had such pretty wings, gold with purple splotches. Mother declared it was the most beautiful butterfly she'd ever seen. She praised Gabrielle for being so gentle with one of God's creatures as she walked to the window and let it fly away.

Yesterday Gabrielle had gathered flowers from the hill outside the castle walls. The scent of heather and honey had surrounded her, and she thought the lovely aroma even more pleasing than her mother's special oils and perfumes. Gabrielle had tied a pretty ribbon around the stems and tried to fashion a nice bow, but she didn't know how and she'd made a mess of it. The ribbon had come undone before she handed the bouquet to her mother.

Rocks were Mother's favorite treasures. She kept a basketful that Gabrielle had collected for her on a table next to her bed, and she would love this rock most of all.

Gabrielle wasn't worried about today's visit. Her mother had promised that she wouldn't go away to heaven any time soon, and she never broke her promises.

The sun cast shadows along the stone walls and floor. If Gabrielle hadn't been on an errand with her rock, she would have liked to chase the shadows and try to capture one. The long corridor was one of her favorite places to play. She loved to hop on one foot from one stone to another and see how far she could get before falling. She hadn't made it to the second arched window yet, and there were five more windows to go.

Sometimes she closed her eyes, stretched her arms out wide, and spun and spun until she lost her balance and tumbled to the floor, so dizzy the walls seemed to fly about her head.

Most of all, she loved to run down the corridor, especially when her father was home. He was such a big, grand man, taller than any of the pillars in the church. Her papa would call to her and wait until she reached him. Then he scooped her up into his arms and lifted her high above his head. If they were in the courtyard, she raised her hands to the sky, certain she could almost touch a cloud. Papa always pretended to lose his grip so that she would think he was about to drop her. She knew he never would, but she squealed with delight over the possibility. She wrapped her arms around his neck and held tight as he strode toward her mother's rooms. When he was in an especially happy mood he would sing. Papa had a terrible singing voice, and sometimes Gabrielle giggled and covered her ears it was so awful, but she never really laughed. She didn't want to hurt his tender feelings.

Papa wasn't at home today. He had left Wellingshire to visit his uncle Morgan in northern England, and he wouldn't be home for several days. Gabrielle wasn't concerned. Mother wouldn't die without him by her side.

Stephen, the leader of the guards, opened the door to her mother's chamber and coaxed Gabrielle to enter by giving her a gentle little nudge between her shoulder blades. "Go on, Princess," he urged.

She turned around with a disgruntled frown. "Papa says you're to call my mama Princess Genevieve, and you're supposed to call me Lady Gabrielle."

"Here in England, you are Lady Gabrielle,"

He tapped the crest emblazoned on his tunic, "But in St. Biel, you are our princess. Now go, your mother is waiting."

Seeing Gabrielle, her mother called out. Her voice was weak, and she looked terribly pale. For as long as Gabrielle could remember, her mother had stayed in bed. Her legs had forgotten how to walk, she'd explained to Gabrielle, but she was hopeful, praying that they would one day remember. If that miracle were to happen, she promised Gabrielle that she would stand barefoot in the clear stream to gather stones with her daughter.

And she would dance with Papa, too.

The chamber was crowded with people. They made a narrow path for her. The priest, Father Gartner, was chanting his prayer in a low whisper near the alcove, and the royal physician, who always frowned and liked to make her mother bleed with his black, slimy bugs, was also in attendance. Gabrielle was thankful he hadn't put any bugs on her mother's arms today.

The maids, the stewards, and the house-keeper hovered beside the bed. Mother put down her tapestry and needle, shooed the servants away, and motioned to Gabrielle.

"Come and sit with me," she ordered.

Gabrielle ran across the room, climbed up onto the platform, and thrust the rock at her mother.

"Oh, it's beautiful," she whispered as she took the rock and carefully examined it. "This is the best one yet," she added with a nod.

"Mother, you say that every time I bring you a rock. It's always the best one."

Her mother patted a spot next to her. Gabrielle scooted closer and said, "You can't die today. Remember? You promised."

"I remember."

"Papa will be awful angry, too, so you better not."

"Lean closer, Gabrielle," her mother said. "I have need to whisper."

The sparkle in her eyes told Gabrielle she was playing her game again.

"A secret? Are you going to tell me a secret?"

The crowd moved forward. All were eager to hear what she would say.

Gabrielle looked around the room. "Mother, why are all these people here? Why?"

Her mother kissed her cheek. "They think that I know where a great treasure is hidden, and they hope that I will tell you where it is."

Gabrielle giggled. She liked this game. "Are you going to tell me?"

"Not today," she answered.

"Not today," Gabrielle repeated so that the curious onlookers would hear.

Her mother struggled to sit up. The housekeeper rushed forward to place pillows behind her back. A moment later the physician announced that her color was improving.

"I am feeling much better," she said. "Leave us now," she ordered, her voice growing stronger with each word. "I would like a moment alone with my daughter."

The physician looked as though he wanted to protest, but he kept silent as he ushered the group from the chamber. He motioned for two maids to stay behind. The women waited by the door to do their mistress's bidding.

"Are you feeling so much better you can tell me a story today?" Gabrielle asked.

"I am," she replied. "Which story would you like to hear?"

"The princess story," she eagerly answered.

Her mother wasn't surprised. Gabrielle always asked for the same story.

"There once was a princess who lived in a faraway land called St. Biel," her mother began. "Her home was a magnificent white castle high on the top of a mountain. Her uncle was the king. He was very kind to the princess, and she was very happy."

When her mother paused, Gabrielle blurted impatiently, "You're the princess."

"Gabrielle, you know that I am and that this story is about your father and me."

"I know, but I like to hear you tell it."

Her mother continued. "When the princess was of age, a bargain was struck with Baron Geoffrey of Wellingshire. The princess was to marry the baron and live with him in England."

Because she knew that her daughter loved to hear about the wedding ceremony, the gowns, and the music, she went into great detail. The little girl clapped her hands with delight when she heard about the banquet feast, especially the description of the fruit tarts and honey cakes. By the end of the story, the mother's narrative had become slow and labored. Exhaustion was catching up with her. The little girl took notice and, as was her ritual, she again made her mother promise she wouldn't die today.

"I promise. Now it is your turn to tell me the story I taught you."

"Every word just like you taught me, Mother? And just like your mother taught you?"

She smiled. "Every word. And you will remember it and tell your daughters one day so they will know of their family and St. Biel."

Gabrielle grew solemn and closed her eyes to concentrate. She knew she must not forget a word of the story. This was her heritage, and her mother assured her that one day she would understand what that meant. She folded her hands in her lap and then opened her eyes again. Focusing on her mother's encouraging smile, she began.

"Once upon a time in the year of the violent storms that tore in from the sea . . ."

TWO

EVERYONE WHO WAS ANYONE IN ENGLAND KNEW about the feud. Baron Coswold of Axholm, one of King John's closest advisers, and Baron Percy of Werke, also called friend and confidant by the king, had spent the last ten years trying to destroy each other. The competition between the two men was fierce. Each wanted more wealth than the other, more power, more prestige, and certainly more favoritism from the king. They fought bitterly over everything, and they coveted one prize most of all: Princess Gabrielle. At the mere mention of her name they became as rabid as mad dogs. Both barons were determined to marry this prized beauty.

The king was amused by their fits of jealousy. At every opportunity, he pitted one against the other. In his mind, they were his pets who would do any trick he requested just to please him. He knew about their obsession with Baron Geoffrey's daughter, Gabrielle, but he had no intention of giving her to either. She was far too valuable. He preferred, instead, whenever it suited his needs, to dangle the possibility that each man might still have a chance to win her hand in marriage.

Everyone who was anyone in England knew who Gabrielle was. Her beauty was legendary. She had grown up in Wellingshire not far from the king's palace. Her life there was quiet and relatively secluded until she came of age and was presented to the court. With her protective father, Baron Geoffrey of Wellingshire, at her side, she had endured an audience with King John that lasted no more than ten minutes at the most, yet that was all it took for the king to become completely enchanted.

John was in the habit of taking what he wanted when he wanted it. His reputation for lechery was well known. It wasn't unusual for him to seduce the willing—and the unwilling—wives and daughters of his barons, and then, the morning after, boast of his conquest. However, he didn't touch Gabrielle, for her father was one of the most powerful and influential barons in England.

John had enough conflicts on his hands. He didn't need another. He was being assaulted from all sides, and he believed that none of the conflicts were of his doing. His problems with Pope Innocent III had recently increased tenfold. Because John refused to accept the pope's choice of Stephen Langton as archbishop of Canterbury, the pope had placed an interdict on England. All church services were banned except for baptisms and confessions, and since bishops and priests had fled their churches to get away from John's wrath, finding one to perform either of those two sacraments was nearly impossible.

The interdict infuriated King John, and he had responded by confiscating all church property.

The pope's reaction was severe. He excommunicated John, thereby undermining his ability to rule his country. Not only did the excommunication damn John's already black soul to the eternal fires of Hell, but it also absolved his subjects from their oaths of allegiance. In effect, the barons no longer had to be loyal.

Through reliable sources John knew that the king of France had his eye on the English throne and was being urged by some of the traitorous barons to prepare an invasion. While King John believed he had the men and the resources to meet this threat, it was still an expensive undertaking and one that would require his full attention.

There were minor problems plaguing him as well. The outbursts in Wales and in Scotland were becoming more and more organized. King William of Scotland wasn't a problem. He had already pledged his fealty to John. Nay, it was the Highlanders who were out for blood. Though King William believed he had them under his control, the chieftains didn't much care about answering to anyone but their own clansmen. The farther north one traveled, the more violent and ruthless the clans became. There were so many feuds going on it was impossible to keep track of them all.

There was only one laird in the northern

Highlands who wasn't a threat to the others and who actually garnered a bit of respect: Laird Alan Monroe. He was an older man, soft-spoken, with an easy disposition, traits that were unheard of in a Highland chieftain. He was content with his life and didn't have any designs to increase his holdings. Perhaps that was why he was somewhat liked.

In a surprising attempt to appease some of his more influential barons, and taking to heart a suggestion from Scotland's King William, King John ordered a marriage between Lady Gabrielle and Laird Monroe. Though he had no need to, he sweetened her dowry with a large piece of land in the Highlands called Finney's Flat, which he had acquired years ago. Laird Monroe's home was at the southeast corner of this coveted property.

John's worries about a gathering army from the Highlands with many of the border lairds wishing to join in, all bent on attacking England, would be put to rest for the time being, and King William would no longer have to worry about a possible insurrection. Already restless and sympathetic to their northern neighbors, there was a fear that some of the lowlanders would add to the rebellion.

When the proposition to marry Gabrielle was put to Laird Monroe, he eagerly agreed. He also believed that with John's royal edict the fight among the lairds for control of Finney's Flat would end, and there would be peace in the area.

Only two would raise their voices against the marriage, Percy and Coswold, but John would ignore the pathetic pleas and protests by the two barons.

Gabrielle's father, Baron Geoffrey, was also in favor of the marriage. As much as he would have liked for his daughter to marry a proper English baron and live in England where he would occasionally see her, and his future grandchildren as well, he knew that Gabrielle wouldn't be safe as long as John was king. Baron Geoffrey had seen the lust in the king's eyes as he watched Gabrielle. He'd acted very much like a spider patiently waiting to ensnare and devour his prey. And from what Geoffrey had heard from his distant relatives in Scotland, the Buchanans, Gabrielle's intended was a good man who would treat her kindly. This was high praise indeed for Laird Monroe, as the Buchanans didn't much like anyone out-side of their own clan. Baron Geoffrey and

Laird Buchanan were related by marriage, but the laird could barely tolerate Gabrielle's father, though ironically, Laird Buchanan, who hated all things English, had married an English lady.

With King John's blessing and Baron Geoffrey's approval, the wedding was scheduled. The only person who didn't have a say in the matter and the last one to hear about the upcoming ceremony was Princess Gabrielle.

THREE

THE DAY BEFORE BARON COSWOLD WAS SCHED-uled to leave St. Biel, he became a believer.

King John had sent him on this fool's errand, and Coswold was determined to get the task done as quickly as possible, for the king had finally promised him that, when he returned to England, Gabrielle would be his. And while Gabrielle's father despised Coswold, the king had assured him that he wouldn't have any trouble forcing Baron Geoffrey to accept the marriage.

Coswold also knew that the king had sent his rival, Baron Percy, on an errand into the northern wilderness to meet with Scotland's

King William. His duties would take some time, and Coswold hoped to get back to England and quickly marry Gabrielle before Percy found out about it.

Coswold's orders were specific. He was to check on and verify that the steward King John had placed in charge of St. Biel, a whiny little man named Emerly, wasn't stealing from him.

John had invaded the country several years ago, and in the fierce battle for possession had nearly destroyed it. As soon as St. Biel was under his control, he set about looting the palace and the churches. If there was anything of value left, John wanted to know about it. The king didn't trust anyone, even the man he had personally chosen to oversee the country that now belonged to the crown.

The king was still intrigued by the rumors of hidden gold, though when pressed, he admitted he thought they were all nonsense; still, on the off chance there was a fragment of truth in them, he wanted Coswold to investigate. John didn't have faith in Emerly's report.

When Emerly had first arrived at the port of St. Biel, he had dragged forth each man and woman over the age of twenty who might have heard something about hidden treasure. Every single one admitted to having heard the rumors, and all of them thought the treasure probably had existed. Some thought the gold had gone to the pope, others that King John had stolen it. Nothing was conclusive, and after his own inquiry, Coswold's findings were no different.

It was late afternoon, and there was a decided chill in the air as Coswold strolled across St. Biel's palace grounds to stretch his legs. The path led down a gentle slope to the harbor, and he could see his men moving his possessions onto the ship that would take him back to England. Before nightfall he would be in his cabin awaiting the tide.

Coswold wrapped his heavy cloak tighter around his shoulders and pulled the hood over his ears. He couldn't wait to be away from this godforsaken place.

He was walking past one of the thatched cottages when he spotted an old man carrying branches in his arms, no doubt for tonight's fire.

The stranger noticed the shivering Coswold and said, "Only men without blood would think this mild weather be cold."

"You are impertinent," Coswold snapped.

"Don't you know who I am?" Evidently the man was unaware that Coswold wielded the power of King John, and with just one word could end his life. "Even the steward, Emerly, would do well to fear me," Coswold boasted.

The old man looked unimpressed. " 'Tis the truth, I don't know you," he admitted, "but I've been near the top of the mountain tending to the ill. I've only just returned."

"You are a physician?"

"Nay, I'm a priest. I look after the souls here, and I'm one of the few priests left in St. Biel. My name is Father Alphonse."

The baron cocked his head and studied the priest's face. His skin had been ravaged by age and climate, but his eyes shone like those of a young man.

Coswold walked over to face the man, blocking his way. "As a priest you cannot tell a lie, can you?"

If the clergyman thought the question peculiar, he didn't let on. "No, I certainly cannot. It is a sin to lie."

Coswold nodded, pleased with the answer. "Put those branches down and walk with me. I have questions to put to you."

The priest didn't argue. Dropping the branches by the door of the closest cottage, he clasped his hands behind his back and fell into step beside the baron.

"How long have you been assigned to St. Biel?" Coswold asked.

"Oh my, it's been so long now I can't recall the exact number of years. I am most content. St. Biel has become my home, and I would be sorry to leave."

"So you were here during the upheaval?"

"Is that what you call English soldiers ripping our country apart, killing our beloved King Grenier II, and destroying the monarchy? 'An upheaval'?" he scoffed.

"Guard your words and your manner with me, priest, and answer the question."

"Yes, I was here."

"Did you know King Grenier before he died?"

Father Alphonse let his anger show. "Don't you mean before he was killed?" Before Coswold could respond, he said, "Yes, I knew him."

"Did you ever speak to him?"

"Of course."

"Did you know Princess Genevieve?"

The priest's expression softened. "Yes, I knew her. She was the king's niece . . . his younger brother's daughter. The people of

St. Biel loved her so. They didn't like the English baron taking her away."

"Baron Geoffrey of Wellingshire."

"Yes."

"The wedding was here, wasn't it?"

"That's right, it was, and everyone in St. Biel was invited."

"Did you know that Princess Genevieve had a daughter?"

"Everyone here knows. We are not so isolated. News travels here just as quickly as everywhere else. Her name is Gabrielle, and she is our royalty."

"King John is your royalty," Coswold reminded him.

"Why are you asking me all of these questions?"

"Never you mind. Living here all this time you must have heard the rumors of hidden gold."

"Ah, so that is what this is about," the priest muttered.

"Answer the question."

"Yes, I've heard the rumor."

"Is there any truth in it?"

The holy man considered his answer carefully. "I can tell you there once was a large sum of gold in the king's treasury."

"I know this already. Your countrymen have told me of the heavy toll your king collected from those who traveled over your mountains, and they also told me about his homage to St. Biel and his offering to the pope."

"Ah, St. Biel." The old man nodded. "Our patron and our protector. We have a great love for him."

"That is apparent," Coswold answered mockingly. He swept his hand around in a wide gesture. "Look at the place," he sneered in disgust. "Your saint is everywhere. One cannot step foot on the soil of this wretched land without being followed by those prying eyes and that smug expression. If the pope were to hear that this country worships a saint, he would excommunicate all of you."

Father Alphonse slowly shook his head. "We don't worship any saint. We pray to God; we honor the pope, but we believe we owe St. Biel a great debt. He is our patron saint. He has watched over us through many adversities."

"All right then," he muttered. "In honor of your patron saint, was all the gold sent to the pope?"

The priest didn't answer.

"Tell me," he demanded, "did you ever see the gold?"

"Over the years I've seen several gold coins. Princess Genevieve had one."

He was deliberately being vague, but Coswold pressed on. "Did you see the gold in the treasury?"

"Only once," Father Alphonse said.

"Was this before or after the donation to the pope?"

The priest paused for several seconds. "It has been so many years. My mind is not as clear as it once was."

Coswold's curiosity was piqued by the evasive response. "Your mind is clear enough, old man. I demand in the name of John, your king, to tell me. When did you see the gold?"

Father Alphonse didn't answer quickly enough. Coswold grabbed the neck of the priest's robe and yanked him forward.

"If you don't tell me," he snarled, "I swear you will not see another day in your beloved country, and I'll have every image of your holy saint destroyed and dumped into the sea."

Father Alphonse gasped for air. The look in Coswold's eyes told him that he would carry out his threat.

"I saw the gold coins in the treasury after a donation had been sent to the pope."

"I would hear the details," he said.

The priest sighed. "I had only been here a short while when I was given an audience with King Grenier I. He was a kind and clever man. He showed me his palace and the grounds—"

"He showed you the treasury?"

"Yes," he said, "but I believe it was by accident. I don't think the king meant for me to see it. As we strolled down the hall conversing quite pleasantly, we passed the treasury. The doors were open and two men were stacking bags of gold on top of other bags. The gold coins filled the shelves and the floor with only a narrow path to the door. Neither the king nor I acknowledged what we had seen."

"And? Get on with it. Tell me more."

"Time passed, and I was called to the king's bedside to administer the sacrament of the last rites, for he was dying. His son was by his side and had spent the last hours with him, receiving instructions for the care of his kingdom. Again, the treasury doors were open as I happened by on my way to the chapel. But now the room was empty.

There wasn't any gold, not even one coin, anywhere."

"How much was hidden away?'

"I don't know."

"Guess," he ordered.

"There is speculation that there was enough to win a war. Gold is power. It can buy anything . . . even a kingdom."

"So where is the gold now?"

"I don't know. It just . . . disappeared. Perhaps it was all sent to the pope." He backed away from Coswold and bowed. "If there aren't other questions, I would like to go home and rest these weary bones."

"Go," Coswold said. "But keep this conversation to yourself."

The priest nodded his agreement and started back up the hill.

Coswold let out a scornful chuckle. How could a treasure so large just vanish with no one to account for it? He shouted after the old man, "So this stupid king of yours hid his gold away and told no one. He took his secret to his grave. How cunning was that?"

Father Alphonse turned around, barely controlling his anger. "Why would you think he didn't tell anyone?"

FOUR

BARON COSWOLD WAS OUTRAGED. HE HAD ONLY just returned from St. Biel when he was given the news by one of the king's messengers that Lady Gabrielle was to be married to Laird Monroe at Arbane Abbey in just three months' time. How could this be? The news stunned him. The royal messenger also had orders to give Coswold from King John, but the baron found it nearly impossible to concentrate. He asked the messenger several times to repeat himself.

The baron barely managed to control his anger until he returned home. Then he let loose. He was furious with the king for once again breaking his promise. He stormed into the great hall, picked up a pitcher and a bowl, and hurled both into the hearth.

Isla, his sister's daughter, was there to greet him. She was a timid creature who had idolized Coswold and had hung on his every word since the day he'd taken her in. Isla had witnessed several of her uncle's tantrums in the past and knew to cower in the corner of the hall until he was finished.

In his fury he forgot she was even in the room. He paced about, kicking and throwing anything in his path, acting like a spoiled child who wasn't getting his way. He swept a goblet and pitcher from the top of a chest and smirked with perverse satisfaction as it shattered against the wall.

"I have no one to blame but myself," he ranted. "I'm the fool here for believing that lying son of a whore. Why did I think this time would be any different? When has the bastard pretender king ever told the truth? When?" he shouted.

Isla nervously tugged on her bliaut and took a timid step away from the wall. Dare she answer him? Did he even want her to? She nibbled on her lower lip while she thought about it. If she made a wrong decision, her

uncle might turn his wrath on her. It had happened once before, and for nearly a month
she'd carried the bruises on her arms where
he grabbed her and shook her. That memory
helped her make up her mind. Isla remained
silent until Coswold calmed down.

Ten minutes later he collapsed into a chair
at the table and demanded wine. A servant
rushed into the hall with a goblet and a
pitcher to replace the ones he'd broken. The
goblet was filled to the rim with the bloodred
liquid. Some of it sloshed over the side as
she placed it on the table. She quickly wiped
the spill with a cloth, bowed low, and backed
away from the baron.

He took a long gulp, leaned back in his
chair, and let out a loud sigh. "There are no
honest men in England these days. None at
all."

Spent now, he turned, noticed Isla, and
called out to her. "Come, sit with me. Tell me
what news you have collected while I've
been away. What of Percy? What has that
bastard been up to?"

A plain woman, Isla was happy for the
attention. She rushed to the table and took
her seat at the opposite end facing her
uncle.

"Baron Percy was sent to the Highlands just as you left for St. Biel."

"I already knew that," he said impatiently. "Is he back yet?"

"Aye, he is," she answered. "But I have heard from his squire that he is preparing to leave for Arbane Abbey within the next few weeks. He was most unhappy about Lady Gabrielle's coming marriage and was said to carry on something terrible. The squire told me he cried."

It was the first bit of good news he'd heard since Coswold stepped off the miserable ship. He chuckled as he thought about Percy weeping like an old woman. "He truly did cry? Did anyone see him? Tell me more."

Isla was about to tell him that she had heard that Percy had kicked and screamed and thrown things when he had heard that the lady was to wed Laird Monroe, but then she realized Coswold had just finished doing the very same thing. He might not take kindly to the comparison.

"He vowed that he would marry her with or without the king's permission and with or without her father's permission."

Coswold snorted with laughter. "He has always had lofty dreams."

She bowed her head. "I wish that he would lower his expectations of a wife."

He paid no attention to her remark. Coswold gulped down the rest of the wine from his goblet, used his sleeve to wipe the drips from his chin, then poured himself more. "Did Percy tell anyone how he planned to accomplish such an amazing feat?"

"Do you mean how he plans to marry Lady Gabrielle without gaining permission?"

"Aye, that's what I mean."

Before he could chastise her for letting her mind wander and not paying attention, she blurted, "Nay, he didn't explain to anyone. The same squire told me that if the king does not attend the ceremony, then Baron Percy will represent him."

"So King John is planning to go to Arbane Abbey?"

She nodded. "But the baron doesn't believe the king will make it there in time, for His Highness told him he has many other commitments he must see to first."

"And Percy's hoping John *won't* attend, isn't that right?" He scowled as he asked the question.

Once again Isla nodded. "Percy boasted that the king has given him full power to speak in his name and make decisions with his blessings as well."

Coswold's good mood was dampered by the news. "Baron Percy can make any decision he wishes?" he muttered. "This is true?"

"That is what I've been told." Isla dropped her folded hands on the table and cried out, "You must marry Gabrielle, Uncle. For even though it is wrong, I have feelings for Baron Percy. You know this well. Do you not see how I suffer?"

Coswold rubbed his jaw. "He flatters you, Isla, because he sees how a kind word will turn your head and win your loyalty."

Her hand flew to her heart. "I shall always be loyal to you. When my father died, you took me in and made certain that all my needs were met. I love you, and I would never ever be disloyal to you." In a rush, she added, "But I know how much you want Lady Gabrielle, and if you were to marry her, then perhaps Baron Percy will look to me for a wife. I know that I'm not as pretty as most, but if you are married, then I will also be related to her, won't I? And won't that count for something with Percy?"

He hardly knew how to answer. He almost felt sorry for her, because she had such impossible dreams. Percy would never marry the likes of her. Coswold doubted that any man would give her the time of day, for she was most unattractive. Her skin was sallow and pockmarked, and her lips were but thin lines that seemed to disappear when she spoke. She had made Coswold a good servant and a companion now that she was grown, and he wouldn't be averse to keeping her in his home until he or she died. But if Isla longed for marriage, who could Coswold find to marry her? She didn't have much of a dowry unless he added to what her father had left her. He knew that if the dowry were large enough, she would have many suitors, but he was unwilling to give up any of what he had. Now that her parents were dead, Coswold was Isla's only family. When she realized her uncle wouldn't increase her dowry, she would get upset, of course, but it would pass, and she would eventually accept her lowly lot. She had nowhere else to go.

"One must always have hope," he muttered for lack of anything better to say. "Remember, Percy and I are enemies. I don't think he will forget our animosity, especially if I should marry Gabrielle. It seems, however, that Laird Monroe will be winning that prize."

"You could change that," Isla said. "You're cunning and so clever. You could find a way to marry her. I've been told she doesn't even know she's to marry the laird yet."

"I think perhaps you have false hope, but I won't discourage you."

"And if I should win Percy's heart, you would give him permission to wed me?" she asked eagerly.

"I would."

"Thank you, Uncle," she whispered. Content now that she had gained his promise, she remembered' her manners. "How was your journey? Did it go well?"

Coswold loosened the belt around his waist and, stretching his feet out in front of him, slouched back in his chair. "St. Biel is a miserable place. It's cold when it should be warm and burning hot when it should be cold."

"Did you find the treasure for the king?"

"I did not."

"Does it exist?"

His answer was immediate. "No."

There was no point in telling her what he really thought. As besotted as she was with Percy, Isla could very well let anything he said slip out at the wrong moment. Love made women foolish.

Coswold wasn't telling anyone that he believed the treasure existed. He planned to find it and keep it all for himself. He certainly wasn't going to share a single gold coin with King John, who had lied to him for the last time. With such a vast fortune at his finger-tips, Coswold could build an army and take whatever he wanted when he wanted it. Ah, the thought of such freedom made his head spin.

To achieve his dreams, he had to be practi-cal. Gabrielle held the key to the whereabouts of the gold. He was certain the secret of the hidden treasure had been passed down from one generation to the next. If he couldn't have her, in order to glean the information from her, then he would make certain Gabrielle was given to someone he could manipulate. And he had the perfect man in mind.

"In a few days I must go on another long journey," Coswold remarked.

"Must you go far?"

He nodded. "All the way to the Highlands."

She gasped. "You're going to Arbane Abbey?"

"I must first meet with King John to answer his questions about St. Biel. Fortunately, he's in the north now, and when we are finished with our meeting, I'll continue on to the Highlands."

"To the abbey." She nodded as she made the statement.

"I have another destination in mind, but when I'm finished there, I will head to the abbey. I should arrive in plenty of time for the wedding."

Isla took a deep breath to summon her courage. "I know it's wrong for me to ask for anything more, but is there a chance I might go with you? I would love to see the princess marry. I'm certain it will be a grand ceremony."

Now *she* was lying to him. She wasn't interested in seeing Lady Gabrielle wed. Percy would be there, and she wanted to see him. Coswold was about to refuse her request, then changed his mind. His niece might be of help to him.

She lowered her head in dejection, accepting his refusal before he had even given it.

"Aye, you may come."

Her head snapped up. Overjoyed, tears

immediately welled in her eyes. Soon she would see the love of her life, and perhaps she would find a way to make him love her. Anything was possible. And Isla would do anything to marry Baron Percy.

Anything.

FIVE

THEY WERE GOING TO BURY THE MACHUGH'S brother in the center of the battlefield, and to amuse themselves, they decided to bury him alive.

The field chosen for his execution was called Finney's Flat, hallowed ground for the MacKennas. The clan was now calling the valley Glen MacKenna, for so many of their own fine soldiers had been slaughtered there. When the last battle had ended, the ground was stained black with MacKenna blood.

Laird Colm MacHugh had been responsible for the carnage. The mighty chieftain and his fierce warriors had poured down the mountain like a cauldron of oil boiling over, their scalding fury destroying everything in their path. Their gleaming swords raised, their united battle cry vibrated the jagged rocks. To the MacKenna soldiers waiting below to do battle, it had been a terrifying sight.

MacHugh was the most spine-chilling sight of all. Until that day some of the MacKenna soldiers had refused to believe the laird actually existed, for the tales of his ruthlessness in battle and his feats of Herculean strength couldn't possibly be accurate . . . unless, as some of the whispered rumors alleged, the MacHugh was in fact more beast than man.

Some who had gotten a glimpse of him swore he was half lion, half man: his chiseled face, his golden hair similar in color to a lion's mane, and his ferocity in battle like that of an animal. Invisible one second, he pounced the next, methodically ripping his prey apart limb by limb.

Or so it was told.

The more enlightened warriors scoffed at such a fanciful notion. The MacHugh was but a shadow with supernatural power, they argued. He disappeared at will, but when his shadow approached, a poor soul could ward off death only by dropping to his knees and praying for mercy. The MacHugh was invincible, impossible to grasp or capture. The only warning that he was about to strike was the music that came before. Shadow music. His battle cry blended in perfect harmony with the whistle of his blade as his sword sliced through the air. When a soldier heard that sound, he was already dead.

Laird Owen MacKenna knew all too well that Colm MacHugh was flesh and bone. Twice in the past year MacKenna had stood in the same great hall with him and twenty other lairds. They had gathered for meetings at the request of Scotland's king. The mighty MacHugh hadn't directly spoken to him either time, but MacKenna felt the sting of his words just the same. When matters affecting their adjoining lands were brought forth, the king and the other lairds turned to MacHugh for direction, as though his land and his strength held more importance than MacKenna's. And always in contention was Finney's Flat. The valley ran adjacent to both the MacHugh and the MacKenna holdings. The land was fertile with nary a rock in sight, perfect for their sheep to graze and perhaps a bit of barley planting, but neither clan could claim it. It belonged to John, king of England, granted to him years earlier by the king of Scotland as a conciliatory gesture. Each time MacKenna tried to take a piece of the land for himself, MacHugh saw to it that he was pushed back.

Oh, MacKenna despised this man. With every breath he took, his hatred grew until it threatened to consume him. Not one day passed without at least one dark thought about the laird, and what was most galling for Owen was the knowledge that MacHugh wasted not one minute thinking about any of the MacKennas. They weren't even important enough to hate.

Owen recognized this sin of jealousy. Envy was eating him alive, and he felt powerless to do anything about it. He dreamed of destroying MacHugh, and though he wouldn't dare admit his sin to his confessor, he would gladly sell his soul to the devil to get what he wanted.

His list of wants was long. He wanted MacHugh's power. He wanted his allies: the Buchanans, the Maitlands, and the Sinclairs. He wanted his strength and his discipline.

He wanted the fear the laird instilled in his enemies; he wanted the loyalty he commanded from his friends. He wanted his lands and everything else MacHugh controlled. Most of all, Owen craved revenge.

Today was the day he would finally rid himself of his jealousy. Today was the day he would get justice.

And what a glorious day it was for an execution . . . or many executions if all went well and a large number of MacHughs were killed. Pity he couldn't watch, but he had to separate himself from the executioners so that when he was accused of the crime, he could protest his innocence and have holy witnesses at Arbane Abbey to vouch for his presence.

Owen had carefully thought out the plan and had handpicked the soldier who would oversee the burial.

"Timing," he had explained, "is most important. You must wait until you see Laird MacHugh up on the ridge overlooking the flat before you bury his brother. He'll know who it is, but he won't be able to stop it. Have no worries. His arrows cannot travel such a distance, and his steed cannot fly. By the time he reaches his fallen brother's side, it will be too late, and you and your good men, will have gone into hiding.

"A contingent of soldiers will be waiting to the west behind the line of trees. As soon as MacHugh gets close enough, they'll circle and attack."

He rubbed his hands with malicious glee as he added, "If all goes well, Laird Colm MacHugh and his brother Liam will both be in the ground before nightfall."

The soldier Owen had placed in charge of the burial was a thick-shouldered, thick-headed man named Gordon. Owen had made him repeat his orders to make certain he fully appreciated the importance of timing the burial just right.

The warriors had little trouble capturing Liam MacHugh. They ambushed him just as he passed through a thick grove of trees. They beat him severely and removed his boots, tied a thick rope around his ankles, and dragged him behind his horse to the deep narrow hole they'd dug in preparation.

While they nervously waited for MacHugh to reach the ridge and also waited for Liam to regain consciousness so he would know what was going to happen, six of the seven soldiers got into a discussion regarding the burial.

The discussion turned into an argument. Three soldiers wanted MacHugh's brother buried headfirst with only his feet above the ground. When his toes stopped wiggling, they would know for a certainty that he was dead. Three other soldiers were in favor of dropping him into the hole feetfirst. They wanted to hear him scream and beg for mercy until the last shovel of dirt was thrown across the top of his head.

"He might not wake up," a soldier argued. "I'm in favor of stuffing his head in first."

"He didn't even give up a whimper while we were beating him. Why do you think he'd start in screaming now?" another asked.

"Look at the mist coming on. It's already covering the ground and creeping up my boots. You won't be able to see his head anyway if this muck gets any thicker."

"Pull that hood off and toss some water on his face and he'll wake up," yet another suggested.

"He's going in headfirst."

"Feetfirst," a soldier shouted, shoving one of the men who had disagreed with him.

Gordon knew the argument would soon

turn physical. He kept his eye on the top of the ridge and announced that he would be the deciding vote.

Liam MacHugh would go to his grave feet-first.

SIX

IT WASN'T UNUSUAL FOR A BRIDE TO MEET HER groom for the first time at their wedding ceremony, but Gabrielle hoped to at least get a glimpse of the man before then. The only piece of information she had about Laird Monroe was that he was an older man. No one had told her *how* much older, though, and she was filled with trepidation. What if he turned out to be an ogre? Or so old he couldn't stand straight? Or had no teeth and could only eat mush? She knew that his age and appearance shouldn't be important to her, but what if his manners were atrocious? Or worse, what if he was cruel to those around him? Could she live with someone who mistreated the men and women who depended on him?

Her mother had often told her that she worried too much, but wasn't the unknown always a worry? To Gabrielle it was. Oh, how she wished her mother were here to offer advice now. She would calm Gabrielle's fears. But her mother had died in the winter two years ago. While Gabrielle knew that she had been blessed to have her in her life for so many years, there were times when she physically ached to talk to her. Today was one of those times, for Gabrielle was on her way to her wedding.

Twenty soldiers along with staff and servants accompanied Gabrielle and her father to the Highlands of Scotland. Their destination was Arbane Abbey, where her wedding ceremony would take place in one week. Rooms would be provided at the abbey for the travel-weary group.

The procession up the mountain was slow and arduous. The closer they came to their destination, the more withdrawn Gabrielle became.

The trail was narrow and broken, but her father was able to ride by her side once they had rounded a sharp turn. Baron Geoffrey tried to think of a way to lighten her concerns about the future.

He motioned to the lush valley below. "Do you notice how green everything is here, Gabrielle?"

"Yes, Father, I do," she replied without enthusiasm.

"And do you notice how invigorating the brisk air is in the Highlands?"

"I do," she said.

The good baron was determined to raise his daughter's spirits. "There are those Highlanders who believe that we are high enough to touch heaven. What do you think?"

It wasn't like Gabrielle's father to be so fanciful. Her mother had been the fanciful one, full of dreams that she had passed on to her daughter. But her father wasn't a dreamer. He was a leader of men, a protector, and a terribly practical man.

"I would think they were mistaken," she answered. "We aren't high enough to touch heaven here. Only in St. Biel would that be possible."

"And how would you know this?"

"Mother," she answered.

"Ah," Baron Geoffrey said with a melancholy smile. "And what exactly did she tell you?"

"She always said the same thing, that when she stood next to the statue of St. Biel that overlooks the harbor, she was as close to heaven as she could be on earth."

Gabrielle's fingers brushed across the gold medallion she wore on a chain around her neck. It had been fashioned from a coin and bore the likeness of St. Biel. She'd had it for as long as she could remember. Her mother had been buried with one just like it.

He noticed the gesture. "I miss her, too," he said. "But she will always be in our hearts." Then with a sigh he said, "Do you notice how blue the sky is? As blue as your mother's eyes."

"I do notice," she said. "And I have also noticed how you have pointed out again and again how lovely this land is. Could you possibly have a motive?" she teased.

"I want you to appreciate your surroundings, and I want you to be content here and content in your marriage as well, Gabrielle."

She wanted to argue. Was contentment the ultimate to be wished for? Were passion and love and excitement only for dreams? Was it ever possible to have it all? She longed to pose these questions to her father, but she could not. She held her tongue. As they continued on, she made up her mind to be more practical, like her father. She was a grown woman, soon to become a wife. It was time for her to put her childish dreams away.

"I'll try to be content," she promised.

Their pace was slowed once again because of the rocky incline. Her father saw the look on her face and the sadness in her eyes. "Daughter," he said in exasperation, "you are not going to a funeral. It's your wedding. Try to be joyful."

"I will try," she promised.

An hour later when the caravan stopped so that the horses could rest and they could stretch their legs, her father asked Gabrielle to walk with him.

Neither said a word until they stopped to rest beneath a clump of birch trees near a flowing brook.

"I have met Laird Monroe and some of his family. He will be kind to you."

She didn't want to talk about her future husband, but her father seemed determined.

"Then I shall be kind to him," she said.

The baron shook his head. "You are a willful daughter."

She turned to face him. "Father, what is it you're finding so difficult to tell me?"

He sighed. "Your life is going to change when you become a wife. You won't be equal in your marriage, and you must accept this."

"Mother was your equal, wasn't she?"

He smiled. "That she was," he admitted, "but she was the exception."

"Perhaps I will be the exception, too."

"In time perhaps you will," he agreed. "I don't want you to worry about your future husband. I have been assured that he will never raise a hand against you, and as you know, there are husbands who would be cruel to their wives." There was disgust in his voice when he added that fact.

"Father, I think you're more concerned about this marriage than I am. Do you actually wonder what I would do if my husband, or any man for that matter, were to raise a hand against me?"

Somewhat chagrined, he replied, "No, I don't wonder. I know exactly what you would do because I saw to your training."

Before she could interrupt, he continued, "However, there will be changes when you marry. You'll no longer be free to do what you wish. You'll have to take your husband's feelings and needs into consideration. You have been self-reliant in many ways, but now you must learn restraint."

"Are you telling me I must give up my freedom?"

He sighed. His daughter sounded appalled by the notion. "Of a sort," he hedged.

"Of a sort?"

"And when you are married," Baron Geoffrey continued, "you will share your husband's bed and—" Too late he realized where he'd taken the conversation. He stopped, then coughed to cover his embarrassment. What had he been thinking to bring up this topic? Talking about the marriage bed with his daughter was impossible for him. After a moment's consideration he decided that he would ask one of the older women to explain what would happen on her wedding night. He simply wasn't up to the task.

"You were saying?" she prodded.

"We're close to the abbey now," he stammered. "Just an hour or so away I'd wager, and just as close to Finney's Flat if we were to ride in the opposite direction."

"It's early in the day. There's time before dark for us to look at the flat."

"Have you forgotten that I must pay my respects to Laird Buchanan?" He nodded to the west. "When we reach the next rise, I'll leave you. It will be going on darkness by the time I reach his home. You and the others will continue on to the abbey."

"Would it be possible for my guard and me to go to the flat while the others continue on? I'm certain it won't take us any time at all to catch up with them. I am most curious to see this dowry that King John has given me."

He considered her request a long minute before agreeing. "As long as you take all four guards with you, and as long as you carry your bow and arrows, and as long as you are cautious to a fault. And you must promise me that you will not let the time get away from you and that it will be an uneventful ride. Then I will allow it."

She held her smile. "Uneventful, Father?"

Seeing the sparkle in her eyes, Baron Geoffrey was suddenly feeling quite in awe of his daughter. With her black hair and her violet blue eyes, so like her mother's, Gabrielle had grown into a beautiful and delightful young lady. His chest swelled with pride as he thought of her many accomplishments. She could read and write, speak four languages, and speak them well. Her mother had seen that Gabrielle was well-versed in the feminine pursuits, and he had seen that she was well-trained in more practical matters. She could sit her horse as well as any man, and she wasn't squeamish with her bow and arrows. Truth be told, she was more accurate with her targets than he was.

"Uneventful, Father?" Gabrielle repeated, wondering why he was so distracted.

He shook himself out of his contemplations. "You know what I mean. Do not play the innocent with me. You're prone to mischief."

She protested. "I cannot imagine why you would think—"

He interrupted. "Promise me it will be an uneventful ride and that there will be no mischief. I'll have your word on this, Daughter."

She nodded. "I promise. There will be no mischief, and it will be an uneventful afternoon."

Uncomfortable with showing affection, Baron Geoffrey awkwardly patted her on her shoulder and then headed back to the horses.

Gabrielle hurried to catch up. "Father, you

worry too much. I'll be careful as I have promised, so please quit your frown. Nothing's going to happen."

Two hours later she had to kill a man.

SEVEN

GABRIELLE INTERRUPTED A MURDER.

She had wanted a bit of excitement to take her mind off her worries, but she most certainly hadn't wanted to witness anything this horrifying.

The ride began quite pleasantly, invigorating in fact. After she had dutifully kissed her father on his whiskered cheek and bid him a safe journey to the Buchanans to pay his respects, she forced herself to walk, not run, to her horse, Rogue. She even allowed the soldier Stephen to assist her into her saddle. Rogue pranced in anticipation, sensing that he would soon be allowed to soar into the wind.

Certain that Baron Geoffrey was watching, Gabrielle played the meek maiden and wouldn't allow Rogue to break into a gallop as was the spirited horse's custom. She forced him to start out at a much slower gait. She had the feeling that her father knew exactly what she was doing, and so she held her smile as she turned and waved to him one last time before she was out of sight.

When she was free to do as she pleased, Gabrielle loosened the grip on the reins and gently nudged Rogue. The horse lunged into a full gallop, and by the time they reached the top of the nearest hill, Gabrielle felt as though she were flying. She laughed over the sheer joy she felt at that very moment. The burdens pressing down on her began to drift away.

As usual, Stephen took the lead. Christien and Lucien flanked her sides, and Faust, the youngest, rode last, protecting her back. The four soldiers could have been brothers, so alike in appearance were they with their white-blond hair, blue eyes, and deeply tanned, weathered skin. They dressed alike as well, in a soldier's uniform, all in black, but with a small, barely noticeable emblem of the royal house of St. Biel just above their hearts.

Their personalities were quite different, though. Perhaps because he was the oldest and the commander over the other three guards, Stephen was the most serious and rarely smiled. Christien spoke his mind more often and was the easiest to rile; Lucien had a wonderful sense of humor, and Faust was the quiet one.

All spoke in their native tongue. Like Gabrielle, they could understand and speak Gaelic, though they preferred not to.

Gabrielle knew how fortunate she was to have the loyalty of these four men. They had been her protectors most of her life. They had shielded her when her adventurous nature took her into precarious situations, and had kept her secrets—even from her father when she didn't want him to find out about some of her escapades. Her safety was always their primary objective, but she valued their confidence as well. On numerous occasions they had saved her from peril, even at the risk of their own lives.

Just last month Faust came to her defense at the village market. She was making her way among the stalls when two drunken men began to follow her, their smirks divulging their lascivious intentions.

The minute they moved in her direction, Faust stepped in front of her and laid the men on the ground before they knew what happened.

She also recalled an incident that occurred last year. She was heading toward her father's stables to see the new foal that had been born. Just as she was rounding the corner of the stable, the hitch on the grain wagon at the top of the hill broke, sending the cart careening down at her with ferocious speed. She had barely turned to see it coming before Christien grabbed her shoulders and threw her out of its path, taking the impact of the wheel on his leg. His ankle was so bruised and swollen, he couldn't walk on it for weeks.

She cringed at the thought of the trouble she had caused these steadfast men, but then she smiled thinking about some of the other times they had been there to look after her. There were the nights when she was a little girl that Stephen kept watch so that she could sneak out of her chamber and listen to the musicians in the courtyard. She also remembered the afternoon that, despite her father's warnings, she and her friend Elizabeth climbed a willow tree by the river and fell into the muddy waters. Lucien had rushed the little girls to the cook to be washed and given clean clothes before Baron Geoffrey was ever the wiser. And she could never forget when she was nine years old and the band of ragged wanderers made camp in the meadow next to her father's castle. She had been cautioned to stay away from them, but she indignantly felt that all visitors were guests and should be treated as such. The cook had been baking berry tarts for the evening meal, and so Gabrielle waited until they were placed in the open window to cool and then gathered them in her skirts. She was happy to see the guests gobble down the treats with great relish, and she would have lingered to visit, and might even have accepted their invitation to ride with them for a while, had she not turned to see Christien and Lucien standing ten feet behind her with their arms crossed and scowls on their faces. When her maidservant questioned the unusual stains on Gabriel's skirt that night, the guards did not mention her disobedience, but later when they were alone with the little girl, they warned her about the harsh ways of the world.

Christien and Faust were the newest

members of her guard, but Stephen and Lucien had been with her for as long as she could remember. Through all of the important, as well as the trivial, events of her life, one or more of them had been by her side. Even in her lowest moments, they were there. When her mother took a turn for the worse and Gabrielle was once again summoned to her bed, Gabriel knew in her heart that this would be her final visit. For two long, sad days, she and her father sat with the dying woman, holding her hand and stroking her brow. Many servants and physicians came and went during that time, but outside the chamber door, for every minute of those two days, all four of Gabrielle's guards stood watch. Not one would leave his post.

As Gabrielle now rode with them toward Finney's Flat thinking of all that they had done for her, she said a prayer of thanksgiving for these dear friends.

Stephen pulled her attention from her thoughts when he veered to the east. Gabrielle followed. After the horses had a good run, she slowed the pace. The rugged landscape surrounding her was craggy and covered with a dazzling green blanket. There were spills of bright purple heather, white chickweed, and milkwort dripping down the hills. Her father had told her that all of Scotland was lovely, but Gabrielle, looking over the vast landscape, thought the Highlands were stunning.

The higher they rode, the colder the air became. The scent of pine was thick, and the cold wind felt wonderful against her face.

They had been climbing almost two hours when they suddenly reached the tip of a plateau. Stephen had already scouted the area and explained to Gabrielle that there was really only one way to get to their destination.

"Since we're coming from the south, the direct route would be straight ahead, but as you can see, the way is thick with trees, and it might be difficult to get our horses through. We could probably manage it, though."

"And if we can't manage it?" Christien asked.

"Then we'll go another way," Lucien answered.

"Finney's Flat is on the other side of those trees?" she asked.

"Yes, Princess."

She blocked the sun from her eyes with her hand and looked to the east and then the west. The line of trees seemed to extend for as far as the eye could see. The plateau was massive.

"How deep are the trees?" she asked.

"I didn't try to go all the way through," Stephen said. He glanced up at the sky to note the position of the sun and then said, "We have quite enough daylight to find out."

"If the closeness of the trees is a concern, could we approach Finney's Flat from the east or the west? Would that be quicker?" Lucien posed the question.

Christien answered. "Princess Gabrielle's father told us that there were woods on the east side of the flats, and beyond those woods is Loch Kaenich. There are also thick woods lining the west side of Finney's Flat, and beyond those woods live the wild Buchanans."

"*Wild* Buchanans?" Lucien was curious about Christien's description of the clan.

"That is what Baron Geoffrey calls them, and from some of the stories he's told, I don't think the name's an exaggeration."

"It's my understanding that none of the clans allow trespassers," Faust interjected.

Gabrielle frowned as she turned to look at the soft-spoken guard. "Faust, we're on

MacKenna land now, and no one has tried to stop us."

"Nay, Princess," he answered. "We aren't on MacKenna land. 'Tis true that their holding does border Finney's Flat on the south, but we're on the southeast tip, and that little piece of land is controlled by Laird Monroe, your future husband. That is why we have been left alone."

She slowly scanned the horizon. The area looked completely deserted to her. Since they had begun their long journey across the Highlands, she hadn't seen another soul. Were the people who lived in this vast wilderness in hiding so they wouldn't have to interact with outsiders, or were they simply few and far between?

"Stephen, what if we were to try to cut through the east and approach Finney's Flat from the north side?" she asked.

"Princess, do you not see the mountain straight north of us?" he asked. "The Buchanan laird told your father that toward the bottom of the mountain there is a limey cliff with a wide stone overhang above Finney's Flat . . ."

"Your father, the baron, told us that the path winding down from the overhang is the only way to get to the bottom, and it is heavily guarded. If you squint against the sun, you can see it," Lucien explained.

"The mountain from the base of the trail to the land above is controlled by the clan MacHugh, and they do not suffer trespassers." Faust made this comment.

"Suffer trespassers?" She smiled as she repeated his words.

"They are . . . quick to rile," Christien said. "And quick to react."

"We could not allow you to go there," Stephen said.

"Laird MacHugh is a dangerous man," Faust said.

"Aye, we have heard the MacHugh clan is quite fierce, and their leader is a savage," Christien told her.

She shook her head. "I would not be so quick to judge a man because someone has spoken ill of him."

"What is your pleasure then, Princess?" Stephen asked. "How would you have us proceed?"

"We'll walk through the forest directly ahead of us," she said. "It is the fastest route, is it not? And it will be good for us to stretch our legs."

Stephen bowed his head. "As you wish, Princess. I would suggest that we ride as far as we can into the woods so that our horses will be hidden from the curious who happen by. Faust, you will stay with the mounts when we are forced to walk."

As it happened, they were able to ride a fair distance into the woods, though there were a few tight squeezes through prickly brush. Twice they had to backtrack to find another way around, but once they had crossed a narrow creek, they were able to gather speed. When they reached the last crush of trees, they dismounted. Handing over the reins of her horse to Faust, Gabrielle followed Stephen who parted the brush ahead of them.

The clearing was only a few yards away when Stephen suddenly stopped and put his arm out to block Gabrielle from going any farther. She stood beside him, straining to hear the sounds of the forest. As she waited, she silently adjusted the strap holding her pouch of arrows over her shoulder and shifted her bow to her left hand in preparation. A few seconds later she heard a harsh bellow of laughter followed by a loud blasphemy.

She stayed perfectly still. She heard men talking, but their voices were muffled and it was impossible to understand the conversation.

Raising her hand to her guards so that she would get no argument, she slowly crept forward. She was well-hidden by the trees, but when she shifted ever so slightly to the left, she had an unobstructed view of the flat land beyond. She spied seven men, all dressed in monks' garb with their brown hoods pulled up over their heads.

For a moment she thought they were standing over one of their own, praying for his soul before they buried him. They were clustered together near what appeared to be a pit. Near the hole was a fresh mound of dirt. When their true intentions became clear, she nearly gasped. An eighth man was on the ground. He wasn't dressed as a monk but wore a muted plaid. His hands and feet were bound, and he was covered in blood.

Gabrielle moved closer. She felt Stephen's hand on her shoulder, but she shook her head and continued on. Still shielded by the trees, she watched and listened to the discussion under way.

The men were arguing over which way to drop the bound man into the hole. Three wanted him to go in headfirst. Others vehemently disagreed, wanting the captive tossed in feetfirst. The one who had been silent, most likely their leader, made the final decision.

All were in agreement on one issue: they wanted their captive to wake up so that he would know what they were about to do to him.

Gabrielle was sickened and appalled by the snippets of conversation the wind brought her. What sin was their captive guilty of? What was his transgression? She decided that it didn't matter what he had done, for no crime, no matter how heinous, deserved such a sadistic punishment. It was inhuman.

As she listened to their escalating argument, she discovered the truth. The only sin their captive was guilty of was one of association. He was Laird Colm MacHugh's brother.

The leader finally spoke. "Hamish, keep your eyes on that ledge. We can't put Liam MacHugh in the ground until we see his brother."

"Gordon, I ain't deaf. You already told me what to do, and I'm doing it. I got my eyes peeled on that ledge. I'm still wanting to know what we're supposed to do if Laird MacHugh don't come to save his brother."

"He'll be coming all right," one of the others answered. "And when he makes the turn at the lookout, he'll see what's happening, but no matter how fast he rides, he won't get here in time. His brother will be long dead, and we'll be long gone back to the border."

"And how will he be able to tell it's his brother going in the ground?" yet another asked.

Gordon answered. "Word's reached him by now that his brother's in trouble. He won't be able to see his face from such a distance, but he'll recognize the plaid."

"What if he don't recognize the plaid from so far away?" Hamish asked.

"He'll still see us dumping Liam into the hole and burying him. He'll know."

"If he can't see his face, then he can't be seeing our faces, either. So how come we have to wear these robes? They're scratching my skin. I feel like I got bugs crawling on me. It smells, too, like pig swill."

"Quit your complaining, Kenneth," Gordon

ordered. "We're wearing the robes we stole because we aren't going to take any chances MacHugh might see our faces."

"If he ever finds out we did this . . ." Hamish visibly shivered. "He'll do worse than bury us alive."

There was a grumble of agreement. "Maybe we ought to just leave him and take off now," Kenneth said. He was nervously backing away from the hole.

"Don't talk stupid," Gordon said. "Laird MacHugh is never going to find out who we are. Why do you think we were brought up from the lowlands?" He added in a rush before there could be another complaint, "And paid handsomely. Are you willing to give that up?"

"No, but—" Hamish began.

"Enough talk of running away," he snapped. He turned to the soldier standing over the unconscious warrior and said, "Kick him, Roger. See if he stirs. I want him awake when he goes in the hole."

Roger did as ordered, swiftly kicking him in his side. Liam didn't move.

"I don't think he's going to wake up this time," Kenneth said. "I'm guessing he's dying now."

"You shouldn't have beat him so hard, Gordon," Hamish muttered.

"We all took a turn," Roger reminded him.

"We only did what we were told to do," another interjected.

Gordon nodded. "That's right. We were only following orders, like the good soldiers we are."

Kenneth pushed the hood on his robe back, scratching his ear. "Tell me again. What did Liam MacHugh do?"

"I've told you ten times already," Gordon shouted as he gave Kenneth a mighty shove, nearly knocking him into the hole.

The soldier scrambled to regain his balance. "Tell me again," he said.

"We caught Liam, and we're killing him to bring his brother down off the mountain so the soldiers hiding in the east woods can catch him unawares."

Kenneth scratched his ear again as though to remove a pesky bug. "What are they gonna do with him when they catch him?"

Gordon shook his head. "Kill him, you simpleton, and bury him next to his brother."

Kenneth wasn't offended by the name calling. "What clan are the soldiers from?

You know, the ones hiding over there." He waved his hand toward the east, squinting to see if he could spy any of them.

"Never you mind what clan they belong to," he answered. "The less you know, the better for you."

"Look! Liam might be waking up," another soldier announced, nudging their captive with his foot.

Roger cackled with delight. "Good. He'll be knowing what's happening when we dump him into the hole. Have any more water to throw on his face, Manus? Get him good and awake."

Before he could get an answer, Kenneth said, "He never waked up. I've been watching his face, and his eyes haven't even fluttered open once. He's as good as dead."

"But maybe like Gordon said, if we threw water on his face . . ." another soldier suggested.

"I used up the last of it," Manus said. "We could spit on his face."

The men thought that was a fine idea and began to laugh. Gabrielle heard the last two names as they pushed and shoved one another, acting like they were at a festival. Fergus and Cuthbert. She knew it was important for her to remember all seven names, for one day there would be retribution.

Hamish's snorts of laughter stopped when he happened to look up and spot Laird MacHugh.

"There he is! There he is!" Hamish shouted as he struggled to get his hood up over his head. "There's the MacHugh!"

Everyone, including Gabrielle, looked to the ledge. A silhouette of a warrior on horseback moved like a golden blur against the sun.

"We've got plenty of time," Kenneth said. "The MacHugh can't fly down here."

"Look at all the men following him. I'm counting up to twenty already," Manus shouted, his voice trembling with fear.

Gordon was getting jumpy. He thought he'd heard a noise behind him. He whirled around, his hand poised on the hilt of his sword. When he couldn't see a threat, he turned again to look to the east and then the west. Nothing.

"We've wasted enough time," he said. "Get him in the hole. We've got to cover him with dirt and be on our way."

Roger and Cuthbert rushed to Liam and

hauled him to his feet. The captive's head dropped forward. Fergus grabbed him by his hair and jerked his head back. "His eyes are closed again," he said, obviously disappointed.

"His eyes were never open," Kenneth replied.

They were dragging Liam to the hole when a far-off rumble caught their attention. In unison all seven turned just as warriors on horseback broke through the trees at the far end of the glen. Their horses pounded the ground as they closed the distance. So far away, they were but dots on the horizon.

"It could be the Buchanans," Manus shouted. "Can't see them good at all yet, but I'm guessing it's them."

"They'll kill us! They'll kill us all!" Hamish screamed. He twirled in a circle like a cornered wood mouse trying to decide which way to scurry. "Where can we hide? Where?"

Cuthbert and Manus dropped Liam's limp body. Urgency cracked Gordon's voice when he ordered, "Get him up. Hurry, damn you. Get him up. When I was pulling him off his horse, his eyes opened, so I'm the only one he's seen. I've got to kill him before he goes

into the hole. There isn't time to bury him
and let him suffocate."

Cuthbert and Manus didn't obey the
order. Neither did Roger or Kenneth or
Hamish or Fergus, for all of them had
already run for cover.

Gordon drew his sword. At the same time,
Gabrielle reached for an arrow and notched
it to her bow in anticipation.

The Buchanan warriors were still too far
away for their arrows to reach the seven
men, and the MacHugh warriors racing
down the mountain were also too far away to
save one of their own.

Suddenly, there was another commotion. Soldiers waiting to ambush the
MacHugh broke through the trees and
headed across the flats toward the
Buchanans. A full-scale battle was about to
erupt. If they didn't hurry, Gabrielle and her
guards would soon find themselves in the
thick of it.

Gabrielle kept her gaze locked on Gordon, the leader of this pack of rats. His captive wasn't moving. Liam was down on the
ground, lying on his side, and Gordon kept
nervously glancing to the north. He took a

couple of steps back, hesitated, and then moved forward again. Gabrielle knew Gordon couldn't run away and leave Liam, who had seen his face.

"Stephen," she whispered. "If I miss—"

"You won't."

"But if I do . . . be ready."

Gordon made up his mind. Turning in her direction, he swung his sword back, his intent to slice Liam in half.

Gabrielle's arrow stopped him. Her aim was true, and the tip of the arrow cut through flesh and rib, piercing his black heart.

Seconds later the ground seemed to buckle beneath her feet as the Buchanans and their enemies clashed on the battlefield. The sound of metal slamming into metal was earsplitting. The killing had begun.

The pandemonium moved toward her. Gabrielle prayed that Liam MacHugh wouldn't be trampled by horses or men before she could get to him. Blessedly, Christien and Faust made quick time and arrived at her side with the horses. Gabrielle climbed onto Rogue's back and started toward the open field, pulling her cape over her head, hoping in the chaos that no one would see her.

Stephen blocked her. He knew what she wanted done. "Christien and I will see to the task. Lucien and Faust will take you back to the stream we crossed. Hurry, Princess. You must get away from here."

She didn't waste time arguing. She prodded Rogue with her foot and headed back through the forest. Moments later at the stream, Stephen and Christien caught up with them. Gabrielle thanked God they hadn't gotten trapped by the battle.

"Is he alive?" She dismounted and rushed to Stephen's side. Liam MacHugh was draped over his steed's saddle.

"He's still breathing," he answered.

"Hurry then. I know where we can get help."

EIGHT

ANOTHER GRISLY BATTLE CRY RENT THE AIR. TOR-
tured screams followed.

The MacHughs had joined the fight.
Forming an impenetrable line, they
advanced. The Buchanans followed their
lead, and within minutes the two clans had
trapped the enemy between them. They
showed no mercy. It was an eye for an eye,
and when it was over, the field was littered
with bodies.

The frantic search for Liam MacHugh
began then. Colm MacHugh leapt from his
horse and ran to the hole the enemies had
prepared for his brother. His relief was great

when he saw the hole was empty. There was only one body on the ground near the mound of dirt. Colm didn't recognize him. He was studying the unusual markings on the arrow embedded in the man's chest when Laird Brodick Buchanan joined him.

"Who the hell is he?" Colm asked.

Brodick shook his head. "I've never seen him before."

Colm jerked the arrow from the dead man's chest. "Is this a Buchanan arrow?"

"No. I thought it was yours."

"MacKenna's behind this," he said.

Brodick shook his head. "Those aren't his soldiers on the ground, and this isn't one of their arrows. The markings . . . I've never seen one like this before. There's no sign of MacKenna here." He picked up a piece of rope. There was blood on it. "They tied your brother with this."

"I still think this is somehow MacKenna's doing," Colm insisted.

"Without proof, you cannot accuse him," Brodick reasoned.

"Liam couldn't have gotten far." Colm scanned the woods surrounding them. "We'll keep looking until we find him and whoever has him."

"The Buchanans are with you," Brodick pledged. "As long as it takes to avenge this black-hearted deed."

The two lairds divided their men into smaller units to scour the area, but after hours of searching, each group reported that they had thoroughly covered the flats and the forests, but to no avail.

Liam MacHugh had vanished into thin air.

NINE

LIAM MACHUGH WAS IN SORRY SHAPE. SOMEONE had taken a whip to his back, and his skin had been shredded into bloody ribbons. His legs and the bottoms of his feet had also taken a beating, and blood dripped from the deep gash on the right side of his head.

Gabrielle knew she could get help for the warrior at Arbane Abbey, and though she was in a hurry to get there, the injured man's immediate needs came first.

They rode along the bank of the stream until they were far enough away from the fighting to stop. Stephen lifted the lifeless body of Liam MacHugh from his horse and placed him on the ground next to Gabrielle. She gently laid his head in her lap and pressed a cloth to the wound at his temple, trying to stop the bleeding, and then she quickly cleaned the other cuts as best she could with a strip of linen she'd torn from her undergarment and dipped in cold water. The man needed medicine to ward off infection and a soothing salve for his back. He also needed someone to put a needle and thread to him to pull together the ragged edges of skin around the gash. She didn't want to be the one to sew him back together, for she didn't wish to cause him any more pain.

The turn of the stream was tucked in between the pines a fair distance away from Finney's Flat. They were isolated and she hoped safe from intruders. While Lucien and Faust guarded the area, Stephen and Christien stayed close to her. Just as she was about to call for her guards to move him, Liam's head wound started bleeding again.

"Princess, you've got blood all over your gown," Stephen remarked.

"I'm not bothered by it," she replied. "But I worry about this poor man. He's lost so much blood."

"I don't think he's going to make it,"

Christien said. "And we should be prepared for that possibility. What would you have us do with the body?"

Gabrielle wasn't shocked by Christien's bluntness. He wasn't being callous. He was a compassionate man, but he was also the most pragmatic of the four guards.

"If he dies, then it is God's will, but I will do everything in my power to help him survive."

"As will we," Stephen assured her. "However, Christien has made a valid point. This MacHugh warrior has not seen you."

Her smile was gentle. "How could he? He has yet to open his eyes."

"You don't understand our meaning," Christien said. "You could be in great danger."

Stephen agreed. "We don't know who these people are or if any of them may have seen us. Your arrow killed the leader of the men at the grave, but the others got away. If they find out you're responsible for his death, they might seek revenge. No one must ever know you were there."

Gabrielle glanced around at the somber faces of her four guards and realized Stephen was right. But it wasn't for her safety alone that she was concerned. If the men at Finney's Flat found out she had killed one of their own, they wouldn't just come after her; they would retaliate against her guards as well. She couldn't let that happen.

"What do you propose I do?" she asked.

"When we get closer to Arbane Abbey, Lucien and Faust will accompany you inside and escort you to your quarters," Stephen suggested.

"You could use your cloak to hide the blood on your gown," Christien said.

"And what of this injured man?" she asked.

"We'll find another way to get him into the abbey. The monks will surely have the medicine he needs."

Christien nodded. "If he dies, there is the possibility that Laird MacHugh might blame you. You heard what those cowards said about him."

"They called him ruthless," she said. "Yet they were going to bury an innocent man alive. Why would I believe a word any of them said?"

She stopped them before they could argue. "This man is now our responsibility. I won't hand him over to anyone. We will all find a way into the abbey that will not draw attention. Only when I am assured that he is well cared for will I leave his side."

"But Princess—" Christien began.

She continued. "These monks are men of God, are they not? I will simply ask them to keep silent as to how Liam came to be at the abbey. If I can get them to promise, they cannot and will not break their word."

"There are other ramifications," Stephen said. "You cannot get in the middle of a war."

She knew they weren't going to let up. "We shall compromise. Once Liam is safe and looked after, I will separate myself."

"And you will tell no one what happened?"

"I will tell no one."

TEN

IT WAS SURPRISINGLY EASY TO GET INSIDE THE abbey unseen. Not only was the door on the south end of the curtain wall that surrounded the monastic buildings unlatched, but it was also propped open. A priest had placed a stone in front of the door so that it would be easier for him to carry in bags of grain from the wagon across the path.

Gabrielle and her guards watched him from the cover of the trees behind the abbey. She thought the bags looked like they weighed more than the priest did. He wasn't quite an old man yet, possibly still in his early forties, she guessed, but he didn't have much muscle. He first tried to put the bag on one shoulder, nearly toppled over, and ended up wrapping his arms around the middle of the bag and letting the bottom drag between his legs.

Reining her horse into the open, she called out to him. "Father, would you allow some help?"

He was at first startled, and then he nodded vigorously. "I would be most thankful for assistance," he called out.

Lucien and Faust had already dismounted and were headed to the wagon. Lucien noticed how the priest struggled under the weight of the bag and took it from him. "Where would you like this?" he asked.

"Just inside the door on the left is a storage building. If you stack the grain there, I would be most appreciative." He pulled a cloth from the belt of his robes and mopped the sweat from the back of his neck. Smiling, he started toward Gabrielle. "Welcome, I'm Father Gelroy."

He'd just crossed the path when he noticed the injured man draped across Stephen's saddle.

"What have we here?" he demanded. He rushed to Stephen's side to get a better look, and he was so shocked by the man's condition he made a hasty sign of the cross. "What happened to this poor fellow? Is he alive?"

"He is," Christien answered.

Stephen dismounted and lifted Liam into his arms. "This man is in need of assistance as you can clearly see. Is there a healer here?"

"Aye, there is, and more than one," he answered in a rush. "Come. Follow me."

Lucien and Faust made quick work of unloading the grain. Gabrielle dismounted and handed the reins to Lucien.

The priest hurried to the door ahead of them. "Does this man have a name?"

Gabrielle answered. "His name is Liam MacHugh."

Father Gelroy's reaction was swift. He came to such an abrupt stop he actually swayed, then whirled around. His expression was one of disbelief, and the color had disappeared from his face.

"Did I hear you say MacHugh?" He was so rattled, he'd shouted the question. "Tell me I didn't, but did I?"

"Father, please, lower your voice," Stephen instructed.

The priest put his hand to his forehead. Gabrielle noticed it trembled.

"My God. You've got Liam MacHugh and he's barely alive. If he dies . . ."

Gabrielle stepped forward. "We are hopeful with the healer's help he won't die," she said quietly.

Father Gelroy forced himself to calm down. "Yes, yes, we must all be hopeful," he stammered. "I'll tell you this. There will be hell to pay if he dies. Quickly now. Inside with him. The room next to mine is empty. We'll put him in there. Once I've shown you the way I'll go in search of Father Franklin. He's more skilled, I believe, than the others."

Lucien and Faust stayed with the horses while Stephen and Christien, carrying Liam, followed Gabrielle and the priest into the abbey. The corridor he led them down was dark, narrow, and smelled like the inside of a wet cave. All the doors were of dry splintered wood in arched frames. Father nodded to one as he rushed past and said, "That's my room."

He stopped in front of the next door, gently rapped on it with his knuckles to make certain it was still unoccupied, and then lifted the latch. He pushed the door, stepped inside, and held it open for them.

The room was tiny, with a small window set high above a wooden pallet that served as a bed. A gray wool blanket covered the straw mattress. A stool and a small chest were the room's only other pieces of furniture. A water bowl and pitcher flanked by two candles sat on top of the chest.

"Put him on the bed. Gently now," the priest said. "Let him sleep on his side so his back . . . good Lord, his poor back . . ." He took a breath and slowly let it out. "I believe Father Franklin is at vespers. I'll tell him to bring his medicines. When I come back, I'll fetch my stole and oils and give Liam MacHugh the last rites."

Gabrielle protested. "But that sacrament is only for those who are dying."

"Can you tell me he isn't dying?"

She bowed her head. "Nay, I cannot."

"Then he must have the sacrament of Extreme Unction so that he can go to heaven unblemished."

He turned to leave, but Christien stepped in front of the door, blocking his exit.

"Father, it would be for the better if no one knew how this man came to be here."

"Then I must first know if any of you had

anything to do with his injuries. It's a foul question, but I must have an answer."

"He was in this condition when we came upon him," Christien told him.

"I thought as much, for why else would you carry such a burden?" the priest returned. "I promise you I won't be saying a word to anyone about Laird MacHugh's brother, but I would like to know what happened."

"Will you keep our confidence as well?" Christien asked. "It would be for the better if you don't know who we are."

The priest shook his head. "I'm afraid it's too late for that. The second I saw this beautiful lady I knew who she was. There have been whispers of her coming for weeks now."

He turned to her and bowed low. "It is a pleasure to meet you, Lady Gabrielle. Have no worries, for if I am introduced to you in the future, I will be pleased to meet you then as though for the first time. Your secrets are safe with me."

"Thank you, Father," she said, but she doubted he heard her, for he had already rushed out of the room.

"It's time for you to leave, Princess," Stephen said.

Christien nodded agreement. "Aye, it's time."

The two guards looked worried, and she was sorry to disappoint them.

"I cannot leave him just yet. He's too vulnerable. Someone must watch over him while he is in this weakened state. Before I go, I must be certain that he is in capable hands and that he has the proper medicines."

She wouldn't be swayed. The argument that Father Franklin would be one more man they would have to trust to keep their confidence wasn't valid in her opinion. Father Franklin was also a man of God and would not break the promise they would get from him.

"The more people who know, the better the chance of the trail leading back to the man you killed . . ." Stephen began.

"This man's life is more important."

"We cannot agree, Princess," Christien said, "but we will do your bidding."

Liam still hadn't opened his eyes or made any sounds at all, not even a groan when Father Franklin, who Gabrielle had to admit was quite capable, sewed his skin together. He'd wanted to forgo the stitches and sear the wound with a hot poker, but she wouldn't allow it. There seemed no need since the bleeding had stopped at last. There was another reason. Though she doubted the warrior would care about appearance, he was quite handsome, and a scar from stitches wouldn't be as terrible as a burn scar.

Once she was assured that nothing more could be done for the wounded man, Gabrielle finally consented to trust his care to the two priests.

The sun was setting when Gabrielle finally left Liam's side.

ELEVEN

GABRIELLE'S ARRIVAL AT THE FRONT GATES OF arbane Abbey was met with great jubilation.

The abbot had given orders to summon him the minute she appeared, and he now hurriedly rushed forward, tying his cincture around his rotund stomach and breathlessly calling out for food and drink.

With a grand bow, he stammered, "Such an honor. It is such an honor to offer you our humble hospitality, milady. Yes, we're truly, truly honored."

He clasped her hand and squeezed. He didn't let go until she forcefully pulled her hand back.

She introduced her guards to the abbot and said, "We thank you for opening your rooms to us, and I thank you for allowing my wedding to take place here."

"We are thrilled to have the honor. Everyone has been making preparations for the holy sacrament for some time, and now, to think it's only a week away. This union will surely secure a peaceful and lasting bond between our two noble countries." Snapping his fingers, he motioned for a servant to hurry and make preparations. "You must be hungry and thirsty. Come inside. We have refreshments for you and your soldiers. I understand they do not leave your side when you are away from home. Is that not true?"

"It is true, but I am happy for their company."

A pretty young woman rushed forward and thrust a bouquet of flowers in Gabrielle's face. Gabrielle took them and thanked her, smiling when the woman made a quick and awkward curtsy.

"These are lovely," she called out as the woman scurried away.

"Was your journey pleasant?" the abbot asked.

Gabrielle didn't laugh, but she wanted to, wondering what he would think if she blurted the truth about their journey. They had been inside the abbey for hours now, but the abbot couldn't know that. Gabrielle and her guards had gotten back on their horses and had circled through the forest so they could approach Arbane Abbey by its front gate. Their trip had taken a few minutes at the most, but since they were keeping silent about Liam MacHugh, she could only say, "It was most pleasant, but I would like to change my gown before I have refreshments."

The cloak hid the stains from Liam's blood. Since the weather was still warm, the abbot must have thought she was ill to be wearing such a heavy garment.

"Yes, of course. Brother Anselm waits inside to show you the way to your rooms. I pray they meet with your satisfaction."

"I'm certain I will be most comfortable."

"We began to worry when the time passed and you hadn't arrived. We expected you hours ago."

"I'm sorry to have caused you concern. Your countryside is so lovely I lost track of the time."

The abbot seemed satisfied with her answer. He took her arm and started walking.

"Guests have been arriving and setting up their camps outside of our monastery for days. Most are from England as one would expect, but some came from as far away as France and Spain, all bearing gifts to mark this auspicious occasion. The contingent from your family's homeland of St. Biel brought the most wonderful gift of all, I believe. It is a lovely sculpture of your patron saint. They have asked us to hold it in our chapel's sacristy for safekeeping until the wedding, and I'm sure Laird Monroe will want to set it in a sacred place of honor in his own chapel. You'll see some of the other offerings at the banquet . . ."

Gabrielle smiled and nodded as the abbot continued to chatter on about the gifts and the visitors and the feasts. It was apparent the abbey had never seen such a celebration, and she was happy to indulge his enthusiasm.

They'd just entered the commons when the abbot stopped and motioned to a man crossing their path.

"You must meet Laird MacKenna. He, too,

is a guest, but he's leaving shortly. Laird," he called out, "come and meet Lady Gabrielle. She has finally arrived."

The man turned and walked toward them with a smile that seemed genuine and warm. His stride was long, and he carried himself proudly. His wavy black hair was swept back from his high forehead, and there wasn't a single scar on his flawless features. He must lead a charmed life, she decided.

He bowed to her. "I have heard it said that you are a beauty, and I must say it was not an exaggeration."

"I thank you for the compliment."

"I know you are aware that Lady Gabrielle is to be married here to Laird Monroe," the abbot said.

"Of course, I know," Laird MacKenna answered. "He's my friend," he said to Gabrielle, "and I will attend the celebration at his request. It will be a great day for both of our countries. Returning the glen . . . I mean Finney's Flat . . . to a Highlander will bring peace among the clans, for Laird Monroe will see that it is used wisely. I look forward to the ceremony." He bowed again. "Until then . . ." he said and took his leave.

The abbot waited until he was out of sight

and then said, "Laird MacKenna surprised us with such an act of kindness. He brought us a wagon full of grain from his fields. He's never been so generous before, and we were quite stunned and pleased. The laird has become a thoughtful man. Ah, here is Brother Anselm. He will show you the way."

The two rooms assigned to Gabrielle were in the largest wing of the abbey. They were surprisingly spacious and had connecting doors on either side. Servants were busy unpacking her clothes in preparation for the festivities ahead. Gabrielle kept her cloak wrapped around her until she was alone in her room. She wasn't sure what to do about the blood on her cream-colored bliaut, and she couldn't come up with a plausible explanation as to why it was there. She ended up folding the garment and hiding it in the bottom of one of her trunks.

Later that evening, after her maids had gone to bed, Faust and Lucien led Gabrielle to Liam's room to check on him. Father Franklin and Father Gelroy were both there and in the middle of a heated argument.

"Has he awakened yet?" she asked in a whisper so as not to disturb the patient.

Franklin smiled at her. "No, he hasn't, but

he's done some moaning, and I've a good feeling he'll wake up soon."

"Or he won't," Gelroy said, scowling. "He isn't out of danger, now is he, Franklin?"

"One must have hope, Gelroy."

"If he dies, Colm MacHugh will tear this place apart, sacred or not. It won't matter to him. He needs to be told that his brother is here. Hopefully he'll come to fetch him before Liam dies."

"*If* he dies," Franklin snapped. "But I don't think he will. I do agree that Laird MacHugh should be told Liam is here. I think you should leave with morning light."

"I would be happy to take over your duties while you make the trip to the MacHugh holding," Gelroy responded.

"I'm too old and feeble to make this journey," he whispered.

Gelroy snorted. "You're neither too old nor too feeble. What you are is afraid, Franklin. Aye, that's what you are."

"And you're not?"

"Of course I'm afraid. In fact, I'm more afraid than you are," he boasted in a low voice. "And older by two years, which is why you should go on this errand, and I should stay. My heart couldn't take Laird MacHugh's disappointment."

Before Franklin could work up a rebuttal, Gelroy turned to Gabrielle. "We've been bickering about this for over an hour now."

Frowning, she said, "I don't understand your hesitance. I would think that Laird MacHugh would be overjoyed to learn that his brother is alive."

"Perhaps," Franklin allowed. "But what if Liam were to die before Colm MacHugh could get here? And after Gelroy has told him Liam's alive. What then?"

"You mean to say after *you* tell him Liam's alive," Gelroy snapped.

"I believe you're borrowing trouble," she said. "And this Colm MacHugh must be told. He's surely frantic by now. If someone I loved disappeared, I don't know what I would do."

Though they had been discussing the issue in low voices, Gabrielle felt they should move into the hallway so they wouldn't disturb Liam.

"He can't hear us," Franklin said. "He's still in a deep sleep."

Gelroy followed Gabrielle into the hall and

closed the door behind him. "I promise you, milady, that Franklin and I will work this out. Have no worries. One of us will make certain Colm MacHugh is informed of his brother's whereabouts."

"My guards have asked me to inquire if you would like their assistance sitting with Liam during the nights ahead. He shouldn't be left alone."

Gelroy was both pleased and relieved by the offer. "I would be most appreciative for their help. Franklin and I promised you that we wouldn't tell anyone how this poor soul came to be here, but we have also decided that it would be for the best if we didn't mention Liam at all. There would be too many questions and speculations. We'll keep his presence secret for as long as possible. So you see, we cannot ask any of the others to sit with him because the secret will then be out."

Franklin stepped forward. "Gelroy told me that he doesn't know what happened to Liam or who inflicted the severe beating, but he and I promise you, whoever it was won't get another opportunity to do him harm while he is a guest here. With the help of your guards we will all make certain he remains safe."

"I wish I could be more helpful and take a turn sitting with him, but I realize—"

Lucien interrupted. "You cannot, Princess."

"It wouldn't be proper for you to be in a man's room, no matter if he were sleeping or not," Franklin told her.

She didn't argue, for she knew he was right.

Turning to Gelroy, she said, "And one of you will go to the MacHugh holding?"

His shoulders slumped. "Aye. One of us will go."

"You understand, milady. Whoever goes won't be coming back," Franklin said matter-of-factly.

Gelroy was nodding agreement when Franklin patted him on his shoulder. "I'll miss you, Gelroy."

"It is a dangerous journey?" she asked.

"Not particularly," Franklin answered.

"Will it take long to get there then?"

"Not overly long," Gelroy answered.

"It isn't the getting there that's the worry, milady. It's the getting out of there that has us worried."

Gabrielle was certain their fears of the MacHughs were exaggerated. They couldn't be as fearsome as the priests were insinuating.

"You'll go soon?" she pressed.

"Very soon," Gelroy promised.

The priest's definition of very soon was different from Gabrielle's. It took him three full days and nights to gather his courage to head out. By that time Liam had improved enough that Gelroy could feel confident he would survive, but the priest was still apprehensive. Even though he knew he must carry the news to Laird MacHugh, he still had his doubts that he would be returning to Arbane Abbey.

Father Gelroy finally rode out on a borrowed mount, but his destination wasn't the MacHugh holding. After putting considerable thought into the matter, he decided instead to go to MacHugh's loyal ally, Laird Buchanan. Gelroy foolishly believed that Brodick Buchanan would be easier to talk to and less likely to physically react to the news that Laird MacHugh's brother had been severely beaten.

The closer he got to the Buchanan land, the more violent his trembling became until he feared he would shake himself off his horse. But God took mercy on him. As he was resting under a huge oak tree just below the Buchanan holding, he spotted a horse and rider coming down the broken trail.

Now he had a dilemma on his hands. He didn't know if the rider was friend or foe. Should he try to hide? No, the rider had already spotted him. Gelroy said a prayer and decided to hope for the best.

Lo and behold, it was Baron Geoffrey riding toward him. He made the sign of the cross in thanksgiving, and as soon as the baron was within shouting distance, Gelroy called out to him. He reminded him that they had met before at the abbey, nearly two years ago. Without mentioning the baron's daughter, Gelroy asked the baron if he had been with the Buchanans. "It seemed to me you were coming from their land."

"I was," Baron Geoffrey answered.

"Do you know the Buchanans well?"

"We are distantly related, and though I had thought to pay my respects and not linger more than one night, a tragedy occurred. A warrior was missing. The men were out searching for him and were expected to come back to the holding yesterday but were delayed by a terrible rainstorm the night before. I had to wait for Laird Buchanan to return home."

"Could the warrior's name be Liam MacHugh?" he asked mildly.

"Aye. So you have heard what happened."

"I've seen him," he said. "He was brought to the abbey, the poor soul."

The baron was rendered speechless. Gelroy took advantage of his condition.

"You'll be getting a high place in heaven, even though you're English, if you'll go back and tell Laird Buchanan this news so that he can tell Laird MacHugh."

While Baron Geoffrey was reeling from the information given so casually, Father Gelroy turned around and nudged his mount into a trot down the mountain.

"Wait," the baron shouted. "You cannot go without—Is Liam still alive?"

Gelroy slapped his horse's hindquarters to get it to speed up. Without glancing back, he called over his shoulder, "Oh God, I hope so."

TWELVE

THE LAIRDS WHO LIVED IN THE NORTHERN HIGH-lands were a prickly group. They were known to be unpredictable, unreasonable, and ungracious. They were also known to be savages upon occasion. Yet if Baron Geoffrey were to accuse any of them of these flaws, they would believe he was flattering them.

Aye, they were a peculiar lot, and no one, Geoffrey believed, was more peculiar or hardheaded than Laird Brodick Buchanan. Brodick didn't have any problem letting Geoffrey know that, even though they were related, he still disliked him intensely because he was English. Since Brodick's wife also happened to be from England and was Geoffrey's cousin, Brodick explained very bluntly that he couldn't come right out and say that he hated all the English, just some.

The rude laird also told Geoffrey that he didn't want him stepping foot on his land, yet Geoffrey knew that if he honored the laird's wishes and didn't pay his respects when he was in the area—and every laird in the Highlands would know that he was—then Brodick would consider the slight a grave insult and would have no choice but to retaliate.

The baron had only visited once before, just after Brodick married Lady Gillian. He had been asked by his uncle Morgan to check on Gillian's well-being. Morgan, Geoffrey's father's youngest brother, was a cranky, reclusive old man, who couldn't believe that Gillian would be content living in the Highlands among the wild Buchanans. To Geoffrey's surprise, he found Gillian not only content but quite happy. She could not have been more gracious to him, and her kindness more than made up for her husband's hostility.

Although he would never admit it to Brodick, Geoffrey was impressed with him and his wife. They didn't live in a fine castle but rather a small cottage no bigger than Geoffrey's steward's home. It was apparent that neither Brodick nor Gillian cared about impressing outsiders but, rather, concentrated on more important issues. Brodick's sole duty was to protect his wife and his clan. Gillian's duty, at the moment anyway, was to protect her unborn child. She wanted to attend Gabrielle's wedding, of course, but from the moment she had informed Brodick that he was going to become a father, leaving their holding was out of the question.

The priest who had intercepted Geoffrey and given him the news about Liam MacHugh acted as though he had a pack of wild dogs on his tail. As soon as he had blurted out the news, he had turned and urged his mount into a full gallop and had disappeared into the trees.

Geoffrey headed back to the Buchanan holding, but Brodick wasn't happy to see him again so soon. He certainly wasn't in the mood to put up with another social call.

The laird was an intimidating sight as he stormed toward Geoffrey. Tall and muscular, he was fair-haired and battle-scarred, and he wore a scowl as black as night. His first in command, a fierce warrior named Dylan, followed in his laird's wake. Then two more warriors joined the procession.

Geoffrey rested his hands on the pommel of his saddle and waited for Brodick to reach him. The laird's greeting wasn't pleasant, but then Geoffrey didn't expect it to be.

"I thought I was rid of you, Baron."

Geoffrey ignored the insult. "Liam MacHugh is at Arbane Abbey."

His announcement took the scowl off Brodick's face. "Is he alive?"

The baron quickly recounted what the priest had told him, and when he was finished, Brodick asked, "What in thunder does 'I hope so' mean? Liam's either alive or he isn't."

"He must have meant that Liam was alive the last time he saw him," Geoffrey suggested. "You'll tell Laird MacHugh?"

"I will."

Brodick turned around and walked away from Geoffrey, dismissing him. He was barking orders to his men. He would go with MacHugh to the abbey. There was no doubt in his mind that Colm MacHugh would stop at nothing to find out who had done this to his brother. If God was merciful, Liam MacHugh would be alive when they got there.

THIRTEEN

WHILE GELROY HAD BEEN WORKING UP THE courage to make the trip to inform Liam's family of his whereabouts, Gabrielle had been filling her days with social obligations and preparations for the wedding. In the late of night she would leave her chamber to look in on Liam while he slept. Her guards stood watch at his door. Father Franklin explained to his patient when he finally opened his eyes that, even though the abbey was a sanctuary and was therefore considered holy ground by all good, God-fearing men and women, he wasn't going to take any chances that a heathen might sneak in and do Liam further injury. He told Liam that Lady Gabrielle had arrived for her wedding with a contingent of guards, and he had asked for their help. In his weakened condition, Liam didn't protest. He was aware that they were watching over him, but he didn't speak to them, and when they spoke to one another, it was in a language that Liam had never heard and couldn't understand.

ONCE LIAM WAS CONSCIOUS, Father Gelroy announced that he would be leaving to deliver his message, and he set out the following dawn. He returned at nightfall. When he knocked on Gabrielle's door, she was happy to see him, but she was surprised that he had returned from his important errand so quickly. She made him comfortable in a chair on the balcony, offered him refreshment, and then took her seat across from him.

"You are well, Father?" she asked.

"I am," he replied. "And you, milady?"

"I am most well," she replied, "but I am quite curious. May I ask, how were you able to complete your errand in such a short time?"

"I rode hard and fast," he boasted.

A servant stood in the doorway with a tray. Gabrielle mo-tioned to her, and she offered a goblet of cool water to the priest. Father Gelroy thanked her with a smile and a nod and then took a hefty drink.

"Was Laird MacHugh overjoyed with the news about his brother? Was he relieved?"

"I imagine he was overjoyed and relieved," he answered. "You see, I didn't go to the MacHugh holding. I thought it would be more prudent . . . yes, prudent," he repeated, "to go to the Buchanan holding and give Laird Buchanan the news so that he could have the honor of telling Laird MacHugh. The Buchanans are allies of the MacHughs, and their holding is much closer to the abbey."

"I see." Gabrielle folded her hands in her lap and asked, "And was Laird Buchanan overjoyed and relieved with the news?"

"I imagine he was," he said a bit sheep-ishly.

"You don't know?" she asked, thoroughly confused.

He cleared his throat. "As it turned out, I didn't need to go all the way to the Buchanan holding. Your father was just leav-ing their land by the only safe route, and I was able to intercept the baron and give him the joyful news. I'm certain he was happy to tell Laird Buchanan."

It seemed to Gabrielle that the priest had made a simple errand quite complicated. His fear of Laird MacHugh was most unreasonable. After all, the priest had good news to relay to the laird. Why would he worry that the man would do him harm?

"Yes, I'm certain he was," she said.

"Your father should be here soon now," he remarked.

"I'll be happy to see him. Perhaps he will go riding with me in the countryside. I don't wish to complain, but I would love to leave the abbey for a little while."

"The countryside is crowded these days," he said. "There are envoys from many countries who have arrived for the wedding. Several barons from England have set up camp here. And as you know, when they travel, they bring all the comforts of home. I have heard that one tent is as big as our church. Your wedding to Laird Monroe promises to be a grand occasion."

"I'm amazed they would travel this long distance for the ceremony," she said.

"This is an important event for many people," he explained.

Father Franklin interrupted with a hard knock on the door. As soon as the servant bid him enter, the priest rushed into the chamber. When he saw Gelroy, he came to a quick stop and motioned for him to join him.

"It appears Franklin's wanting a private word with me. I think I know what this is about. I missed noon prayers," he explained. "And I imagine he's wanting to give me a good lecture."

A moment later the two priests were in deep discussion, whispering back and forth. Gabrielle's attention was drawn to the commons below. She leaned over the railing and saw a priest running and shouting to two others coming out of the chapel, but she couldn't make out what he was saying. The commons quickly filled with men, and all of them seemed highly agitated, waving their arms and shaking their heads. A few priests made the sign of the cross, knelt down, and began to pray.

Something terrible had happened.

"Lady Gabrielle?"

Father Gelroy begged her attention. The look on his face didn't leave any doubt. The news was bad.

Her mind raced with dark possibilities.

Was it her father? Had something happened to him? Dear God, please, no.

She forced a serene expression and waited for one of the priests to explain.

Gelroy nudged Franklin. "You tell her."

"It's Laird Monroe, milady. He cannot marry you."

"Of course he can't marry her," Franklin muttered.

"He cannot?" she asked, trying to understand.

"No, milady, he cannot," Gelroy blurted. "He's dead."

FOURTEEN

IT WAS A PITY HE DIDN'T HAVE TIME TO MAKE THE murder look like an accident. It would have made his life so much easier. He had considered the possibility of suffocating Monroe, but a dying man could very well summon the strength of ten when he was fighting for his life. No, suffocation was too risky.

And so was drowning. What if he were a stronger swimmer? Or a screamer? One loud shout could bring him help. Drowning, he had decided, was also out of the question.

He had considered several other methods that would pass for accidents, but he eventually ruled all of them out. Some were too complicated, others relied too heavily on strength and timing.

In the end he had settled on using a knife. A sharp blade was a quick and easy kill. Unfortunately, no one would ever believe it was an accident. How could anyone accidentally fall on a knife five or six times? It took several good thrusts to kill Laird Monroe.

He had killed before, but never like this. Because of his position of power he would usually give such an unpleasant duty to someone else. But this was different. He didn't dare trust anyone else with this onerous task. He had to do it alone. It was the only way to make certain the trail wouldn't lead back to him.

Fortunately Monroe had become complacent in recent years. He didn't take care like he should, and his followers had become just as lax in their guard. They didn't expect trouble because their laird didn't have enemies. How could he? He never took sides with one clan against another, and he never wanted more than what he already had. The laird had absolutely no ambition and was as lukewarm as old bathwater.

The laird never varied his routine. Every

night just before sundown he took a long stroll, no matter what the weather, no matter where he was staying. He always walked alone.

Crouching in the darkness and waiting for Monroe had been uncomfortable and tedious, but once the rustle of leaves told him Monroe was coming, he gripped his knife tightly and patiently waited for the perfect time to spring.

It was unfortunate, but it was unavoidable. Laird Monroe had experienced a very unpleasant death.

FIFTEEN

THE FUNERAL MASS WAS SAID IN THE ABBEY'S north chapel. Many of the Monroe clan had been on their way to the wedding when they received news of the laird's sudden demise, and their happy journey of celebration had turned into a mournful and somber procession instead. Several Highland lairds attended the funeral, but many more would have ridden the distance to pay their last respects had they known about Monroe's death. The ritual—one day after his death—had to be hurried due to the unusually warm weather and the rapidly deteriorating condition of the body.

The English weren't welcome, though it was doubtful that any of the barons would have wanted to sit and listen to the priest extol the virtues of the dead man. He was, after all, a Highlander, which in their view made him inferior and not worthy of their prayers.

Baron Geoffrey of Wellingshire and his daughter, Lady Gabrielle, were the only exceptions. The Monroe family allowed their presence because the lady had been pledged to marry their laird. She was allowed to hear mass with them, but she and her father were seated in the last row. Although there was plenty of room, no one would sit next to them.

Gabrielle didn't expect special consideration. She was thankful that she was given the chance to pray for Laird Monroe's soul. Her father and others held the laird in such high regard and praised him because he was such a good and kind man. Why would anyone want to harm him? His murder didn't make any sense. Robbery wasn't the motive, for nothing had been taken from his body. His gold ring and jeweled dirk were still on him when he was found. Was he killed just for the sport of it?

Her mind wandered, and she thought about Liam MacHugh and the terrible men who had made him suffer so. How could one man treat another with such depravity?

Mass ended and Monroe's body, wrapped in white linen, was carried out. Gabrielle kept her head bowed as the procession of mourners filed from the chapel. She happened to glance up once and noticed that most of them were glaring at her as they walked by.

When the last couple, a young man with an older woman, reached her, they stopped. Gabrielle could feel the woman's piercing eyes, and she raised her head.

"Go home. You have no place here," the woman hissed. Her words spewed out like poisonous venom.

The young man quickly took the woman's shoulder and gently turned her toward the procession. "Come, Mother, my uncle wouldn't want anger."

Gabrielle's face burned. She had never heard such contempt before.

As they slowly made their way down the aisle, the man turned to give Gabrielle a sympathetic smile.

Her father laid his hand on her arm to

keep her from standing to leave. "We'll wait until the Monroes are gone," he cautioned. "That woman was Laird Monroe's sister. I think it would be best that we not follow them. There could be other insults."

"Why would they want to insult me?" she asked incredulously.

"The Monroe clan has decided that you are the reason their laird is dead."

She stared at him as though he was speaking nonsense.

"They hold you responsible for their laird's death," her father restated.

She was appalled. "They think I killed him? How could they think such a thing?"

"You misunderstand, Gabrielle. They don't think you stabbed him, but they do believe that if their laird had stayed home and hadn't agreed to marry you, he would still be alive. Monroe and his followers were camped in a nearby glen the night he was murdered, and since he was on his way here to the abbey to marry you, they believe you caused his death."

"But that's ridiculous."

He patted her hand. "Yes, it is. Don't let their foolishness bother you."

She straightened. "I can withstand their

insults. I'm not so weak that I would fall apart over a cruel word or two."

"You have tender feelings, daughter, whether you will admit it or not."

The door opened behind them, and Stephen stepped inside. "It's safe now. The Monroe mourners have left, and the baron who was waiting at the door has returned to his camp."

Her father nodded. "Then we can go. Come, Gabrielle. Your guards will escort you back to your rooms."

"Stephen, what baron was at the door?"

Her father answered her. "Percy." He stepped into the aisle and moved back so Gabrielle could walk in front of him.

"I don't understand why he came for the wedding? He isn't your friend or ally, and I doubt he knew Laird Monroe," she said.

Her father sighed. "I should have explained this a long time ago. Percy says he was sent by the king's command to witness the cere-mony, but I'm sure he had other motives. I had thought to shield you. Baron Percy and Baron Coswold are two very manipulative men who will stop at nothing to get what they want. I had hoped that once you were married they would give up their obsession."

He motioned for Stephen to open the doors.

"Was I right, Stephen?" he asked as they walked down the steps. "Was Percy waiting for a chance to speak with Gabrielle?"

"Aye, Baron. He was lurking by the side of the chapel, and he had his friends with him. I haven't seen Baron Coswold yet."

"Coswold traveled to Scotland. I'm sure of that. But God only knows what he's up to."

"Why would either one of them want to speak to me?" Gabrielle asked.

"I will explain what needs be told later," her father said. "Go now and have your servants pack your things. You'll be going back to England tomorrow morning. If it were not so late in the day, I would have you leave now."

"But aren't you going with me, Father?" Gabrielle asked.

"No, I must go to the king first. He has been told of Monroe's death by now, and I will need to get his approval for our return to England. I will catch up with you in a few days."

"Are Coswold and Percy the reason you're so anxious to go home?" she asked.

"Yes, they are the reason," he answered grimly.

They entered the commons, walking side by side, with Stephen and Faust trailing behind.

"I haven't told you what I have learned about these two and their obscene competition, but it appears that whatever one baron wants, the other must also have. Everything becomes a game to them to see who will win and who will lose."

He shook his head in disgust. "I thought you would be rid of them once you married Laird Monroe, and I cannot tell you how stunned I was to find that Percy had arrived here for the wedding and had set up camp outside the abbey. I expect Coswold will appear at any time."

"Dead men can't marry," Faust remarked. "How fortuitous for them that Laird Monroe was murdered."

Stephen nodded. " 'Tis most convenient, isn't it?"

Baron Geoffrey turned to him. "I was thinking the same thing."

"Are you suggesting . . ." she began.

"You have been sheltered from the evil in this world, and so you cannot imagine what men are capable of. Let me tell you what I encountered when I arrived at the

Buchanans. Laird Buchanan and many of his soldiers were with their allies, the MacHughs, searching for Laird MacHugh's brother."

Her father didn't spare the details when he explained what the monsters who had captured Liam had wanted to do.

"I was told there was blood on the rope they bound him with and a hole was dug to bury him."

"Do they know who these men were, my lord?" Stephen asked.

"Nay, they do not. Brodick and Laird MacHugh found one of them on the ground near the hole, but no one recognized him. He didn't wear the colors of any clan to iden- tify him. Brodick returned home for a short while. I was waiting for him."

"Did you search with him, Father?"

"Heavens no. He would never allow it, but as it turned out, MacHugh's brother was found. As I was leaving Brodick's land, out of the forest came a priest with joyful news. He asked me to tell Laird Buchanan that Liam MacHugh was here at the abbey."

Her father smiled. "The poor priest couldn't get away fast enough, and he wouldn't answer my questions. I imagine the MacHugh clan will be overjoyed to hear that

Liam is alive and safe. Has the abbot mentioned anything about this poor injured soul being here?"

Gabrielle cast a furtive glance over her father's shoulder at Stephen before answering. "No, the abbot has told us nothing of him."

"It's just as well," her father said. "The less of this brutality you see, the better."

"I choose to believe that there is more good than evil in this world," she said.

"You have your mother's kind heart, Gabrielle." Baron Geoffrey kissed her lightly on the cheek before he left her. "I must make haste and speak to my soldiers. There's much to be done before I leave, but I will make certain to say farewell to the abbot."

As soon as her father had turned the corner, she looked at Stephen. "I feel as though I have deceived my father by not telling him how we found Liam."

"You protect the baron by not telling him. None of us could know the ramifications of killing one man and saving another. They are both strangers to us. Your father should not be put in the middle, and that could very well happen. It is best that we are going home."

She agreed. "This has been a sad journey."

Sixteen

GABRIELLE WAS ABOUT TO GO INTO HER ROOM when Father Gelroy called to her.

"Milady, a word, please?"

He ran toward her, robes flapping against his ankles. His face was bright red, and he was frowning intently.

She didn't think she could handle more bad news. Bracing herself, she walked toward him. "Yes, Father?"

"They're here." He was panting so rapidly, he could barely get the words out.

"Who's here?" she asked.

"The MacHugh laird and the Buchanan laird. Both have their warriors with them.

They're at the top of the hill overlooking the abbey."

"This is good news, isn't it?"

"Oh, no, no. I mean yes," he stuttered. "They've come for Liam, and that's very good."

"Then you should go and greet them, shouldn't you? And take Laird MacHugh to his brother?"

"That won't be necessary," Gelroy answered.

"I don't understand. Of course it's necessary. Laird MacHugh has come all this way, and he should be taken to see his brother," she insisted.

"Oh, he'll see him. I'm sure of that," Gelroy asserted. "But the laird won't be taken to him."

Gabrielle was more confused than ever. "Then how will he see him?"

"Liam's waiting outside the gates," the priest blurted.

Shocked, Gabrielle said, "That poor man hasn't been able to rise from his bed since he got here. How could he possibly get outside the gates of the abbey?"

Gelroy couldn't look her in the eye when he answered. "Father Franklin and I carried him."

"And you just left him there?" She couldn't believe what the priest was telling her.

"You don't understand. Laird MacHugh is a mighty warrior. Everyone has heard of his amazing strength . . . and his amazing temper."

Suddenly the situation became clear to her. "You're afraid of him."

"Only a fool is unafraid of Laird MacHugh."

"But just abandoning the poor man—" she began.

"Come with me," Gelroy said. "I think you'll understand when you see for yourself. Don't worry. They won't be able to see you. We'll climb the wall and peek out. I'll show you the way."

The priest led Gabrielle outside and up the narrow steps to an opening carved out of the thick stone wall.

Gelroy pointed to the hill. "Can you see them?"

Her sharply indrawn breath answered his question. The sight of the warriors had rendered her speechless, and she could only summon a quick nod.

She didn't have any trouble locating the lairds. The two men were in front of their followers, each atop a magnificent horse, one black, the other gray. Both men looked as though they'd been fashioned by a god of ancient times. She knew that Zeus never actually existed, but when she looked at these giants, she couldn't help but think that maybe . . .

"The one on the right is Laird MacHugh," Gelroy said.

Was he real? She closed her eyes, opened them again, and he was still there.

"He's quite . . . large, isn't he? They both are actually," she said, glancing from MacHugh to Buchanan.

The priest laughed. "They're Highlanders," he said, as though that explained everything. "They are not as civilized as the rest of us."

"They have come here for one of their own, which tells me they are capable of brotherly love. They are human, Father," she said with a hint of disapproval at the priest's negative judgment.

"There's Liam," he whispered, even though he surely knew they couldn't possibly hear him.

"We'll get to see their joyful reunion," she said. "Is it wrong of us to intrude?"

"I don't believe so. Besides, they'll never know."

They watched another minute or two, and then she whispered, "Liam's having trouble walking. Do you see how he's trying not to limp? He's favoring his right foot, isn't he? He's slowing down, too. How will he ever climb the hill?"

"Pride will get him there."

"But pride is a sin."

"Not to a Highlander."

Gabrielle stared at Laird MacHugh. His expression was rigid. There was no trace of feeling in his eyes as he watched his brother struggle to move forward.

Barbarian, she decided. MacHugh was a barbarian. Had he no feelings for his own brother? He'd come this far for him. Why wouldn't he help him now? Why wouldn't any of them help poor Liam?

They were *all* barbarians, she decided. Every last one of them.

Liam tried to stand erect, but when he moved his foot forward to take a step, he swayed and stumbled backward. Laird MacHugh immediately swung down from his horse and handed the reins to Laird Buchanan.

"My faith has been restored," she said. "I was wrong to think ill of the laird. He's going to help Liam after all." Gabrielle smiled as she added, " 'Tis brotherly love."

She watched in anticipation as the laird strode toward the weakened man. He didn't stop to speak to him; he didn't smile at him, and he certainly didn't embrace him.

What he did do was give his brother the full force of his fist.

SEVENTEEN

BRODICK COULDN'T BELIEVE HE WAS THE VOICE OF reason. He was usually the hot-tempered one. But not today.

Today his duty was clear: to keep Colm from doing anything reckless, and that was no easy task. It had taken a great deal of talking for Brodick to convince him not to storm into the abbey and tear it apart room by room in order to find out what had happened to his brother.

Colm had been resistant, but managed to control his anger on the ride to the abbey. Then he saw Liam leaning against the abbey gate, and he began to burn with fury.

"Good God," Brodick whispered when he saw Liam. He took a breath, remembered he had to be the rational one, and added, "He's alive."

Colm didn't respond. He could only watch Liam's faltering attempts to walk for one agonizing minute before he swung down from his mount and headed to fetch him. With one blow to his jaw, Liam teetered and collapsed across his brother's waiting shoulder.

Once Colm had situated his brother on the back of a horse, he motioned for two riders to flank his sides and sent them ahead.

"Someone knows what happened to my brother, Brodick. Whoever brought him to the abbey had to have witnessed something. There's no way in hell that Liam got up and walked away from that field. He had to be carried. Look at him, Brodick." The MacHugh nodded to the abbey and added, "Liam didn't get there on his own. He had help."

"He could have been left at the gate."

"Or he could have been taken inside. If someone in the abbey knows what happened, I'll find him, and I'll make him tell me what he knows, no matter how much force I have to use."

Brodick motioned to the tents set up outside the walls. "With all of these people around, you need to use your head. You can't just force your way inside the abbey. It's sacred, for God's sake. You can't even carry your sword or any other weapon with you when you walk through those gates."

Colm didn't appreciate being told what he could and could not do. He glanced at Brodick. "Since when do you pay attention to rules? Marriage has made you weak."

"My wife would not be married to a weak man."

Colm swung up on his horse, grabbed the reins, and started back up the hill.

"Perhaps she's turned you into a weakling because she's weak. Most women are."

The insult amused Brodick. "You *have* met my wife, haven't you?"

Colm shrugged. "Aye, we've met." There was a hint of a smile in his voice when he added, "She's a strong woman. A rarity, that."

"That's right, she is strong, and trying to antagonize me won't work. I'm not going to help you wage war on a group of old men."

"I have no intention of waging war on the

priests. I'm simply going to find out what happened."

"Before you do anything, perhaps you should talk to your brother."

"That's where I'm headed."

"You probably shouldn't have hit him so hard. How long do you think it will take him to wake up?"

"Some water on his face will bring him around."

As the column of riders slowly made their way down the other side of the hill, Colm said, "Did you see what was done to him?"

"I saw," Brodick answered quietly.

It would be a long time before Colm would be able to let go of the memory of his brother trying to walk toward him. It appeared that almost every inch of skin on his brother's back and legs had been torn or ripped off of him.

No, he would not soon forget that godawful sight.

"Your men should take Liam to Kevin Drummond's cottage. His wife has a way with healing."

"Nay, they're taking him home. He'll get the care he needs there. I want you to understand, after I've questioned him, I'm going into the abbey."

"I know," he replied. "I'm going with you."

"No, you're not. I'm already in your debt. Those bastards would have buried Liam if you and your men hadn't shown up when you did. I never would have gotten to him in time."

"The dead one near the hole with the arrow in his chest . . . that wasn't done by one of ours," Brodick reminded him.

"I still owe you a tremendous debt."

Brodick smiled. "Aye, you do."

They caught up with the others. Dylan, Brodick's first in command, trailed behind MacHugh's soldiers. He heard Brodick's shrill whistle and stopped the procession.

There were a dozen from the MacHugh clan and almost as many Buchanans sur-rounding Liam.

Since they were so close to Duncan's Bluffs, they decided to let Liam rest for a few minutes before continuing on. Colm's brother was still groggy from the blow he took to the jaw. He refused assistance as he dismounted and nearly fell to his knees. Everyone saw that the bottoms of his feet were caked with blood, but no one rushed forward to help him. They waited for him to straighten himself and follow Colm to the flat rocks overlooking the valley.

Liam tried not to wince with each slow and painful step. When he finally reached the bluff, he dropped to the ground and leaned his shoulder against a smooth rock.

Colm's greeting to his brother was blunt. "Who did this to you?" He stepped in front of Liam and folded his arms across his chest as he waited for him to answer.

"If I knew who did this, I would have killed them by now," Liam answered.

It was an empty boast, and both of them knew it. His brother wasn't in any condition to kill anyone. His face was so gray, Colm thought he might pass out again. But Liam's pride was at issue, and for that reason Colm went along with his arrogant claim.

"Aye, you would have," he agreed. "Tell me what happened."

"I don't remember much," he said. "I was leaving Monroe's holding, heading for home across the flats, but I stayed to the east by the water. I know I was still on Monroe's land. Yes, I'm sure I was. Something struck me on the side of my head, and I think maybe I was hit again in the back. The blows stunned me, and when I came to my senses, my hands and feet were bound. There was a hood over my head."

He closed his eyes for a moment, trying to reclaim his memory. "There were at least four of them. I came to for a while, but I had to let them think I was still unconscious. I heard them talking before I passed out again. I'm certain there were four distinct voices . . . no, wait." He sighed then, his frustration mounting. "There could have been more."

He rubbed the back of his neck and closed his eyes again.

"Did any of them speak directly to you?" Braeden, Colm's first in command, asked as he and some of the others circled.

"No, I don't think so." Liam's voice grew hoarse and more difficult to understand with each answer he gave. "Why can't I remember? It's damned irritating."

To Colm, it was obvious why Liam's memory was so spotty. He'd taken several blows to the head.

"You said you heard them talking. What were they saying?" Brodick asked.

"That they hoped to kill as many MacHughs as they could."

"If there were only four or so captors, how could they possibly kill seasoned MacHugh warriors?" Brodick asked.

Braeden handed Liam his leather water pouch. Liam took a long drink, nodded his appreciation to the commander, and then answered. "There were men hiding in the woods, waiting to attack. They'd been told to get as many MacHughs as they could. The more they killed, the higher the reward."

He took another swallow before continuing. "Another one of them worried that there really weren't troops waiting in the woods to help them, and they would be all alone to face Colm's wrath. He wanted to kill me and be done with it, but the one in charge kept telling him they had to wait."

"Wait for what?" Colm asked.

"I don't know."

"Did you hear any of their names?" Brodick asked.

"If I did, I don't remember."

Colm continued to question his brother, hoping for some clue as to who was behind this atrocity, but Liam wasn't much help.

"Do you remember being taken to the abbey?" he asked.

"No, but I remember waking up there. I

was in a little room. Two priests were with me. One was a healer, and the other wore his stole and prayed over me. I think he thought I was dying."

"Who were these priests?" Braeden asked.

"Father Franklin was the healer. I asked him how I'd gotten there, and he said he didn't know."

"Did you believe him?" Colm asked.

"Yes, I did, after he explained. He told me that Father Gelroy came to him and asked him for his help. Gelroy was the priest praying over me," he added.

"And Father Franklin wasn't curious to know how you'd gotten there?" Brodick asked.

"Aye, he was curious. He asked me how I'd been injured, and I told him I couldn't remember. I heard him ask Gelroy the same question, and Gelroy told him it was best if he didn't know the details."

"What about this priest Gelroy? What did he tell you?"

"He said he was outside unloading a wagon of grain when he happened to look up, and there I was."

"There you were? That's it? No one was with you?" Colm asked.

"I asked Gelroy that very question, and he couldn't give me an exact answer. When I asked him to explain what he meant, he said that he couldn't say yes and he couldn't say no."

"He speaks in riddles," Colm snapped.

Liam tried to stand. Bracing his hand against the rock, he made it to his knees before falling back. Cursing his weakness, he rested another moment before trying again.

"This priest Gelroy will not speak in riddles to me," Colm said. "He will tell me what I wish to know."

"Colm, you need to understand. Gelroy sought to protect me. He was concerned that whoever had injured me might come inside the abbey—"

"To kill you." Brodick nodded as he finished Liam's thought.

"Yes," he said. "Gelroy believed that the demons, as he called the men who attacked me, would not respect sanctuary. He and Franklin agreed to keep my presence secret as a safety measure until you arrived, Colm, but there was a problem. The two of them could not stand guard over me day and night without raising suspicion, and neither would be very effective against an intruder."

"And how was this problem solved?" Colm asked.

"Gelroy enlisted the help of a few good men he knew to protect me while I slept. He explained to me that he wanted men who understood the ways of fighting."

"Priests would have no such training," Braeden interjected.

"No, they wouldn't," Colm agreed.

He stopped pacing in front of his brother. "Who did this priest find to watch over you?"

"He asked soldiers who were there for Laird Monroe's wedding."

"What clan were these men from?" Brodick asked.

Before Liam could answer, Colm asked, "Were these men Highlanders?"

"No, they were not, but Gelroy trusted them completely."

"Then they had to be Highlanders," Brodick reasoned.

All of the warriors listening to the conversation immediately nodded their agreement. Only Highlanders were to be trusted, and even then with caution.

"I'm telling you they were not Highlanders. I don't know where they came from, but Gelroy must have known them well to trust them."

Colm knew he had to hurry with his questions, for he wanted to get as much information as he could from his weary brother before exhaustion caught up with him. Liam was already drowsy. He could barely keep his eyes open, and he was having trouble concentrating.

"How many were there?" he asked.

"How many what?" Liam asked wearily.

Colm held his patience. "Soldiers, Liam. How many soldiers watched over you?"

"Four. There were always two either inside the room with me or just outside my door."

Brodick glanced at Colm when he asked, "And these men carried weapons?"

Liam actually smiled. "No, they did not."

"The question amuses you?" Brodick asked, trying to understand Liam's reaction.

"Aye, it does. When you see these men, you will understand why. But I will assure you of this, Laird Buchanan. They do not need weapons."

"They are invincible? Is that what you suggest?" Braeden asked as though the notion of such praise of an outsider's strength should be taken as a personal affront to his own might.

"No man is invincible," Colm snapped. "What did these soldiers tell you, Liam? Did they explain how you came to the abbey?"

"No. They talked to one another, but they wouldn't talk to me."

Both Colm and Brodick waited for Liam to explain further. When he didn't, Brodick asked, "Why wouldn't they talk to you?"

"I don't think they understood me," he said finally. "And I certainly didn't understand them. They spoke a language I've never heard before."

Colm was becoming even more frustrated. "Gelroy must have understood them."

"I'm not sure he did. I never heard him speak to them."

"Then how did he—" Colm stopped. It was pointless to continue questioning his brother. Liam needed rest, and Colm hoped that when his brother grew stronger, he would be able to remember more about the men who had taken him captive.

Besides, he reasoned, Gelroy would tell him what he wanted to know.

He removed his sword and sheath and

handed both to Braeden. "Take Liam home," he ordered.

He went to his horse to get his bow and arrows and gave those to Braeden as well. "And send the Buchanans home." With a glance at Brodick, he added, "All the Buchanans."

Before Colm could argue, Brodick swung up onto his mount and said, "I am going back to the abbey with you."

Braeden nodded. "Do you want any of us to go inside the abbey with you?"

"I do not." Colm's voice was unyielding.

Braeden was used to his laird's gruff ways. "Then may I suggest that half of our men take Liam home, and I and the others will wait outside the gates with your weapons, Laird."

Brodick's commander stepped forward to stand beside Braeden. "And since my Laird Buchanan is going with you, I suggest that I also wait with our laird's weapons outside the gates. The other Buchanan soldiers will see Liam safely home."

Brodick agreed. "It would be to our advantage to take our swords should we have the good fortune to run into the men who tortured your brother."

"I prefer to use my hands," Colm said.

"Even if others have swords?"

Colm gave him a hard look. "What do you think?"

Brodick shook his head. "I think you're just itching to kill someone, aren't you?"

"I am going to kill whoever did this to my brother," Colm answered.

This wasn't a hope or a promise. It was a solemn vow.

EIGHTEEN

THE COMPETITION BETWEEN BARON COSWOLD and baron Percy had turned deadly. Or so it seemed.

Each man went to great lengths to find out what devious schemes the other was plotting. Spies were everywhere. Certainly not all of Baron Percy's companions were loyal to him. One—William, his herald in fact—was secretly in the employ of Baron Coswold. The herald was a well-compensated informer who committed to memory every word said and every action taken by Percy and his conspirators, and reported back to Coswold.

When word of Laird Monroe's murder reached Percy's camp, the traitorous herald left the abbey on a false errand and rushed to give Coswold the news. The baron had made certain that William knew where he would be at all times, and the informer was therefore able to catch up with him just as he sat down to supper with Laird MacKenna in MacKenna's palatial great hall.

The terrible news didn't get the reaction William expected. Neither Coswold nor MacKenna seemed the least surprised. Coswold merely shrugged indifference and MacKenna, apparently just as unaffected, looked bored as he reached for a chunk of black bread and popped a wedge into his mouth.

Baron Percy had seemed just as uninterested when he'd heard the news. Had both barons expected this to happen? Had they anticipated Monroe's death, or had they simply wished for it? And why was Laird MacKenna also indifferent? One of his own countrymen had been murdered; the herald had thought there might have been at least a hint of remorse.

Coswold pushed the chair back from the table and motioned for the herald to follow him outside. When they were alone, he ordered him to return to Percy's camp to keep his eyes and ears open for further developments.

"Go now, while there is still light to guide you. You can make some of the distance back before darkness falls. I'll arrive at the abbey tomorrow."

The herald watched Coswold strut back inside and then stood there a long moment scratching his head in confusion. Although he'd wanted to, he didn't dare ask the baron the question plaguing him. Monroe had been a powerful, and from all accounts a well-liked, laird who was shockingly murdered in the night.

Why wasn't anyone surprised?

NINETEEN

BRODICK WAS IN WHOLEHEARTED AGREEMENT with colm. If given the opportunity, he, too, would kill the bastards who had attacked Liam. The MacHughs were the Buchanans' allies, and their enemies were, therefore, the Buchanans' enemies as well. Over a year ago, Brodick had ventured into dangerous English territory on a mission to help his wife. The MacHughs had come to the Buchanans' aid then, and it was now the Buchanans' turn to reciprocate.

The MacHugh was a loner, though. He refused to acknowledge the benefit of having anyone other than his own clan fight by his side. Brodick used to feel the same way, and it had nearly taken a war with England to change his attitude. He now recognized the value of these ties, and he considered not only MacHugh but the Maitlands and the Sinclairs, two of the most powerful clans in the Highlands, his closest allies. These lairds had also become Brodick's good friends.

The two men did not speak for most of the ride back to the abbey. Then, urging his horse alongside Colm's, Brodick asked, "Do you know how I met my wife?"

An odd question, Colm thought. "She was bringing Laird Ramsey Sinclair's brother home to him," he replied.

"That's right. The boy was only five or six at the time. One of the men in the Sinclair clan thought he should have been named laird over Ramsey. He conspired to take over the clan, and he used the boy to draw Ramsey into the open with the intent of killing him."

"Why are you bringing this up now?"

"Perhaps Liam was taken for the same purpose. To draw you out."

"Perhaps, twice now in the past month my soldiers protecting my border have been ambushed."

"Did you lose any men?"

MacHugh was insulted by the question. "Of course not. My warriors are trained to expect the unexpected."

"And the men who attacked?"

"Unfortunately, none lived long enough to tell me who sent them, but they were not Highlanders."

"Outcasts then? Looking to steal what they could?"

He shook his head. "You heard what Liam told us. The orders were to kill as many MacHughs as possible. Outcasts would not be so organized. They thrive on chaos, and like rats they steal and run."

" 'Tis the truth you speak," Brodick said. "Ramsey's brother was but a child, but Liam is a grown man. He is nearly as old as you are, is he not?"

"Five years younger but still full-grown."

"Then why didn't he expect the unexpected? He has been trained as well as the others."

"I'll be asking my brother that very question as soon as he recovers his wits."

"Whoever is behind these attacks wants to be rid of all the MacHughs, then?"

"So it would seem."

"Finney's Flat. That's what these attacks are about."

"Aye," Colm answered. "MacKenna's behind this. I'm sure of it."

"But you have no proof."

"MacKenna is a greedy man. He wants the land for himself, and I'm not going to let him have it. I could not abide having any of the MacKennas any closer to my border. The flats have always been our planting fields, and also a buffer between the MacKennas and us."

"King John was gifted the land by our king years ago. He owns it until the woman he has chosen marries Laird Monroe. She brings Finney's Flat as her dowry."

"I am aware of this pact."

"Yes, but are you aware that this woman is from my wife's family. Her father is Baron Geoffrey of Wellingshire."

"You admit to having English relatives?"

"Reluctantly, I admit it. I have become more lenient in my opinions, for if you will remember, my wife used to be English."

"It doesn't matter to me what she is."

"Can you abide having the Monroe clan to look down on from your mountain?"

"What about you?" Colm countered. "Can

you abide having them so close? The Buchanans border Finney's Flat on the west."

"Aye, but we have a forest of trees between us."

"I have no grudge against the Monroes. As long as their laird doesn't interfere when we plant the fields on the north end of the flat, I won't mind his presence."

They'd reached the top of the hill above the abbey and could see the crowd of tents to the south.

"Those tents belong to the English," Brodick said.

"They cannot all be here for Monroe's wedding, unless your English relatives invited them."

"Not this number," Brodick answered. "Monroe wouldn't want them here, either. Nay, there must be another celebration at the abbey."

Once down the hill, they passed off their horses to Braeden and Dylan.

"Be on guard," Colm said as they walked to the gates.

"I'm always on guard," Brodick assured him. He pulled the rope to ring the bell. A moment later, a priest opened the massive wooden door.

The abbot, a shiny little man, who from the size of his belly never missed a meal, motioned them forward. He had already jumped to his own conclusions as to why the two were there.

"You've come to offer your condolences, haven't you?"

Before either laird could respond, the abbot continued, "You must be terribly disappointed to have missed the funeral mass, but with the unusually mild weather it was necessary for his family to take him home and put him in the ground as quickly as possible. Did you think you might speak to the family? A pity you missed them. Shall I show you to the chapel so you might pray for his soul?"

Colm and Brodick looked at each other, and then Colm turned to the abbot. Though addressing a man of God, he didn't guard his words.

"What in God's name are you talking about?"

The abbot took a quick step back and patted his chest in an attempt to calm himself. He had lived a quiet, contemplative life in the monastery for years, and the excitement and turmoil of the last few days was taking its toll on his nerves.

"You don't know? I just assumed . . . it's Laird Monroe," he rushed on when he saw the mean look in Laird MacHugh's eyes. "He's dead. Isn't that why you came here? To express your sympathy?"

"Monroe's dead?" Brodick was staggered by the priest's announcement.

"How did he die?" Colm wanted to know.

The abbot lowered his voice when he answered. "He was murdered." He paused to make the sign of the cross before adding, "Murdered he was, and in the black of night."

"When did this happen?" Brodick asked.

"How was he murdered?" Colm asked at the same time.

The look in the lairds' eyes frightened the abbot. Laird MacHugh seemed the more threatening of the two, angrier as well. The priest's voice trembled as he gave his answers, but he could barely keep up with the rapidly fired questions from the two giants.

Colm noticed that every time he moved, the abbot flinched. He clasped his hands behind his back as a sign of trust, so the meek abbot would know he meant him no harm.

The abbot rushed to explain. "Here I was

thinking you came all this way to pay your last respects, and it's apparent you didn't know about Laird Monroe's tragic death. Now I see what has happened. I've misunderstood, haven't I? I'm so sorry I greeted you with such sad news when it is clearly evident you have come here for a much more joyful occasion, the wedding."

"How can there be a wedding if the groom has been murdered?" Brodick asked. He was beginning to think the abbot was missing part of his mind.

"Laird Monroe is no longer the groom . . . since he's been murdered," he hastily concluded.

"We're not here about any wedding—or any funeral for that matter," Colm said. "We're here about my brother."

The abbot responded with a quizzical look. "Your brother?"

Colm considered grabbing the man by his neck and shaking him but knew it wouldn't be prudent to attack a man of God. From the abbot's blank stare, it was apparent he knew nothing of Liam.

The abbot was sweating profusely. He wiped his wet hands down the sides of his robe. The laird's eyes had turned a dark gray, the color of a brewing storm.

"Things have been happening so fast. We're not used to this much activity in our monastery. Another match for Lady Gabrielle is just now being decided upon. It's chaos." He lowered his voice to a conspiratorial whisper. "Two barons from England are now in the great hall, each claiming to be speaking on King John's behalf. A crowd of English is gathering in the commons. I recommend that you wait upstairs if you don't want to become involved."

"What are the barons fighting about?" Brodick asked.

"We need not concern ourselves with their petty squabbles," Colm said. "Remember the reason we are here." He addressed the abbot once again. "You have a priest here named Gelroy. I wish to speak to him as soon as possible."

"May I inquire as to your reason for speaking to him?"

"You may not."

The abbot was taken aback by the blunt denial. Then he nodded, thinking he understood why the laird had refused to explain.

"Oh, I see. You wish to say your confession. I apologize. I shouldn't have asked. Why don't you go on upstairs, and I'll send Father Gelroy to you. I believe I know just where he is. He'll show you the way to the chapel so that you may rid yourself of your sins."

Yet again the abbot had jumped to the wrong conclusion, but neither laird set him straight.

"It shouldn't take any time at all," he remarked, turning to lead them to the steps.

Brodick nodded his head toward Colm. "With his number of sins, I wouldn't count on it."

Colm was not amused. He shoved Brodick out of his way. "I'm not here for confession. I'm here for some answers about my brother. I just want to get this over and done with and get out of here. Perhaps I can convince Father Gelroy to come with us. I can't think or breathe with this many English surrounding me."

"I doubt Gelroy will want to leave with us. But you can ask," Brodick said.

"Ask? Why would I ask?"

Brodick shrugged. Colm would do what he wanted regardless of how Brodick felt. Besides, Brodick may well have done the same had it been his own brother. Still, dragging a priest out of his sanctuary for the sole purpose of browbeating him into telling what he knew about Liam's captors . . . and saviors . . . was probably going to blacken their battered souls a little more.

The abbot was so intent on overhearing their conversation he didn't realize he'd reached the top of the wall surrounding the commons. Out of breath, he pointed. "Here we are."

The abbot turned to go back downstairs and fetch Gelroy, but Brodick stopped him with a question.

"I'm curious, Abbot. Are Baron Geoffrey and his daughter still here, or have they started back to England?"

"Baron Geoffrey? You know these English?"

Brodick sighed. "It is an embarrassment to admit they are related . . . on my wife's side," he hastily added.

"It is still an embarrassment," Colm remarked.

Brodick silently reminded himself that Colm was his ally. "I've never met the daughter," he told the abbot.

The abbot replied, "The baron has left on

a journey to meet with his king, and his daughter has been preparing to leave for England, but I believe she will be detained."

"Why will she be detained?" Brodick asked.

"You don't understand," the abbot said. "All this chaos concerns the lady and whom she is to marry."

"Is her father aware of this?" Brodick wondered.

"No. He left before the two barons came together."

"And when is Baron Geoffrey expected to return?" Though the future of Lady Gabrielle was of no concern to Brodick, he felt a gnawing obligation.

"I doubt anyone has had time to send a messenger to her father. It's as though the barons deliberately waited until he was away from the abbey before springing this marriage on his daughter. They're both acting as though this is a most urgent matter. From what I've heard of their argument, they want her married before her father finds out and causes an upset." Darting a glance to the left and then to the right he said, "Trickery. Aye, it's trickery if you ask me. But the lady is protected by her guards and she is safe in our monastery. No harm will come to her while she is here."

The naïve belief irritated Colm. The abbey was overrun with strangers, and most were English. How could he believe the likes of them would honor sanctuary? Even the priest Gelroy had had his doubts, for he had asked soldiers to guard Liam while he slept. Colm wondered what this jumpy abbot would think if he found out that Liam had been a guest here.

"Is Lady Gabrielle agreeable to a new match?" Brodick asked.

"She doesn't know yet. They'll call for her soon." Shaking his head, the abbot sighed. "She'll find out about this mischief when she answers their summons."

TWENTY

BARON COSWOLD HAD STORMED INTO THE ABBEY that afternoon with his coterie of drones. He had quite an assemblage of sycophants trailing behind him, twenty-three in all. The large number was deliberate, for Coswold hoped to intimidate and overwhelm Percy.

Coswold felt incredibly powerful. He carried a writ proclaiming that he and he alone spoke on the king's behalf.

But Percy was neither intimidated nor overwhelmed. Like Coswold, he, too, had his spies, and although he didn't yet know about the new writ, Percy had learned that his enemy was going to try to take charge of

Finney's Flat and Lady Gabrielle's future. He believed that Coswold planned to use force to get what he wanted.

Percy was ready for him. His own horde of mindless miscreants followed him as he rushed into the hall to confront Coswold. Percy wasn't about to back down or be pushed aside, and he wasn't the least concerned that he might not get what he wanted. He had a writ signed by the king that he and he alone could act on John's behalf. The king had sent him to the abbey to witness the wedding between Monroe and Gabrielle, but now that the groom was out of the way, Percy was confident that he could decide Gabrielle's future.

Each power-hungry man had a trick or two up his sleeve.

The two barons met in the center of the visitors' hall. The doors to the courtyard had been thrown open. This was not to be a private fight. Each wanted witnesses to hear.

Percy attacked first. Stabbing the air between them with a long bony finger, he said, "Don't you dare try to interfere in my decisions here or I'll have you thrown out. I speak on King John's behalf, and I am going to decide Lady Gabrielle's future."

"Her future with you?" Coswold scoffed. "And Finney's Flat becomes yours as well? Is that what you think will happen, you fool? You most certainly will not have her. I will see to that."

"You have no power, Coswold. I am going to escort the lady back to England. Aye, she goes with me." Percy didn't bother to add the important fact that he planned to force her to marry him first.

Coswold took a step closer. "You no longer speak on the king's behalf, for I have a writ signed by John giving me full power here. I will speak and act in his stead."

Percy was outraged. The veins on his forehead bulged when he responded. "Nay, I have the writ, and it was truly signed by King John. You cannot dupe me. I know what you want, and you will not get her."

The verbal sparring increased until both barons were ceaselessly shouting at each other. The fight moved outdoors as more and more of the curious joined the crowd.

The dividing line between the two camps was marked by a stone cross in the middle of the open lawn: Percy and his followers on one side, and Coswold and his supporters on the other.

"Would you like to see the writ?" Coswold asked. "The king's seal is there, and so is the date, Percy. If you do not step aside, I will have you thrown out."

Percy snorted. "When was this writ signed?" he demanded, and before Coswold could answer, he added, "I know where you've been, and I know all about the dark bargain you've struck with the laird."

Coswold ignored this comment. He snapped his fingers toward one of his supporters, and the scroll was promptly produced. He snatched it from his hands and waved it in Percy's face. "Here it is. King John has assigned power to me."

Colm and Brodick rested their arms on top of a parapet, watching and listening to the debacle taking place beneath them. Colm was simply biding his time until Father Gelroy arrived. The abbot had indicated to them that it wouldn't take long to locate him, but obviously he'd been mistaken.

Impatient to grab the priest and get away from these foul English barons, Colm muttered, "Where is that blasted priest Gelroy?"

"Surely he's on his way," Brodick replied.

Colm scanned the crowd below. He noticed the number of ordained men in robes and said, "There are so many of them. If I knew what Gelroy looked like, I'd drag him out of here."

Brodick grinned. "You know how I mentioned you can't start a war against a priest? Well, you also cannot drag one of them out of here, unless the priest is willing to go, and I doubt Gelroy would be. You and I . . ."

"You and I what?"

"According to my wife, we tend to frighten people."

Another shout drew their attention. "The English, they're loud, aren't they?" Brodick commented. "It's a pity we don't have our bows and arrows. We could rid the world of a few of them."

Colm smiled. "Aye, we could."

At that moment Coswold clapped his hands for attention and bellowed, "Bring Lady Gabrielle to me. We will settle this here and now." He turned to the group behind him, gave a quick nod, and then turned back to face Percy. "I have made my decision. By this day's end, she will be married."

TWENTY-ONE

THE ABBOT FOUND GABRIELLE STROLLING WITH Father Gelroy in the garden. She had already expressed her gratitude to Father Franklin and was about to give her thanks to Gelroy for keeping her confidence when the abbot rushed into the garden calling to her.

"Lady Gabrielle, there's a furor." Panting for breath from the exertion of running, he could barely breathe and speak at the same time.

Gabrielle led him to a stone bench and suggested that he sit for a moment.

Nodding, he plopped himself down and wheezed, "Ah, that's better."

Gelroy clasped his hands behind his back. "You mentioned a furor?"

"Oh, yes. You have been summoned to the courtyard. Father Gelroy, perhaps you should accompany her. Such fighting. Terrible, just terrible the way they're carrying on. And inside this holy monastery of all places. Shame upon their souls."

"Who is fighting?" Gabrielle asked.

"Two barons from England. One is named Coswold I believe, and the other—"

"Percy."

"Yes, that's right, milady. Baron Percy."

"And these two barons have called for Gabrielle?" Gelroy asked.

"Baron Coswold made the demand."

Gabrielle was indignant. "I answer to neither of them, and I have no wish to see or speak to them. I'm ready to leave for home now, and I see no reason to delay my departure."

Gelroy agreed with a quick nod. "Her guards are even now bringing the horses to the front gate, for Gabrielle is planning to leave the abbey momentarily. Her possessions have already been packed."

The abbot shook his head. "I don't think the barons will allow her to leave."

"There's more to this than meets the eye, isn't there?" Gelroy asked.

He sighed. "There is. Each baron carries a writ proclaiming to be speaking and acting on the king's behalf. Coswold's writ is more current if you believe the date written down. The king's seal is on both writs, or so I've been told." All of a sudden the abbot bounded to his feet. "Oh, Lord, I forgot. With all the commotion and the shouting, my errand completely slipped my mind. And how could it? With the worry about those two—Father Gelroy, I was on my way to search for you when Baron Coswold called out to me."

"Why were you searching for me?" he asked.

"I promised to send you to the top of the wall. You see, there are two . . ." He paused.

"Two? Two what?" Gelroy asked.

"Lairds," he answered reluctantly. "Buchanan and MacHugh. They didn't say why they need to speak to you, but Laird MacHugh mentioned something about his brother. Do you know anything about this?"

Panic and dread flashed across Gelroy's face. "I've a fair idea."

"I will hear your explanation later as the

lairds have been kept waiting long enough. They don't look the patient sort." He smiled as he added, "I also heard one of them—I believe it was MacHugh, but I can't be certain—mention something about taking you away with him."

Gelroy swallowed loudly. "You did?"

"Perhaps one of them will offer you the chance to join his clan as a spiritual leader. I know you want to have your own church one day, is that not so? And you also wish to save as many souls as possible. Is that not also so?"

Gelroy frantically nodded agreement. He did want his own church and his own flock—what priest wouldn't?—but not among these brutal lairds and their unruly clans. He didn't want to live the rest of his life in the state of perpetual terror.

"I am content to pray for lost souls here, Abbot," he said in a whisper. "Do you want me to escort Lady Gabrielle to face the barons, or do you want me to speak to the lairds?"

"I will go with her, and you hurry to the lairds. More and more of their clansmen have come inside. The sooner you talk to them, the better."

There was no getting out of it, Gelroy knew. "Best get it done," he said.

He said his good-bye to Gabrielle one last time and left on his dreaded mission.

Gabrielle was going to continue to refuse to meet with the barons, but she abruptly changed her mind. She didn't want to put the abbot in the awkward position of having to explain why she ignored the summons.

"I'll see what the barons want, and then I'll leave the abbey with all possible haste. Abbot, I would like to thank you once again for your hospitality and your kindness to my father and me. We are most appreciative."

She began to walk around the abbot to go to the commons, but he blocked her.

"I'm going to escort you, milady, but shouldn't we wait for your guards? They would certainly want to stand by your side when you speak to these barons."

She shook her head. "My guards are too busy to be bothered with this nonsense, and I'm certain the meeting won't take any time at all."

He couldn't dissuade her. Gabrielle had another reason for keeping her guards away from the barons. Her father didn't trust these men, and neither would she. She was concerned that Coswold and Percy might have their underlings provoke a fight, and though her guards were well-trained, they could be overwhelmed by the sheer number of men attacking.

She did wish her father was by her side, though. He knew what these men were capable of, and he would know what to expect. She tried to think of the worst that could happen so that she would be prepared, but never in her wildest thoughts could she have imagined what was coming.

TWENTY-TWO

GELROY DRAGGED HIS FEET AND PRAYED HIS WAY up the stairs. When he reached the last step and took a good look around, his knees buckled. He had to lean against the wall to keep from tumbling backward.

Good Lord, there were so many of them! And all were watching him.

His voice sounded like the squeak of a rusty door hinge when he called out, "Did someone wish to speak to me?"

Two Highlanders were coming his way. Their long strides quickly consumed the distance between them. Gelroy clung to the wall and waited. Someone gave him a push from the rear. Startled, the priest turned. Another Highlander was standing on the stairs behind him. How had the man gotten there so quickly?

"You are the priest Gelroy?" a booming voice at the top of the stairs asked.

He looked up again. The two giants stood side by side. They were of equal height, and both wore the scars of their past. Gelroy took a tentative step toward them. "I am Father Gelroy."

Brodick noticed the priest was twitching and rapidly losing the color in his face. "We mean you no harm, priest," he said in an attempt to help Gelroy get over his scare.

"I am Laird MacHugh," Colm said.

Gelroy nodded. "Yes, you resemble your brother."

"And I am Laird Buchanan."

The priest managed a bit of a smile as he looked up at Brodick. "Yes, I know. You are the wild Buchanan."

"What did you call me?" He was too surprised to be angry.

"She calls you the wild Buchanan."

Brodick raised an eyebrow. "Who calls me this?"

"Lady Gabrielle," he answered. "Don't you

know who she is?" He rushed on, "She's the daughter of Baron Geoffrey of Wellingshire, and they are your family through your wife."

Brodick's pleasant mood was ruined. He felt as though he was constantly being reminded that he had English relatives. It was damned humiliating.

"I have questions to put to you," Colm said impatiently.

"Yes?"

"It's my understanding that you tended to my brother when he was brought here."

"No, I didn't tend to him, for I have never learned the ways of healing. It was Father Franklin who tended to Liam, but I helped as much as I could. His injuries were severe, and for a time, I'm ashamed to admit, I didn't think he would survive."

Colm nodded. "Who brought him here?"

"I cannot say."

Colm tilted his head and stared at Gelroy for several seconds. "You cannot or you will not?" he demanded.

"Cannot." Gelroy was able to look directly into the laird's eyes because he was telling the truth. He *couldn't* say. He had promised Lady Gabrielle that he would hold her secret, and he could not break his word to her. He didn't understand why she didn't want anyone to know that she and her guards had helped Liam, but he would respect her wishes.

The questions continued, but Gelroy knew that Laird MacHugh didn't believe he was telling him everything because he kept circling back to the same question: How had Liam gotten to the abbey?

"Did anyone else see Liam being carried inside?" Brodick asked.

"No. I don't believe so, and I did my best to keep his presence secret."

"Did you lift him and carry him in, priest?" Colm folded his arms across his chest and waited for his answer.

Gelroy was feeling sick to his stomach. What was he going to do? In order to protect the promise he'd made, he would have to lie to the laird. What a mess. He wished he had time to talk to his confessor, for he didn't have any idea what kind of sin he was about to commit. Was it a mild infraction that would be considered a venial sin, or was it far more damning because a priest was telling the lie? Could it be a mortal sin then? No, surely not. Gelroy thought he would have to do something much more serious, like kill a man, to make a mortal spot on his soul. Still, a sin was a sin.

Gelroy was sinking in a quagmire, and he saw no way out.

"What would you say if I told you I might have lifted him and carried him inside?"

Colm looked at Brodick. "Is he jesting?"

Brodick shook his head. "I don't think so."

Gelroy asked, "What if I were to tell you I cannot remember?"

Colm let the priest see his annoyance. "You cannot remember lifting a man who weighs at least twice as much as you do? You cannot remember that amazing feat?"

Gelroy bowed his head. He gave up trying to be clever. "I'm sorry, Laird, but I cannot tell you anything more. I have given my word to keep silent, and I must keep it."

Colm was furious. "Did you give your word to the men who tried to kill my brother?"

"I did not, and I have no idea who those terrible men are. I would not hold their secrets unless they came to me in confession." He hastily put his hands up. "And none of them did confess to me. I swear to you I know nothing about them. I don't even know what happened to your brother. I only saw the result of the punishment they inflicted."

Brodick was distracted by the noise from the courtyard. A Buchanan warrior called to him. "There's trouble below."

One of MacHugh's men looked down at the people assembled below. "You should see this," he told Colm.

"Why do I care about the English and their troubles?" Brodick asked as he strode to the parapet.

"Baron Geoffrey's daughter is at the heart of the trouble."

TWENTY-THREE

GABRIELLE LED THE WAY TO THE COMMONS. SHE was determined to end this meeting and be on her way home as quickly as possible. The abbot followed as she hurried up the small knoll past the monks' sleeping quarters and around the smaller chapel adjacent to the baking house. She was about to enter the commons through an archway when she noticed a woman standing in the shadows watching her. Gabrielle instinctively smiled and nodded a greeting, but the woman did not respond in kind. There was loathing in her expression, and her ferretlike eyes glowed with hatred.

Gabrielle was so taken aback, she abruptly stopped. Although she had never met the woman before, she had a fair idea who she was. Such a vile reaction could only come from a Monroe. Her father had told her that most of the Monroe clan blamed her for their laird's death. The ridiculous idea made no sense to her, and she considered saying something to the woman and pointing out that her attitude was most unreasonable, but before she could speak, the strange woman picked up her skirts and ran away.

The abbot caught up with Gabrielle in time to see what had happened. "Do you know that woman?"

"No, I don't," she replied. "She seemed most upset, didn't she?"

"Aye, she did. Upset with you from the look she was wearing on her face."

Gabrielle nodded. "She must be a Monroe because the Monroes dislike me intensely."

"Oh, no, Lady Gabrielle, that isn't so."

"It's not?" she asked, a bit relieved. The idea of an entire clan hating her was upsetting. "The Monroes don't hate me?" she asked eagerly.

"Oh, yes, they do. They most certainly do," he answered matter-of-factly, sounding almost cheerful. "But you see, that woman isn't a Monroe. I can't recall her name, but I remember being introduced to her, and I believe she's related to one of the barons. With all the strangers I've met in the past few days, I can't keep all of them straight in my head. These English all tend to look alike."

Lovely, she thought. The Monroes' hatred had spilled all the way down to England.

"I won't allow myself to be concerned about their foolish opinions."

The abbot gestured toward the passage into the courtyard. "Shouldn't we continue on?"

"Yes," Gabrielle agreed. "But you needn't come with me. I'm certain you have more important matters to attend to, and I don't want you to waste another minute worrying about me. I prefer to face the barons alone."

She stepped through a short hallway and found herself in the middle of a dogfight. It was difficult for her to locate the two barons because the area was filled with people, everyone in the assembled crowd trying to shout louder than everyone else. It was pandemonium. Something urgent must be happening, she thought, to provoke such vehement arguing. She drew back into the shadows, waiting for the noise to die down.

She searched the crowd for the two barons, and when she happened to look up, her breath caught in her throat and she nearly lost her balance. Liam's brother stood looking down from the top of the wall. He now appeared even larger and more menacing than the first time she had seen him on the hill. It wasn't just his size that made Colm MacHugh so intimidating but his rigid stance and his stony expression. He was the most fearsome man she had ever seen.

The laird next to him was also a daunting figure. She recognized him as well. This was the wild Buchanan.

Concerned that she would lose what courage she had if she continued to stare at the two Highlanders, she turned her attention back to the fighting throng in front of her.

Suddenly one man noticed her, then another and another, and within seconds a hush had fallen over the crowd.

Baron Coswold spotted her before Percy did. He bowed low and held out his hand to bid her to come forward.

"Lady Gabrielle, it is so good of you to join

us. We've met before in King John's court. I'm sure you remember me, don't you?"

Gabrielle didn't acknowledge Coswold's question. She simply looked at him and waited for him to explain the purpose of the meeting.

"I speak on the king's behalf," he stammered, unnerved by her silence.

She walked toward him, and the baron silently cursed himself for the devil pact he had made with MacKenna. What had he been thinking? How could he give her to another man? Since he'd last seen her, she'd grown even more beautiful.

Everyone remained quiet as the lady made her way to the center of the courtyard.

Colm MacHugh had been watching the melee unfolding below him with both amusement and disgust. What asses the English were, arguing over who had the right to speak. When the screaming suddenly subsided, he wondered what could have quieted their absurd tirade. And then he saw her. She moved through the crowd with her head held high and her hands at her sides.

Baron Percy broke the silence. "My lady, I

can see you don't remember Coswold," he said, a snicker in his voice. "We have also met before, when you were presented to King John."

Percy knew better than to ask her if she remembered meeting him, for he had the feeling that he would get the same cold, silent response she'd given Coswold.

"And Coswold is mistaken," Percy continued. "He doesn't speak on the king's behalf. I do."

The statement was the spark that once again ignited the fiery argument.

Coswold waved a document in the air. "I have a writ signed by King John giving me his power to decide your future. Percy's writ is no longer valid. The date marked by the king, later than Percy's worthless paper, proves that I am in charge."

Percy wasn't about to let the woman slip through his fingers. "As is his habit, Baron Coswold speaks nonsense. I have already decided that since Laird Monroe is dead, you will return to England with me. We shall let King John decide your future."

Coswold turned to Percy. "Everyone here knows what you're planning. You plan to wed the lady before you leave the abbey, but she isn't going anywhere with you."

"I will have her!" Percy screamed.

Gabrielle could hardly believe her ears. Were they both mad? They sickened her. How dare they fight over her as though she were a piece of meat thrown to ravenous dogs? She knew she couldn't be that important to either of them. Nay, it was Finney's Flat they were after. Both barons wanted the valuable land.

Several MacHugh and Buchanan men joined their lairds at the wall to observe the commotion in the courtyard, but Colm's gaze was fixed on the woman at the center of the storm. He wondered what was going on inside her mind. Gabrielle hid her feelings well. Her regal bearing and her composure impressed him.

Coswold clapped his hands to regain everyone's attention. He then turned to the group of men behind him, gave a quick nod, and said, "I'll settle this here and now."

The crowd parted, and Laird Owen MacKenna stepped forward. He nodded to several men as he passed them. Looking up at the top of the wall, he saw MacHugh and

Buchanan watching him, and stiffened in reaction.

"Look who just crawled out from under his rock," Brodick said. "It's our old friend."

"The arrogant swine," Colm scoffed.

Baron Percy did not know Laird MacKenna. "Who is this man who dares to interrupt this proceeding?"

"I am Laird MacKenna, and I have agreed to marry Lady Gabrielle and accept her dowry. From this day forward, Finney's Flat will be called Glen MacKenna."

Coswold wore a smug look. "Aye, Finney's Flat will be yours."

Up above, Colm reacted with a start. "The hell it will."

Brodick straightened. "No, we can't let that happen." He looked at Gabrielle and wondered why she hadn't protested the barons' high-handed methods. Was she flattered or insulted? If she were anything like her father, she was railing inside, Brodick thought.

MacKenna approached Gabrielle with a warm smile. She didn't return the smile. She seemed to be looking through him, and MacKenna thought she must be overwhelmed by all the attention she was receiving. After all, she was about to be married to a powerful laird. Aye, far more powerful than poor dead Monroe could have hoped to be. And MacKenna was much more handsome. Women liked attractive men. Perhaps her good fortune just hadn't sunk in yet.

"Laird MacKenna and Lady Gabrielle will be married before this day ends," Coswold called out.

Another shout from behind the throng of people interrupted his proclamation. "MacKenna, you have no right to her. I am Harold Monroe, and I will soon become laird of the Monroe clan. It is my duty and my right to marry this woman. My right by primogeniture."

The throng stepped aside to let him through. Gabrielle recognized the man. He had been with the spiteful woman at the funeral.

As Monroe made his way to them, MacKenna challenged him. "You are not the firstborn son of Laird Monroe. He had no sons. You, therefore, cannot claim primogeniture."

"I am his brother's firstborn son," he shouted. "And since my uncle is now deceased, I claim Lady Gabrielle and Finney's Flat for myself. From this day forward, the land will be called Glen Monroe."

Coswold was determined to take control again. "You can demand all you want, but you aren't getting her, nor are you getting Finney's Flat."

"Glen MacKenna," MacKenna corrected. "As of today, it's Glen MacKenna."

"What deceit is this?" Percy hissed at Coswold. "What kind of a pact have you made with this man? Does he know you want her for yourself?"

"You are a fool, Percy, a damn fool."

Neither one was going to get her, Coswold had realized. He'd given up the possibility of marrying Gabrielle. The king had put one obstacle after another in his path, and as lustful as Coswold was for Gabrielle, he wanted the gold every bit as much. Aye, he lusted after the treasure. And so he had made his deal with MacKenna. The laird would get her and the land, and in return Coswold would have access to her. He was convinced she had knowledge of St. Biel's treasure, and, whether with charm or with torture, he would get it out of her.

Fortunately for him, Percy didn't even know the treasure existed and neither did

MacKenna or King John. MacKenna was such a greedy pig, he hadn't shown any curiosity when Coswold insisted that he be able to see Gabrielle whenever he wanted. All the laird was interested in was controlling Finney's Flat.

Coswold wasn't worried that MacKenna might not live up to his part of the bargain. If necessary, Coswold could summon enough soldiers to destroy the entire MacKenna clan.

Harold Monroe wasn't about to go away quietly. He had to scream to be heard over the chaos that had erupted. "I claim the right to marry the lady and be given Glen Monroe!"

Everyone in the crowd seemed to have an opinion and decided to express it.

Coswold raised his hand for silence. The command was ignored.

"Quiet, everyone! Baron Coswold wants quiet now so he can be heard." In an attempt to be helpful, Henry Willis, one of Coswold's henchmen, shouted the demand from directly behind Coswold's back. He added several obscene curses as well when the crowd didn't immediately obey.

At the sound of Henry's voice, Coswold

flinched, then whirled around to glare at the offender.

"Do not scream in my ear," he demanded.

Henry gritted his teeth. He didn't like being corrected in front of an audience, and he especially didn't like disappointing the baron. Coswold was his liberator. He'd liberated him from a trip to the gallows, and Henry idolized him, for the baron had given him an identity and made him an important man.

Henry knew what he was. In appearance he certainly wasn't much to look at. He was a wide-necked brute of a man with a flat face, small ears, and thick lips. His eyes were no bigger than two beads of perspiration. His hands were big though. Big and strong. Perhaps because he knew he was so unattractive, he wore a perpetual sneer.

He made up for his unpleasant appearance with his special talents. He could snap a man's neck quicker than he could drop to his knees, and he would do so without any provocation or a moment's remorse. There were only a handful of men in the world he feared, and Coswold was one. Henry knew that Coswold used him and his cohorts, Cyril and Malcolm, to do his unpleasant work, but they were well-paid and given respect by the baron's peers.

Henry heard Malcolm snicker and shoved an elbow in his side. Since Coswold was still glaring at him, Henry said, "I won't be yelling again, but Baron," he continued in a rush to redeem himself, "maybe if you used force, you'd get them to do what you wanted."

Coswold was exasperated. "We had to leave our weapons outside the gates, remember? Oh, to have my sword now. I'd run it through Percy just to shut him up."

"I'd be honored to run him through for you," Malcolm blurted. The hireling only came to Henry's shoulder and had to push his way to the front so he could be seen by the baron.

"What if you were to bring more of your people inside the abbey? Even without weapons they'd be giving Percy a message of how powerful you are. Besides, look at those Highlanders strolling in here as if they owned the place. I lost count, there are so many of them," Henry said.

"They aren't important and have no interest in this proceeding. I certainly have no interest in them. Now both of you be quiet while I finish this. I have no need for more of your suggestions."

Both Malcolm and Henry bowed their heads. "Aye, Baron."

Percy strained to hear the conversation between Coswold and his men, but the clamor of voices surrounding him drowned them out. When Coswold turned back to him, he screamed, "You will not decide anything!"

Percy screeched like a trapped bird, Coswold thought. "I have already decided her future."

Percy's face turned bloodred. "I want her and I will have her."

Gabrielle had had enough. She couldn't bear to hear another word from either of these repulsive men.

"May I have your attention?"

Gabrielle had not raised her voice, and only a few men standing near her heard what she said. One of them yelled, "The lady is wanting your attention, Baron."

Coswold and Percy both turned to her. MacKenna stood between them. All three smiled at her like starry-eyed suitors.

"Which baron do you wish to address?" Percy cooed.

"Both."

Everyone eagerly waited for her to speak. She would surely choose one over the other, and Coswold was confident that she would obey the king's writ and abide by his decisions. Percy held the same view, confident she would place her future in his hands.

"Yes, Lady Gabrielle?" Coswold said.

"There seems to be some confusion here," she began.

"Aye, with all the shouting Percy's doing," Coswold interrupted.

"Let her speak!" someone from the crowd shouted.

"All right. All right." Coswold nodded. "You were saying, milady?"

"I believe I can settle this dispute. You see, I will not marry anyone today."

"But I have agreed to marry you," MacKenna said, staggered by her refusal.

"Yes, but I have not agreed to marry you."

His mouth dropped open. He was astounded and turned to Coswold for help. "Can she refuse?"

"She cannot," he snapped. "Don't be difficult, Gabrielle, for I speak on King John's behalf . . ."

Gabrielle was weary of their pompous

declarations. "Yes, you've mentioned that fact several times now."

Did she mock him? Coswold's eyes narrowed. He couldn't be certain. She looked so angelic, and there was no bite to her voice.

"Baron Coswold is mistaken. I speak for the king," Percy insisted.

She turned her attention to him. "So you have also said countless times. May I ask both of you a question? Where was my father while all of these decisions were being made?"

No one would answer.

"Did you wait for my father to leave to carry out this obscenity?"

"Obscenity?" Coswold roared. "How dare you speak to me in such a way."

Percy was just as outraged by her attitude, and MacKenna looked like he wanted to strike her, but she held her ground and budged not one inch.

MacKenna considered grabbing Gabrielle by her arm and forcing her to his side, but he looked up and saw MacHugh and Buchanan still watching. Best not touch her, he decided, for he had no wish to make a scene. For the time being, he was forced to treat her with courtesy. Later, he promised himself, when he had Gabrielle alone, he would show her how to be respectful.

"Lady Gabrielle, I am afraid this isn't your decision to make," Percy told her.

"I agree."

Coswold and Percy glanced at each other. "You agree?" Coswold said. "Then why this fuss?"

"It isn't my decision. It's my father's. It's his right to decide my future, certainly not yours."

"Are you refusing . . ." MacKenna began.

Lord, he was as thickheaded as both barons appeared to be. She held herself even straighter. "Let me make my position clear so that there will be no more confusion. My father will decide my future."

How many times would she have to say it before they believed she meant every word? She wasn't going to marry anyone today.

"You would go against your king's wishes?" Percy demanded.

She looked him in the eye. "I know not what my king's wishes are. He has yet to tell me."

"I've just told you that I speak on his behalf," Percy cried.

"Yes, you have, but then so has Baron

Coswold. Who am I to believe? I think I must wait for my father to decide."

She bowed to the barons and had every intention of leaving, but a woman's sudden shout stopped her.

"This is a mockery. A mockery! She's making fools of all of you. This cannot go on."

Gabrielle turned to see the woman who had glared at her outside the commons make her way toward them.

Isla ran to Coswold. He looked horrified by the intrusion.

"What are you doing?" he hissed under his breath.

She couldn't look at him. Lowering her head, Isla cried out, "Pray forgive me for not speaking out sooner, but I couldn't . . . it's . . . it's so horrible."

"Who is this woman?" a man in Percy's group asked.

"She's Baron Coswold's niece," Percy answered.

"Isla, what's come over you?" Appalled by her behavior, Coswold grabbed Isla's arm, squeezing as hard as he could. What was she thinking to make such a scene?

"Uncle, I'm so sorry to upset you, but the truth must come out before you or Baron

Percy decide her future. I will not let her humiliate you." Although there were no tears in evidence, Isla let out a loud dramatic sob. "It would be blasphemy for an honorable man to marry her."

"Why? What are you saying?" Percy demanded. He sounded more confused than angry. "What blasphemy do you speak of?"

Isla pointed to Gabrielle and screamed, "She's unclean. She's . . . she's a whore!"

TWENTY-FOUR

THE DAMNING SILENCE THAT FOLLOWED ISLA'S horrible accusation lasted only as long as it took for everyone in the commons to draw a deep, gasping breath. Then the crowd erupted into bursts of anger and outrage. Within minutes, sides were taken, those for and those against Gabrielle.

Gabrielle couldn't move. How could she respond to such an absurdity? It was preposterous.

"Let's hear what she has to say." Percy waved his arms and demanded the crowd quiet down.

Coswold's voice shook with fury. "Yes,

everyone be silent now. I would hear what Isla has to say for herself." His niece was ruining all of his carefully thought out plans, but all eyes were on her now, and he couldn't ignore her. "Isla, why would you call the Lady Gabrielle such a foul name?"

Isla timidly glanced up and saw that everyone was closing in on her. "Because it's true," she answered in a meek voice.

"Speak up," Percy said. "Tell us why you made this outrageous claim."

Isla raised her voice slightly and repeated, "Because it's true."

Murmurs spread through the crowd.

"How do you know this?" Percy demanded.

"I saw her," Isla said.

The murmurs grew louder.

"Go on," Coswold ordered. "Tell us what you saw."

It was easy for Isla to cry real tears now. Her uncle had such a tight grip on her arm, her skin was burning.

"It was the middle of the night three nights ago, and I was awakened by a noise in the hall. I opened my door to see what it was." She pointed to Gabrielle. "She was sneaking around the corner. I knew I shouldn't, but I was curious and decided to fol-low her. I stayed well behind her because I didn't want her to see me."

"How could you see where you were going in the dark? Did the lady carry a candle?"

She hesitated for the barest of seconds and then blurted, "The moon was bright. There was no need for a candle."

She struggled to get away from her uncle, but he wouldn't release her. In fact, he tightened his hold.

"Where did Lady Gabrielle lead you?" MacKenna asked the question.

"She stopped in front of a door and tapped lightly. I hid behind a pillar. The door opened, and after looking both ways, she went inside."

"Did you see who opened the door?" Percy asked.

Isla dropped her gaze to the ground again. "It was a man."

"And do you know this man?" her uncle asked.

"No," Isla said, "but I had seen him at the banquet that night. I believe he was the envoy from France."

Percy called to his followers. "Find him. Bring him to us."

One of them answered immediately. "He's no longer here. He and his companions left yesterday."

MacKenna grew impatient. "If it was dark, how could you recognize the man?" he asked Isla. "Perhaps it was her father. Perhaps it wasn't a man at all, but a maidservant." He was grasping for an explanation. If Isla's accusations were taken seriously, his entire scheme would be destroyed. He could feel Glen MacKenna slipping through his fingers.

Isla's courage was gaining strength. "It *was* a man," she stated emphatically. Pointing at Gabrielle again, she said, "And what she was doing makes her unclean."

MacKenna scanned the crowd as everyone reacted to the shocking news. When he looked up, he saw MacHugh and Buchanan watching with scowls on their faces. His mind raced. How much had they heard? Once again, his reputation and his authority were at stake. If he was going to emerge from this situation with his dignity and his plan intact, he had to think fast.

He looked at Isla with mock compassion when he said, "I'm sure your intentions are noble, but perhaps you are mistaken, my dear. Is it possible that you could have confused what you saw for something innocent?"

"It was no mistake," Isla said defiantly. "I saw her when she came out of the room. Her hair was down and her gown was unlaced. The man came to the door, and he wore no tunic or shirt."

Gabrielle was so shocked by the woman's absurd claims, she was speechless. At this last hideous allegation, however, she could remain silent no longer.

"That's a lie!" she shouted. "I don't know why this woman is saying these things, but nothing she's told you is true."

"It is true!" Isla shouted back. "I saw you, and you were giving yourself to a man."

An uproar swelled among the onlookers. It took MacKenna several minutes to get them to calm down so that he could be heard.

"It appears," he said to Isla, "that this is your word against Lady Gabrielle's."

Almost everyone in the crowd nodded agreement. Only a few people knew Baron Coswold's niece, so her words held little credence with most.

Suddenly, a man standing behind Laird MacKenna spoke up. "The woman speaks the truth."

Everyone turned toward the voice. A young monk with his head covered by his hood and his arms folded inside the sleeves of his robe slowly moved forward.

"What are you saying?" MacKenna questioned. "Who is telling the truth? What do you know of this?"

Unaccustomed to having so much attention paid to him, the monk hesitated a moment before answering, then said, "Lady Isla is being truthful. I know this because I, too, saw Lady Gabrielle."

The circle at the stone cross expanded so that everyone could see and hear the monk. He took a tentative step forward then halted as though he suddenly realized the magnitude of his actions.

"I saw the lady . . ." he began.

"Go on," Percy demanded impatiently.

"I had just come out of the chapel at midnight after my hour of adoration and I saw someone hurrying toward the sleeping quarters where a few of the guests were staying. At first I saw only a dark figure, but as she passed under the candlelight shining from the chapel window, I recognized Lady Gabrielle." He looked over at the astonished Isla and said, "Lady Isla is not lying."

"She's a whore!" someone behind Percy shouted.

"Unfit to marry anyone!" a member of the Monroe clan yelled.

Before long, dozens of angry voices joined together in condemning her.

Gabrielle was numb. She felt as though she'd just been thrown over a cliff and the wolves were waiting at the bottom to tear her apart. She had been judged and damned.

She tried to make sense out of the insanity. How could this be happening? How could people be saying such vile things about her? Isla had to be demented to be making such ludicrous accusations. But what of the monk? Why did he agree with Isla? What could possibly make him confirm that Gabrielle had done these wicked deeds?

Liam. Dear God, it was Liam. Maybe the monk had seen her on her way to look in on the sick man. But she was never alone when she left her rooms. At least one guard accompanied her, but if he had stepped ahead and the monk happened to look up just as she was walking past, he might have assumed she was alone. That could be the only explanation.

If she tried to defend herself, tried to tell

the truth, no one would believe she was simply visiting a sick man and nothing improper had happened.

Two people had accused her. And that was enough to prove her guilt.

"Have you nothing to say for yourself?" Coswold shouted at Gabrielle.

She refused to answer. The incensed crowd had already passed judgment.

She had given her word that she would tell no one about her part in saving Liam, and even if she hadn't promised, what would the reaction of the mob be if they knew that she was responsible for killing a man at Finney's Flat? Who would turn against her and her guards then? She could neither do nor say anything that would end this nightmare. Tears flooded her eyes, but she would not let them spill down her cheeks. She would not respond to the slurs these people were hurling at her.

Baron Coswold's anger toward his niece subsided, and he released his grip on her arm. Isla's motives for coming forward were now clear to him. She was only trying to save him from the humiliation that would surely come when the truth about Lady Gabrielle was revealed, for inevitably it would be known. Even if the monk stayed silent and never uttered a word about her sin, surely Baron MacKenna would be enraged when he discovered his new bride was not a virgin. No, Isla may not have chosen the most appropriate time to speak up, but she was only trying to protect him.

The turmoil over Gabrielle's future had suddenly shifted. Just moments ago four men had been vying for her hand, but with this revelation everything had changed. For who among them would step forward to accept her now? Who would take a harlot as a wife?

Twenty-five

Coswold was enraged. It was true. It was all true. Gabrielle was a whore. She had tricked him. She'd tricked them all into believing she was pure. Her appearance made it so easy for her to dupe men. Her angelic face and those eyes, those bewitching violet eyes . . . she was so beautiful. What man would even consider that she might be anything but innocent?

What a fool he had been to want her. How many men had she given herself to? It made him sick to think about it.

Coswold looked at Percy to see how he was taking the news. A look of horror seemed frozen on his face. His mouth was open as though he were about to speak, but he uttered not one word.

Even if he had said something, he wouldn't have been heard over MacKenna's roar. The laird was ranting about his good name and the shame Gabrielle would have brought to it. With each statement in his tirade, he'd look up at the wall. Did he expect the Highlanders watching to applaud his refusal to marry Gabrielle?

"She has no value now," Percy said when MacKenna paused to take a breath. "King John won't give her a dowry. Finney's Flat is no longer yours for the taking, MacKenna. The same goes for you, Monroe."

"Do you think I still want her?" Monroe spat on the ground in front of Gabrielle. "The devil take her." He turned and walked away. As he passed MacKenna, he said, "She's all yours, MacKenna, as long as you don't mind the mocking behind your back. You heard the baron. You can have the whore, but you won't be getting Finney's Flat."

MacKenna had never felt so humiliated. His wrath turned on Coswold. "Did you know she was a whore when you struck your bargain with me? You did, didn't you?"

Indignant, Coswold responded, "I most certainly did not. I believed her to be innocent, as everyone else did. I knew you wanted Finney's Flat. You were already calling the land Glen MacKenna before I even suggested the bargain, and I wanted—"

He stopped in the middle of his sentence before he accidentally blurted out the promise he'd forced MacKenna to give to seal the bargain.

MacKenna didn't want anyone to know the particulars of their agreement. He pulled Coswold aside and turned his back to the others. "You demanded that I agree to let you see her whenever you wanted, but you refused to explain why. Tell me, were you one of the men she'd already given herself to? Were you planning to continue to bed her? Was she your mistress?"

With each question he posed, his complexion turned a darker shade of purple.

Coswold had almost forgotten about the gold. Gabrielle's shocking conduct had pushed every other thought aside. Coswold didn't want her any longer, but he was still determined to get the treasure. His mind raced for a solution. If he was ever going to find out where the treasure was hidden, he needed access to Gabrielle, but if he took her back to King John, she would be lost to him. The king would probably be so furious he'd order her execution, and if he were in one of his rare forgiving moods, he would most likely use her until he became bored and then pass her on to his favored underlings. Either way, Coswold wouldn't be able to see her.

Percy wasn't as worried. While he would have preferred to have Gabrielle in marriage, he was prepared to take her as his mistress. His obsession did not require a public ceremony. If Gabrielle were banished, she would be free for the taking, and he could have her whenever and however he wanted. All he had to do was wait until Coswold washed his hands of her.

Coswold had devised a plan, too, and knew exactly what he would do. He had to act quickly because Gabrielle was still in a state of shock. He feared that she would react with a vengeance and perhaps even try to escape to her father for protection. He couldn't let that happen.

"I think it's a waste of my time to take the woman back to England and wait for King John to return. Since I speak on his behalf, I will decide her fate this very minute."

"You will not kill her," Percy shouted.

Isla's hand flew to her chest. "Why do you care what happens to her?" she cried. "You can't possibly still want her."

"Can't you shut her up, Coswold? No one wants to hear anything more from her."

"Be silent," Coswold ordered as he shoved Isla away from him. "Percy's right. You've said enough."

"I mean what I say, Coswold," Percy warned. "You cannot kill Gabrielle."

Coswold sneered at his adversary. "No, I won't kill her. I want her to suffer for the rest of her life, however short that might be."

He turned his full attention to Gabrielle then and took a step toward her. The crowd gave him a wide berth.

"With the power bestowed on me by King John, I hereby banish you."

The assemblage cheered the punishment. Some clapped, others shouted approval. "Good riddance." "She's getting what she deserves."

Coswold waited for everyone to settle down before he continued.

"Do you understand what this means, Gabrielle? From this moment on, you are an outcast. You have no home, no country, no king, and no title. King John and his faithful subjects no longer acknowledge your existence. You are nothing."

"Does she answer to the king?" someone shouted.

"She does not, for she has no king," Coswold answered.

"What about Baron Geoffrey?" Percy asked. "Don't you wonder what he'll do when he hears his daughter has been banished?"

"By the time he finds out, it will be too late."

Percy was desperately trying not to show his joy. Gabrielle would be forced outside the walls, and he planned to follow her. Once she was far enough away from the abbey and no one could see her, Percy would take her. He had enough men to ambush her guards and overwhelm them. No one would even know or care what happened to her, and if Percy wanted to, he could lock her in the bowels of his castle and keep her there for as long as he wished.

Coswold had the same intention. "Isla, go and tell my servants to prepare to leave," he commanded in a whisper.

She nodded and hurried to do his bidding.

But as she passed the scorned woman, she slowed her pace and turned her head so that only Gabrielle could witness her sly smile.

TWENTY-SIX

WHAT MALICIOUS REASON DID THE WOMAN HAVE to lie? What was her purpose? And what about the monk? Why did he substantiate her lies? What did he have to gain?

Brodick didn't have any answers. The only fact he knew to be true was that in less than ten minutes' time the two of them had destroyed Gabrielle's life. They had disgraced and dishonored her, snatched her future from her, and shamed and humiliated her father. Both Baron Geoffrey and his daughter would no doubt suffer King John's displeasure, for she was no longer of any value to him. Brodick knew there was a good chance that the baron's lands would be con-fiscated—John was notorious for taking what belonged to others, including wives and daughters—and with his twisted mind and his unpredictable temper, there was also a possibility that he would have Baron Geoffrey executed to make an example of him.

And Gabrielle? What would he do to her?

"We're seeing the English in all their depravity," Colm said with disgust.

"Gabrielle is innocent." Father Gelroy had tears in his eyes, so great was his distress. "She's kind and gentle," he insisted. "If only you knew . . ."

The priest stopped in the nick of time. He was about to blurt out that, if Colm and Brodick were aware of the lengths Gabrielle had gone to to protect Liam and save his life, they would know for a certainty that she would never do anything to disgrace her family's name.

"If we only knew what?" Colm asked.

"If you only knew her," he hastily said. "She is innocent of these terrible accusations."

Colm turned to the priest. "We already know she's innocent."

"Aye, we do," Brodick agreed.

"You do?"

Brodick sighed. "We do," he repeated. "But at the moment, that doesn't matter, does it? Look at them. They have all condemned her."

"Yes, they have." Gelroy was wringing his hands. He stared at Gabrielle as he whispered, "Terrible things will happen to her if they take her back to England and hand her over to King John. That lecherous man is capable of vile deeds, and I will tell you this, when he is finished with her, he'll . . ." He couldn't go on. Gabrielle's future was too horrible to speak of.

"The woman who accused her . . ." Brodick began.

"Isla," Gelroy said. "I heard them say her name."

"She lies," Colm said.

Gelroy agreed with a nod. "She will have to answer to God for this."

"But what about the monk?" Brodick asked. "Why did he confirm her lies?"

"I don't know."

"Do you know this monk?" Brodick asked.

"I do. He's young and eager to serve, and I believe him to be an honest man. I can't imagine why he would say that he had seen Gabrielle. It has to be a mistake, and I'll seek him out and ask him to tell me exactly what he thinks he saw."

"The damage is already done," Brodick said.

Gelroy's shoulders slumped. "Yes it is. They have ruined Lady Gabrielle's life. Shame to them."

"Priest?"

"Yes, Laird MacHugh?"

"When I leave the abbey, you're coming with me."

Gelroy had the sudden urge to throw himself over the parapet. He took a step back, judged the distance to the steps, and then found a bit of courage. He wouldn't run. He would politely decline.

"You're inviting me to serve your clan . . ."

"If you choose to think of it as an invitation, you may."

"And if I decline?" the priest gulped.

"You won't."

The lump in Gelroy's throat made it difficult for him to speak, and it took every ounce of self-control he possessed to stand before the MacHugh. Praying that the laird had indeed come to the abbey to seek a priest, and not, as Gelroy feared, to exact revenge for his brother, he rasped, "I will be happy to go with you."

Brodick laughed. "Now who's telling lies? Your face gives you away."

Embarrassed, Gelroy admitted, "I do have trepidation, but I will do my best to minister to the MacHugh clan."

"Go and gather what you wish to take with you," MacHugh ordered.

Brodick waited until the priest was out of sight before speaking. "I've heard it said that once a priest finds a home with any clan, it's impossible to get rid of him. I've a feeling you're going to be stuck with Gelroy for the rest of your days."

Had Gelroy heard Brodick's prediction, he wouldn't have agreed. The sooner he could complete his duty and be away from the MacHughs, the better.

He didn't wish to irritate the laird by dragging his feet, and so he ran all the way back to his quarters to pack his holy water and oils, his stole, and the rest of his possessions. Laird MacHugh had ordered one of his younger soldiers to accompany the priest, and Gelroy thought the laird did so to make certain he wouldn't try to run away.

God only knew Gelroy wanted to flee, but with Lady Gabrielle in such need, he had to put his own fears aside. All he could think about was finding a way to help her.

He thought she would be worried about her guards waiting for her. It wouldn't do for them to join in this monstrous persecution. Four guards and one woman standing against a hundred incensed men . . . no, no. The guards must stay outside the gates until this dreadful drama was over. Then, God willing, they could help Gabrielle find shelter away from these terrible people.

Gelroy headed for the front gates. The warrior blocked him. "You're to go back to Laird MacHugh," he said as he took the two bags filled with Gelroy's things. "I'll see that these get tied to one of our saddles."

"Pray be patient with me," Gelroy replied. "I must give Gabrielle's guards orders to continue to wait. She would not want them to come inside the abbey, for there is danger here. It will take but a minute."

The warrior agreed with a quick nod.

Stephen stood with Gabrielle's horse just north of the gate. He came forward when he spotted Gelroy with the Highlander.

"Gabrielle will be joining you soon. Do you

have her clothes and other necessaries with you?" Father Gelroy asked.

Stephen shook his head. "We have some of her things. Her maids packed her trunks. We plan to catch up to them by late this afternoon. Why do you ask?"

He hated to lie, but Gelroy excused the sin by telling God he was only protecting the guards and Gabrielle from a mob wanting blood.

"She wanted me to make certain because her plans have changed. She will tell you in just a few minutes when she joins you. She bids you stay and wait for her here."

Stephen had no reason to doubt the priest, for he knew that Gelroy had become a friend to Gabrielle.

As Gelroy hurried back to the wall, the MacHugh clansman accompanying him remarked, "You lied to that man. Why?"

"To protect him and the others. The lady would want it so," he added. "She wouldn't wish for them to try to interfere in this debacle, as they would be sorely outnumbered."

His escort continued to follow Gelroy and wouldn't leave his side until the priest was halfway up the stairs. Gelroy knew that the man was also suspicious that he might decide to hide. When he reached the top step, he stopped and waited for one of the lairds to bid him to come forward. Brodick noticed him and motioned to him.

Gelroy cleared his throat to get MacHugh's attention and said, "Laird, I cannot leave until I know that Lady Gabrielle will be safe from these monsters. With your permission, I'll go and stand by her side."

Before MacHugh could respond, Gelroy straightened his shoulders and turned to Brodick. "Laird Buchanan, Gabrielle's father isn't here to defend her honor, and you are her only relative. You must help her."

"Do not tell me my duty, priest." Brodick's voice was harsh. "I know it well."

"Yes, of course you do," he said, nodding vigorously.

Dismissing Gelroy, Brodick watched the crowd below. They were being whipped into a frenzy by Coswold and Percy.

"Colm, I'll take her home with me. I can protect her there."

"Keeping her safe won't restore her honor," Colm said grimly.

Brodick agreed. "She deserves better."

"Her father . . . he isn't like those barons?"

"I wouldn't allow him on my land if he

were," he replied. "I know him to be a right-eous man."

"Send word to him that his daughter is staying with you, and he'll come and get her."

"It isn't that simple. Baron Geoffrey will have to gather his vassals and prepare for war. If the king confiscates his property—"

"He'll be powerless."

"Yes," he agreed. "Gabrielle needs a strong protector. She's my wife's cousin. It's expected that I would shield her, but that wouldn't prove she is innocent."

"What do you care what others think?"

"I don't care," he countered, "but if Gabrielle were my wife, I would kill any man who would dare attack her honor."

"As would I," Colm said.

"But she has no husband to defend her honor."

"No, she doesn't."

"I think perhaps you should take her home with you."

Frowning, Colm said, "And what would that accomplish? What difference would it make if I offered her my protection instead of you? You're as strong as I am."

"I cannot marry her."

The statement lay between them for a long moment before Colm responded. He knew exactly what Brodick wanted. "You ask too much of me."

"You have a debt to repay. I ask what you can give."

"Marriage? No. It's out of the question."

Brodick shrugged. "It makes sense to me. If you marry her, everyone will know you believe her to be innocent. You would not marry a whore. You're respected and feared by most of the other clans. You could restore her honor by giving her your name."

"No. You will have to come up with another solution," Colm answered emphatically.

Brodick wasn't deterred. He knew Colm MacHugh would eventually do the honorable thing.

"Do you suggest there might be another laird more powerful than you who hasn't taken a wife yet?"

"I am not suggesting anything, Buchanan. This is your problem to solve, not mine."

"A wife for a brother. You save her life as I helped save your brother."

Colm's jaw was clenched tight.

A Buchanan called out. "Lairds, Lady

Gabrielle is leaving. They've opened the gates."

Brodick looked at the commons just as a man stepped forward and spit on the ground in front of Gabrielle.

Colm saw another man pushing his way through the throng as Gabrielle was walking toward the gates. The man called out to her, but she ignored him and continued on. He grabbed her arm then, swung her around, and hit her face with his fist. Had he not had a firm grip on her, she would have dropped to the ground.

Colm was already heading for the stairs with Brodick right behind him as he called out to one of his men, "Find out who he is."

All the warriors, both Buchanans and MacHughs, understood the command. Gelroy didn't. He hadn't seen what happened below.

"Who is he talking about? What does he want?" the priest asked one of the men who was pushing his way past.

The man didn't slow his descent. "He wants to know who struck Lady Gabrielle."

"Someone struck her? Oh dear Lord," Gelroy replied. He pivoted on the step and rushed behind the others. "But why does he—"

The last warrior to leave answered. "The MacHugh wants to know the name of the man he's going to kill."

TWENTY-SEVEN

SHE WAS TRAPPED IN A NIGHTMARE.

An hour ago she was Lady Gabrielle, daughter of Baron Geoffrey of Wellingshire and Princess Genevieve of St. Biel. She had been loved, happy, and hopeful for her future. Now Gabrielle was hated, treated like a leper, and she had no future.

It was too much to take in. Survival was what mattered right now. She had to find a safe place for her and her guards. And though she didn't have a destination in mind, she wanted to get as far away as possible from the heinous barons and their henchmen. Then perhaps she would be able to make sense out of what had just happened.

First, however, she needed time to calm down and quiet her racing heart. She could barely breathe. Strangers screamed foul names at her as she passed them on the long, seemingly endless walk to the front gates.

The humiliation and shame were unbearable. It took all of her concentration to show no emotion. She didn't hurry her pace—though God knows she wanted to run—and she didn't allow a single tear to fall, for to do either would have given the rabid crowd satisfaction. Pride was all she had left. She would not let them take that from her.

The side of her face throbbed from the hit she'd taken. She'd seen the fist coming and tried to step back from her attacker, a brute of a man with hatred smeared all over his ugly face, but he latched on to her and wouldn't let her retreat. Fortunately, she was able to twist away and lessen the impact. He was more than twice her size and weight. If she hadn't moved, his fist surely would have broken her jaw.

"Don't damage her," Coswold had bellowed a scant second before the attacker's fist slammed into her face.

The blow had stunned her, and she had staggered back just as a stone struck her from behind. She quickly righted herself and kept walking. Another stone and then another hit her. Though dazed, she still heard the baron's shout. Damage her? What a ludicrous command. Coswold, Isla, and Percy had already destroyed her reputation and attacked her character. She had been stripped of everything. In the eyes of her countrymen, she no longer existed, and she belonged nowhere. What difference did it make if they disfigured her as well?

The abbot was waiting for her at the gate. He pulled it open, bowed his head, and whispered, "God be with you."

Did he believe the lies? There were tears in his eyes, but she couldn't tell if they were tears of sympathy or shame.

She stepped outside, heard the huge door shut behind her, and then the harsh sound of the bolt slipping into place.

Stephen let out a shout when he saw her. He leaped from his horse and ran to her while Faust, Lucien, and Christien all drew their swords in preparation for a fight.

She knew she must look awful. A stone had cut her skin just below her right eye, and she felt blood trickling down her cheek. Her jaw was sore and probably already beginning to swell and bruise.

"Princess, what happened to you?" Stephen asked, appalled.

"I'm all right," she answered, her voice surprisingly strong, "but we must leave. Now."

"You're bleeding!" Christien's face was red with anger as he swung toward the closed gates. "Who did this to you? We will kill him."

"No, you will not go back into the abbey," she demanded.

Faust pulled his tunic over his head and doused it with water from his leather pouch. Leaning down from his saddle, he handed the wet cloth to Gabrielle. "Does it hurt?" he asked.

"No," she assured him, quickly wiping the blood from her cheek. "I'll tell you everything, but please, we must be away from here with all possible haste."

They heard the urgency in her voice and

didn't question the command. Stephen lifted her onto Rogue's back, handed her the reins, then swung up on his mount. Assuming she wanted to catch up with her father's staff, he turned south.

"No," she cried out. "We must go north."

"Won't your father—" Lucien began.

"You don't understand. If the barons change their minds and decide to take me to the king—their King John," she corrected, "they will look for us to the south. They'll never find us hidden in the forest."

"But why—" Stephen began.

"No questions now," she said. "When we are away from here, I will explain."

Stephen nodded. "We go north."

Christien was the last in the procession and the first to feel the ground shake beneath him. The Highlanders approached from the hill below. He called to the others riding ahead of him.

When she turned and saw the approaching horde, Gabrielle panicked, thinking her enemies were in pursuit. But as they drew closer, she recognized the two men leading them: Buchanan and MacHugh. They looked wild and ferocious and proud . . . and dangerous. A magnificent sight: like a bolt of lightning, beautiful to observe from a distance but terrifying up close.

The sound of the pounding hooves was deafening.

"Let them pass," she shouted to her guards. She guided Rogue to the left to give the charging Highlanders room, but they didn't go around. They fanned out. Gabrielle urged Rogue into a full gallop, yet they gained on her, surrounding her and her guards and swallowing them into their midst. Enclosed in this thick circle of warriors, they rolled over one hill and climbed the next.

Anyone looking out from the abbey would have seen only the clansmen heading back to their homes. Gabrielle and her guards were completely hidden from view.

Was that their intent? She was so relieved and thankful to be getting farther and farther away from the barons, she wasn't going to worry about the Highlanders' motives. Besides, she'd already spotted Father Gelroy bouncing along on his mount. A grimace on his face, the poor priest appeared to be hanging on to the pommel of his saddle for dear life. If any of them meant to do harm, would they have brought a priest along to witness their dark deeds?

They veered to the northwest. When they reached the edge of Finney's Flat, a good two hours' ride from the abbey, she heard one of the men shout that they were on Buchanan land. Rogue was more than ready to rest, and Gabrielle wasn't going to push her horse any farther without a respite.

She was surprised the Highlanders didn't trample her when she abruptly pulled up. They stopped with her, but before she even had time to dismount, they were on the ground, surrounding her.

Her guards stood at attention, ready for what might come. Their hands were at their sides, but their stance wasn't relaxed. They knew that if they even looked as though they were going to reach for their swords, it would be their last earthly act. The Highland warriors would kill to protect their lairds, just as the guards would fight to the death for their princess. As long as the Highlanders didn't press in on them, they would stand their ground.

Knowing her guards wouldn't back down, no matter how many men they were up against, Gabrielle worried for their lives. She heard one of the Highlanders give the command to fall back. She hoped it was the wild

Buchanan she'd heard, but when the soldiers parted, she saw that it wasn't her cousin who had spoken. It was the other laird, the ruthless man who had greeted his long-lost brother with his fist.

He was as big and ferocious-looking as she remembered, but there was something else surprising about him. One might even say he was actually handsome, if one liked the rugged, flawed, somewhat scarred type. She didn't. But if there was anything she did like about his appearance, it was the color of his hair. It was blond, with a hint of red. It framed a face stern and rigid, reminding her of a Viking from the stories of times past. Most likely he was just as mean and barbaric.

Colm MacHugh stopped when he was barely a foot away from Stephen. The two men sized each other up, then Colm ordered, "Get out of my way."

Stephen moved not an inch. Colm was at least a head taller and much more muscular, but the guard didn't give. He took orders from no one but Princess Gabrielle. The same went for his fellow guards. Faust and Christien moved to stand with Stephen, while Lucien stood with his back to hers.

Brodick joined Colm as Gabrielle said, "They mean us no harm."

A part of her actually believed that to be true, that the Highlanders had followed them to help, not hurt. Still, after today's horror, anything was possible.

"Step aside and let me speak to them," she ordered.

Her guards moved away, cautiously keeping an eye on the Highlanders.

"What language are you speaking?" Brodick asked the question in Gaelic.

She responded in kind. "It is the language of my mother's homeland, St. Biel."

Her command of their language was excellent. Brodick assumed her father had taught her. His wife, Gillian, would do well to take a lesson from Gabrielle. His men still occasionally winced when she spoke to them.

Turning to Colm, he remarked, "She isn't all English, just half."

Why Brodick thought that fact would matter was beyond Colm. Half English was the same as all English to him. Colm's response was a noncommittal shrug.

Brodick stepped toward Gabrielle. When her guards reacted, he glared at them. His followers also took offense and moved forward.

"Enough!" Gabrielle called out. She raised her hand and repeated the command: "Enough."

Since she'd spoken Gaelic, it was obvious to Brodick and Colm that she hadn't given the order to her guards but to their soldiers. Her assertiveness amused Brodick, but it irritated Colm.

Only after a signal from their lairds did the men move back, but all intently watched her protectors. Gabrielle thought perhaps they were waiting for an opportunity to pounce.

"Do you know who we are?" Brodick asked.

She nodded. "You're the wild—that is to say, you're my cousin, Laird Buchanan. I've heard stories about you." The comment didn't remove his scowl. "They were most impressive stories about your cunning and your strength."

He clasped his hands behind his back. "Who told you these stories?"

"My father, Baron Geoffrey."

"Then the stories are true. He would not lie."

She knew she was going to have to

acknowledge the other laird, and a shiver of dread rushed through her when she finally turned and met MacHugh's piercing eyes.

"I also know who you are."

His response was a slightly raised eyebrow. She wasn't deterred. "You're Laird MacHugh, and you have a most peculiar way of greeting your brother."

Colm didn't understand her meaning. "How do I greet him?"

"With your fist."

Ah. So she'd been watching Liam leave the abbey.

For the briefest of seconds Gabrielle saw a hint of warmth in his eyes. It was long enough for her to realize he wasn't a complete ogre.

Father Gelroy pushed his way through the clansmen. He bowed to Gabrielle and then turned to address Colm. "Laird MacHugh, these are the good men who protected your brother while he was recovering from his injuries at the abbey. I mentioned them to you before, but I wanted to make certain you hadn't forgotten."

The priest had a little courage deep inside him after all, Colm thought. Gelroy dared to remind him that he owed these men his

gratitude. Colm hated owing anyone anything. The debt always weighed heavily until
it was repaid.

He didn't thank the guards, but nodded in
acknowledgment of what they had done. The
other Buchanans and MacHughs, hearing
what the priest had said, also relaxed their
positions.

"Did anyone try to get to my brother while
you were guarding him?" he asked the four.

Gabrielle started to answer no, but
decided she should let them speak for themselves.

"Stephen, did anyone try to hurt Liam
while you or the others were protecting
him?"

He hesitated before answering, then gave
a quick nod. "Two men came that first night."

"What did he say?" Brodick asked
Gabrielle.

Gabrielle was so surprised by the guard's
answer she ignored Brodick. "Why didn't you
tell me?"

"We didn't feel it necessary to tell you,"
Lucien said.

"You asked us to guard him, and that's
what we did," Stephen said.

"We took care of the matter," Faust added.

Brodick and Colm had waited long enough to get an answer.

"You will tell us what they said," Colm ordered.

She quickly apologized and asked Stephen and the others to speak directly to the lairds.

Stephen turned to Colm and in Gaelic said, "Laird MacHugh, two men came for your brother the first night we guarded him."

If the lairds were surprised that Gabrielle's guards were also proficient in their language, they didn't show it. Colm folded his arms and waited for further explanation.

"They were dressed as monks, but carried knives in their sleeves," Lucien said.

"Lucien and I were on watch," Christien explained.

"We waited until we were certain they meant to murder your brother before we acted," Lucien said.

"And what did you do when you realized what they were about?" Brodick asked.

"We killed them," Christien answered frankly.

Colm nodded approval. "Did they speak? Did you hear their names?" he asked.

"Did they mention where they were from or who sent them?" Brodick asked.

"No," Lucien answered. "They spoke your language, but differently from the way you speak it."

"Describe these men," Brodick ordered.

Lucien told of two men with long hair and beards who were burly but not exceptionally tall.

After he had finished, Christien added, "They were ordinary."

"No marks on their skin or their weapons," Lucien explained.

"My brother slept through this fight?" Colm asked.

Christien was offended by the question. "There was no fight. We didn't give them time to fight us."

"A surprise attack then," Brodick said, nodding approval.

"No," Lucien said, "they saw us coming."

Colm admired their conceit. "What did you do with the bodies?"

"We couldn't leave Liam unprotected, so we kept the bodies in the corner of his room until Stephen and Faust arrived to relieve us," Christien said. "Then, Lucien and I carried the bodies outside the abbey and threw them in the ravine. It was still dark; I'm certain no one saw us."

"We tossed dirt over them, but by now the animals have probably gotten to them."

The questions continued, but Gabrielle wasn't paying attention. She was still reeling from the casual admission that her guards had killed two intruders. Honest to heaven, she didn't think she could take any more shocks. She was worn out; all she wanted to do was find a quiet spot and sit for a few minutes. Her world was crashing down around her, and she needed time to sort out the horrific events of the day before she tried to make plans.

Understanding these horrific events would take much, much longer.

When it appeared that the lairds' questions were at last finished, she called to Stephen. "May I have a word?" she asked.

Gabrielle led Stephen away from the others so she wouldn't be overheard, but just to be absolutely certain, she spoke the language of St. Biel.

"Why didn't you tell me about these attackers?"

"I'm sorry, Princess, but I felt that if their

bodies were found, you would be safer having no knowledge of them."

"Did you recognize them? Could they have been at Finney's Flat?"

"We all got a good look at them, but none of us thought so. Remember, Princess, you are the only one who saw all of their faces."

"The description I just heard Lucien give the lairds didn't sound like any of the men I saw. Still, I thought perhaps they had followed us to the abbey."

Stephen shook his head. "That isn't possible. Christien kept backtracking to make certain we weren't being followed. He would have seen them."

"Then how did those men know Liam was there?"

"Someone must have seen him, or seen us carrying him inside. It's difficult to keep secrets in such a large place with so many strangers coming and going."

"Yes, that is so, but he's safe now, isn't he? And that is all that matters."

"And you, Princess? From the cuts and bruises I see, I must assume you are not safe. Will you tell me what happened?"

Dreading the task, she confessed to

Stephen what had transpired in the commons. She couldn't look at him as she repeated the foul names she'd been called, and her voice broke when she spoke of the monk who had confirmed Isla's story.

Stephen came to the same conclusion that she had, saying, "He must have seen you when you were on your way to look in on Liam."

Of the four guards, Stephen was the most pragmatic, and in a crisis, the most unruffled, but he could not contain his ire. "It is our duty to keep you safe, Princess, and you deliberately kept us in the dark. Had we known what was happening inside the abbey—"

She interrupted. "You would have been killed because you and the others would have tried to defend me. I couldn't let that happen."

Frustrated, he answered sharply. "It is our responsibility to defend you."

Christien, Lucien, and Faust came running. Faust looked horrified when he said, "Stephen, you raised your voice to Princess Gabrielle."

"When you hear what she has just told me, you'll share my anger. Men dared to throw stones at her!" he railed.

Gabrielle was saved from having to relive the nightmare once again when an unhappy Laird MacHugh approached.

"I have yet to find out how my brother came to be at the abbey. In the time you were there, did you hear anything?"

Gabrielle answered, "Please keep in mind, Laird, very few people knew he was in the monks' quarters. Perhaps Liam will remember something. I suggest you ask him."

Colm turned his attention to her four guards. "My brother said he tried to talk to you. Why didn't any of you answer? Liam thought you didn't understand him, but since you clearly understand Gaelic, I want to know why you wouldn't speak to him."

Faust looked to Stephen. Receiving his permission with a quick nod, he said, "We didn't want to."

TWENTY-EIGHT

GABRIELLE'S GUARDS WERE ARROGANT, RUDE, insulting, blunt, and brutally honest. Colm couldn't help but like them. Had he not known better, he would have thought they were born and bred Highlanders. And since he didn't consider any of these traits flaws, there was no need to shove his fist down Faust's throat because of his insolent attitude.

There was much he wanted to know about their involvement with Liam, but he decided to put that matter aside for a moment and concentrate on Gabrielle. The sooner he explained what was going to happen to her, the better. He had a debt to repay, and by all that was holy, he would see it done.

While the others prepared to resume their journey, he waited for the guards to return to their horses before he addressed her. "Gabrielle."

"Yes, Laird MacHugh?"

"You will walk with me."

It wasn't a request. It was an order, given in a harsh voice.

"I will?"

He nodded. "Aye, you will."

The laird was used to getting his way. And why not? Gabrielle thought. He looked strong enough to lift a horse and not break a sweat. She could see the power in the way he moved, in his arrogant swagger, but she didn't feel threatened or frightened by it. His strength somehow made her feel secure. And what sense did that make?

But then, today had been one of the worst days of her life. Nothing made any sense to her.

"You will speak only Gaelic when you are with me," Colm ordered.

She tried not to take exception to his biting command. The laird was accustomed to his clan following his orders without question, but had he forgotten she wasn't a MacHugh? If he continued to be so abrasive, she would remind him of that fact.

Without a word, she walked across the small clearing to the shade of a bank of trees. She felt the soldiers' eyes on her.

She stopped and turned to face the laird.

Standing just a few feet from her, Colm gave her his full attention. He tried not to react physically, but that proved to be impossible. She was beautiful: long, softly curling hair the color of midnight, skin as pure as cream, eyes so violet and expressive they seemed to sparkle, and that mouth, dear God, that mouth could give any man fantasies. Even with the bruised jaw and the bloody cut on her cheek, she was irresistible.

Colm could not let his mind digress like this. The last thing he needed was a woman confusing his thoughts. In time, he was certain he would get used to her appearance, but he wasn't as certain about his followers. Even now his men were gawking. He turned to signal his disapproval, but none would spare him a glance; they were fully occupied watching her. If they were closer, he would slam some heads together—that would get their attention.

Gabrielle waited patiently for Laird MacHugh to speak. The way he was staring so intently at her made her feel uneasy.

She attempted a smile and said, "What is it you wish to say?"

He saw no reason to ease into the topic. "You are going home with me."

She was certain she hadn't heard correctly. "I'm sorry. Would you mind repeating what you just said?"

"You're going home with me."

Totally bewildered, she asked, "Why?"

Frowning, he said, "Because I have decided so."

"But why would you want to take me home with you?" she asked again.

He let out a long, drawn-out sigh. He should have known it wouldn't be easy. Things having to do with the Buchanans always ended up being complicated, and this obviously wasn't going to be any different.

"It has been suggested by your cousin . . ."

"The wild Buchanan?"

"Yes . . ."

"What exactly did he suggest?"

"Stop interrupting me."

She was immediately contrite. "I apologize, Laird. Your announcement took me by surprise, and I—" She stopped. "I make no excuses."

Embarrassment made her cheeks flush, and Colm knew that if he didn't stop noticing such things, he would never get through this. Clasping his hands behind his back, he scowled and tried once again.

"Brodick suggested that you would be safe living with my clan under my protection."

She folded her arms and waited a few seconds before responding. "Why would Laird Buchanan make any suggestions regarding my welfare?"

"Your father wasn't at the abbey, and because Brodick is related, the duty to protect you fell on his shoulders."

"Brodick isn't my guardian. My father is."

Colm nodded. "Yes, that is so," he said impatiently. "But he wasn't there, was he?" Before she could answer, he added, "We were."

"Yes, I know you were. When I walked into the commons, I looked up and I saw you, but I thought . . . that is to say, I assumed you were leaving just then." Suddenly completely rattled, she took a step back and shook her head. "Why did I think that? Why did I assume you were leaving? I never even looked up at the wall again once the shouting started." Frantic now, she whispered, "When did you leave?"

"After you did."

She felt sick. "Then you witnessed . . ." She couldn't finish the question.

"Yes."

She took another step back. Had all the men with the lairds also heard and seen her humiliation? Yes, of course they had. That was why they were all staring at her now. Did they think she was a whore? A Jezebel? Why weren't they shouting obscenities at her like the others?

She stopped retreating and straightened her shoulders. She decided she wouldn't defend herself or protest her innocence. She wouldn't cower, either. If, like the mob hurling insults and stones, they wanted to think the worst of her, so be it. She summoned every last ounce of courage she possessed, but there was so little left. She was once again overwhelmed with shame for something she hadn't done.

Colm saw the sadness enter her eyes and the color drain from her face. He had the crazy urge to try to make her feel better. "You are a confusing woman," he muttered.

Gabrielle could not argue with his opinion, for her thoughts whirled in every direction. Why would this man offer her his home? What could he possibly gain from this? Nothing made sense.

She and her guards certainly needed a safe haven while she planned for their future. Living with the MacHughs would be a sound, but temporary solution, providing she understood the laird's reasons for offering. In her present state of mind, she didn't dare trust anyone to do the right thing. Was MacHugh honorable, or did he have twisted motives of his own?

"I think you must be a good man and an honorable leader—" she began.

"How could you possibly know what I am?"

It was the opening she was looking for. "I couldn't possibly know—"

"You just said—"

"And since I couldn't possibly know, you cannot take offense to my demand to understand your true motives. I ask you again, Laird, 'Why do you want me—' "

"I don't want you. Wanting has nothing to do with this. I'm paying a debt to Brodick Buchanan, and that is all."

"Oh." She didn't know whether to be relieved or offended. Things had been happening so fast, she hadn't had time to think. "You don't want . . . that is to say, you're paying a debt?"

Hadn't he just said as much? The woman was the most confounding creature Colm had ever met. Her emotions had gone from mortification to fear and despair, and now, damned if the woman didn't look disgruntled. He had assumed she wouldn't act favorably to being told she was to live with him, but he hadn't suspected such a bizarre reaction. This was proving even more difficult than he had anticipated.

"Thank you, Laird, for offering your home. Have no worries, you won't have to put up with the inconvenience for more than a few days."

"I'm not offering temporary lodging, and you won't be leaving in a few days. You're coming home with me to stay."

One of his men called to him. Colm answered by putting his hand up for silence and responding to the man, "You will wait to speak until I've finished with this."

Finished with this? Apparently, Gabrielle thought, she was the "this" he was referring to.

"I thank you for your offer of hospitality," she said, "but I cannot go with you."

Declining his invitation seemed the logical thing to do because she had just come up with another destination. She and her guards would go home with Laird Buchanan. The Buchanans could keep her just as safe as the MacHughs.

But why hadn't Buchanan offered?

Colm wasn't certain how to proceed. In truth, he was astonished that she would turn down his protection. Didn't the daft woman realize the danger she was in? Did she understand what being an outcast meant?

He decided to enlighten her, but before he could explain how precarious and bleak her situation was, she asked, "Why didn't Laird Buchanan offer his home and his protection? I am related to him."

Colm glanced over his shoulder, found Brodick in the crowd of men straining to overhear the conversation, and tilted his head toward Gabrielle.

From the look on Colm's face, Brodick knew the discussion wasn't going well. He crossed the clearing, and with his gaze locked on Gabrielle, he asked, "Why is this taking so long?"

"She's being difficult," Colm told him.

She immediately protested. "I must disagree, Laird. I don't believe I'm being in the least bit difficult."

"Then what's the problem?" Brodick asked Colm. "Did you tell her what's going to happen?"

Ah, that's where he went wrong. He'd told her Brodick's suggestion instead of commanding her obedience.

"Laird MacHugh kindly offered—"

"I what?" he roared.

"You kindly . . ." she began again.

When his eyes narrowed and the creases in his brow deepened, she understood. Using the word "kindly" was obviously some sort of an insult. What a strange group of men these Highlanders were. She would be relieved to be rid of them.

She didn't dare smile. "Laird MacHugh offered me his protection, and I declined. I *politely* declined," she stressed.

"She wants to know why you didn't offer her your home and your protection, Brodick," Colm said.

"You didn't fully explain the plan?"

"I never got that far. This woman is prone to interrupting."

"Gabrielle," Brodick began, using what he believed was his most reasonable tone of voice. "I could offer you my home and my protection—and I'll admit my wife would be happy for your company. You would be safe—"

"I will be pleased to accept your offer as long as you understand that it will be only for a few days. Is that agreeable?"

She hadn't given him time to tell her that MacHugh could do more than protect her; he could give her his name. Instead, she had accepted an invitation he hadn't extended.

"The woman's hell-bent on refusing help," Colm said.

Brodick nodded agreement.

Colm addressed Gabrielle. "What happens in a few days? What is it you plan to do?"

"First, I must find my father and warn him of the danger."

"Find him? You don't know where he is?" Brodick asked.

She shook her head. "He was going to

King John to give his account of what happened to Monroe, and he was going to catch up with me on my way back to England."

"Do you think to roam the land until you happen upon him?" Colm asked.

"Even if you do find him, you wouldn't be able to follow him into England. You've been exiled," Brodick reminded her. "If you're caught, you'll be executed, and if you're captured with your father, he'll also pay a high price."

They were forcing her to face reality, but she still couldn't abide the idea of anyone having to rescue her for something she hadn't done.

"My father must be told what happened."

"He's probably hearing about it even now," Brodick suggested. "Or he will hear soon. Bad news travels fast. He'll also hear that we were there," he added with a nod toward Colm, "and I would wager he'll come to me looking for you."

This made sense to her. "Yes, that is what he would do, and that is yet another reason I should go home with you."

Brodick sighed in frustration. He didn't know how to make her understand.

"You know, in a dire, dire situation . . . where there is no other possible solution— none at all—and it is life-threatening," he stressed, "you can come to my home, for you are my wife's cousin. However—"

Colm interrupted him. "We've wasted enough time here, Brodick. If you don't tell her, I will."

Frowning, she asked Colm, "Tell me what, Laird?"

Brodick answered. "If you go near your father, you'll put him in harm's way. Is that what you want, Gabrielle?"

"No, no, of course not, but I . . ."

And then it struck her. The enormity of the situation finally penetrated. Dear God, what was she going to do? No one was safe with her. Even the Buchanans and the MacHughs were at risk.

MacHugh's first in command, Braeden, called out to him. Colm turned and saw another of his soldiers talking to Braeden, and both were staring at Gabrielle. Then Brodick's commander, Dylan, joined their discussion.

"What is it?" Colm shouted.

Braeden explained as he walked toward him. "The English." He glanced at Gabrielle before he continued. "Both barons are searching for her, and both have small armies with them."

Brodick asked, "Are they heading this way?"

"No, Laird," he answered. "One of the barons leads his men to the south, and the other is heading toward the Monroes."

"Eventually, when they can't find Gabrielle, they'll backtrack and come this way," Brodick said.

Colm agreed. He took Braeden aside to give him orders and finally turned back to her.

"Now do you understand?" He asked irritably.

Apparently she didn't. "Why would they be looking for me? You were there. You heard what they called me, and you surely heard that I was condemned in King John's name. Didn't they say that in their eyes I no longer exist?"

"You're now vulnerable," Brodick explained.

Colm was going to have to be more direct. "Any man who is strong enough to fight off the others can have you now. Need I be more explicit?"

Horrified, she frantically shook her head.

"Since you no longer answer to any king nor belong to any country, you have no one to protect you from predators," Brodick explained, his voice much kinder than Colm's had been.

She bowed her head while fighting the terror inside. "How will I protect my father and my guards? They'll kill them." She whispered her fears.

"You worry about others instead of yourself?" Brodick asked.

She didn't answer. Instead, she took a deep breath and looked at the lairds. "You must leave immediately. Yes, that's what you must do." Her voice was strong now, determined. "All of you are in danger as long as you are with me. Go. Leave me now."

"Did she just dismiss us?" Colm looked incredulous.

"Aye, she did," Brodick said. "I don't think she knows any better."

After a moment's thought, Colm decided Gabrielle hadn't realized she was insulting them by suggesting that they would run at the first hint of trouble. Both he and Brodick welcomed the opportunity to fight with the English, but neither would give in to the temptation as long as Gabrielle swas in their care.

Exasperated, Colm said, "Gabrielle, you will not question my authority in the future."

She was slow to catch on. "In the future? What future?"

"Your future as my wife."

TWENTY-NINE

THERE WAS NO DISCUSSION. MACHUGH SIMPLY told her what was going to happen and then walked away.

All things considered, Gabrielle thought she handled herself quite well. She didn't scream or faint when the laird calmly announced that she would be spending the rest of her life with him. She might have paled, but she did not faint.

She took solace in one certainty: no way in Hell would she marry Laird MacHugh. She didn't like the man, and she knew he didn't like her. The debt he had to pay to Brodick must be staggering, for why else would he ruin his life by marrying a woman he barely knew and had heard such terrible lies about? As far as she knew, MacHugh thought she was a whore.

No, marriage was out of the question.

How terrible would it be if, just for a little while, Gabrielle let MacHugh think she was agreeable? This small deception would give her time to work on a plan for her future. After two or three days, she would tell him the truth . . . as she was leaving, of course.

She weighed the good against the bad. On the one hand, she and her guards would be safe from the barons. They would have shelter and protection. If the barons found out where she was staying, they wouldn't dare ride onto MacHugh land, for they would surely know they wouldn't come out alive.

On the other hand, she would be living with . . . him.

Laird Buchanan seemed most pleased with his friend's decision. Smiling and in good cheer, he motioned to his men that it was now time to leave. Gabrielle tapped on his shoulder. She was about to ruin his good mood.

"Cousin Brodick?"

His smile vanished. "It isn't necessary for you to call me cousin."

"Do you have a moment to answer a question?"

"What is it?" he asked warily.

"I understand why you would feel responsible for me, since I'm your cousin."

Gabrielle wondered why he grimaced at her reference to their relationship. Did he need to be reminded that he had married a woman from England? Did he grimace every time his wife spoke to him?

She decided to get right to the heart of her question. "What debt is he paying that he must be responsible for me? He doesn't even know me."

"Put the question to him," he suggested. "If he wants to explain, he will."

"And Laird," she continued, "if you should hear from my father, will you please tell him not to come after me?"

Brodick started to turn away, then changed his mind. "Gabrielle, MacHugh won't let anything happen to you. He protects what belongs to him."

That said, he went on his way, leaving Gabrielle aghast. Belongs to him? She was now a possession?

Despite the sinking feeling in the pit of her stomach, she told herself to stay strong. She would keep an open mind about MacHugh. If she didn't draw attention to herself, maybe he would pay no attention to her or her guards, and if she stayed out of his way, perhaps he would stay away.

"Gabrielle, it's time to leave." MacHugh spoke from directly behind her. She nearly fell into his arms when she whirled around.

"I didn't hear you approach," she stammered. "You move like a lion."

Amused, he asked, "Have you ever seen a lion?"

"As a matter of fact, I have. In St. Biel, my father once showed me two lions. They were quite beautiful."

And fierce, she silently qualified. *Much like you.*

Gabrielle followed him to the horses. "Laird, I want you to know that I will not defend myself. I don't care if you believe what the barons said."

"Yes, you do care," he replied as he kept walking. "We know the woman lied."

Her hand flew to her heart, and she stopped. "You do?"

"Of course. I knew she was lying from the beginning."

Apparently he was finished talking about

it. Before she realized what he was going to do, he picked her up and all but tossed her onto Rogue's back. Braeden handed her the reins.

"Your guards will be allowed to accompany you," Colm said.

Did he honestly believe she would go with him if her guards were *not* allowed to go with her? He had already swung onto his horse and ridden away before she could ask.

The others fell into formation behind him. Riding hard through the valleys, their pace slowed once they reached the hills. The riders formed a single line to climb the narrow, treacherous trail ahead of them. After making one harrowing turn, she discovered they were on a bluff overlooking Finney's Flat. This was the spot the scoundrels who were holding Liam had watched as they waited for MacHugh to show himself. She squinted against the sun to see if she would be able to recognize anyone from such a distance. Impossible, she thought. Only an eagle could have seen Liam's face.

Realizing she was holding up the procession, she continued on. Rogue faltered near the first crevice, and stones rumbled down the steep cliff on the right. Gabrielle looked over the side and cringed. It was a sheer drop to the bottom of an abyss. Her horse continued to have trouble finding his footing. She let him go at his own pace, but still he stumbled twice more before the path finally widened and leveled. By then, her heart was racing.

When they reached a grassy slope she leaned down and whispered praise to Rogue as she patted him. When she straightened, she saw MacHugh watching her with a puzzled expression.

And on they continued. The weather turned damp and cold, and Gabrielle felt it in her bones. Without her heavy cloak, she was shivering in no time at all. She didn't think anyone noticed how miserable she was until MacHugh ordered Lucien to move out of his way so he could ride next to Gabrielle. Her guard had no choice in the matter. MacHugh's stallion would have trampled him if he hadn't moved back.

"You're cold," he stated.

Was it an accusation? She couldn't tell. "Yes, I'm cold." She added, "Glaring at me won't make the shivers go away, Laird. Perhaps—"

She might have yelped. She couldn't be

certain. It all happened so fast. One second he was listening to her, and the next he was lifting her from Rogue, settling her on his lap, and wrapping her in his plaid.

His chest was like a rock, a warm rock. So were his thighs. The heat radiating from him warmed her. Exhausted, she let herself relax against him. His scent was pleasant, like heather and the woods. The barons who had come for the wedding at the abbey drenched themselves in perfumes and oils, thinking the heavy fragrances would cover the foul stench of not bathing. Gabrielle found it nauseating to be in the same room with them. MacHugh was nothing like the barons.

She was suddenly plagued with guilt. It was wrong to deceive him, no matter what her reasons were.

"I have deceived you," she blurted. "I will only be staying with you for two or three days, Laird, and I have no intention of ever marrying you. I wouldn't blame you if you threw me off your horse this very minute. I hope you won't, but I wouldn't blame you."

His response wasn't what she expected. He pulled the plaid over her face and ignored her.

Lucien rode up next to the laird's horse

and with a threatening look at Colm said, "Princess Gabrielle, do you need my help?"

She pushed the plaid away from her face. "I'm warm now, Lucien. There is no cause to be concerned." She gave Colm a glance that was cross and reproachful, but when she turned back toward Lucien, there was a faint smile on her lips.

MacHugh tightened his hold. The woman had gone through Hell today, and still she could smile. If she was afraid of what tomorrow would bring, she wasn't letting it show.

Colm had lost his train of thought for a second or two, but he quickly regained his stern composure and said, "I don't need your guard's permission to touch you."

"No, you don't," she agreed. "You need mine."

Her comment obviously wasn't worthy of a response, she decided, unless a grunt meant something.

They rounded another hill, and suddenly his fortress loomed ahead of them. The watchtower was so tall it seemed to disappear in a cloud. A stone wall surrounded his holding, and a wooden drawbridge crossed a wide moat filled with water, black from the river stones deep in its bed.

Colm motioned for her guards to follow his soldiers inside. It was his ritual to be the last to cross the bridge. As soon as he had cleared the wooden planks, he signaled by raising his fist, and the drawbridge was lifted. The clanking sound of metal scraping against metal gave Gabrielle the feeling of being sealed inside a dungeon. She closed her eyes and forced the dark image from her mind. This was her sanctuary, not a prison.

The sun was setting as they crossed the lower bailey and started up the incline to the castle. The cottages they passed were dappled gold by the sun, and the grass on the slope ahead of them took on a fiery hue.

Clansmen stopped their chores and came outside to call to their laird and to stare at her. Children ran after them. Some of the women smiled. That would soon change, she thought, when they found out what she'd been condemned for. Hopefully, she would be gone before then.

His home was not impressive by St. Biel's standards, or her father's, for that matter. The square structure wasn't large, but an addition was being constructed. Three sides were built of stone, and the remaining side, made of wood, was in the process of being reinforced with massive rocks. Scaffolding had been erected next to the keep with a winch and a treadmill to haul the stones up to the top floor.

"Your fortress is different from the ones in England."

"How is it different?"

"The castles in England usually have two walls. The outer wall surrounds the bailey, but then there's another defensive wall between the lower and the upper bailey. Sometimes there is even a drawbridge to further separate the lord's home from all the others."

"I have no need for two walls."

"And you have only one watchtower," she pointed out.

"I have need for only one."

"I hope you don't think I'm criticizing your home. I was just pointing out the differences. I'm certain I shall be most content here."

When he didn't agree, she assumed he had his mind on more important matters. Father Gelroy waved to her as he passed, and if her arms hadn't been trapped inside MacHugh's plaid, she would have waved back.

The stables were halfway between the

lower and the upper bailey, and they passed the garrison on the way to the laird's courtyard. There wasn't anyone waiting at his door to greet him. Did he have other family besides Liam? She hadn't thought to ask that question. She'd find out soon enough, she supposed.

MacHugh dismounted with her in his arms. The second he let go of her, she stepped back to put some distance between them.

"Where will my guards and I have rooms? Inside your home with you? Or do you want us to take two of the empty cottages? Are there any empty?" Dear God, she was nervous. She couldn't stop talking. "That is to say, I'd like to rest. I just need to know where I am to stay."

Father Gelroy saved her from continuing to ramble. "Princess Gabrielle, are you as tired and hungry as I am?"

She latched on to his arm as though it was her lifeline. "Yes, I am," she said much more enthusiastically than necessary. "I was just asking the laird where we should take our shelter for the night."

"You'll sleep inside," Colm said as soon as he could get a word in.

Braeden rushed ahead to the tall door made of oak timbers and thrust it open. Gabrielle thanked him as she walked past, but she came to a quick stop on the threshold. It was so dark inside, she couldn't see her way. Colm took her hand and pulled her along.

The wooden floor sagged under his weight, and the men's boots made a clatter in the cavernous space. Light filtered in through the open door. As Gabrielle's eyes adjusted to the darkness, she made out a room with a low ceiling. There was a large storeroom on her right. Shelves were filled with sacks of grain and barley, and there were barrels of wine stacked high. From the number of bags, it looked as though the MacHugh clan could hold off a siege for a good six months, perhaps more, though Gabrielle doubted their enemies would get all the way to the castle with the treacherous trail they would have to climb.

An opening in the wall on her left led to stairs, the steps surprisingly wide and deep. On the second level was the great hall. It was spacious, and a fireplace with a huge hearth took up much of the far wall. A welcoming fire warmed the room.

The housekeeper—a stout, older woman named Maurna—made them welcome and bid them to rest by the fire. After giving instructions, Colm left the hall. Stephen and Lucien went with him to see to the horses.

Another set of steps continued up to a third level, which, Maurna explained, held the armory. Laird MacHugh had ordered that her guards should sleep there and so could Father Gelroy until further arrangements could be made. Gabrielle was to be given the room next to it.

Gabrielle wouldn't have cared if she was given a stall in the stables. The day had caught up with her. Tired and hungry and dusty from the journey, a room next to the armory sounded like a blissful refuge. When Maurna announced that she had prepared a meal and would show them where they could wash their hands and faces, Gabrielle thanked her profusely.

At supper, Father Gelroy sat next to her and seemed agitated.

"There isn't a chapel here," he whispered. "I didn't see one on the ride up to the court-yard, so I asked the housekeeper, and she told me there isn't one. I worry they may all be heathens. If that is the situation, I have my work cut out for me."

"It will be a challenge, but I believe you'll do well here," she assured him.

He leaned closer and whispered, "I don't think the laird brought me here to look after his followers' souls. I think he's wanting me to explain how Liam came to be in the abbey. He knows I didn't tell him everything about his brother."

"Surely he won't coerce you."

Maurna interrupted their discussion. "Is there something wrong with the food, milady? You've barely taken a bite."

"The food is excellent," she said. "I'm just not as hungry as I thought."

"Sleep is what you're needing, if I may be so bold to suggest. Would you like me to show you to your chamber?"

Gabrielle nodded. Saying good night to Father Gelroy and to Christien and Faust, she followed Maurna upstairs. Lucien caught up with her. He carried her satchel, which held two changes of clothes and the other essentials she had needed for her trip back to England.

"Is the laird's brother here?" he asked Maurna.

"He is indeed. And sleeping soundly since his return. Our healer is watching over him."

The first door they passed was the laird's chamber, Maurna pointed out.

The room Gabrielle was assigned had been used for storage. It was damp and musty. Maurna rushed ahead to light several more candles and placed them on the table across from the bed.

"I tried to air the room for you, but it seems all I've done is make it colder in here. Would you like me to pull the tapestry down over the window?"

"I'll take care of it."

"I've got the bed ready for you and put extra blankets on top. There's water to wash with on the chest behind the door, and if you'll give me a few mintues, I'll see to lighting a fire in the hearth. My man, Danal, already carried up dry wood and put it in the box."

"I'll light the fire later."

"But milady, should you be doing common work?"

She smiled. "Of course I should."

Maurna was frowning intently. "It's probably not my place to mention it, but I couldn't help but notice you've got blood on the back of your gown up high by your shoulder. Did you cut yourself?"

Gabrielle wondered what the woman would say if she told her the truth, that the stones the mob had thrown at her had caused the bleeding.

"I must have," she answered.

Maurna wiped her hands on the cloth she had tucked into her belt and walked toward Gabrielle. "Since you don't have a maid to assist you, I'll be doing it. Let me help you get that gown off so I can see the damage."

There was no talking her out of it. "I don't want to be a bother," Gabrielle protested. "I can take care of myself."

"And how are you going to do that?" Maurna asked as she tugged the bliaut over Gabrielle's head. "How are you going to reach behind you and clean your cut?"

She stopped arguing. "Thank you, Maurna."

When the housekeeper saw Gabrielle's back, she clucked like a mother hen. "You poor dear. Your back is one big bruise." She rushed to the basin and dabbed a clean cloth into the water. She hurried back to Gabrielle. "How did this happen? Did you take a spill?" Deciding that was exactly what must have happened, she went on, "Of course you did. You sit down and wait while I go get some healing salve to put on those cuts. Wrap yourself in a blanket so you won't catch cold. I'll be right back."

Letting someone else take care of her was nice, Gabrielle admitted. It reminded her of home.

Homesickness and worry for her father suddenly overwhelmed her. She said a quick prayer to God to watch over him, and then, exhausted, she sat on the bed, closed her eyes, and waited for the housekeeper to return. It was quiet at last, and since there weren't any distractions, Gabrielle could replay in her mind the events of the day. Maybe she could sort them out and make sense of them.

Impossible. It was simply impossible to understand—as though she was missing an important piece of a very bizarre puzzle. The barons had been so quick to condemn her. It couldn't all be about Finney's Flat, could it? Yet what more was there that the greedy pigs would want?

Maurna returned with the salve, and after she'd tended to Gabrielle's back, she insisted on washing her face as though she were a child. Dabbing a bit of the salve on the cut under her eye, Maurna said, "You hit your face when you fell, didn't you?"

Gabrielle nodded.

"Does it pain you?" Her voice was filled with sympathy.

"Not at all," Gabrielle insisted. It did hurt, but she didn't want the housekeeper to worry over her. Or hover.

"Is there anything more I can do for you?"

"No, thank you, Maurna. You've been most kind."

The woman's blush was as bright red as her hair. "I'm only doing what I was told to do, milady. Our laird wants you to be comfortable here. Might I ask a question that's been nagging me?"

"Yes?"

"What am I to call you? I heard the soldiers who came with you and the priest address you as 'princess.' Are you a princess?"

"I used to be, but no longer."

The answer didn't make a lick of sense to the housekeeper, and she fretted that perhaps milady had struck her head in the fall.

"Are you seeing two of me, milady?"

Though Gabrielle thought the question

was odd, she didn't laugh, for the house-keeper's expression showed her concern. "No," she assured her. "Just one of you."

Maurna looked relieved. "You're plain worn out, aren't you? You rest well, milady."

The second the door closed, Gabrielle went to the window to pull the tapestry down. She usually loved cold weather, but tonight she wanted to bury herself under the covers and sleep. It was pitch black outside with nary a star in sight. She could see tiny golden lights glowing from the cottages dotting the hillside. Families preparing for bed, no doubt, tired from the day's labors, but content. She tried to picture the ideal family. There would be children, a healthy mother and father, and laughter. Aye, they would be happy and safe.

Again, her thoughts raced back to her father. Was he safe? Had he heard what the barons had done?

Only when the chill became unbearable did she pull the drape and climb into bed. Too tired to light the fire, she snuggled under the MacHugh plaid and fell asleep saying her nightly prayers.

She awakened once during the night. The room was warm. A fire blazed in the hearth.

How had that happened? She rolled over and drifted back into a deep slumber.

The following morning, Stephen was waiting for Gabrielle in the great hall. She greeted him and then asked him if he or one of the other guards had come into her room during the night.

"Laird MacHugh asked the housekeeper to look in on you before she went to bed."

"Why would he do that?"

"Apparently Maurna went into great detail about the bruises and cuts on your back. Perhaps the laird was worried."

"Then Maurna started the fire?"

Stephen shook his head. "She reported to the laird that your room was near to freezing, so he went in."

"He came into my room?" She couldn't hide her shock.

"Yes, he did," he replied. "He started the fire in the hearth. Faust couldn't stop him, and so he went with him and stood with his back to your bed, blocking the laird's view, though he reported that you were so hidden under the covers, no one could see anything."

Stephen sounded unconcerned about the matter. "How did Faust try to stop him?" she asked as she crossed the great hall to sit at the table.

"He told me he got in the laird's way."

Hesitantly she asked, "And what did the laird do?"

"According to Faust, the laird got him out of his way. He didn't explain how." Stephens lips curled slightly in an uncharacteristic grin.

"Warming the room was a thoughtful act," she admitted.

"But improper," he said disapprovingly. "If you will excuse me, I'll see to the other guards. The laird wishes to speak to you after you've had your breakfast."

"Where is he?"

"I don't know, Princess. He asked that you wait here."

And wait she did, for over an hour, before the laird joined her. Gabrielle was standing with Maurna and the cook, a sweet-tempered woman named Willa, as the two women discussed the advantages of boiling a pheasant over roasting it on a fire—a subject Gabrielle knew absolutely nothing about—when she heard a door slam. A few seconds later, she heard men talking and then footsteps on the stone.

"That should be our laird," Maurna said. "Willa and I will be about our chores so that you two can have your privacy."

Braeden and another soldier accompanied their laird. They bowed as they crossed the hall and continued on to the buttery.

MacHugh stood on the top step observing her. She was a fair sight. Her hair gently curled around her angelic face and fell in silky waves across her shoulders. His eyes moved down. It was impossible not to notice the soft curves of her body.

He wanted her, and the acknowledgment didn't please him. Gabrielle was a complication and a nuisance he didn't need in his life.

Gabrielle took a step toward him when he entered the great hall. Even though he was frowning—his usual expression, she decided—she smiled and bid him good morning.

He wasn't much for pleasantries. "Sit down, Gabrielle, while I talk to you about your future."

Why would he want to talk to her about her future? She had explained to him that she would be a guest for only two more nights. Had he forgotten?

She pulled a chair out from the table, sat

down, and demurely folded her hands in her lap. He'd sounded so serious, she began to worry that he'd changed his mind and wasn't going to let her and her guards stay another night.

Colm wasn't fooled by the serene expression she'd plastered on her face. He could tell she was nervous. Her folded hands were turning white, she was gripping them so tightly. And she sat rigidly straight and wouldn't look him in the eye.

He stood at the hearth with his arms folded in front of him while he considered her.

"Do you wish to say something to me, Laird?" she asked after a long silence.

"Yes, I do. Gabrielle, no matter how I try to stop it, the clan will hear about your situation."

He didn't think it was possible, but her back straightened even more. He expected her to snap at any second.

"Don't you mean to say that they'll hear I'm a harlot?"

His eyes narrowed. "You will not say that word again." He waited for her agreement before continuing. "There is a way to stop the rumors."

"Why do you care what people say about me? I'll only be here for a short time. Unless you would prefer that I leave today. Is that it? Is that what you want?"

"And you will go to the Buchanans," he said in exasperation.

"Yes, but only for one night or two. I'm rested now, and I have already decided upon a plan for my future."

"Is that right? And what might that plan be?"

"I'm going to St. Biel."

His sigh was long and drawn out. "The English control St. Biel, don't they?"

"Yes, but in the mountains I could—"

He didn't let her finish. "And how are you planning to get there? Will you swim across the ocean?"

"No, of course not. I thought—"

"Do you even know how to swim?"

"I won't swim across." In frustration, she raised her voice. "I'll go by ship."

"What ship's commander would allow you passage?" he asked. "If caught, the penalty would be his death . . . and yours and your guards," he thought to add. "And if you were able to convince someone to take you, how could you trust him? Have you considered the possibility that he might have your guards killed, and then he and his men would spend the voyage taking turns with you?"

Noticing how the blood had drained from her face, he said, "Have I shocked you? Men are capable of such behavior. Have you forgotten the look in those barons' eyes when they watched you? What do you think they would have done if they'd gotten hold of you?"

He continued to fire questions at her, determined to make her realize it was a fool's dream to think she could live in peace in St. Biel.

"There are good people who would help me," she protested.

"You would put those good people in jeopardy? You would let them risk their lives for you?"

"No, I couldn't do that."

Colm destroyed every argument she gave, and within minutes any hope of leaving was gone.

"You're going to marry me, Gabrielle."

Her shoulders dropped and she sank back in her chair. "Is there something in the air up here that is making every man I meet talk of marriage? In the past two days, I've been told that I'm to marry two obscene barons, one Monroe upstart, and a despicable laird named MacHenley."

He flashed a smile. "The despicable laird you speak of is named MacKenna."

She shrugged indifference. "Since I'm not ever going to speak to the vile man again, I don't care what his name is."

"It is decided," he announced. "You will marry me, and no one will dare call you anything but Lady Gabrielle."

"You aren't asking me."

He looked affronted. "Of course not. I'm telling you."

His audacity was outrageous. Gabrielle felt the blood rushing back to her face, and it was difficult not to shout at him, though the urge was nearly overwhelming.

Colm could tell she was furious with him. Her hands were in fists in her lap now, and he knew it was only a matter of time before she lost her temper. He wondered if she realized how easy she was to read. Probably not, he decided, or else she wouldn't go to such lengths to try to hide her feelings.

Braeden interrupted. "Laird, they're waiting for you."

Colm nodded. "I'll be there in a minute."

Giving Gabrielle his undivided attention once again, he asked impatiently, "Are there any other questions?"

Was he serious? Of course she had questions. Hundreds of them.

"I don't have a dowry," she said.

"I don't need or want a dowry."

"That makes you different from the others. All they wanted was Finney's Flat."

"Don't compare me to those bastards." Anger flashed across his face.

She wasn't intimidated. "To pay a debt to Laird Buchanan, you're willing to give up your future. I don't understand why you would do this."

He didn't know what misconception to address first. "Do you think Finney's Flat is the only reason those men wanted you?"

"What more could there be?"

Her question, though naïve, was an innocent one. She really didn't know her own appeal, and therefore had obviously never used her beauty to get her way.

"I won't waste time discussing their twisted motives," he said.

"And you? You would ruin your life—"

"Gabrielle, I would never allow any

woman to have that kind of power over me," he said unequivocally.

"No, I don't suppose you would."

"I don't know how the barons in England treat their wives, but I have a suspicion that most misuse them."

"Not most," she countered.

"We do not mistreat our women here. I will never hurt you, and you will be well-protected."

She believed him. And suddenly marriage didn't sound so terrible after all. Perhaps because she had nowhere else to go.

"Did you have a date in mind for this marriage?"

"You have a choice," he said as he once again glanced toward the entrance. He was becoming more impatient to get this discussion over and done.

"Explain this choice, please."

"We'll marry now or in six months. However, if we marry now, we won't live as man and wife until six months have passed."

Thoroughly confused, she asked, "Why six months?"

"So that the clan will know the only child you carry is mine."

He'd rendered her speechless. When she found her voice again, she said, "You told me you didn't believe the lies—"

He interrupted. "The suggestion came from Brodick. He doesn't want anyone to question who the father is if you were to be with child right after we're wed."

Appalled and embarrassed by his bluntness, she could only shake her head when he asked if there were any other questions he needed to answer before he took his leave.

Halfway to the stairs he remembered the other matter he wanted to talk to her about.

"Gabrielle, I allowed your guards to accompany you here so that you would know that you are safe. But they cannot stay."

She bounded to her feet. "They must stay."

He was astounded by her outburst. She'd been so cooperative when he explained her future, but now she was belligerent and combative.

"No, they cannot stay," he said quietly. "It's my duty and the duty of my soldiers to protect you now that you are to live here, and it would be an insult for an outsider to interfere."

"You don't understand. You must—"

"This isn't open for discussion," he snapped. "Your guards will be handsomely rewarded because they protected my brother."

"Reward them by letting them stay here with me."

He shook his head. "Shouting at me won't change my mind. I have another duty that is far more pressing, but when I return, I will talk to your guards. I'm not in the habit of justifying my decisions, but in this instance, I will. Once I've made my position clear, my men will escort them down the mountain. You'll have until then to say your good-bye."

He walked down two steps, turned around, and commanded, "I will have your acquiescence."

She looked at him for several seconds, then affected a perfect curtsy.

"As you say."

Relieved that there hadn't been any tears, Colm was in good spirits when he left the holding. Three hours later, upon his return, he was informed that Lady Gabrielle was gone.

THIRTY

MACHUGH CAUGHT UP WITH HER NEAR THE BASE of his mountain. She was still on his land, though just barely. Had he returned to his holding an hour later to hear of her departure, Gabrielle would have already started across Finney's Flat and been a fair target for the predators who waited for the cover of nightfall to crawl out from their holes.

What in God's name was the daft woman thinking to go out into the wilderness with but four men for protection? Didn't she realize what a temptation she was?

But she was safe, he told himself as he rode toward her. Safe from everyone but him, he qualified, for in his present mood, he was thinking hard about throwing her over his shoulder and carrying her back to his keep. Dragging her back didn't sound all that unappealing, either.

Gabrielle heard his horse thundering toward her. She had stopped to water the horse and had walked far enough away from Rogue to know she couldn't get back to her horse before Colm caught up with her.

There was no guessing what his mood might be. The man was angry all right. The fire in his eyes and the clenched jaw were obvious indicators. He leaped from his horse before the animal had fully stopped, and though she had a strong desire to back away, she stood her ground and held her chin up as he stomped toward her.

Her guards naturally took a defensive position to block the laird, but Gabrielle knew MacHugh wouldn't retreat. She'd been in his company long enough to learn that much about him. But then her guards wouldn't retreat, either. It was up to her to stop the confrontation before it started.

"Please move out of my way. I wish to speak to the laird."

Faust was worried. "Princess," he whispered, "it is our duty to make certain he won't harm you."

Stephen, like Gabrielle, was a good judge of character, and he'd already determined what the laird was all about. He had noticed the way MacHugh's clan had greeted him when the laird returned home. They were genuinely happy to see him, not afraid. Their homes were sturdy, there was firewood outside each door, and children didn't run away and hide when MacHugh and his soldiers came up the hill. MacHugh protected those he cared about, and the relief Stephen saw in the laird's eyes as he now spotted Gabrielle told the guard that he cared, even if just a little, about her.

Stephen prodded his friends' shoulders and ordered, "Get out of the laird's way. Our princess is safe with him."

Colm paid no attention to her guards. His gaze was locked on Gabrielle, and he stopped just an arm's length from her. "I would have a word with you, Gabrielle." His voice had a noticeable bite to it.

The laird towered over her, and she retreated several steps so she would not have to crane her neck to look at him. "What is it you wish to say?"

"What part of our discussion this morning didn't you understand? I would like to know so that I may clarify it for you."

"Discussion? I don't believe it was much of a discussion. You gave orders."

"Which I expected you to obey."

"Why?"

Her question sounded impudent, but he didn't believe that to be her intent. She really didn't understand, and though it had been a long while since anyone had asked him to explain himself, he allowed it.

"Because I have said so."

"That isn't a sufficient answer. Why would you think I should obey your commands? I'm not a member of your clan."

He was determined not to lose his patience with her. "You are to obey my commands because you will soon become my wife and, therefore, soon become a MacHugh."

He couldn't have been any more clear or concise, and she couldn't possibly have any more questions or arguments, for there was nothing more to argue about.

"But Laird, I never agreed to become your wife."

"You are a frustrating and aggravating woman," he snapped, "and I suspect more stubborn than all the women here combined."

His insults were meant to make her realize that *he* was in charge, not she, and he was totally nonplussed by her response.

"You're no prize, either, Laird. But unlike you, I don't feel it necessary to list your many faults."

She had the gall to smile at him. He damned near laughed, he was so stunned by her insolent behavior. The woman gave as good as she got. He guessed he was going to have to drag her back to his keep after all. He took a threatening step toward her and she didn't back away. She looked him right in the eye and waited to see what he would do.

She didn't cower, and that pleased him considerably. He decided he would try to gain her cooperation one last time before he resorted to carrying her back to his home to do his bidding.

"While I understand that not wishing to marry me was your reason for leaving my home, I want you to understand—"

She interrupted. "That isn't why I left."

"Then what in God's name was your reason?"

"You ordered my guards to leave, and I couldn't allow that to happen. I tried to explain why they must stay with me, but you didn't want to listen."

"And so you left."

"Yes, I left. What other choice did I have?" she replied, and before he could start in on her again, she added, "And yes, I was going to the Buchanans with the intent of pleading with my cousin to release you from your promise. My hope is that he will find something else for you to do to pay your debt to him, whatever that might be."

Speaking to the Buchanan on his behalf? Unthinkable . . . and appalling.

"You will not speak to anyone on my behalf. Is that understood?"

She supposed she'd inadvertently insulted him. She quelled his anger with a quick nod. "I promise. In fact, I won't even mention you. I'll simply explain that my guards weren't allowed to stay, and so I left your holding." She turned and walked away from him.

He followed. "Not speaking to him at all will satisfy me."

Then he wasn't going to be satisfied, she decided as she quickened her pace.

"You said I refused to listen to your explanation as to why your guards must stay with you."

"Yes, that is so."

"I'll hear your reasons now," he announced. "But I will tell you this, Gabrielle. English soldiers living with my men will not work."

"They aren't English soldiers, and they would be highly insulted to hear you think they are. They're from St. Biel, and the emblem they wear over their hearts signifies that they are part of the royal guard."

Gabrielle was so intent on making the laird understand, she didn't realize she was heading into a thick woods. Colm stayed right behind her, and twice he reached over her head to lift a branch out of her way.

"My mother was Lady Genevieve, princess of the royal house of St. Biel. When she married my father, guards accompanied her to her new home in England, and only when they became convinced that she was well-protected by her husband did they return to their country. My mother told me that at first Father wasn't happy to have them in his home, but in time he not only accepted them, he came to depend on them."

"How long did it take for her guards to become convinced that your mother was well-protected?"

She turned around to answer.

"Three years. They stayed three years." Colm flinched. Irritated by his response, she was about to poke him in his chest, but thought better of it and stopped herself in time—though he had to wonder why she was pointing her finger at him.

She put her hand behind her back. "My father was sorry to see them go."

"I think perhaps you exaggerate."

"Father trusted them," she insisted.

"You said that the guards returned to St. Biel after three years with your mother, yet now there are four guards with you."

"A month after I was born, four guards arrived at Wellingshire. They had been sent by my uncle, who was still the king. Their duty was clear. They were to protect me. Over time the guards have changed. Stephen has been with me the longest. Then Lucien came. Christien and Faust arrived a few years later."

"Who sent them? England has ruled their country for many years now."

"The people of St. Biel. The English may occupy their land, but the people are still very loyal to my mother's family."

"Stephen has called your mother Lady Genevieve, but you are called Princess Gabrielle. Was she not also a princess?"

"In St. Biel a princess isn't addressed as such. I should be called Lady Gabrielle. When I was a child, the guards called me Little Princess. The name has stayed with me. It doesn't matter now, does it?"

"No, it doesn't," he agreed before moving on to another question.

"Why did it take four guards to look after one little girl?"

"One guard would have been enough," she said. "Though my father would disagree. He insists that I liked to get into mischief, and it took all four of them to watch over me. I wasn't willful," she insisted. "I was just curious."

She waited for him to comment, and when he remained silent, she continued. "Father never worried about me as long as my guards were with me. They saved my life too many times to count."

Gabrielle only just then realized she had

no idea where she was. The forest was closing in on her.

"What happens if I refuse to let them
stay? What will they do?" Colm asked.

"Stay anyway. They've taken an oath, and
they are honor-bound."

"Even if staying means their death?"

"Even then," she whispered. "But they
would die with honor, and whoever kills them
would have no honor at all."

Hell, he was going to be stuck with them.
"They can stay, but they damn well better not
take three years to figure out I can protect
you."

Gabrielle was overjoyed. Colm MacHugh
was a good and reasonable man. "Then I
shall marry you, Laird, in six months' time.
You have my word."

She leaned up on tiptoes to seal her promise with a kiss. Her lips barely brushed over
his, but his surprise was evident in his expression. "It isn't appropriate to kiss like this?" she
asked. She could feel her face burning. She
had acted impulsively and had obviously over-
stepped the bounds of propriety. She should
have made a curtsy to seal her promise.

"It is appropriate," he said quietly. "But I
prefer to kiss like this."

He didn't grab her or wrap her in his arms. Nay, he simply lowered his head and kissed her senseless. His mouth covered hers completely. His warm lips parted and when she imitated him and parted her lips, he deepened the kiss. His tongue stroked hers, sending shivers through her. It was shocking and thrilling at the same time. And sinfully arousing.

One kiss was all it was, yet when he lifted his head, her heart was thundering in her ears and her legs were trembling so, she was afraid she was going to fall on her face. She had never been kissed like this before.

Gabrielle tried to read his eyes. Evidently, the kiss didn't have the same effect on him.

She lowered her head. "It is a good thing that we are alone. It isn't seemly to kiss as we just did without being married. It's probably a sin."

She didn't sound too worried about it, he noticed. "We're soon to be married, so it isn't a sin, and we aren't alone." Without turning around, he called, "Stephen?"

"Yes, Laird?"

"How many soldiers are watching us?"

"I count seven."

Colm was disappointed. He expected the

experienced guard to be more observant. "Nay. There are eight."

Stephen stepped forward. "There were eight watching. Seven now."

"What happened to the eighth?"

There was satisfaction in Stephen's voice when he answered. "Christien happened to him. Your soldier wanted to follow our princess too closely. Christien didn't think he should, so he stopped him. He didn't kill him," he added. "He just put him to sleep."

Colm muttered something under his breath and strode back to the horses. Gabrielle would have had to run to keep up with him. When he noticed she wasn't behind him, he waited for her, then took hold of her hand and pulled her along, forcing her to keep up.

"Laird, if you knew your men were watching, why did you kiss me so . . ."

"So what?"

"Soundly."

"It is my right," he answered. "And Gabrielle, since we are to be married, you may call me Colm." He didn't look back at her as he continued, "And another thing, when we return to my home, you will not ever argue with me again. You and I have come to an agreement regarding your guards, but that is all I will concede. I cannot spend my days chasing after a stubborn wife. I have more important duties to see to."

"I am never to argue or disagree with you?"

That sounded good to him. He nodded. "I will have your agreement now, Gabrielle."

She bowed her head. "As you say."

THIRTY-ONE

TO SARAH TOBIAS, GOSSIP WAS AS ADDICTIVE AS sweet butter biscuits. She craved it. She loved being the first to spread the latest rumors and didn't care if the stories she repeated were true or false. The telling was all that mattered to her. By the time she reached the end of her tales, Sarah felt such a rush that her face was flushed, the palms of her hands were sweating, and her breath came in short gasps. Gossip, she had discovered, was every bit as good as sex. Sometimes even better.

Sarah rarely spread stories about anyone's good works or good fortune. What was the point? There was nothing exciting about that. Sin was always much more fulfilling, and when the sin was one of lust, it became titillating as well.

One evening during supper her brother Niall happened to mention what he had heard about the incident at Arbane Abbey.

Sarah ate two biscuits listening to the tale, then gobbled down three more while she whittled every possible detail out of him. When Niall had finished relating what he had heard, Sarah was dizzy with excitement and stuffing the last biscuit into her mouth.

Before noon the following day everyone in the Dunbar clan knew about Gabrielle. Then Sarah, giddy with power, branched out. After baking a double batch of her sweet biscuits, she took them to her second cousin Hilda, who was married to a Boswell. She didn't leave the Boswell holding until she had made certain everyone in the clan knew about the infamous incident.

Besides spreading vicious gossip, Sarah's other weakness was that she liked to embellish. After telling the story thirty or forty times, she no longer felt the same rush. Her heart didn't race, and her palms didn't sweat. The gossip had become old news, and so she began to add a few extra little lies of her own. Nothing outrageous, of course. Just enough to spice up the telling. What harm was there in that?

Two weeks later the lies had spread to the MacHugh clan.

Gabrielle felt the difference in the atmosphere. Women who usually smiled as they walked past now avoided looking at her. They turned their heads and scurried away. Before anyone told her, she knew that they had heard the horrible lies. And from the way they were behaving, she also knew they believed them to be true.

Colm returned home from a long day of hunting to find Braeden waiting for him in front of the stables. The look on his commander's face told Colm the news wasn't good. His first thought was for Gabrielle. Had something happened to her?

He hadn't even dismounted when he asked, "Is Gabrielle all right?"

Braeden knew his laird didn't realize how telling the question was. "She's fine. No harm has come to her."

Colm's second question was just as revealing. "What's she done now?"

"Nothing that I know of," he assured him.

Colm swung down from his horse and tossed the reins to the stablemaster as he addressed Braeden. "She hasn't tried to leave again?"

Braeden smiled. "No, at least not today, anyway." He looked to the sky before adding, "The sun's still out, though. She still has time."

Gabrielle was having trouble adjusting to her new home. Every day it was something new. In the past week she'd tried to leave the holding twice, and twice Colm had had to bring her back. She'd insisted she wasn't running away. Her first excuse was that she wanted to go riding across Finney's Flat. The second excuse was that she wanted to do a "spot" of hunting, whatever that meant.

"Lady Gabrielle just needs time to understand the rules we live by here," Braeden said, trying to defend her.

Colm scoffed at the notion. "She knows the rules. She just doesn't pay any attention to them, which is why twice now I've had to stop what I was doing to chase after her."

"May I point out that I offered to go after her, as did several other soldiers."

"She's my responsibility and therefore my problem. I won't foist her on anyone else."

Braeden knew that wasn't the reason. Although Gabrielle had only been with them fourteen days, Colm had already become quite possessive of her. He didn't like anyone else near her. He barely tolerated her guards. As far as he was concerned, they were useless. They only answered to Gabrielle and only obeyed her commands. Colm believed he'd put up with their behavior long enough, even though he grudgingly had to admit they did guard her well.

"None of us consider Lady Gabrielle a problem. The men are infatuated with her, and the women like her as well, for she has a kind word and a smile for everyone she meets."

"Does she distract the men from their duties?"

"She does," he admitted. "Though not deliberately. Have you had a chance, Colm, to notice how pretty she is?"

Exasperated, he answered, "Of course I have."

"The men have also noticed. They like looking at her."

He stiffened. "Then I'll double their duties. If they train from sun up to sun down, they won't have time to stare at her."

"You speak like a jealous man."

From the dark look Colm shot him, Braeden realized he shouldn't have spoken the thought out loud.

"I am your friend for many years," Braeden reminded him. "I don't mean to rile you, only to speak truthfully. Word has spread that you are going to marry her, but if I could suggest, I think you should make the announcement to the entire clan soon."

"I'm a busy man," he barked.

Colm knew it was a poor excuse. He should have told his followers of his intention to take Gabrielle for his wife the day he had brought her home with him, but instead he had spent the last two weeks trying to stay away from her, telling himself that he had other duties that were far more important.

He could have made time for her. Colm wasn't one to avoid unpleasant tasks. He had a debt hanging over his head, and it would be paid as soon as he married her. And since he hated being in debt to anyone, he should have been eager to wed her. Why, then, wasn't he?

This morning he finally admitted the truth: Gabrielle was a dangerous woman. He didn't like the way she made him feel, turning his mind upside down. It started with a kiss. The damned kiss had awakened emotions he thought were long dead. The way she smiled at him only made it worse. She would turn him into a besotted fool if he let her, and no way in hell was he ever going to let another woman make him vulnerable.

"I hope you will make the announcement soon, Laird."

Colm responded sharply. "What is it you have to report?"

As he asked the question, he noticed two horses tethered to a tree branch, and from the markings on their hindquarters he knew who they belonged to.

"What in thunder are the Boswells doing here?"

"Spreading lies."

"What say you?"

"The lies about Lady Gabrielle have reached our clan, and two men from the Boswell clan are responsible. Kinnon Boswell claimed that he needed to speak to his cousin Rebecca, who as you know is married to one of our soldiers. He told the guards manning the tower that the matter was urgent, yet when he was allowed entrance, he didn't bother to go to her cottage. It seems both he and his friend Edward were determined to see Lady Gabrielle."

Furious, Colm demanded, "Did they see her?"

"No, they did not," he assured him.

Colm relaxed. "Then they just might get out of here alive."

Braeden continued with his report. "I was in the west field training the younger soldiers when one of Lady Gabrielle's guards came to me and told me there was a problem."

"Which guard?"

"Lucien."

"At least one of them is learning to follow the chain of command," he said drily. "What did he tell you?"

"He asked me if we were allies with the Boswells, and when I asked him why he wanted to know, he explained that he was about to kill two of them."

"Did you let him?"

"No, but I swear to you, Laird, when I heard what they were saying about Lady Gabrielle, I wanted to. I was about to throw them out when you returned."

"Where's Gabrielle now?"

"In the great hall."

"Find the Boswells," he ordered, "and

bring them to me. I want them to tell me what they've been saying about Gabrielle."

After giving the command, Colm continued on. He was in a hurry to get to Gabrielle before she heard about the Boswells. Gabrielle had been through enough heartache. She didn't need any more.

Damn it all, this was his fault. He should already have married her. That was the only sure way to stop this slander. No one would dare say a word against his wife . . . unless, of course, he had a death wish.

As he approached the courtyard, Colm spotted Gabrielle. Her back was to him and she was talking to someone. A few steps farther, Colm saw the Boswells facing her. He cursed as he quickened his step. The young men seemed so intent on what they were telling her, they didn't notice him. Nor did they hear Lucien and Faust coming up behind them. The guards were running toward the two men, but stopped when Gabrielle raised her hand slightly to signal them.

The action was noticed by Kinnon. He took a step toward her and asked, "What are you doing?"

She smiled as she answered. "Saving your life."

Edward was slow to catch on, but Kinnon was more astute. He whirled around and came face-to-face with Lucien. Instantly he turned back to Gabrielle and with a shaky voice said, "I was only telling you what everyone else was saying about you. I thought you would want to know. They can't kill us for that, can they?"

"They can't, but I can," said Colm. Had he not been so angry, he probably would have thought their reaction to his voice comical. They jerked back and bumped into each other looking for a way to escape.

Gabrielle feared Colm might actually carry through on his threat and kill the Boswells, and she didn't want that to happen. Kinnon and Edward were stupid young men with nothing better to do with their time than to come all this way just to see her reaction to their stories, but they should not have to die because of their ignorance.

They should have to do some squirming, though.

"Laird, I'm so happy you're home," she said ever so sweetly. "Come and listen to the stories the Boswells are telling me. You're certain to be amused."

Kinnon's face looked like it had been

scorched by the sun, while Edward's appeared to have lost all color. He resembled a corpse. 'Twas the truth, he smelled like one, too.

"I doubt I'll be amused," Colm said.

He threw his arm around her, pulled her to his side, and kissed her while the Boswells watched with wide eyes and gaping mouths. Then he turned and gave them his full attention.

"I will hear what you have said to Lady Gabrielle, soon to be my wife."

"Soon to be . . ." Kinnon swallowed hard.

"Your wife?" Edward said. "We didn't know. We never would have . . ."

"You would not have slandered Lady Gabrielle? Is that what you mean to say?" Colm asked.

He was so furious he could barely keep from strangling the fools. He was inadvertently squeezing Gabrielle instead, and only when she pinched him did he realize what he was doing and loosen his grip.

"We wanted to see what she looked like. We had heard she bewitches men and we wanted to see for ourselves," Kinnon explained.

"We were only repeating the stories we

heard," Edward said, his voice so high-pitched it neared a screech.

Lucien and Faust moved closer to Kinnon and Edward, who surely felt them breathing down their necks. Both guards were watching Colm, hoping that he would give the signal to dispose of the pests.

Gabrielle felt the Boswells had been sufficiently punished. "Kinnon and Edward have both convinced me that I am an amazing woman. It seems that I have given birth to four children, out of wedlock of course, and all in the span of one year," she explained. "And with four different men." She laughed before adding, "I must be very affectionate."

"The stories are falsehoods," Kinnon stammered. "We realize that now. Don't we, Edward?"

His friend nodded vigorously. "We do. Yes, we do."

"If we are allowed to leave, we promise never to say another word about Lady Gabrielle. Except praise," he hastened to add. "We will praise her. That's what we'll do."

"Lucien, Faust, step back. Gabrielle, go inside," Colm ordered.

Gabrielle wanted to ask him what he was

going to do, but knew it would be improper to question him in front of outsiders. He wasn't going to kill them, was he?

She took her time walking away. The Boswells had said terrible things, even repeating words she knew had to be foul because of their leers and dark laughter. She shouldn't feel sorry for them, but she did.

Colm noticed she was dragging her feet and decided he would have to have a word with her about her obedience. When he gave an order, he expected it to be followed immediately. And quickly. She obviously didn't know that. She was half English, he reminded himself, and perhaps that was why she was so headstrong.

He turned his attention to the Boswells, shaking in their boots.

"When you wake up, you will go to your laird, and you will tell him what happened here today. I will know if you don't tell him every word you said to Lady Gabrielle. You will also tell him that the only reason I let you live was because you made my future wife laugh."

Edward nodded. "We'll tell our laird every word," he vowed.

Kinnon scratched his chin. "Laird, did you say when we wake up? Are we to stay—"

He never finished his question. Colm moved so fast, neither Kinnon nor Edward had time to react. One second they were standing, and the next they were crumpled on the ground.

Lucien nodded approval while Faust grinned.

Colm stared down at the Boswells as he ordered, "Tie them to their horses and get them the hell off my land."

Walking toward the forge a few minutes later, Colm was still furious. How dare the Boswells, or anyone for that matter, say slanderous things about Gabrielle? Anyone who met her knew she was an innocent, sweet, kind woman. He should have killed them, he decided. Gabrielle may have been upset, but it certainly would have lightened his mood.

He stopped abruptly. When had that happened? When had her feelings become important to him?

Colm tried to put Gabrielle out of his thoughts. He had work to do. He reached the forge and spent an hour with the smith discussing modifications he wanted made to the sword blades and then walked up to the crest overlooking the field where the men were sparring. The younger warriors were training. They held shields, but none of them were using them properly. A few were actually using them as weapons while their swords hung idly at their sides.

They shouldn't be training with any weapon yet, Colm concluded. They were too inexperienced. Braeden was bellowing at them, but wasn't getting the results he wanted. When one of the younger ones made the mistake of grinning, Braeden promptly knocked him to the ground. Why was it that the inexperienced were the most arrogant? On a battlefield they would be a hindrance, and the seasoned warriors would have to protect them as well as fight the enemy. The distraction could prove deadly.

Stephen and Christien walked over to stand beside Colm.

"Lucien told us what happened to the men from the Boswell clan," Stephen said.

Colm didn't acknowledge the comment. Then Christien said, "Why didn't you kill them? I would have."

"Our princess would have been unhappy

if they were killed," Stephen explained. "I think that is why they're still alive."

The three remained quiet as they watched the exercises on the field. One young soldier dropped his sword.

"For the love of God," Colm muttered. "I should let them kill each other and be done with them."

"They should first learn to fight with their bare hands. They shouldn't be fighting with weapons." Christien voiced the criticism.

Colm nodded. Weapons could become crutches, and if disarmed, the warrior would be powerless against his enemy unless he possessed other skills. What in God's name was Braeden thinking to let them use swords? By day's end there would be severed limbs everywhere.

There were over a hundred clansmen on the field now, and that number didn't include the unskilled beginners. Braeden couldn't be in five places at the same time, and Colm realized he needed to delegate more responsibility to other worthy, seasoned warriors. No one would want to take on the beginners. Colm started back down the hill when an unexpected solution presented itself.

"Stephen, I think it's time for you and the other guards to earn your keep here."

"What did you have in mind?"

"I've yet to see your skill on the field. Tomorrow you will spar with some of my warriors. If I think you're up to the duty, you will help train the young ones."

Colm didn't have to look at Christien to know he was smiling. Come morning he would knock some of that arrogance out of him.

THIRTY-TWO

GABRIELLE HAD BEEN IN A FINE MOOD UNTIL SHE stepped outside to get a bit of fresh air and met the Boswells. Kinnon and Edward had taken delight in sharing the stories they'd heard about her. The tales were so outrageous she couldn't help but laugh.

The humor of the situation eluded her now. How could anyone get joy from saying terrible things about another person? There was no excuse for such cruelty. She pondered the sad fact as she climbed the stairs and entered the great hall. Her frame of mind had turned quite gloomy.

Though it wasn't logical, she decided to

place the blame for her misery on Colm. She had been living with the MacHughs for two weeks, and if their laird had bothered to tell his clan that he was planning to marry her, word would have spread to the other clans by now, and the Boswells wouldn't have dared to taunt her.

But he hadn't told anyone, had he? There was only one conclusion she could draw from his silence. He didn't want to marry her, and he was so dreading it, he couldn't bring himself to say the words. He didn't even like being in the same room with her. Aside from lecturing her every now and then about something he felt she'd done wrong, he hadn't had a decent conversation with her.

On one of her many walks with Father Gelroy she had discussed her concern about Colm. The priest suggested that she try to be more understanding. Colm's responsibilities as laird of his clan were sizable.

"I do realize his clan comes first," she told him, "and I am an outsider."

"They will come to love you," he assured her.

She wasn't as certain. Patience wasn't one of her virtues. She decided she would give Colm one more week to make a formal announcement.

"One week. Then I'll leave this place and go where he will never find me."

Voicing her thoughts made her feel better and more in control. She straightened her shoulders and walked across the hall to the bench where she'd left her needlework.

"Did you say something?" Liam MacHugh asked the question.

Gabrielle was so surprised and pleased to see him, she didn't mind that he had heard her mumbling to herself.

"Good day to you, Liam," she called out.

Colm's brother had been sprawled in one of two tall chairs flanking the fireplace. He stood as she crossed the room.

"Lady Gabrielle. Please, come and sit with me."

She took the chair on the other side of the hearth and noticed that Liam didn't grimace when he sat down. The cuts on the backs of his legs had obviously healed. There were a few wounds still visible just below his knees, but she didn't think he would carry the marks the rest of his life. The deep cuts on his back, however, would surely leave scars. Lucky for

Liam, his face had been untouched. He actually looked quite fit.

"Father Gelroy has told me all about you," he said, smiling.

"How is it that I have been here two weeks, and this is the first I've seen you?"

"I didn't want to see anyone until I was stronger. I've been up and about."

"Are you feeling better?"

Her concern seemed genuine to him. "Yes," he assured her. He studied her face for several seconds and then asked, "And how is it that you seem so familiar to me? I know we have never met, for I would remember such a beautiful woman. Perhaps I dreamed of you. The guards who traveled with you watched over me while I slept. I must thank you for allowing them to do so."

"They didn't need my permission, and they are the ones who should hear your gratitude."

"Yes, you're right," he agreed. He then repeated what the priest had told him about the royal guard and was curious to hear more. He was also interested in hearing about St. Biel, and Gabrielle was happy to answer his questions.

She liked him. Unlike his brother, Liam was easy to talk to and quite charming. Women must flock to him, she thought, because of his easy smile and his good looks. He also had a roguish sense of humor. He made her laugh telling stories about pranks he and Colm pulled when they were boys. Spending the afternoon with Liam was the most pleasant time she'd had since arriving at the MacHugh holding. Best of all, Liam never mentioned the reason she was there, and for that she was most thankful.

GABRIELLE WAS ACCUSTOMED to eating her meals alone. That evening both Colm and Liam joined her. Colm, sitting at the head of the table, and Liam, sitting at the opposite end, stood when she entered the hall with Father Gelroy trailing behind. Liam beckoned to her while Colm, stone-faced as always, simply waited for her to sit down. She made a choice without giving it much thought. She smiled at Liam as she walked to Colm and took the seat adjacent to him.

Father Gelroy glanced in both directions before taking a chair next to Liam.

The room was quiet until Maurna carried

in trenchers fashioned from day-old bread and filled with herring, salt cod, mutton, and salt beef. Last to be placed on the table were fat loaves of fresh brown bread. Still hot from the oven, the bread's aroma filled the hall.

Determined to engage Colm in conversation, she asked, "Laird, how did your hunting go today?"

"As expected."

She waited for him to elaborate, but he didn't seem inclined. She took the wedge of bread Father Gelroy offered her and tore off a piece as she tried to think of something else to talk about.

The men ate their meal in silence, while, occupied in thought, she continued to tear the bread into shreds.

Finally, Gabrielle spoke. "What are your plans for tomorrow?"

"Why do you ask?"

"I was but curious."

Father Gelroy began to tell an amusing story, and Gabrielle looked down at the table. She'd torn the bread into a million crumbs and made a mess. Thinking no one had noticed, she scooped up the crumbs and dropped handfuls onto the trencher.

Once the priest had finished his story, she

turned to Colm and asked, "Is the weather unusually mild this time of year?"

"No."

Gabrielle was frustrated. Nothing was working. Surely there was a topic that would get his attention. She moved on to a question about the new addition being built.

Liam was talking quietly to the priest, but he heard what she asked and leaned forward to answer.

Gabrielle sighed and reached for another wedge of bread, but Colm stopped her by putting his hand on top of hers. His voice was whisper soft. "Why are you so nervous with me tonight?"

Tonight? She was *always* nervous when she was with him. But why? There was no reason for this feeling, unless, of course, it was a purely physical reaction, which didn't make any sense at all. Of the two brothers, Liam was the good-looking one. He was the complete opposite in appearance and temperament from his brother, and yet it was Colm she was attracted to. There had to be something wrong with her, she decided, to prefer such a flawed and rude man.

"Gabrielle, answer me."

"Should I give you one-word answers like

you've been giving me? I have been trying to have a decent conversation with you."

Liam interrupted them. "Colm, did you find out anything about Monroe?"

"There are rumors but nothing of substance yet."

Liam looked from the priest to Gabrielle as he explained. "Laird Monroe was murdered."

"We know," Father Gelroy said. "Lady Gabrielle was supposed to marry the laird."

"That's right, she was. I heard about the marriage before I left the Monroe holding, not long before I was ambushed."

"May I ask why you were there?" Gelroy said.

Liam smiled. "I was meeting someone."

"Who?" Gelroy prodded.

"Just someone."

The priest was about to ask another question, but Liam stopped him when he said, "A woman, Father. I was meeting a woman. I won't give you her name."

Gelroy blushed. "If only there was a chapel, you could go to confession."

Liam shrugged. "Did you hear that the Monroes are fighting over who will be the next laird? Braeden believes there will be war among them."

For the next ten minutes the brothers debated who should take over leadership of the clan.

"Do you think they will ever find out who killed the laird?" Gabrielle asked.

"We won't rest until we find the culprit," Liam said.

"We?" Father Gelroy inquired.

"Lairds Buchanan, Sinclair, Maitland, and MacHugh," he answered. "They have already come together to share information."

Gabrielle hoped there would be justice for Laird Monroe. "No man should die from a knife in his back," she said.

"It is a cowardly act," Colm agreed.

She stared at his hand resting on top of hers. It was twice the size of hers and warm, wonderfully warm. How could a simple touch please her so? Was she so starved for affection that his nearness would evoke such a reaction? He probably wasn't even aware of what he was doing. Disgusted with herself, she turned away from him and listened to Fathery Gelroy telling about life at the abbey.

At every opportunity, Gelroy would make a comment or two about the benefits of having a chapel for the clan. He gave several examples, thinking he was being subtle.

"A chapel would provide a holy and proper place to hear Liam's confession and to absolve him of any sins he may have committed with the Monroe woman," he assured Colm. "And you, Laird," he continued, "I could hear your confession anytime you wished . . . even twice a day if necessary."

Gabrielle burst into laughter. "Father, I think perhaps you should just ask our laird to build you a chapel."

"*Our* laird?" Liam asked.

She lifted her shoulders and looked at Colm. "It would seem that you are Father Gelroy's laird now . . . and mine as well. Is that not so?"

His expression was inscrutable when he answered. "It is so."

Liam frowned. "Am I missing something here? Why is it so?" he asked. "And are you thinking about building the priest a church?"

"Perhaps," he allowed.

"There are souls in need of saving here," Gelroy said with a pointed look at Liam.

"Building a church will save our souls?" Colm asked, grinning.

"It would be a step in the right direction. Your clan would have to be encouraged to go inside, get down on their knees, and pray God's forgiveness for their past sins." Wagging his finger at Liam, he added, "And mean it . . . with a sincere heart. After what happened to you, I would think you would want to be in God's good graces."

In the blink of an eye the conversation turned serious. "Colm, Father has not been able to tell me how I got from Finney's Flat to the abbey."

"You could have walked," Gelroy suggested.

"No, I could not."

Gelroy sighed. "I have already explained that I cannot tell you."

"But you know, don't you?" Colm asked.

"Have you found the men who hurt Liam?" Gabrielle asked in a rush.

"You would know if I had."

"But you won't give up searching, will you?" she asked.

"No, I won't."

"You've still to answer my question, Father," Liam said. "You do know how I got to the abbey, don't you? Were you perchance near Finney's Flat when I was there?"

"You cannot think this dear priest had anything to do with—"

Colm squeezed her hand. "No, we don't think he was involved. It's our hope that he might have seen the men who tried to kill Liam."

"I was at the abbey before Liam came to us," Gelroy said.

"I know you're holding something back, and I want to know what it is," Colm demanded.

Gabrielle's mind raced. She had hoped to have a private moment with Colm to tell him that she was the one who shot Liam's attacker and that her guards had carried him to Arbane Abbey, but now he was forcing the issue.

"I must tell you—" she began.

He shot her a daunting look that stopped her from continuing. "I'm talking to the priest, Gabrielle. It's time for the truth."

Father Gelroy seemed to shrink in his chair, recoiling from the laird's anger.

"Well, Father, what is it? Are you going to tell us, or do we have to resort to more forceful measures?" Liam asked.

Gabrielle bolted to her feet, upsetting her chair in her haste.

"I cannot believe you would ask Father Gelroy to tell you what he cannot."

"Cannot? Or will not?" Liam asked.

"Cannot," she snapped, glaring at him. "I will not allow you to bully Father Gelroy. He's a man of the cloth. He has explained more than once that he cannot tell you. Leave him alone, or you will have to answer to me."

Before anyone could respond to her outburst, Braeden appeared at the stairs and called out. "They're ready, Laird."

Colm reached down and picked up Gabrielle's chair and moved it to the side.

"Come with me, Gabrielle," he ordered as he took her hand and pulled her behind him.

He didn't explain where he was leading her, but she was happy to oblige. A moment alone with him would give her the opportunity to explain what had happened at Finney's Flat.

They were halfway to the entrance when Colm called over his shoulder, "Liam, I'm marrying Gabrielle."

Liam was stunned. "You're getting married?"

Gabrielle's reaction was more intense. "You didn't even tell your brother? I've been here two weeks, and you couldn't make time—"

He was all but dragging her toward the steps now. "I have seen my brother as often as you have in the past two weeks."

"That isn't an acceptable excuse," she muttered.

Exasperated, he pulled her along down the stairs. "I don't make excuses."

A soldier stood at the door. When he saw them coming, he bowed to Gabrielle and pulled the door open. She thought his action most peculiar. He should have shown deference to his laird, not her.

A blast of cold air brushed over her face. Colm let go of her and walked outside. He stopped on the top step and beckoned her to come to him.

The golden light of sunset spilled over a sea of faces watching her. The courtyard was filled with his clan, and more of them covered the hills beyond.

Gabrielle was so shocked, she could barely keep her wits about her. There seemed to be a thousand men and women staring at her. She tried to catch her breath. No one was smiling. She noticed that right away. Oh, no, had the Boswells gotten to all of these people? She pushed the horrid thought aside. But why did they all look so somber? Since they were crowded together, she couldn't see if they were holding anything in their hands.

She moved closer to Colm. Her arm brushed his. She looked up and whispered, "Am I about to be stoned again?"

"For the love of . . ." He stopped. He couldn't be angry with her. Of course she would expect the worst. He hadn't told her what was going to happen, and God knows, after what she'd been through in the last few weeks, why wouldn't she be frightened?

"Do you think I would let anyone harm you? You belong to me now, Gabrielle."

Colm turned to his followers, raised one hand high into the air, and said, "After much deliberation, Lady Gabrielle has finally agreed to become my wife. I am fortunate to marry such a passionate and spirited, beautiful and innocent lady. You will welcome her and honor her as you honor me."

The crowd erupted into cheers and shouts. All of them were smiling now. Colm pulled her into his arms, tilted her chin up, and kissed her.

She was overwhelmed. He only kissed her long enough for her to want more, and when he lifted his head, she trembled. The noise swirled around her, and there was but one thought in her mind: there weren't any stones.

THIRTY-THREE

COLM HADN'T GIVEN HER ANY WARNING. HAD GA-
brielle known he was going to call his clan
together to make his announcement, she
would have changed her gown and brushed
her hair. She didn't even have time to
pinch her cheeks to give them color. The
door opened, and there they all were, staring at her.

An astonished Liam had followed them
outside and stood on Colm's right as he
spoke to the clan. Liam seemed pleased by
what he called "remarkable news." Once the
cheering had died down and the crowd had

dispersed, he slapped his brother on the shoulder and hugged Gabrielle.

"I thought Gabrielle was our guest because of the help her guards gave me at the abbey, but it appears there's much more to this visit." He laughed and gave Colm a shove as they headed back inside. "You've been holding out on me, brother. Just how long *did* I sleep? Evidently I've been missing a great deal. I must hear the details."

"I'll explain another time," Colm said.

Liam took Gabrielle's hand and with a wink said, "Are you sure you've chosen the right MacHugh, Gabrielle? Colm can be a bear to live with, you know. Perhaps you should reconsider."

Colm answered. "There is nothing to reconsider, Liam. Gabrielle is quite happy." He turned to her. "Aren't you, Gabrielle?"

"Why . . . I . . ." How could she answer him? Happy? With all that had occurred in the past two weeks, thoughts of happiness had not entered her mind.

Liam saved her from coming up with an answer. "Need I pester Lady Gabrielle for details?"

"No, you need not," Colm replied firmly.

Gabrielle was relieved when Liam bid

them good night and went upstairs. She didn't want to answer any questions. There was a more pressing matter on her mind. The time had come for her to face Colm with the truth. She needed to be alone with him. Her heart started pounding.

"Colm . . ."

"You look exhausted, Gabrielle. Get some rest." Dismissing her, he headed for the door.

She followed him. "May I have a word with you? There is something I must tell you."

"Can it wait?" He pulled a torch from its wall bracket to take outside.

The door swung open and Braeden and Stephen entered. She hoped they would pass through, but neither did. They waited to speak to Colm. He was a busy man with many responsibilities and burdens, she reminded herself.

"I wanted to . . . that is to say . . . I suppose I could wait until tomorrow. Perhaps early in the morning?" she asked.

Colm nodded, and Gabrielle, feeling weak with relief because she wouldn't have to tell him tonight, hurried up the steps.

Father Gelroy was waiting to offer his congratulations, but she didn't give him the chance. She motioned for him to come closer and then whispered, "I'm so sorry I haven't told Colm yet. I have twice tried to explain that I and my guards brought Liam to the abbey, but both times we have been interrupted. I think it best if I tell him in private. You had to suffer his anger, and Liam's, too, because of the promise I forced on you."

"The longer you wait, the harder the telling."

"Yes, I know, but I do dread it."

"Laird MacHugh will be pleased to know that you found his brother and sought help for him."

"There is more to the telling than you know, but have no worries. By tomorrow night, Colm will know everything."

"As will I?"

"Yes."

She had hoped to tell him in confession, but if she did, she would have to say she was sorry for taking a man's life, and God would know she wasn't sincere.

That man had really needed killing.

MAURNA WAS THRILLED that Gabrielle was going to marry their laird and told her so several times while serving breakfast.

"No one believed that foolishness the Boswell boys were spouting, and we were right not to pay them any mind since our laird is making you his wife. He declared you innocent, milady, but we already knew it. Didn't we, Willa?" she called over her shoulder.

The cook peeked out from the buttery. "We did. We surely did."

"I thank you both for your faith in me." Gabrielle stared down at a bowl of what appeared to be a thick gray paste.

"No lady as holy as you are would commit such terrible sins, and besides, our laird wouldn't be marrying you if those sins were true . . . which they aren't," she hastened to add.

Willa brought out bread and put it next to the paste. "You eat up now. You could stand to put some fat on those bones."

Gabrielle didn't want to hurt the cook's feelings, but she had to ask what the paste was before she put any of it in her mouth. It would be more hurtful, she thought, if she started gagging.

"What do you call this, Willa?" she asked.

"Breakfast."

Maurna brushed some crumbs from the

table onto her open hand. "You take your bread, and you dab it in the mush."

"Mush?"

"It's good for you, milady," Willa insisted. "It's made with cooked oats and some of my special spices."

"We'll leave you alone so you can eat while it's warm," Maurna said.

Gabrielle reluctantly picked up her spoon and dipped it into the thick goo. "Maurna, could you explain what you meant when you said no one was as holy—"

"As you are."

"Why would you think I was holy?"

"Not just me, milady. Everyone thinks it."

"I think it," Willa said.

"I'm supposing it's because you spend so much of your time walking with Father Gelroy. You're praying with him, aren't you?"

She laughed. "Goodness, no. Father has been rather lonely, and that is why I've been walking with him, but we're both getting accustomed to our new surroundings and feeling more comfortable now. Everyone is so friendly."

The two women beamed at her praise for their clan.

"Your breakfast is getting cold on you," Willa warned.

"I thought I might wait for our laird."

"He's been up and gone quite some time now."

When the women left her alone to eat the mush, Gabrielle forced herself to try it and was surprised that it wasn't vile. In fact, it didn't have much taste at all.

She finished quickly and then went looking for Colm. The man must get up at the crack of dawn, she thought.

Faust caught up with her as she was heading to the stables. "Where are you going, Princess?"

"I'm looking for Colm."

"He's in the fields with his soldiers. Would you like to sit on the hill and watch the sparring?" he asked eagerly.

Faust obviously wanted to watch, and since she couldn't talk to Colm until later, she decided to accommodate her guard.

"Lead the way, Faust."

"I think you will enjoy watching, Princess. I know I will."

"I don't understand your enthusiasm. You've seen my father's men training nearly every day at Wellingshire."

"They did train almost every day, and for good reason, for they, like all good vassals, must keep their skills sharpened."

"I know that, in England, a knight's primary duty is to protect his liege lord. I think it must be the same here."

"No, it's different. I think as long as they win, most barons don't care how many men die fighting for them, but MacHugh would take it as a personal affront if he lost one man or twenty."

She lifted her skirts and quickened her step to keep up with him. "Do you think you will learn new techniques by watching today?"

"Perhaps, but that isn't the reason for my eagerness. You will understand soon enough. We'll sit high on the hill between the two fields where we'll have a good view."

Faust led her up a worn path winding through the trees; it was a steep incline. When she reached the ridge, a panoramic view of the fields opened up below her.

There were two fields almost of equal dimension and separated by mounded stacks of hay. On one side the archers practiced accuracy. Their targets were so far away it was difficult to see the center. Next to them men were throwing axes at targets. As far as she was from the field, Gabrielle could still hear the whistle of the heavy weapons slicing through the air. On the other field, men sparred with swords and shields. Circling them were rows of clansmen, young and old, waiting for their chance to demonstrate their skills.

There were at least a hundred men on the field, yet she easily spotted Colm. He was by far the most impressive warrior there. He stood at the far end of the circle, arms across his chest and feet braced apart. Even from her vantage point, Gabrielle saw his scowl, indicating he didn't like what he was seeing.

She stared in fascination. His bronzed skin glistened with sweat, and the bulging muscles in his upper arms and legs exuded raw power. While she knew it was indecent for her to notice such things, she couldn't make herself look away.

"Would you like me to fetch a blanket for you to sit on? Or do you think you will not want to stay that long?" Faust asked.

"I don't need a blanket," she replied, sitting down. She tucked her legs under her and adjusted her skirt; all the while her violet blue eyes were fixed on Colm.

"Do you see Stephen? He stands next to the laird." Faust pointed him out.

"I see him. What's he doing?"

"He's watching Lucien spar."

She searched the field and located her guard. "And why is Lucien sparring?"

"The laird invited him to," Faust answered. "If he thinks we are capable, he will have us train the beginners. His seasoned warriors find it all beneath them, though of course they would do whatever their laird ordered them to. Stephen says the laird wants us to earn our keep, and we are happy to oblige."

Gabrielle watched Lucien. Her guard's movements were fluid and graceful. He held his own against the MacHugh soldier without seeming to exert much effort. Neither gained an advantage.

"Stephen bested all the others with bow and arrow. The laird wouldn't give him time to fetch his own, so he had to use Braeden's. I think you could best them all, too, Princess."

She laughed. "Your faith in me is misplaced. Tell me this, Faust, what did the laird and his commander think of Stephen defeating their soldiers?"

"They were impressed with his skill. Braeden and Stephen aren't adversaries. They respect each other's ability and have, in fact, become friends of a sort. The laird has placed Stephen in charge of training the young ones with bow and arrow under Braeden's watchful eye."

"What about you?" Gabrielle asked.

"I will spar tomorrow."

"You needn't sit here with me. You will know I'm safe. You can see me from either field."

"The distance is too great."

"If I can see Colm's frown, you'll certainly be able to see me."

"Tomorrow will be soon enough to take my turn. Besides, Christien will be fighting soon, and I don't want to miss that. Lucien's almost finished," he added with a nod toward the guard. "I think he's going to let the MacHugh soldier best him this day."

"Why would you think that?"

"He should have finished him by now. He's holding back because the man he fights is older by at least fifteen or more years. Lucien won't humiliate him in front of his laird. It's what I would do."

Next to the combatants, Stephen had made the same observation. He stepped back and spoke to Braeden. A few minutes later, Colm stopped the match. New opponents moved forward to take their places on the field.

"Lucien, come here," Colm commanded.

The guard ran to him. "Yes, Laird?"

"Stephen has suggested that you didn't put your full strength in your fight. Is that true?"

"It is."

Colm expected to hear an excuse and was surprised by his honesty. "Give me your reason."

"He is my elder by many years. I didn't want to embarrass him."

"That is the most ridiculous reason I've yet to hear. Am I to assume that if an old man were to attack Gabrielle, you would be considerate of his age as you try to protect her?"

"No, I would kill him if he tried to harm my princess, no matter what his age."

"You insult my clansmen when you do not give your best. Tomorrow I will see that you do."

Colm gave the command, and the swords and shields were put aside. There would be hand-to-hand combat now. Groups of experienced warriors took the field. Each man's goal was to pin the other to the ground. Cunning as well as raw strength were required, and several times during the challenges Colm intervened to show the combatants their mistakes.

Christien joined Stephen to watch. "They don't fight like us."

Colm heard his remark and called to him. "Show me the difference."

"I'm sorry, Laird, but I must decline." He sounded disheartened when he added, "I cannot fight you."

Astounded by the guard's refusal, Colm asked, "Why is it you think you have a choice?"

Stephen stepped forward to explain. "Now that you are betrothed to marry our princess Gabrielle, none of her guard can fight you."

Christien nodded. "We must protect you now just as we protect our princess."

Braeden took offense. "The laird's warriors protect him."

Stephen nodded. "Yes, and we protect the man who will marry Princess Gabrielle."

Christien glanced up at the crest of the hill where Gabrielle was sitting. "Besides, she would not like to see us sparring with you. She is beginning to have affection for you."

Colm looked up and saw Gabrielle watching. She was beginning to care for him? Not likely. The guard was wrong. A woman who cared about a man didn't run him in circles and ignore his every command.

He pushed his thoughts aside. "If you cannot fight me, Christien, then you will fight someone else."

He motioned to one of his clansmen. A thick-necked warrior immediately stepped forward.

"Ewen, tell Christien how old you are."

"Laird?"

Colm repeated the command. Ewen, though puzzled by the odd order, quickly obeyed. He and Christien were only months apart in age.

"I trust Ewen isn't too old for you to fight," Colm said sardonically.

The two men went to opposite sides of the field. Braeden gave the signal, and Ewen, head down, charged. Christien met him in the center, and before the MacHugh soldier could get in a punch, Christien spun on one foot and used the flat of his other foot to slam him to the ground.

Christien waited several seconds to see if Ewen was going to get up. When he didn't, the guard walked over to him and offered him his hand. Ewen pushed his hand aside, stood, and shook his head to clear it. He charged again. And again. It was painful to watch, and irritating as hell for Colm. After Ewen had been knocked to the ground for a fourth time, Colm strode onto the field, hauled the battered man to his feet with one hand, and gave him a good shove.

"Four times Christen has flattened you the very same way. Haven't you figured out that you need to come up with another way to attack?"

Ewen frowned. "I knew he was going to kick me with his foot again, but I thought I could be quicker."

Colm shoved him again. "Obviously you were not quicker, were you?"

"No, I wasn't."

"Why didn't you try to block the attack?"

Colm showed him how it could be done, but Ewen was a slow learner, and twice more Christien knocked him down using the same method.

Three other soldiers met Ewen's fate. Then the more experienced clansmen challenged Christien. The second man not only blocked his attack, but he landed a good punch to the guard's middle. Christien fell to the ground. The next time Christien changed his maneuver and felled this worthier opponent.

Colm ordered Christien to try both techniques on him so that he could show his soldiers how to block the attack and gain the advantage. The laird was much quicker than Christien. The third time Colm sent the guard flying backward, Christien landed on his stomach, rolled over, and sat up. Blood trickled from the corner of his mouth. He wiped it away, looked up at Colm, and began to laugh.

"Again, Laird?" he asked as in one motion he gained his feet.

"This isn't a game, Christien," he snapped. "Tomorrow you will help train the younger soldiers." He pointed a finger at him and added, "Before then, I suggest you rid yourself of your arrogance. In battle, these men won't get second chances. It's your duty to teach them how to survive. When they're ready, Braeden and I will teach them how to win."

THIRTY-FOUR

AFTER THE TRAINING SESSION, COLM WENT TO the lake and washed the sweat from his body, then headed toward the great hall. He was walking past the stables just as Gabrielle led her horse out of a stall. The steed was already saddled.

He stopped outside the gate and watched her. She brushed a loose strand of hair from her face as she closed the gate behind Rogue.

"Where do you think you're going?" Colm asked.

Startled, Gabrielle glanced in his direction. "Good day to you, Colm."

If she was trying to get him to waste his time on pleasantries, she was in for a disappointment.

"I asked you a question."

"I'm going riding. Rogue needs to stretch his legs."

"And where exactly are you planning to ride?"

"Here and there."

"Across Finney's Flat perchance?"

It seemed he could read her mind. "Yes. I thought I would pay Laird Buchanan a visit. I would like to meet his wife. I am related to her, if you'll remember."

"No."

"No, you don't remember?"

"No, you're not to leave this holding. You can ride in the hills here, but you will not leave the mountain." Clasping his hands behind his back, he said, "I will have your word."

She bowed her head. "As you say."

Colm turned away from the stables and started toward the courtyard, then stopped. He turned and looked at his betrothed. She stood next to the horse, holding Rogue's reins and waiting for Colm to walk away. He knew exactly what she was doing. Once he was out of sight, she would head to Finney's Flat.

"Oh no, Gabrielle. You're not pulling that on me again."

"Excuse me?"

He walked back to her. "Don't play the innocent with me. I know that 'as you say' means that you're going to do whatever you damn well want to do. You will now give me your promise. You will say 'I give you my word,' and you will mean it."

Gabrielle was not about to let him intimidate her. He wasn't the only one who had something to be cross about. She took a bold step toward him.

"You were supposed to set aside a moment of your time this morning, for I have something important to tell you, but when I came downstairs, you were gone. Did you wait at all?"

He stepped in her direction.

"I couldn't spend half my morning waiting for you to wake up. Get up earlier, and I'll listen to what you have to say."

Stubbornly, she moved forward. "You are an aggravating man."

"And you have yet to give me your promise."

"I promise," she said with a hint of defiance.

They were now so close she felt his warm breath. "I want your promise to set aside some time tonight," she said. "I must speak to you in private."

"Tell me now."

"This isn't private."

He put his hands on her shoulders and pulled her toward him. "I don't know how I will ever get along with such a stubborn woman."

His mouth brushed hers when she whispered, "I don't either."

He meant to give her only a brief kiss, but once his mouth covered hers, his intentions changed. Her lips were so soft and warm. At his insistence, she opened her mouth for him, and the kiss deepened as he wrapped his arms around her and pressed her tightly against him.

For Gabrielle, the world ceased to exist. There was only Colm's magical touch. She returned his kiss with a passion she hadn't known she possessed.

He came to his senses before she did and abruptly ended the kiss. He took a deep shuddering breath. She was so dazed she didn't realize she was clinging to him until he gently pulled away.

Colm had to put some distance between them before he gave in to temptation and kissed her again. He knew exactly where that would lead, and he wasn't about to dishonor Gabrielle and take her to his bed before their marriage, but she wasn't making it easy for him to walk away. No woman had ever affected him so deeply.

He grabbed her horse's reins, pulling Rogue closer to lift Gabrielle onto the saddle. With a slap on the horse's hindquarters, Colm sent her on her way.

THIRTY-FIVE

COSWOLD'S SEARCH FOR GABRIELLE BEGAN THE moment she was banished. He spent several days canvassing the area around the abbey, but she was nowhere to be found.

His spies told him that Percy was also in pursuit, but it wasn't long before he gave up. No surprise there, Coswold thought. Percy was, and always would be, a quitter. He had, no doubt, returned to King John to whine about how unjustly he'd been treated.

Coswold was not that easily discouraged. Thinking that Gabrielle had no alternative but to go home, he headed south, speeding in the direction her servants had taken. He intercepted their caravan near the English border where they had made camp for the night. After hours of threats and bullying, Coswold was finally convinced they knew nothing. He allowed the frightened band of travelers to continue on their journey, but not before he confiscated Gabrielle's trunks, claiming that they should be held at Arbane Abbey until such time that Gabrielle would come to fetch them.

Frustrated but not deterred, he returned to the Highlands. Gabrielle was hiding somewhere in this uncivilized, godforsaken land, and Baron Coswold would find her.

In the week that followed, he spent most of his time watching and listening. The rumors were many, and with each scrap of information Coswold became more convinced that Gabrielle had remained in the Highlands.

One rumor persisted. Coswold heard third-hand that Gabrielle had been taken in by the MacHugh clan, but he was unsure how to make certain the information was correct. The Highlanders were a close-knit group, and Coswold knew that if he sent out inquiries on her whereabouts, word would reach Laird MacHugh in no time at all, and the laird would hide Gabrielle away where no one could find her. The risk was too great. The baron had spent a good deal of time coming up with a plan to lure Gabrielle into the open.

He was ready for his next step: verifying that Gabrielle was indeed with the MacHughs. For this, he called on Laird MacKenna. The laird knew men who would not be recognized in this part of the Highlands and who would do anything for money. Once MacKenna's men were gathered in front of him, Coswold explained what he wanted done.

"The plan is simple," he told the men. "You will carry Gabrielle's things to the MacHugh holding. You will insist on seeing Gabrielle before handing them over. Explain that you must be certain she receives them."

"But what if they won't let us see her?" one of the men asked.

"Tell them the order came from the abbot. That her trunks had been returned to the abbey and that he had been holding them in safekeeping until he knew where she was."

"What do we do when we've seen her?"

"You do nothing," Coswold stressed. "Leave her things with her, return to me, and receive your payment."

"Payment of gold and women?"

"Yes."

"What if she ain't there?" another asked.

"Then you will bring her things back to me."

"Will we still get paid in coin and women?"

Coswold assured them that they would, and sent them on their way. He didn't anticipate any problems. His plan was flawless.

Nothing could go wrong.

THIRTY-SIX

TWO MORE DAYS PASSED WITHOUT THE PROMISED meeting, and Gabrielle still hadn't had an opportunity to speak to Colm in private. No matter how early she got up in the morning, he was already gone. And when he came in late at night, he took his meals alone, then disappeared.

She was beginning to think he never went to bed, but he didn't look as if he lacked sleep—unless she considered his mood an indicator. In the brief encounters they'd had in passing, he'd either ignored her or had grumbled about something she had done to displease him.

She had convinced herself that he was deliberately avoiding her, but then Maurna changed her mind. The housekeeper was in a chatty mood as she swept the hall on that third morning.

"The laird has not had a minute's peace since Liam was taken," she said, shaking her head. "He says he won't rest until he finds the men responsible. He's led men out every day looking for anyone who knows something." Maurna moved a stool aside as she continued. "And then word came three days ago that thieves had stolen cattle from Seamus MacAlister's valley, so the laird and his men have been out searching for those culprits as well. He didn't find them until yesterday . . . and if those worries aren't enough, he arrived home last night to find a war brewing between Heckert, the smith, and Edwin, the butcher. Those two are always at odds about something . . ."

She chattered on and on about various incidents involving the laird, and Gabrielle listened patiently. She was tremendously relieved to discover that she was not the reason he was absent, but she was also anxious to find a time to talk to him. Gabrielle was becoming desperate to unburden her conscience.

She felt so alone. There was no one she could confide in or share her problems with. Most nights she would have supper with Liam, and spend the evening playing a table game. His favorite was Fox and Geese, and he would rush to get the board and pegs the minute the trenchers had been cleared away. Gabrielle enjoyed his company, but their conversation never turned to serious matters. She couldn't tell him about her role in his rescue. Colm was the laird, the man who had taken her in, the man who would marry her. She should first tell him her startling news.

She didn't want to burden Father Gelroy with her worries. There wasn't anything he could do about it anyway, except worry with her, and what would that accomplish? She had not spent much time with the priest these last few days. Now that he was trusted by the clan, he was invited into their homes to eat with the families and to bless their children. He was kept very busy and seemed to thrive on the new demands on his time.

Nor could she talk with her guards. It

wouldn't be proper to pour her heart out to them. She would never burden them with her problems.

She fretted in silence.

Her main concern was for her father. Was he safe? Or had the king already imprisoned him? Oh God, she prayed, please keep him from harm. Had Baron Geoffrey had time to gather his vassals, and if he did, would they fight against the king's favored barons and their armies? Brodick had suggested that once her father heard that Gabrielle was still in the Highlands, he would rush to the Buchanans. But she had heard nothing from them. If her father was safe, why hadn't he sent word?

Gabrielle couldn't wait any longer. Tomorrow she would go to the Buchanans. Brodick knew her father, and he might offer some suggestions to help find him.

She didn't worry that Colm would deny her permission to leave the holding because she wasn't going to ask him.

Gabrielle strolled toward the fields as she formulated her plan. Cheers coming from the hill drew her attention. She looked to its crest. Several people—some old, some young—were gathered under the tree where she had recently sat with Faust, watching Colm and his soldiers' exercises.

A girl running to join her friends paused long enough to curtsy to Gabrielle, then dashed away as her friend called to her. "Liam is back in training today," she announced. "He's feeling ever so much better."

And he was looking ever so much better to the girls, too, Gabrielle thought. Eventually Liam would settle down, and God help the woman he chose for his wife. Most certainly she would have her hands full with his mischief.

Gabrielle hurried down the hill. Her stomach grumbled, reminding her that it was the noon hour. Maurna had served her that paste for breakfast again, and Gabrielle had been unable to make herself eat more than two bites. Willa had urged Gabrielle to eat it all, claiming it would stick to her ribs. Why Gabrielle would want that to happen was beyond her. She thought the very idea disgusting.

She had almost reached the courtyard when a woman approached from behind and tapped her on her shoulder.

"Lady Gabrielle?"

Gabrielle turned. "Yes?" There was a time when she would have had a ready smile, but no longer. She had since learned caution and was now wary meeting anyone new.

"I haven't had a chance to meet you," the pretty woman said. "My name is Fiona, and I come from the Dunbar clan. My father is Laird Dunbar. I was recently married. Devin, my husband, is one of Laird MacHugh's most trusted clansmen."

"It is my pleasure to meet you." Gabrielle was polite but tentative with her response.

Fiona didn't smile. She was a hearty woman, with a ruddy complexion, freckles, and green eyes the color of new grass. Her long, red, curly hair was, without a doubt, her best feature. Her eyes slanted down at the corners, giving her a look of overwhelming sadness.

"By now I'm sure you know who my sister is."

"No, I don't believe so. Is she also married to a MacHugh?"

Fiona acted surprised, though Gabrielle could see through her pretense. "What is it you wish to say to me?" Gabrielle asked.

"My sister Joan is betrothed to Laird Mac-Hugh."

Had the woman wanted to shock Gabrielle, she'd accomplished her goal.

But Gabrielle recovered quickly. "Be sure to give your sister my congratulations."

Fiona's eyes widened. "Yes . . . I will."

As Gabrielle walked away, Fiona called out to her, "You'll be able to meet her yourself soon. Joan will be here in a few days."

Gabrielle pretended not to hear. She saw Lucien waiting for her in the courtyard and rushed toward him.

"Princess, your face is bright red, but it isn't warm enough today for the sun to burn you."

"The wind makes my face red," she explained, surprised at how calm she sounded. Inside she was seething. "Do you happen to know where Laird MacHugh is?" *I wish to kill him,* she silently added.

"No, I don't. Would you like me to find him for you?"

She shook her head. "No, I'll let him live a little longer."

She didn't realize she had spoken the thought out loud until Lucien asked her to repeat it.

"I'll find him later," she said. *Then I'll kill him.*

"Did you want to go riding this afternoon?"

"No, I think I'll stay inside and finish my needlework. It's relaxing and gives me something useful to do."

"If you don't need me, I'll go help Faust. He's making arrows and fashioning them like the MacHughs'. Theirs are so much stronger and thinner, which allows for more distance and speed. You'll have to try one, Princess. You're sure to be impressed."

"There is that much difference?"

"Let me get one of mine and one of theirs to show you."

A short time later Lucien came into the hall carrying two arrows. He placed them on the table. Gabrielle had just finished eating a wedge of coarse brown bread with honey. She pushed her trencher aside and took the MacHugh arrow in her hands to feel the weight.

"The shaft is thinner, but seems to be strong. The fletchings are strange to me."

Maurna heard her mistress's comment. She hurried to the table to clear away the food, and leaning over Gabrielle's shoulder said, "Looks to be from a goose to me."

Their attention was drawn to the stairs, as Colm and Liam entered the hall together.

Gabrielle placed the arrow on the table and turned to the brothers.

"There is good news," Liam said. "Your clothes and much more will arrive shortly. There is quite a procession of men carrying the goods. Surely they can't all be garments, can they?"

Gabrielle was puzzled and directed her questions to Colm. "How is that possible? The staff took my possessions back to Wellingshire. How can they be here now?"

"They came from the abbey," he explained.

"Did my father send them back? Is there word from him?" Her face lit up with excitement over the possibility.

Colm hated to disappoint her. "No, there is no word from your father."

Her eyes quickly filled with tears. "I had hoped . . ."

Liam elbowed Colm and tilted his head toward Gabrielle.

"Come here, Gabrielle," Colm commanded.

She blinked her tears away, straightened her shoulders, and crossed the room to face him. "Yes?"

"Perhaps you will hear something from

your father tomorrow," Liam suggested when Colm stayed silent.

"Perhaps," she said softly. *And perhaps the sun will turn black tomorrow, too,* she thought.

Colm tilted her chin up. "Brodick and I are both trying to find out where he is. I know it is difficult, but you must be patient."

"He could still be at Wellingshire."

He nodded. "I have sent a messenger into England."

"You have?"

She was so surprised by his thoughtfulness, she didn't know what to say or think about him. Had she been wrong to judge him so harshly? Maybe he wasn't such an ogre after all.

Then she remembered Joan.

When Gabrielle's tear-filled eyes squinted into a frown, Colm was perplexed. Now what was wrong? He would never understand her. He had thought she would be happy to hear that he was trying to find her father. Aye, she should be damned pleased. She certainly shouldn't be looking like she wanted to strangle him.

Gabrielle decided that now wasn't the

time to talk to him about Joan. She would need privacy for that discussion as well.

"Colm, do you remember I asked for a moment alone with you?"

"I remember."

"I'm going to need a lot more time."

Liam nodded to Lucien, then went to the table and poured himself a goblet of water. He noticed the arrows. "What are those doing here?"

Lucien answered. "I wanted to show the differences between the two. Princess, if you don't mind, I will go help Faust now." Her loyal guard bowed to her and left the hall.

Colm picked up both arrows. "Who do these belong to?" he asked.

"What color is the marking on the fletching?" she asked.

He turned an arrow over in his hand examining it.

Thinking he didn't understand what she meant, she walked over to him, leaned into his side, and pointed to the color in the center of each feather. "Saffron. See? Saffron is Lucien's color."

"Why did he mark it?" Liam asked.

"So that he would know it belonged to him. When we practice, sometimes our arrows are so close together on the target, the only way to know who is dead center is by the color."

"You use a bow?" Colm asked.

"Yes, I do. I don't always practice with my guards, just sometimes. If you'll excuse me, I'd like to go upstairs and find my needlework. I seem to have misplaced it."

She was halfway across the floor when Colm ordered her to stop.

"What color does Faust mark his arrows with?"

"Red."

"Christien?"

"Green."

"And Stephen?"

"Purple."

"And yours?" he asked.

"Blue. I mark mine blue."

Colm stood watching the stairs for a long minute after she had left. Then he went to the stone mantel and picked up the broken arrow he'd pulled from the dead man at Finney's Flat.

The marking was blue.

THIRTY-SEVEN

COLM HELD THE PROOF IN HIS HANDS, AND YET HE still couldn't believe it. Was it possible? Had Gabrielle been at Finney's Flat, and had she witnessed the atrocity?

His sweet and gentle Gabrielle had taken one of her arrows, notched it to her bow, and shot the bastard in the chest.

No, she couldn't have done it. She didn't have the stomach for killing.

Yet the proof was in his hands.

"Colm, what's the matter with you?" Liam asked. "You've been staring at that broken arrow for a good long while."

His mind racing, he didn't answer his

brother. He remembered how Gabrielle had jumped to her feet to defend the priest when he'd been prodded to tell them how Liam had gotten to the abbey.

She was there . . . and so were her guards. Had Stephen or one of the others used one of her arrows to make the kill? Aye, that's what must have happened. Gabrielle didn't have the mettle to take a life.

Colm called to Maurna, asking her to tell Gabrielle he wanted to speak to her. The housekeeper saw the look in her laird's eyes and hurried to do his bidding. Something had riled his temper, and she hoped to heaven Lady Gabrielle wasn't the cause. The genteel lady would be most upset if the laird raised his voice to her.

Maurna tapped on Gabrielle's door. "The laird's waiting to talk to you."

The housekeeper opened the door and peeked in. Gabrielle sat on the bed with her needlework in her lap.

"Milady, I think there's some trouble brewing. The laird's unhappy about something. I wouldn't make him wait on you."

Maurna continued to whisper advice as she followed her mistress down the stairs. "If he shouts, don't you pay any mind. He won't hurt you."

"Has he ever shouted at you, Maurna?"

"No, he hasn't, but there's always the worry that he might. I'd probably faint dead away."

Gabrielle thought the housekeeper's concern for her was sweet. "Don't worry. I won't faint."

"Even so, you might want to sit down while he tells you what's bothering him, just in case you get lightheaded. I don't want you bumping your head falling down. 'Course our laird is quick. He'll probably catch you."

Maurna didn't follow Gabrielle into the hall. "Maybe it's not about you, milady. Maybe he's displeased about something else."

Colm was talking to his brother when Gabrielle walked in. Liam stood and smiled at her, and she could see how tired he was. Getting back his strength was an arduous task. She then turned her attention to Colm. He wasn't smiling.

"Did you wish to speak to me?" she asked.

"Come closer. I have something to show you." He held up the broken arrow. He expected an immediate reaction, but she looked only mildly curious. "Do you recognize this, Gabrielle?"

She moved closer, saw the markings, and said, "It's one of my arrows."

"It's broken."

"I can see that it is," she agreed. "Where did you find it? I haven't hunted with my bow and arrows since I came here."

"I found it at Finney's Flat."

"At Finney's . . ." Her eyes widened, and she took a step back. "At Finney's Flat, you say. How did it get there I wonder."

"I thought perhaps you could tell me. Would you like to know exactly where and when I found it?"

She already knew. "It's broken, Colm. You might as well throw it away."

Liam leaned back against the table, desperately trying to follow the tense conversation.

"Will one of you tell me what's going on?" he demanded.

"This is the arrow I pulled out of the dead man at Finney's Flat, Liam. He was on the ground by the hole the bastards had dug for you."

"Are you saying . . ."

Gabrielle glanced at Liam and said, "It's my arrow. That is what Colm is saying."

"You will now answer my questions without hesitation," Colm ordered. "Were you at Finney's Flat?"

"Yes."

"When I was there?" Liam sounded like he was choking.

Impatience made her voice sharp. "For God's sake, Liam, try to keep up. Yes, I was there when you were."

"Which one of your guards killed the bastard with your arrow?"

"None of them did. I killed him."

Hearing a loud gasp, Gabrielle saw Maurna and Willa peeking out from the buttery.

She leaned around Colm and called out, "The man really did need killing."

Willa's head was bobbing up and down, and Maurna's mouth was gaping open.

Colm threaded his fingers through his hair in agitation. "All this while I've been trying to find out . . . why in God's name didn't you tell . . ." He shook his head in a futile attempt to clear it and said, "Were you ever going to tell me?"

"I have been trying. I've asked you over and over again for a moment of your time."

"There is a difference between sweetly asking me for time and telling me the matter was of the utmost importance."

She poked him in his chest. "How was I to know which magical words I should use to get your attention?"

She was aware that she sounded like a shrew. Maurna had worried how Gabrielle would react if the laird shouted at her, and now she was raising her voice to him.

Stephen took this most inopportune time to enter the hall. "Princess, is there a problem?"

She didn't answer. Colm did. "Damn right, there is."

Gabrielle turned to Stephen. "He knows," she said on a sigh.

"Ah." Her guard looked at Colm as he asked her, "Did you tell him?"

"He figured it out. It was my arrow, Stephen. We forgot to remove it."

"The arrow. Of course. I never thought about the markings. I cannot believe I was so careless."

"You were busy carrying Liam from the field. Do not fault yourself. Colm was bound to find out eventually, and I had already decided it was time for me to tell him the truth."

Colm eyed both of them skeptically. "And just why did you keep this a secret?"

Stephen answered. "We didn't know who the men were or where they came from, and therefore we didn't know what the repercussions would be once the body was found."

"You were concerned about the ramifications because you killed the man?" Colm asked Stephen.

"No, because *I* killed the man," Gabrielle answered.

"Is this true?" he asked Stephen.

"Yes," he said. His pride was evident when he added, "Princess Gabrielle is more accurate with her bow than we are. There was no time to waste or consider consequences. The coward had raised his sword and fully intended to cut Liam in half. She stopped him." Nodding, Stephen said, "It was a clean, quick kill."

Gabrielle watched Colm's face intently as he mulled over what they were telling him. What must he be thinking of her now? Since he'd met her, she had gone from a whore to a cold-blooded killer. What lovely words to describe the woman he was to marry. She almost felt sorry for him.

Colm put his hands on Gabrielle's shoulders and forced her to stand in front of him. "You will explain everything that happened. And when you are finished, Stephen will give me his accounting."

Gabrielle was relieved to finally get it all out in the open. She quickly recounted what she could remember, beginning with her goal to see Finney's Flat.

"As we approached the clearing, we heard voices, so we hid and didn't make ourselves known."

"Did you see any faces?"

"Not at first. They wore robes with hoods. But a couple of them pulled the hoods back, and we did see them."

"And what about names?"

"Yes, they were arguing with one another, and they used their given names, but we didn't hear any names of clans or families. The leader's name was Gordon. He's the man I killed."

"What were they arguing about?"

Gabrielle glanced sympathetically at Colm's brother before answering. "They wanted Liam to wake up so he would know he was being buried alive, and they argued over how they would put him in the grave."

"But they weren't going to bury him until

they saw you on the ridge, Laird," Stephen interjected.

Colm clasped his hands behind his back and paced to the hearth. Deep in thought, he stared at the fire. "Did they say why they needed to see me there?"

"Yes, Laird," Stephen answered. "Liam was the bait. They were using him to get to you."

THIRTY-EIGHT

COLM VOWED HE WOULD FIND THE BASTARDS. HE didn't care how long it took—one year, ten, or a lifetime—he would keep hunting until he had killed every last one of them. And before they died, they would tell him the name of the man who gave them their orders, for surely such a deliberate attack by strangers was masterminded by someone with something to gain. By all that was holy, there would be justice.

As it turned out, it didn't take a lifetime or even a year. Just one afternoon. And Colm didn't have to hunt them down. They came to him.

* * *

AFTER STEPHEN AND GABRIELLE had reported what they had heard at Finney's Flat, Liam paced back and forth venting his fury.

"You heard what Stephen said. They spoke our language, but their accent was different, more guttural. They must have come from the lowlands or the border. I say we call together all of our men and our allies and tear apart every inch of land from here to the border until we find them. Bury me alive? Cut me in half? Son of a whore!" Liam's anger and his impatience for reprisal spilled out in every word.

Arms folded, Colm stood quietly in front of the hearth. He allowed his brother to voice his rage until Liam began describing how he thought each of his attackers should die.

"Gabrielle doesn't need to hear this, Liam."

"They'll suffer. I swear to God, they'll scream for mercy," he vowed. Spent now from his tirade, Liam dropped into a chair.

"You know we'll find them," Colm said.

"Yes," Liam answered. "I know."

With tempers at last under control, the two brothers began to formulate plans.

Since Colm was occupied with Stephen

and Liam, Gabrielle thought this might be the perfect time for her to slip away. Twice she had tried to leave the hall, and twice Colm had pulled her back. He finally anchored her to his side by putting his arm around her. She wasn't going anywhere until he allowed it.

Poor Father Gelroy strolled into the hall seeking his noon meal and was immediately stopped and questioned at length. The priest looked relieved that the truth was out at last, then looked appalled when he found out Gabrielle had taken a man's life.

Gabrielle felt worn thin, but she was also relieved that it was all finally out in the open. Telling Colm the truth had been exhausting work. She leaned against him and relaxed. The terrible burden had been lifted and given to him. She didn't doubt that he would find the men who hurt Liam and was thankful he had stopped his brother from describing the gruesome manner in which they would die.

When Colm let Stephen return to the field and Father Gelroy was allowed to go to the kitchens in search of food, Gabrielle was finally alone with him, but not for long.

He let go of her. "Gabrielle—" he began.

Maurna interrupted. "Begging your pardon, Laird, but they're here. If you don't have time now, I could stand them in the corner and let them squirm until you're ready to punish them."

Following on Maurna's heels was another servant. "The winch is broken, and the men can't get the big stones up to the top. They're thinking you should look at it."

Colm nodded. "I'll be there in just a minute, Emmett."

Gabrielle could have taken her leave then, but she stayed where she was and watched as Maurna half dragged, half pushed two little boys into the hall. Both had their heads down. Colm dismissed Maurna and ordered the boys to tell him what they had done.

He towered over them, and Gabrielle could only imagine what they must be thinking when they looked up at such a giant. Neither seemed afraid, though, as each tried to outtalk the other.

Colm raised his hand. "One at a time. Ethan, you will go first, and Tom, you will stop staring at Lady Gabrielle and pay attention to me."

"Yes, Laird, but is she your lady?" Tom asked.

"Yes she is, now be silent while I hear what Ethan has to say."

"Yes, Laird, but are you going to marry with her?" Ethan asked.

Colm showed remarkable patience. His expression was stern, but the boys felt comfortable with him or they wouldn't have asked so many questions.

Gabrielle thought they were the most adorable boys. They couldn't have been more than five years old, and though they weren't identical, it was apparent they were twins. Both had freckles and big brown eyes with a bit of the devil in them.

Three times Colm had to remind them why they were there, and finally Ethan told his story.

"See, Laird, what we did was . . ." he began.

Those were the only words Gabrielle understood. Tom kept interrupting and correcting, and the story became so convoluted that by the time they finished, she didn't have the faintest idea what their transgression was.

Then Tom, a bit more precocious than Ethan, felt he should have a turn. His explanation was just as nonsensical.

The boys were in constant motion, rocking back and forth and side to side, elbowing each other and peeking at her.

Apparently Colm understood what they had told him. "You will not go into the kitchens unless you are invited."

"Yes, Laird, but could we go inside when we want to play with the cat?"

"No, you may not."

"Yes, Laird," Ethan said. "But could we maybe look inside sometimes?"

"You may go into the kitchen only when you are invited by Willa. Do you understand?"

"Yes, Laird," Tom said. "But could we—"

"No, you could not. Now you will go to Willa and you will apologize to her."

The boys nodded their heads. "Yes, Laird," they recited in unison.

"And then you will go to your aunt and apologize to her."

"Yes, Laird, but we didn't spill her flour."

"You will apologize for getting into mischief."

"Yes, Laird, but could we—"

"Enough, Tom." His tone was deliberately harsher, and he got just the reaction he wanted. Their eyes widened, and they nodded again. Liam coughed to cover his laughter.

Colm said, "I don't want to hear any arguments. I will decide what your punishment will be. Come back to me tomorrow, and I will tell you what you must do."

The boys ran toward the buttery and then made a detour to the table, where Liam was sitting.

"Liam, are you better now?" Ethan asked.

"Yes, I am better."

"Can we see your back?" Tom asked. "Where you got hurt?"

"No, you cannot."

"Yes, Liam, but could we see—"

Liam smiled at the boys and tousled their hair. "You have done something very good today."

The boys beamed at the unexpected praise.

"We have?" Ethan asked in astonishment.

"Yes, you have," Liam said.

"What did we do?" Tom wondered.

"You have shown me that there is still innocence in the world," Liam explained. "Now leave before the laird decides what your punishment is." As soon as they were out of sight, he said, "They lighten my mood."

"They do not seem overly contrite," Gabrielle remarked.

"That's because they aren't," Colm answered.

"What punishment will you give them?" Liam asked.

"I'm open to suggestions. So far they've been banned from the stables, the fields, the hills beyond, the armory, and now the kitchens."

"Where is their father?" Gabrielle asked.

"Gone."

She assumed that meant the man had died and didn't ask for further explanation.

"Begging your indulgence, Laird, but about that winch . . ." Emmett, who had been waiting patiently in the corner, said.

"I'm coming," Colm answered.

Liam pushed himself up from the chair and walked over to Gabrielle. Colm was heading for the stairs, but stopped cold when Liam pulled Gabrielle into his arms and hugged her.

Gabrielle was so startled she stiffened for a few seconds.

"What do you think you're doing?" Colm demanded.

"Showing Lady Gabrielle my appreciation."

Colm felt a rush of possessiveness. No man had the right to touch what belonged to him, not even his brother.

"Let go of her."

Liam ignored him. He kissed Gabrielle's forehead, leaned down close to her ear, and whispered, "Thank you."

Just as Colm was about to rip Liam away from Gabrielle, his brother let go and walked out of the hall.

At first, Gabrielle was taken by surprise by Liam's sudden gesture, but as he left, she realized that showing his gratitude was actually a sweet, thoughtful thing to do. He had been quite gentle when he pulled her to him.

Colm was far from gentle when he grabbed her and wrapped his arms around her. He started to say something, then changed his mind and kissed her instead. His mouth took absolute possession in a kiss meant to melt any resistance she might have had.

Each kiss was more wonderful than the one before, but what happened after remained the same. Colm walked away without sparing her a backward glance, leaving her dazed. Gabrielle stared after him as he disappeared from view. She didn't think she was ever going to understand him.

With the weight of a heavy burden lifted from her shoulders and most of the afternoon still ahead of her, she decided to get some fresh air and walked to the stable to give Rogue a sweet treat. Then she went in search of Faust and Lucien. She found them sitting on a knoll behind the keep, working on their arrows. Lucien was using a rag to oil the shaft of an arrow while Faust attached the fletching to another arrow. She sat next to Faust and helped with the feathers. The two men spoke in their native tongue, and she listened while Faust told Lucien that Colm now knew that they'd been at Finney's Flat. After a pleasant hour had passed, Gabrielle asked the two guards if they would ride with her outside the holding. Lucien wanted to keep working, so Faust saddled two horses for them.

Gabrielle could tell Rogue was eager to run. As soon as they were past the fortress wall, she turned north, gave him his head, and let him race to the top of the first hill, then she slowed his gait as she rode beside Faust into the open countryside.

"Should we head back?" Faust asked after a few minutes passed. "The caravan with your trunks should be here soon. I wonder if the abbot remembered to send the statue of St. Biel. Father Gelroy will want to put it in front of the chapel."

"The chapel that doesn't exist yet," she said. "It can stay in the storage room until one is built."

"Maybe someday your father will send the larger statue of our saint, the one that stood in the courtyard outside your mother's room. It was a gift from your grandfather before she left St. Biel." A fleeting look of sadness passed over his eyes when he added, "There should be snow in the mountains of St. Biel by now."

Gabrielle could see that the guard was becoming nostalgic and perhaps a little homesick, and she felt a pang of guilt for pulling him even farther from his homeland.

"You will return soon, I think," she said.

He smiled. "That is what Stephen says, but you must be married before we leave . . ."

"And you must know that I will be safe."

"We already have faith that your laird won't let any harm come to you."

"Soon then you will be complaining about the bitter cold and snow."

He nodded. "Soon."

They rode down the hills and continued

on to the ridge overlooking Finney's Flat. Gabrielle knew the sentries wouldn't allow her to go farther. She slowed the pace to accommodate the curve in the trail. They rounded a hill to where the path straightened, and Gabrielle suddenly pulled hard on the reins. A procession was heading in their direction. Three narrow carts laden with trunks and bundles led by a half dozen men on horses were less than a stone's throw away.

"Oh God," she whispered.

Before Faust could ask what was wrong, she jerked on the reins to turn Rogue around and goaded him into a gallop.

Faust raced to keep up. When they were almost back to the holding, he called to her, "Princess, what is wrong?"

"Those men . . . they're here. I cannot believe my eyes. Call the others. Hurry, Faust."

When they reached the stables, Gabrielle jumped down and handed Rogue's reins over to a stable boy. Had she had her wits about her, she would have ridden to the courtyard, but she ran instead. Questions raced through her head. She had to be sure. Were these the same men? And if they were, what were they doing at the MacHugh holding? This didn't make sense.

Gabrielle had to be certain before she condemned them. Faust hadn't recognized them because he had stayed with the horses in the forest, but the others had gone with her to the clearing at Finney's Flat. They had seen some of the men, but not as clearly as she had. If only she could hear them speak, then she could know for certain. She would recognize their voices.

Faust called the other guards with two long piercing whistles. Stephen was instructing the young MacHugh warriors and had just notched an arrow to his bow when he heard the whistles. Without a word of explanation, he dropped the bow and arrow and ran.

Christien was just about to show a soldier how to use leverage against an opponent in hand-to-hand combat. When he heard the whistle, he tossed the young man to the ground and leaped over him on his way toward the sound.

Lucien and Faust were with Gabrielle by the time Stephen and Christien arrived. With her guards surrounding her, she told what she had seen.

Stephen agreed that she must be certain before she told the laird.

"They would be fools to come here," Lucien said.

"That is exactly what I was thinking," she said.

"But Princess, why would they be afraid to come here? They don't know we saw them," Christien pointed out.

"Did any of you see their faces clearly?" she asked.

"I didn't see them. I stayed with the horses," Faust said.

"I didn't see all of them," Stephen replied. "I remember moving behind you so you could have a clear shot with your arrow. The hoods of their capes still covered them."

"I don't know if I would remember what they looked like," Lucien admitted.

"The princess saw all of them, and she will remember," Christien said. "Trust yourself," he told Gabrielle.

"When I hear their voices, I will be certain."

The sound of the horses' hooves on the drawbridge drew their attention. The caravan had arrived. Sentries stopped them at the gate. Only the horses pulling the carts were allowed to cross, and the men riding their own mounts were ordered to leave them outside the walls and walk the rest of the way. The men on foot walked ahead of the carts and made their way up the incline toward Gabrielle and her guards. The closer they came, the faster Gabrielle's heart raced. When they were close enough for her to see their faces clearly, fear gripped her.

Unaware that they were walking to their doom, the men laughed and talked to one another. Gabrielle heard their voices, but she already knew: they were indeed the same men.

Stephen didn't take his eyes off them as he asked, "Princess?"

"Yes, now I'm certain," she whispered.

The guards moved protectively closer to her.

"Faust, go and find the laird."

"That be her?" one of the men asked.

"They told us she's got black hair and is fair to look at," another said. "If those men would move away from her, I could get a good look."

"We can't give over the trunks until we know for sure it's her."

One man dropped his voice to a whisper. "Let's get this over with quick. I ain't stayin' around to meet the laird."

Colm had been working with the stone-masons on the winch at the side of the keep. He rounded the corner with a frayed rope in his hands just as Faust called to him.

The visitors formed a line in front of the first cart. The tallest stepped forward and with an air of importance announced, "We brung the Lady Gabrielle's trunks. We'll leave them if you will tell us if that woman be her." He pointed to Gabrielle.

No one answered him.

Colm walked over to Gabrielle. "What's this?" he asked.

His nearness gave her strength, but she couldn't stop her hand from trembling when she touched his arm. "I would like you to meet the men who have brought my things to me." She took a step forward, but Stephen stopped her from taking another. "I am Lady Gabrielle."

The spokesman eyed MacHugh nervously as he said to Gabrielle, "Then these be your trunks."

"Yes, they are."

"We brung them from the abbey."

Gabrielle turned to Colm. "These men will be of interest to you."

Colm looked them over. "Why is that?" he asked.

With her back to the infidels, she whispered, "They like to dig holes."

THIRTY-NINE

"YOU'RE CERTAIN OF THIS, GABRIELLE?" COLM asked.

"Yes."

Gabrielle couldn't tell what Colm was thinking. She whispered, "Do you want me to give you their names? I remember all of them."

He didn't look at her when he answered, "That won't be necessary. Go inside, Gabrielle, and stay there."

His control amazed her. She knew rage had to be surging through his veins, but he wasn't letting anything show.

Without being asked, Christien ran in

search of Braeden, feeling the laird's commander should know what was going on.

As Lucien and Faust were escorting her inside, Gabrielle looked back over her shoulder. Colm walked toward the condemned men. With terror-stricken eyes, they retreated and scrambled around the carts, only to find dozens of armed MacHugh warriors coming up the hill behind them.

The door closed behind her, and she climbed the steps to the great hall. She didn't hear any sounds coming from outside—it was deadly quiet—and neither guard would allow her to look out the window. One hour passed, then another and another. And still not a sound from outside. Despite Lucien's and Faust's attempts to divert her attention, Gabrielle's apprehension grew.

As the sun was setting, Stephen came into the hall. He was alone.

"Princess, your trunks have been placed in the storage room."

"Thank you. Tomorrow will be soon enough to go through them. Do you happen to know if Colm will be coming soon?"

"The laird has left the holding. I doubt he'll be back tonight."

"Milady, your supper's on the table waiting for you," Maurna announced.

"I thought I would wait for the laird and his brother . . ."

"They have both left the holding," Stephen said.

"Just the two of them?"

"No."

He would say nothing more.

Gabrielle learned more from Maurna than from any of her guards.

"A fair number of our clansmen went with our laird. And the strangers who brought your things went with them, too. From the looks of things, I don't think they wanted to go, but you can't say no to the laird, can you?"

It was apparent that Maurna didn't know who these strangers were or what they had done, and Gabrielle wasn't about to tell her.

She went to bed early that night, but sleep didn't come until the early-morning hours.

Colm didn't return to the keep for five long days and nights. And when at last he came, he didn't make a big announcement of his arrival. Gabrielle came down the stairs one morning and there he was, standing in front of the hearth. She was so surprised to see him, she nearly tripped on the last step. She nervously smoothed her gown and adjusted the braided belt resting on her hips. Had she known he was back, she would have taken more time and care with her appearance. She would have worn her emerald green gown, not this faded blue one, and she would have bound her hair up with a pretty ribbon. She wouldn't have let it hang down around her shoulders.

She knew she looked drab, but it was actually his fault, she decided, because he hadn't given her any warning.

"You're home," she said.

Colm turned and his fierce eyes hungrily took her in. Damn, but he had missed her. He missed her smiles, her frown, her laughter, and most of all he missed kissing her.

He wasn't much for honeyed words. "You sleep your mornings away, Gabrielle."

"You cannot even say hello to me before you begin to criticize?"

"Are you ill?"

"She's not sleeping at night, Laird." Maurna made the announcement as she carried a pitcher to the table. She placed it next to four goblets, bowed to her laird, and added, "Some nights she doesn't go upstairs until the wee hours of the morning."

"How do you know when I go upstairs?" Gabrielle asked.

"Garrett told David, and he told Aitken, who told my man, who told me."

"But how would Garrett know?"

"He knew because Nevin told him. Do you want to know how Nevin knew?"

Dear God, no, she didn't. She had a feeling this litany could go on all morning.

"Gabrielle, come here," Colm ordered.

She crossed the hall to stand in front of him. She leaned up on tiptoes and kissed him full on the mouth. It was quick, but still a kiss. She stepped back, looked up at him, and said, "Welcome home, Laird."

And that, she believed, was a proper greeting. She folded her hands and waited for him to do the same.

"Why aren't you sleeping at night?" he asked.

Ignoring the question, she asked, "Are you happy to be home? And if you are, you should tell me so. It is the courteous thing to do."

"Yes, I am happy to be home, you daft woman. Now answer my question."

Since he'd been smiling at her when he called her daft, she didn't take offense.

"I don't know."

"Could you be worried about something?"

"Could I be worrying? What could I have to worry about? Could it be that I fear for my father since I have no notion of where he might be? Or might it be that my future husband leaves and doesn't return for days on end? Could I be worried that something might have happened to him?"

"You would worry about me?"

She jabbed him in the chest. "And you call *me* daft?" She took a deep breath before continuing. "Yes, I was worried about you, but you were last on my list of worries."

"You lie, Gabrielle, and not at all well."

"I know you don't want to marry me," she began, "but—"

"I will marry you," a voice from the entrance called.

Liam strode into the hall.

"No, you will not marry me, Liam," she said in exasperation. "And I am trying to have a private conversation with Colm. Please leave."

Colm put his arm around Gabrielle and pulled her close. "Lady Gabrielle has agreed to marry me."

"Yes, I know she has, but you don't want her, and I do," said Liam. "She didn't save your life, she saved mine, and I am forever in her debt."

Colm was getting angry. "Do you think I would give her up to you or to any other man?"

"Then you do want her?" Liam retorted.

"Damn right, I do!"

Liam nodded, and with the most satisfied grin he said, "You might want to tell her so."

Gabrielle and Colm heard him laughing as he descended the stairs.

Colm turned her in his arms and looked into her eyes. "I will never let you go, Gabrielle."

She didn't know what to say, which was probably just as well, because he didn't give her time to do more than open her mouth.

His mouth covered hers, and his tongue thrust inside, demanding a response. She wrapped her arms around his neck and moved restlessly against him as his mouth slanted over hers again and again. Their kiss became carnal. She aroused him as no other woman could, and Colm knew if he didn't stop now, he would lose all control.

When he ended the kiss, Gabrielle's heart was pounding. She could barely catch her breath. She was jerked from her daze by a man's voice.

"Laird, begging your pardon, but there are more problems with the winch."

The stonemason was standing directly behind her. Colm waved the man away.

"Gabrielle, I noticed you haven't asked me what happened when I left here."

"Would you tell me if I asked?"

"No."

"Then it is good that I don't ask. I don't think I want to hear what happened to those men. I might have nightmares."

"Rest easy," he said. "I did not have them buried alive."

"That is exactly what I was worried about. You know my thoughts as well as I do. Liam was so distraught, and he threatened to do such terrible things." She sighed. "But you did not bury them alive." She tilted her head and studied his face for several seconds then dared to ask, "What did happen to them? Did you let them return home?"

"No."

She knew not to prod him, fearing he would tell her exactly what the punishment had been. Colm wasn't the forgiving sort, nor was Liam.

"Were you able to find out who sent them after Liam?"

Before he could answer, two more clansmen came into the hall, begging his attention. Colm ignored them, but Gabrielle couldn't. "Your clan makes many demands on your time."

"Yes, they do."

"You'd best go."

He nodded. "Yes, I'd best go." He grabbed her hand as he walked past her and pulled her along. "Saddle my horse," he ordered one of the men waiting. To another, he said, "I will not listen to any problems until this afternoon. Make that clear to those waiting."

Gabrielle stepped out of the way to let a clansman carrying a bag of grain over his shoulder enter the open door of the storage room.

He nodded his greeting to her and turned to Colm. "Would you like me to help carry Lady Gabrielle's clothes upstairs?"

Colm looked into the room and saw the trunks stacked on the floor. "You carry far too many possessions," he criticized.

Gabrielle laughed. "Does everyone think these trunks are filled with gowns?"

The young man nodded. "The English have need for more than we do."

"And the MacHughs have need to make judgments without knowing the facts," she countered. "If you have a moment, I would like you to open one of my trunks."

"For what purpose?" Colm asked.

"Open one and see for yourself."

She had captured his curiosity. "Which one would you like me to open?"

"You choose."

Colm pulled one trunk down from the stack and was surprised by the weight.

"Danen, grab one end," he ordered.

"English clothes weigh more than a trunk filled with stone," Danen grunted.

"Clothes don't weigh this much, even English clothes."

There were four latches. Colm unlocked each one, then lifted the lid. Bags stuffed full were packed inside.

Gabrielle suggested he use his dagger to pierce the cloth, and when he did, grains of salt spilled out.

He was astounded. "You bring salt."

"Yes. Salt was one of my gifts to Laird Monroe, and now it's yours."

"Salt is more valuable than the most

precious jewels," Danen stammered. His green eyes were bright with excitement. "And much needed. Isn't that true, Laird?"

Colm agreed with a nod. "Are all these trunks filled with salt?"

"All but one. You are pleased?"

"I am. If anyone had known what was inside these trunks, they never would have gotten here."

He latched the locks and walked outside. A stable boy led Colm's horse across the courtyard. The skittish animal had tried to rear up twice before Colm calmed him. The Black, as he was called, was a magnificent animal. He was twice the size of Rogue, but Gabrielle doubted his disposition was half as sweet. Colm lifted her onto The Black, then swung up behind her and took the reins.

"Where are we going?" she asked.

A woman carrying a basket hurried toward them. "Laird, if you have a minute, I need but a word about—"

"It will have to wait."

He wrapped his arm around Gabrielle's waist and held her tight against him as he nudged the giant horse forward. Gabrielle couldn't imagine what had come over Colm. He wasn't running from her to take care of the demands of his clan. Nay, he seemed now to be running from his clan to be with her.

Once they'd cleared the moat, Colm gave The Black a kick and raced into the wind. They didn't stop until they reached a crest overlooking a beautiful glen with a brook meandering through it. He dismounted and lifted her to the ground. His hands lingered on her waist before he moved away.

"Come sit with me. We need to talk," Colm said.

His tone worried her. "Is it bad news you have? Is that why you wanted me alone, so I wouldn't disgrace you by weeping in front of your clan?"

"You could not disgrace me."

She sat down by a tree and adjusted her skirts to cover her ankles. "I have learned to expect the worst."

He knelt on one knee in front of her and cupped her chin in the palm of his hand.

"I brought you here so that we would not be interrupted, which, as you surely have noticed, happens quite frequently in my holding."

"It happens because you don't delegate. You should, you know. If you would give Braeden and the others, including your brother, more responsibility, you not only would take some of the bur-den off your shoulders, but you also would show them you have trust in them. You aren't the only one who can make a good decision."

"I did not bring you here to have you lecture me."

"But you will consider what I have said?"

He sat down next to her and leaned back against the tree. "I will," he said, stretching his long legs out in front of him, then crossing one foot over the other.

He looked relaxed, she thought, but then so did lions before they pounced.

"If it were good news, you would have told me by now."

"It's neither good nor bad. Here is what I know. The men who brought your trunks would never have come to my home if they had known anyone had seen them at Finney's Flat. I had the opportunity to question them at length."

She didn't ask him to explain what he meant by opportunity. "And they answered your questions?"

Did she possibly think he had given them a choice? Of course they had answered his questions. He made it all but impossible for them to refuse.

"They all insisted that they never knew the name of the man who hired them. Only their leader knew."

"Gordon. He was their leader, and I killed him." She patted his knee as though to console him. "I'm sorry."

"Sorry about what?"

"Sorry you won't ever find out who sent them after Liam."

"MacKenna sent them."

"But how . . ."

"I will explain, and you will hold your questions until I'm finished." He waited for her nod and then said, "Baron Coswold had your trunks taken to the abbey. Almost immediately after you left the abbey, he and his soldiers began their search for you. So did the other one."

"Percy?" Even his name repelled her, and she shivered with disdain. "The two of them are demons."

"From what I understand, they have both been chasing rumors, trying to find you. Coswold heard that you might be living with my clan, and he needed to find out for certain before he acted. What better way than to send your trunks with men who would report back to him."

"The abbot didn't send them?"

"At Coswold's urging, he did. But I'm sure the abbot thought he was doing a kindness. The problem was finding men to take them. Coswold couldn't send English-men. They never would have gotten this far, and if by chance and luck they did, they would never have made it back to report to him."

"But how did he . . ." She realized she was once again interrupting and stopped.

"The men Gordon hired didn't know MacKenna was paying them, but MacKenna knew who they were. Gordon gave him their names."

"How did you get this information?"

"It's amazing what a man will remember when pressured to do so. The one named Hamish told me he heard Coswold and MacKenna had come to some sort of an arrangement. He called it a pact. Coswold knew King John wouldn't give you to him, and so he promised you to MacKenna. He would get Finney's Flat, and in return Coswold would be able to see you whenever he wanted. It's my understanding they intended to share you."

Gabrielle felt ill. "I did not think these men could sicken me any more than they already have, but now you tell me they meant to share me? As they would a wife? Oh, my God . . ."

She tried to get up, but Colm gently pulled her down beside him. "Another one of the outcasts admitted he overheard Coswold whispering to one of his confidants. Yes, Coswold wanted you in his bed, Gabrielle, but he also wanted information he believes you hide."

Colm thought it peculiar that Gabrielle didn't ask him if he had any idea what kind of information Coswold thought she might have.

"You know what he wants, don't you?" he asked.

"Yes."

"Gabrielle?"

She rested against his side. "He wants the treasure of St. Biel."

She told him the legend as it had been told to her countless times.

"It is said that St. Biel's King Grenier did not send all the gold to the pope, but hid it away. It is also believed that the treasure is so vast, whoever finds it will have the power to rule the world. No one has ever found it, but it makes an interesting story."

"So why does Coswold believe it exists?"

"I don't know."

"And why does he think you know where the treasure is?"

"There are some who believe that the secret was passed down from the king to his daughter, and she in turn passed it down to her daughter . . ."

"Did your mother ever talk about this treasure?"

"She told me all the stories. She thought that greed is why some believe this legendary treasure exists."

"What about the people of St. Biel?" he asked. "Do they believe the myth?"

"Some do, others don't. They have few needs. They have enough food to eat with fishing and hunting, and enough wood to heat their homes. They live a simple but rich life."

"In other words, they wouldn't want the gold."

He had wrapped his arm around her waist, and she stroked it with her fingertips while she thought about her mother's homeland.

Her touch was as light as a feather, but had a powerful effect on him.

"Now it is my turn to ask you questions, Colm. You said that Coswold needed to be certain I was living with your clan before he acted. What does that mean? What do you think he intends to do?"

He shook his head. "I have yet to find out what is in his twisted mind, but I will, Gabrielle."

"In the name of King John, he banished me, remember? And Percy was united with Coswold in condemning me. Yet you say, as soon as they left the abbey, they began to search for me?" Her fingers traced the scar on his hand. "How did you know I was innocent? You said you knew that Isla had lied."

"The moon. She said the moon was bright and that she was able to see you, but it rained that night, Gabrielle. There was no moon. I know because I was searching for Liam, and it was too dark to continue. I had to wait until morning light."

"I don't think the monk lied. I believe he saw me when I went to look in on Liam."

"That is what I think as well."

"Are you betrothed to another woman?" She blurted the question before she lost her courage. "Lady Joan? Did you promise to marry her?"

"I was going to marry her."

"When?"

"Three years past."

"What happened?"

"Her father decided another alliance would make him stronger, so she was married to Laird Dunbar. Like Monroe, he was an older man."

"She's coming here, isn't she?"

"I had not heard this, but she will be welcomed. Her sister is married to one of my men."

The question she most wanted him to answer she couldn't ask. Did he love Joan? And if Gabrielle asked, would he tell her the truth?

"What will you do about MacKenna?"

"Kill him."

"Then you will go to war against the MacKenna clan?" she asked, and before he could answer, she added, "What if Coswold adds his army to MacKenna's?"

"You will not worry about Coswold or Percy," he replied. "They have no power over you."

If that were true, why then was she so afraid?

FORTY

KING JOHN WAS DEMANDING AN ACCOUNTING, and Baron Coswold was fit to be tied. He had been ordered to meet with John at Newell's castle, where the king was taking his leisure after a failed campaign against the Welsh. A large number of John's barons were so incensed by their king's attacks that they threatened to rise up against him. Coswold expected John to be in one of his black moods.

Percy had also been summoned to Newell's castle to give his version of what had taken place at Arbane Abbey, and Coswold could only imagine the lies his enemy would tell.

Coswold allowed Isla to accompany him. He had grown accustomed to talking to her about his worries without concern that she would repeat anything he said. Her station in life was solely dependent upon his good graces, and she would do nothing to jeopardize it.

She took good care of him. She saw to his every comfort and made certain the servants ran his home to his liking. Coswold never walked into a chilled room or picked up an empty goblet. She knew what foods he liked and what foods he avoided. Coswold also knew that eventually he would have to take a wife so that he would have heirs, but even then he planned to keep Isla around to continue to do his bidding.

She had become even more solicitous since he'd allowed her to go with him to Arbane Abbey, and now she could barely hide her excitement. He knew why. She had heard that Percy would be there with the king. Oh, what a fool she was to think she would ever have a future with Coswold's enemy. Back at Arbane Abbey when Isla had accused Gabrielle of whorish behavior, at first Coswold was annoyed at the spectacle, but then he realized it might be used to his advantage.

"Are you eager to see Baron Percy again?" he asked her on the trip to Newell's castle.

"It is true that I am."

"Isla, he doesn't even speak to you."

"Yes, he does," she insisted. "Upon occasion."

"You waste your time longing for him."

She hid her smile. "There is talk that he will soon be married."

Coswold shrugged indifference. "Then he must have given up on Lady Gabrielle. It's about time. He could never have her."

"I think he wants another now," she said.

He raised an eyebrow. "How would you know this?"

"Gossip," she said hastily. "Have you heard from the men you told me you sent on an errand? You seemed to be worried when they didn't return immediately."

Coswold had told Isla he had hired men to take care of a matter for him, but he hadn't told her what the errand was.

"No, I have not heard a word. It has been long enough for them to return to me. It is as though they, like my underling, Malcolm, have vanished into thin air."

Isla knew Malcolm was afraid of Coswold. She had seen the big, ugly man at Coswold's side and knew that he would kill if that was what her uncle ordered. Isla had heard that Malcolm had struck Lady Gabrielle with his fist. She was only sorry Malcolm hadn't disfigured Gabrielle. Isla hadn't any guilt over the pain her lie had caused.

"When did you last see Malcolm?" she asked, trying to sound concerned.

"We were searching the hills to the west of the abbey. One minute he was riding beside me, and the next time I looked, he was gone."

"What were you searching for, Uncle?"

"Never you mind. Ah, we have finally arrived. You will be as quiet as a mouse if you are in the presence of King John. It is already going on sunset. I doubt I will have my audience with him until tomorrow."

Coswold was very much mistaken. The king wanted to speak to the baron the minute he arrived. Coswold was not even allowed time to wash the dust from his hands.

Isla followed her uncle to the main hall,

but stood just inside the door. She stood so close to the curtains that, had she wanted to, she could have hidden herself behind them without even being noticed.

The hall was three times the size of Coswold's hall. It boasted two fireplaces, one on each end. The king sat behind a long table covered by a white cloth that was so long the hem touched the floor.

His Highness wore scarlet robes, identical to the color of the wine he spilled on the white cloth when he slammed the goblet down and stood.

John was not a handsome man. He was of average size with a protruding stomach, but to Isla he appeared a towering giant. She believed him to be as powerful as God, for he could destroy an entire country with one command. John had already proven to the world that he did not fear the pope. In fact, he profited from his own excommunication by confiscating church revenues. It was said that King John could steal the purity from a saint.

The dais John stood on made him appear much taller than Coswold, who bowed and then knelt before him. John had just given the baron permission to stand when the doors opened and Baron Percy strutted in. A woman about Isla's age followed. Dressed in fine clothing, she wore sparkling jewels around her neck and in her hair. She did not look to be related to Percy, but then Isla didn't look anything like her uncle. Perhaps the woman was a cousin or even, like Isla, a niece.

The woman was far too arrogant, though. She didn't hide in the shadows but knelt next to Percy and waited until John motioned both of them to stand.

John spoke to Percy first. "I see you have come to your senses and heeded my command," he said, nodding at the woman standing next to the baron.

"Lady Beatrice, go and make yourself comfortable in your chambers." Percy clapped his hands, and two servants immediately appeared to show the lady the way.

Once the elegant woman was out of sight, John discarded his manners. "Do you know the trouble you have caused me?"

"I did what you would have wanted me to do," Percy said.

"Give me your accounting now," the king commanded, "and I will decide if what you did was right or wrong."

Percy quickly recounted what had happened at the abbey. "No one was more surprised than I to learn that Lady Gabrielle had acted as a common whore. I knew that you would want to punish her, and I wanted to bring her to you so that you could decide her fate."

"Now it is your turn, Coswold."

The baron explained what had happened after Monroe's murder was discovered, and when he was finished reciting his version of the events, he said, "I did not think you would want to waste your time with a whore. I knew what must be done."

"And what was that, pray tell?"

"I banished her. In your name, I took everything away from her. She no longer has a king or a country or a family to call her own. She has been cast out into the wilds. I believe her punishment to be worse than a quick execution. Wouldn't you agree, my lord?"

John rubbed his chin. "I do agree," he said at last. "I find it difficult to believe that Baron Geoffrey's beautiful daughter would ruin herself. I will lay siege to Wellingshire and kill her father, for he did not do his duty and protect her innocence. She has no value to me now."

He picked up his goblet and took a long swallow. Wine dripped into his beard, and he used the back of his arm to wipe his chin.

"Perhaps you, too, Coswold, are now over your infatuation with Gabrielle? Percy has moved on, and I suggest you do the same."

Coswold turned to Percy. "What do you have to smirk about?"

"I am to marry Lady Beatrice in two months' time. She brings a handsome dowry to our wedding. Most handsome."

Isla covered her mouth to stop herself from screaming. No, it couldn't be true. Percy was to marry *her.* He had promised.

When Coswold left the hall with King John, Isla didn't follow. Frozen in the shadows, she stared at Percy, who had remained behind.

Percy had seen Isla cowering by the window and decided to get his talk with her over and done with now. He needed to make certain she wouldn't cause him any problems. And if he must threaten her, he would. He walked to the dais, reached up, and poured himself a goblet of the king's wine. He didn't bother to turn around when he said, "Isla, come out of the shadows so that we may talk."

Her legs were stiff as sticks as she crossed the hall. "Who is Lady Beatrice?" she demanded.

"She is my future wife. You heard the conversation. I will be married to her soon."

"But you don't love her. You love me. You said you did, and you promised to marry me."

"Lower your voice," he snapped. He could see she was losing control. "Do you want King John to hear you? You could be locked away in prison for the rest of your miserable days because of what you have done."

"What *I* have done?" she screamed.

He slapped her across the face. "I told you to be quiet! And you know good and well what you did. You destroyed Lady Gabrielle's life with your lies. You were her accuser."

Isla covered her cheek with her hand, though she was numb to the pain. "You told me what to say, and you promised that if I did exactly what you instructed me to do, you would then marry me."

"I would never marry you. You repulse me, Isla. You are Coswold's niece."

She began to sob. "But you promised . . ."

She grabbed his sleeve, but he pushed her back. "Get away from me."

"I lied for you."

"Yes, you did," he admitted. "But no one will ever know the truth now, will they?"

"Why? Why did you have me do it? Why did you want to destroy Lady Gabrielle?"

"I knew I couldn't have her, and I wanted to make sure Coswold couldn't have her, either. Then do you know what I planned to do? I was going to find her and take her to my home. I'd use her every night. Picture it, Isla. I would touch her, caress her, worship her . . ."

She tried to hit him, but he laughed as he fended off her attack.

"What a pathetic creature you are . . . and so gullible. I knew Coswold would come up with a surprise, and he didn't disappoint me. He arrived with a brand-new writ signed by the king. But I was prepared. I had you. Aye, you were *my* little surprise if all else failed. And you came forth at my signal just as I had instructed you. If I couldn't have Gabrielle in marriage, I would get her another way."

"I will tell everyone what you did," she threatened. Her devastation had turned to rage.

"Don't you mean what *you* did? If you tell

anyone you destroyed Lady Gabrielle with your lies, you will be condemned.

"I told you that I might need you to lie so that I could get Finney's Flat and barter it away for gold, and you and I could live a rich, happy life together. How stupid you are. Did you not think that King John would take the land back? Ah, I can see from your eyes that you had not thought it. But then I didn't expect you would. You were fool enough to think I could love you. Why not believe everything else I told you?"

"If you want Gabrielle so much, why are you marrying this Beatrice woman?" Isla sobbed.

"She has wealth," Percy admitted. "She will be very useful to me. And someday I'll resume my search for Gabrielle. I don't give up easily. Your uncle should know that."

"I will tell King John that you made me lie."

He snorted. "He won't believe you."

"Are you so certain I won't believe her, Percy?"

The baron dropped his goblet, so shocked was he to see His Highness standing in the doorway. "You misunderstand our conversation," Percy stammered. "What did you hear, and I will explain—"

"Silence!" the king shouted.

He motioned to two guards. "Make certain Baron Percy stays quiet while I speak to this woman."

Isla was terrified, but her fury at Percy overrode her desire to save herself. Her head was bowed, but out of the corner of her eye she watched the king as he climbed three steps and sat in his royal chair.

"Get to your knees in front of me and tell me about this lie," he ordered her.

She threw herself to the floor and confessed everything, begging for mercy at the end. John was seething. He called Coswold back into the hall and made Isla repeat her story. Isla couldn't look at her uncle, so great was her shame and her fear.

"Get her out of my sight," the king ordered, and as his soldiers were storming toward her, Isla cried out, "Have mercy, please. What is to become of me? Where will I go?"

John motioned to the guards to wait. He eyed Isla coldly. "Did you ever worry what would happen to Lady Gabrielle? Did you wonder where she would go?"

Isla pointed to Percy. "He made me lie."

She was dragged out of the hall, screaming and crying. When the door closed behind her, John considered his barons.

Neither Coswold nor Percy said a word. They waited to hear what their king would decide. Coswold worried the king would blame him for Isla's conduct, and Percy worried his lands would be confiscated.

"Surely both of you are aware of the trouble I face these days. The nobles have been released from their oaths to me because of my excommunication. There is unrest and talk of conspiracy. I must be on guard day and night. Now one of my most powerful barons, Geoffrey of Wellingshire, will plot against me because of you, Coswold, in my name banished his daughter. At this moment Geoffrey surely is gathering his forces."

"Kill him and be done with the worry," Percy suggested.

"You fool. Geoffrey has many influential friends who will be as outraged as he is. They will join him in fighting me. Would you have me kill them all? And will you and Coswold pay their tax to me?"

"You know we cannot," Percy said.

"I have enemies who aid Phillip of France. He would have my crown. I don't need more problems. Where is Lady Gabrielle now? Is she still alive?"

"I believe she is living with a clan high up north. They are a primitive group."

"Do you know if any man has claimed her for his own?"

"No, but what would it matter? You could force her to come back to England," Coswold said.

John shook his head. "You have taken my power over her away, you fool. When you announced that she has no country, you also announced that she does not answer to me."

"But you could still force her—"

"Quiet."

John considered the problem for several minutes before coming to a decision. "I must first make peace with Baron Geoffrey before he gathers allies against me. I will send word to him that I have found out the truth about his innocent daughter. Gabrielle will be given Finney's Flat. If she isn't married, I will find a suitable husband for her."

"And if she is?" Coswold asked.

"Then Finney's Flat will be my wedding gift to her."

"Laird MacKenna would take her for his

wife now that she has been proven innocent," Coswold said.

The king stood. "I believe you did not have a part in this treachery of lies, Coswold. You will continue to be my humble servant. As for Percy, I think you should have time to consider your transgressions. He motioned to his guards. "Take him away."

As Percy was being escorted out of the hall, Coswold stepped in front of him. Percy glowered at his enemy.

"This isn't over," he hissed.

Coswold smirked. "I think it is." In a whisper, he added, "And I win."

FORTY-ONE

COLM WAS HEADING OUTSIDE TO GIVE ORDERS TO his men as Gabrielle was coming down the stairs.

"Good morning," she called out. "It's going to be a fine day today, isn't it?"

He stopped and waited for her to reach him. She was a bonny sight to be sure. Her gown was a royal blue, and though he would have preferred her to wear his colors, she still looked beautiful. Had they already been married, he knew exactly what he would do at this very moment. He would pick her up, carry her back to his bed, and take his time removing her clothes.

There was no way he was going to make it five more months without bedding her, and he decided that as soon as he returned home, he would order the priest to bless their union. When Colm first took her in, Brodick had suggested that Colm delay the marriage, warning that if Gabrielle got pregnant immediately after the wedding, some might believe the babe was from another man. Colm had another solution. He would know the babe was his and kill any man who suggested otherwise.

He thought about telling her now that he would marry her as soon as he returned, then changed his mind. He'd explain while the priest prepared for the ceremony.

"Liam is in charge while I am away, and if you have any problems, go to him. He will know what to do," he told her.

"May I ask where you are going?" Gabrielle said.

The question puzzled him. He had already made his intentions clear to her. Had she forgotten so soon?

"To war, Gabrielle."

She nearly fell over. "*Now?* You're going to war *now*?"

"Why do you act so surprised? I told you what I was going to do."

She grabbed his arm and held tight so that he wouldn't get away from her until he had properly explained. "You said you were going to kill MacKenna."

"Ah, so you do remember. Now let go of me so that I may—"

"You can't just go to war, Colm." Gabrielle couldn't believe what she was hearing. Had he gotten up this morning, eaten his breakfast, called his men to arms, and now thought he would ride into battle? "You are not prepared."

"How am I not prepared?"

Had he never gone to war before? Was that why he didn't know what he was supposed to do?

"You haven't declared war first," she instructed. "Then you must spend weeks, if not months, on preparation. There are weapons to be made and packed in a wagon, food to pack as well to sustain your men during battle, and all other necessary equipment must be carefully placed in wagons and taken along for your comforts."

He contained his laughter and asked, "Explain these necessary comforts to me."

She thought about what the nobles took with them when they went to war. "You will need a strong tent so that you will be sheltered from the rain, and a rug to place inside the tent so that you will not have to step barefoot on the hard ground when you get out of your bed."

"And do I take my bed with me?"

"Some would."

"What about wine? How many barrels should I take with me?"

"As many as you think you will need," she said. "There are rules, Colm, even for you to follow. In a civilized war—"

"War is never civilized, and you have just described to me how the English prepare for war. By now you should have noticed that I am not English."

"You still must prepare."

"I have my sword, my bow, and a sound horse. I have no need for more."

"Then I will pray that you finish your war before you get hungry or thirsty."

She tried to walk away, but he grabbed her and kissed her soundly.

"Will you come back to me?" she asked.

"I will."

And then he was gone.

*   *   *

COLM AND HIS SOLDIERS had been gone from the holding for four days and nights when Lady Joan Dunbar arrived to pay her sister a visit.

Gabrielle was most curious to meet the woman Colm had intended to marry. She made up her mind that, no matter how pretty Joan was or how sweet her disposition, she would not be jealous of her. Colm obviously cared about the woman, or he wouldn't have agreed to marry her. He might even have loved her. But Gabrielle would not be jealous.

Colm didn't love Gabrielle. He had simply been trapped by a stupid debt. He never would have given her a second glance otherwise.

Did Joan love Colm? How could she not? He was a handsome, virile, strong man—a protector. And if Joan loved him, so what? Gabrielle still wouldn't be jealous.

Perhaps she and Joan could even become friends. It would be nice to have a woman with whom to talk of matters that men would have no interest in. And she and Joan did have one thing in common: Colm. Yes, they just might become friends.

But that was not to happen. After spending five minutes with the woman, Gabrielle knew they would never be friends. The reason was simple: Lady Joan was a bitch, and a mean one at that.

Fiona introduced her sister. Joan was much taller and thinner than Gabrielle. She didn't seem to have many curves. She was more statuesque. Her hair was so long it touched her waist, and the color was as pale as her complexion. Long lashes fanned across her azure eyes. She was pretty, and she knew it.

Joan kept sweeping her hair over her shoulder with the back of her hand in a dramatic gesture meant to draw attention to her curls.

"This is Lady Gabrielle, Joan," Fiona said. "I explained to her that you and Laird MacHugh were to marry and then Father formed an alliance with Laird Dunbar and forced you to marry him."

Joan stared at Gabrielle as she asked her sister, "Did you also explain that my husband is dead, and I am now free to marry Colm? And did you explain that I fully intend to do so?"

Lady Joan didn't get quite the reaction

she expected. Gabrielle was so surprised by what she'd said, she burst into laughter.

"Stop laughing," Joan demanded. "I haven't said anything amusing."

"I would offer you my condolences on the loss of your husband, but you seem to have gotten past mourning him."

Joan wagged a finger at Gabrielle. "I've heard all about you."

"It's odd that I haven't heard anything about you."

"Maybe that's because *I'm* not a whore."

Gabrielle shrugged, and that action further incited Joan's anger.

"Colm won't marry a whore, and that's what you are."

Gabrielle knew that Joan wanted her to defend herself, but she wasn't going to accommodate her. "Enjoy your visit," she said and then walked away.

That night, as Gabrielle was pulling the covers back, she thought about Joan and what she had said.

One day, after she was married to Colm, she would tell him she had saved him from a fate worse than death. Aye, she'd saved him from Joan.

FORTY-TWO

THE WAR WASN'T CIVILIZED. IT WAS BLOODY AND hard-fought.

MacHugh made no pretense of a surprise attack. He had made sure that MacKenna knew he was coming by sending word to surrounding clans that he was ready to avenge his brother.

When the news reached the MacKenna holding, the laird rallied his soldiers to battle, but he hadn't had time to call his allies. He swore that the MacHughs would never step foot on MacKenna land. MacKenna would meet the enemy head-on and make the first strike.

MacKenna never varied his strategy, believing what had worked in the past would work again. He would strike and retreat, again and again, with wave after wave of assaults. Although his men weren't as well-trained, they were twice in number, and he could move fresh troops in after each wave. He had another advantage as well: his archers. As the MacHughs poured down the mountain and crossed the flats, there would be no place to hide. Even if they managed to reach the border of the flats, his archers would be waiting to finish them off.

Colm counted on MacKenna's stupidity.

It never occurred to Laird MacKenna that the MacHughs could cross the flats in the dark. Even fools would never try to ride across what they could not see. Without light, their horses could stumble and falter. But the MacHughs didn't ride their horses, they silently led them across. By morning light they had made a wide circle and were in position behind their enemy. They advanced, forcing the MacKennas to engage in battle or run. Most of them ran.

Once they flushed the MacKennas into the open, they fought with their swords and with their fists. The battle was quickly won, for the MacKennas fought like the cowards they were. One even tried to use another as a shield against MacHugh's sword. Colm killed them both with one hard thrust, his blade cutting through two bodies just below their hearts.

Colm was always the first to go into battle. He led his men. MacKenna was always the last, fighting only when there was little actual danger of getting killed.

Bodies covered the field like rushes. Every dead MacKenna was turned over in search of the laird. But he was not to be found. Colm stood in the middle of the carnage, his sword dripping MacKenna blood, enraged that MacKenna had slipped away.

"Find him!" he roared.

The MacKenna keep was blocked off. The hunt continued.

Colm found his enemy three long days later, hiding like a coward in a grotto near the bluff overlooking Loch Gornoch. With swords drawn, two of MacKenna's soldiers stood guard in front of their laird.

Braeden leaped from his horse and ran to Colm's side.

"Stand back," Colm ordered. His eyes locked on MacKenna as the two MacKenna soldiers ran for their lives.

Grasping his sword in both hands, Colm raised his arms high over his head.

The last image Owen MacKenna saw was a looming shadow.

The last sound he heard was the music of the sword.

FORTY-THREE

GABRIELLE STOOD AT THE WINDOW IN HER CHAM-
ber and watched a group of boys fighting
with wooden swords. She heard one of them
yell that it was his turn to play Laird
MacHugh, and she soon learned that meant
he got to win. There were always two win-
ners on their pretend battlefield, Colm and
Liam. She wondered if the laird and his
brother knew how much they were admired
by their clan.

The mischief-makers, Ethan and Tom,
stood on the sidelines begging to be
allowed to join in, but the older boys kept
pushing them back and ignoring them. She

was surprised the little ones gave up so easily. They put their heads together, giggled loudly, and then took off running around the side of the castle. They had already moved on to their next adventure.

Hearing the children's laughter lightened Gabrielle's mood. She had been so melancholy since Colm left, and he had been gone such a long time. Was he safe? Please God, keep him safe.

She knew what evil MacKenna was capable of, for there was proof that he had plotted Liam's torture and murder. In the last few days she had heard numerous stories about Laird MacKenna, and each one painted a picture of a tyrant who used others to carry out his sadistic plans. His loyalty to his clan went only as far as the benefit he received personally. If his followers displeased him, they were expelled, or worse, killed. He even used women and children as shields against hostile neighboring clans. Housing them near the fortress walls, he made sure any laird who dared attack the MacKenna holding knew they were first killing these deterrents.

As Gabrielle listened to each horrendous tale, she thought back to the man she had met at Arbane Abbey. Laird MacKenna's generosity to the monks had no doubt been part of his scheme. The abbot had been deceived, and so had she. At his introduction, Gabrielle had thought the man amiable and attractive, and now that she knew the truth, she admonished herself for making judgments based on appearance. She had been wrong about him, and she had been wrong about Colm as well. Had she only looked at Colm's rough exterior, she would never have seen the heart of the man.

She tried not to think about MacKenna and what must be happening, but late at night when she was huddled under the covers, sleep would elude her, and her imagination would run rampant. All sorts of horrible images would come into her mind. She would imagine Colm lying injured, all alone, with no one to help him.

The possibility that he might die was too unbearable to consider. His clan needed him.

Shoving one worry from her mind, it settled on another. Why hadn't she heard from her father? There had been enough time for him to have gotten word to her or to the Buchanans. The longer she waited to hear, the more convinced she became that Wellingshire was under siege and that King John's soldiers had taken him captive. Gabrielle knew her father would never surrender.

So many were suffering now . . . and all because of a lie. Gabrielle hoped that one day she would know why the woman had said such heinous things about her. How could she so blithely destroy someone she didn't know? Where was her conscience? Had Isla felt any remorse? Or had she, like so many others, discovered a way to justify her evil deeds?

Gabrielle didn't have any answers. She knew only that fear could paralyze her if she allowed it. She needed to keep busy. If she worked hard enough and moved fast enough, there would be no time to worry.

Now, as she straightened up her chamber, she said another prayer that God would watch over her father and Colm.

Feeling a chill in the air, she went to the window to lower the tapestry. Before the heavy fabric fell into place, she glanced once again at the boys playing below. Something caught her eye and she quickly pushed the curtain back.

"Oh, dear Lord."

She picked up her skirts, threw the door open, and ran as fast as she could. She nearly broke her neck flying down the stairs.

Liam was in the hall when he heard her shout. He kicked a chair out of his way as he came running. "Gabrielle, what's wrong?" He caught her as she tried to run past him.

"Ethan . . . Tom . . . with swords," she gasped.

"Yes, I saw the boys playing outside, but what—"

"Real swords," she stammered. "They've got real—"

She didn't have to continue. Liam understood what she was trying to tell him. He was much faster than she was and had already vanished down the second set of stairs. Gabrielle pushed a clump of hair out of her eyes and took a deep breath, then picked up her skirts again and chased after him.

There weren't any blood-curdling screams, which was a good indication the boys hadn't cut themselves. Still, she wanted to make certain they were all right. By the time she reached the first floor, she had picked up a good amount of speed. The door was just closing as she ran outside. It struck her on the hip, knocking her off balance and sending her spinning down the steps into the courtyard. She might have been able to save herself from falling on her face if her legs hadn't gotten caught up in her gown. She tripped over her own feet and once again went flying through the air, though this time she was sure to land on her head.

Colm saved her from breaking her neck. He had Tom wrapped firmly in one arm when he saw her. Tossing the boy to Christien, he grabbed for Gabrielle and she landed against his chest with a thud.

Gabrielle uttered an unladylike expletive she hoped no one heard, looked up, and only then realized she was in Colm's arms. She was so happy to see him, she kissed him. He hadn't shaved, and she felt the bristles of his beard against her cheek. He squeezed her just enough to let her know he was happy to see her, too. At least that is what she wanted to believe.

She stepped back. "You are well?"

"Yes."

"And the battle?"

"Finished."

"And the outcome?"

"As expected."

She knew he wasn't going to tell her anything more, and though she thought he could have been a little less rude about it, she was too happy to see him to let it irritate her.

Liam walked past them with Ethan tucked under his arm. The boy was yelling for Liam to put him down so that he could get his sword. With Tom in tow, Christien followed them inside. The child chattered away and didn't seem to mind that the guard paid no attention.

For a moment Gabrielle and Colm were alone. "I have missed you," she said.

She hoped he would tell her that he had also missed her, but he only gave her a quick nod. And then he broke her heart.

"Gabrielle, I know I told you I would marry you in six months' time . . ." he began.

"Yes, and a month almost has already passed."

"It doesn't matter how long it's been. I can no longer keep my promise."

Willa stopped him from saying more. "Laird, begging a minute of your time . . ." she called as she approached, wiping her hands on her apron. "Those little imps have been at it again. They've gotten into the pens in the back and terrorized my poor hens, and now they won't lay their eggs. I swear I saw one of them hide when Ethan and Tom ran past. I'm afraid you're going to have to ban them from the yard."

"All right, Willa. I'll take care of it," he answered.

Out of the corner of his eye, he saw others coming—the stonemason holding yet another shredded rope in his hands, the smith with the new sword blade ready to be inspected, the young soldier—all with immediate problems to be solved.

He answered several questions and then motioned to everyone else to wait so that he could finish explaining to Gabrielle what he planned to do. She was nowhere in sight.

"What the . . . Gabrielle!" he shouted.

"Begging your indulgence, Laird, but I think your lady is making her way to the stables," the soldier said.

"I saw her guards following," another volunteered.

"Ah, hell." She was at it again. The woman was forever trying to leave him.

Calling for Braeden to take over and

answer the remaining questions, Colm headed for the stables.

Gabrielle had disappeared before he finished his statement, and therefore she did not understand what he had been trying to tell her—that there would be no marriage in five months because he could not wait five months to bed her, and that the last month had been torture and he couldn't continue this way. He couldn't be in the same room with her without thinking about what he wanted to do to her. It was getting ridiculous. She would walk up the stairs; he would walk down. She walked into a room; he walked out. She had no idea the power she held over him, and so he had done everything he could to stay away from her.

Since she was so innocent, she couldn't possibly know how her touch affected him. But after they were married, he would take his time showing her how crazed she could make him.

He caught up with her as she was opening Rogue's stall. He reached around her and kicked the gate shut, then ordered her guards to leave. Without questioning, they filed outside and waited at the stable doors.

Colm wasn't gentle as he forced her to turn around and face him. There were tears in her eyes.

"You are not leaving," he told her.

"As you say."

"No, you are not leaving me."

"But Colm—"

"You are not leaving me." His voice shook with emotion.

She pushed against his chest, but she couldn't budge him. "I cannot stay here," she cried out. "I can't. I won't be able to stop chasing you and kissing you and demanding your attention. I know you think you can keep avoiding me, but you can't, Colm. I can be relentless when it's something I want." She took a breath and whispered, "And I want you."

And there it was, out in the open for him to accept or reject. She looked up at him. He'd gone completely still. She wasn't even sure if he was still breathing. She knew she'd shocked him by pouring her heart out to him. It was unseemly for a lady to admit she felt passion, but it was too late to take the words back, and Gabrielle wouldn't have wanted to anyway.

"You say you cannot marry me, and I will

accept your decision," she said. "But if I stayed, it wouldn't matter if we were married or not. I would still chase you, and eventually I would wear you down. You could not get away from me."

He stroked the side of her face with the back of his hand as he struggled to find the words to give her. "There are times I don't know what to think of you. You constantly astound me. You save my brother's life, and ask nothing in return. I offer you marriage, and you worry that I will ruin my life. You have been dragged through Hell, and you show only kindness. Now you think I reject you, and you open your heart to me. I don't know how this miracle came to pass, but I cannot imagine living the rest of my life without you. I want you, Gabrielle, and I will not wait five months to have you. We will marry now."

FORTY-FOUR

THE WEDDING WOULD TAKE PLACE IN TWO WEEKS. It was as long as Colm was willing to wait, and he believed fourteen days was more than enough time to prepare for the celebration.

Maurna and Willa were frantic. Everything needed to be perfect for their laird and his bride. Maurna took charge of the women who would give the keep a proper scrubbing while Willa and her helpers began making their special recipes. There would be pheasant, fully dressed and trimmed; stuffed pigs; pullets, of course—four dozen would do nicely—meat pies; and berry tarts. Honey would be mixed in almost every sweet dessert. The best wine would be served.

"You'll be a vision, milady, floating down the stairs in your finery," Maurna said. "Father Gelroy will hear you say your vows outside in the courtyard. There will be pretty flowers to garnish your hair and more flowers will be strewn in a circle around you and our laird, and the priest as well. Father thought the ceremony should take place at Arbane Abbey. As he explained, you are a princess of St. Biel and should have a royal wedding, but our laird wouldn't hear of it. He isn't explaining why, but Willa and I think it's because he knows his clan would want to join in the celebration."

"It will be a grand day," Willa predicted, "and here before you know it."

The best-laid plans had a way of changing.

GABRIELLE RECEIVED JOYOUS NEWS from her father. Laird Buchanan came to the MacHugh holding to tell her that he had received a message from Baron Geoffrey.

"Your father is well. He has not been harmed by the king, nor have his estates been seized. He knows that you are living with the MacHugh clan, and he wants you to know that he will be here soon to see you, and to explain what happened with the king.

"There is more news," he added, looking at Colm. "Your father believes you will be going home with him."

"He knows I have been banned. Why would my father think I could go into England with him?" she said.

Brodick had no answer.

Not an hour later, while Colm and Brodick discussed the trouble the new Monroe laird was stirring up, one of the MacHugh soldiers on duty at the drawbridge came to the gate of the courtyard to announce that an envoy from King John was asking permission to speak to Lady Gabrielle.

"There are a bishop and three other holy men, along with a few servants, traveling with the envoy," he said. "They insist that you will want to hear what they have to say. They brought a scroll with them and a gift for Lady Gabrielle."

"And soldiers?" Colm asked. "Did the envoy bring the king's soldiers as well?"

"He did, Laird. Twelve in all. They have already placed their weapons on the ground to show their good intentions."

Colm scoffed. "The English don't have good intentions."

Colm was going to refuse to let any of them cross his drawbridge, but Brodick urged him to reconsider. "Aren't you curious to know what they have to say? And if you don't like what you hear, you could always—" He stopped when he realized Gabrielle was listening.

Colm gave his order: the soldiers would remain outside, but the others could come forward.

The shout to lower the bridge echoed down to the guards.

"Gabrielle, go inside," Colm said.

"As you say."

She wanted to stay. She was as curious as Brodick to find out what the envoy had to say, but she would not oppose Colm in front of his ally and friend. Besides, she knew protesting wouldn't do any good. Once Colm had his jaw set, nothing could change his mind.

Although no command was given, MacHughs began to line up on either side of the worn path from the drawbridge to the courtyard. Most were armed and ready for any outcome. Gabrielle thought they were being overly cautious. What harm could one envoy, some holy men, and a handful of servants cause? None of the priests or servants would be armed, and the envoy would not dare to carry a sword. To do so would be a grave insult to the laird.

Stephen appeared at Gabrielle's shoulder and explained what was happening as they made their way into the castle. "It is believed that the procession is coming for you, Princess, with the intent of taking you away. The clan knows there are English soldiers waiting outside the walls, and word has spread that the envoy brings news to you. He could be carrying an order for you to return to England." He nodded toward the men standing on either side of the path. "The MacHughs are letting it be known that they will not let you be taken away from them without a fight."

"These men came here unarmed, and are few at that," she said.

"But they will report back to the soldiers waiting outside the walls, and those soldiers will tell King John what has happened here today."

"There has been so much deceit of late. How can we even be certain the envoy comes from King John?"

"We must assume that he does and be prepared," Stephen answered gravely.

Just as he reached for the door, Liam pulled it open and came outside. He nodded to Gabrielle, stepped aside so that she could pass, then crossed the courtyard to take his place beside his brother.

They were a fearsome sight. Colm stood in the middle of the warriors. Liam and Braeden were on his left, Brodick to his right. Christien and Lucien joined the line next to Braeden. Faust went to the opposite side to stand beside Brodick.

"Go and take your place with the others," she said to Stephen. "I will stay inside and cause you no worry."

Stephen bowed his head and turned to do as she asked.

The door had just closed behind her when it was flung open again as Father Gelroy ran inside, looking like a pack of wild dogs was on his heels.

"The bishop has come," he told her, "and I'm not ready to receive him!"

He rushed ahead of her to the steps. Then, remembering courtesy, Gelroy stopped suddenly and let her go in front of him. But as soon as they reached the second level, he cut around her and raced up the next flight. He didn't have time to change his robes, but wanted to at least wipe the dust off and wash his hands and face.

Gabrielle paced in the hall while she waited for someone to come and tell her the news.

Panting from his haste, Father Gelroy joined her a moment later. "I'm to stay with you until I am called outside. Our laird will not allow felicitations until the envoy has explained the purpose of his visit."

"I would stand by the window so that I would see what is happening," said Gabrielle, "but those outside would also see me. It would be unseemly."

"Aye, it would," the holy man agreed.

"And it would be wrong to try to overhear what is being said, but if you were to stand slightly closer to the window, you couldn't help but hear some of the conversation. I do not see any wrong if you were to just happen to walk toward the window . . ."

Gelroy nodded. "No, no, of course it wouldn't be wrong, and I am certainly in need of fresh air."

The priest positioned himself at the edge of the window with the hope he wouldn't be noticed.

"I'm just in time to see the procession," he reported. "There is pomp and splendor. The bishop is dressed in his rich finery, riding a docile horse. He's not a young man, but he's not so old, either."

"And the envoy?"

"Walking he is, with a scroll tucked under his arm. His clothes are unremarkable, and I must say he seems the jittery sort, for he keeps darting quick looks to his left and right. I think the poor fellow believes he will be pounced on any minute." Gelroy chuckled as he added, "And well he could. I remember such a feeling myself."

"What of the others?" she asked.

"It is quite a procession. First comes the bishop, then the envoy, then, one at a time, the monks, and last the servants. I recognize a few faces. They are indeed from the abbey."

Gabrielle kept edging closer to Gelroy, hoping she could sneak a peek. The priest shooed her back.

"The bishop can see straight through this window, Lady Gabrielle. Do not let him see you."

"Then tell me what is happening now."

"The bishop is still atop his horse, but he

has stopped. A servant is coming forward to take the reins and aid the bishop."

Gelroy made the sign of the cross and folded his hands as though in prayer. Then he explained. "The bishop decided to give his blessing. If he had hoped the lairds would bow to him, he was mistaken. None of them have moved."

The bishop didn't seem offended that Colm and the others didn't drop to their knees. The servant stood by his side and held the reins, but the bishop didn't dismount.

The envoy came forward. Assuming the warrior standing in the center of the stone-faced men to be Laird MacHugh, he addressed him.

"His Highness, King John of England, sends word to Lady Gabrielle. She is here?"

"She is," Colm answered, "but you will give me the king's message, and I will then decide if you can speak to her."

The envoy was quick to agree. He cleared his throat, straightened his shoulders, and took a step forward. He then began his rehearsed speech as a herald would do, in a loud booming voice so that many would hear.

"There has been a terrible injustice done to Lady Gabrielle. She has been wrongly vilified and persecuted. His Highness now knows and has absolute proof that the lady is innocent. The king wants it known that Baron Geoffrey of Wellingshire will be lauded and richly respected for his vigilance over his daughter, and Lady Gabrielle, a treasure to England, will from this day forward be called Princess Gabrielle of St. Biel and friend to England's king."

The envoy paused to await a response. It was not long in coming.

"Every man here knows Lady Gabrielle is innocent. We do not need your king to tell us so," Colm said.

"King John will be pleased to hear that you and others have seen through the treacherous lies told and wrongly believed by many. He wishes to prove his sincerity."

"And how will he do that?" Colm asked.

The envoy held out the scroll so all could see the seal was unbroken.

"To prove sincerity," he repeated, "and in hopes of forgiveness for this grievous injustice, His Royal Highness hereby confers the land known as Finney's Flat to Princess Gabrielle. He has signed his name and affixed his royal seal as his solemn promise that the land will never belong to England again. He also has had it written that God may strike him if he does not keep his word."

The envoy took another step forward and with both hands held out the scroll. Colm took it and handed it to Liam. "Why do these priests travel with you?" he asked.

"For protection, Laird MacHugh," he answered. "It was hoped . . . sincerely hoped . . . that you would hear the message from my king and not harm the messenger."

Colm glanced at Brodick before speaking to the envoy again. "Holy men would not save you from my fist if I were displeased with your message."

The envoy swallowed loudly, and the bishop, hearing what the laird had just said, gave yet another blessing. "And are you displeased, Laird?" the envoy asked.

"No, I am not, and I do not kill messengers, even when the news is not to my liking. You are welcome here as long as it takes you to refresh yourselves. The others, too."

The envoy was weak with relief. "I thank you, Laird, but there is more of the apology to give, and more needs said about the gift. His Highness wishes to hear Princess

Gabrielle has forgiven him. She must say the words to me so that I may say them to my king."

"My clan will also hear this apology from your king." He signaled to Braeden, who shouted the command.

Within minutes men, women, and children surrounded the courtyard and stood silent, watching.

"Go and get your princess," Colm ordered her guards.

The door was thrown open and held by two of the men who had been standing guard. A moment passed and then another as all eyes watched the entrance.

And then Gabrielle stepped out into the light. An aid sounded a herald's trumpet as the envoy said, "Hail to Princess Gabrielle." He then dropped to his knees and bowed his head. The visitors from the abbey also fell to their knees to show their respect.

Startled, Gabrielle looked at Colm, uncertain of what to do. It was not appropriate for these men to kneel. Colm wasn't giving her any help. He simply stared at her and waited for her to come to him.

She didn't disappoint him. Liam moved back so that she could stand beside Colm.

"You must give them permission to stand," Stephen instructed in a whisper.

Her cheeks flushed with embarrassment. "You may stand."

She surprised everyone then when she gave the envoy instructions. "You bow to Laird MacHugh, for you are on his land by his good graces, but you do not kneel to me. If the laird wants you on your knees, he will tell you so."

A murmur of approval came from the MacHughs.

Colm gave the envoy permission to speak, and the envoy repeated his prepared speech. The cheers were deafening when he finished. He waited until the noise had died down and then asked, "May I tell His Royal Highness that you forgive him?"

Gabrielle was about to answer the envoy and tell him yes, she did forgive the king, but something held her back. Was this another trick?

"I will consider it. You will have your answer before you leave here."

The envoy looked shocked that she didn't immediately agree, but bowed to her wishes. "I will await your answer."

Liam took Gabrielle's hand. "You have

always had the acceptance and respect of this clan, but now you have their love."

Colm knocked his hand away. "You will give your love to another and leave Gabrielle alone."

Liam laughed. He winked at Gabrielle and said, "As you say, Laird."

"Laird, we must celebrate," Braeden said, "for now we have a princess and Finney's Flat."

Colm agreed but didn't want any of the outsiders to come into his home, not even the bishop. With the weather pleasant and no rain cloud in sight, he called for tables and benches to be carried outside and a barrel of ale to be brought from the buttery.

The bishop was finally removed from his horse, and he and his monks were given places at the table. Still suspicious of their English visitors, the MacHughs were reticent to be welcoming to the envoy and his men.

Gabrielle was even more wary than the MacHughs. She kept an eye on the envoy as he made his way through the gathering crowd. Distracted, she barely paid attention to the conversation next to her until she heard Colm praise Father Gelroy. With each word he said, the priest seemed to grow taller.

"Perhaps soon, Laird, you will wish to build Father Gelroy a chapel," Gabrielle suggested.

"Perhaps," he replied.

"The statue of St. Biel the abbot has kept safe for you is soon to come here," the bishop said. "Perhaps you will name your chapel after the saint. I have not heard of him," he admitted, "but so many were sainted before my time. Would you know how many miracles he has performed?"

Gabrielle didn't have the faintest idea. Father Gelroy saw her hesitation and said, "St. Biel was a good and holy man. I'm certain the royal guards could tell us the number of miracles."

When the bishop left to get refreshment, she whispered to Gelroy, "I am ashamed that I have forgotten so much about St. Biel. I, too, will seek instruction from my guards."

Father Gelroy spotted Maurna carrying out a tray of food. "Yes, yes," he said, dismissing the talk of saints. "The meal is ready."

Gabrielle looked around in astonishment as MacHugh women carried huge trenchers filled with meat pies and bread and game birds. One of the women crossed to the courtyard with yet another tray. Everyone was bringing food to share.

She looked around for Colm, but he had disappeared. As she set out to find him her way through the gathering throng was interrupted by well-wishers who wanted to congratulate her. She was patted on her back, her arms, and once on her head by a robust woman.

When she finally had threaded her way to the side of the castle, she looked for a quiet spot. She needed time to think. Something in the back of her mind gnawed at her. Although the envoy's announcement was good news, something wasn't right. What that was she didn't know.

Colm found her sitting on a stone. "Gabrielle, what are you doing?"

"Pondering."

He pulled her into his arms, kissed her, and then tried to get her to go back to the celebration.

"I think there may be trickery by King John, but I don't know what it might be," she told him.

"I will read the scroll carefully, and if you

like, I will ask Liam and Brodick to read it as well," he assured her. "You are right not to trust."

As Colm went to find Brodick and Liam, and head inside, Gabrielle returned to the feast. Maurna forced her to sit and taste some of the offerings. Since she had prepared one of the meat pies, she insisted that Gabrielle be given a good helping.

Conversation whirled around her. There was much excitement about the MacHughs owning Finney's Flat. They could triple their crops even if they let some of the ground lie fallow. Their joyful enthusiasm made her smile. But still she kept a skeptical eye on the envoy.

Why would the king give her Finney's Flat? And how were his lapdogs, the barons, involved? For surely they were. Aye, if there was trickery, they were behind it. The king called the land his gift. The first time she'd heard of Finney's Flat, it was to be her dowry. But now? What could the reason be? Certainly not the king's generosity. He didn't know the meaning of the word.

He wanted her forgiveness. There it was. Suddenly she knew exactly what was in the king's mind. She slapped the top of the table causing quite a startle, then jumped to her feet and stormed over to the envoy.

The celebrating crowd might not have noticed Gabrielle's behavior, but all of them saw her guards racing to her. By the time she reached the envoy, Christien was standing beside her.

"Stand," she ordered the envoy.

The laughter died down and a hush fell over the people.

"You will answer my questions," she demanded. "Do you go directly back to King John?"

"No, I first go to the abbey," the envoy answered, glancing around at the startled faces staring at him. "I will stay the night there and then continue on my journey."

"Are there barons also waiting to hear what news you bring?"

"Yes, Princess, I'm certain there are."

"Perhaps those barons are Coswold and Percy?"

"I do not know all who anxiously wait to hear that you have forgiven King John." Frowning, he added, "And that is why I wait as well."

The crowd edged closer. Gabrielle saw Joan watching her and the bishop standing beside her.

"I know what the king and his barons are about," she said, her voice rising with her anger. "If I accept the king's apology, I am also accepting his rule. Is that not true? I am no longer free of him."

The envoy looked at his shoes when he spoke. "I cannot lie, and so I will tell you that Finney's Flat will be a dowry for you to bring to the man the king will choose for you to marry."

"But if I don't accept his apology, then Finney's Flat returns to the king?"

"I am not certain, but there would be the possibility."

If a bread crumb were to drop to the ground, it would have made more noise than the clan.

"Did the king not consider that I might already be married?"

"He did, and if you were, then Finney's Flat would belong to your husband, and the king would not interfere."

Gabrielle looked around her and raised her voice to proclaim. "I am married this day."

The envoy took what she said as true and asked, "To Laird MacHugh?"

"Yes," she answered. "Finney's Flat belongs to him."

"You are not married this day!" Joan shouted. "You cannot deceive us. You boldly tell a lie in front of the bishop. You will burn in hell for such an offense."

Incensed, Gabrielle brushed past the envoy. "I *am* married this day."

Joan backed away as Gabrielle came closer. The anger she saw in Gabrielle's eyes frightened her, and she feared she would strike her.

"I am married this day, and Finney's Flat belongs to Laird MacHugh," she repeated.

A rumble of agreement rolled through the crowd, growing louder and louder until the sound was deafening.

Once the noise had died down, Gabrielle spoke again. "Would you like proof? All of you wait here, and I will get it for you."

"We know you are married this day and Finney's Flat belongs to our laird," a man called out.

"Aye," another called and another.

Gabrielle stopped in front of the envoy. "But you, I think, require proof."

The envoy nodded. "I must be able to tell King John with a certainty that you are married." He could feel the heat of the crowd's anger and called out, "And Finney's Flat will be Laird MacHugh's."

Christien ran ahead of Gabrielle and held the door for her. "Is the proof inside?" he asked, grinning.

"Yes," she answered.

Followed by her guards, Gabrielle ran up the stairs, paused to make herself presentable by smoothing her bliaut and pushing a strand of hair behind her ear.

"Are you ready to be married this day?' Stephen asked.

She nodded.

In the hall, Colm had just finished reading the scroll. He was handing it to Brodick while Liam and Father Gelroy, goblets in hand, waited their turn.

Gabrielle took a deep breath and entered the hall. "Colm, may I have a moment of your time?"

FORTY-FIVE

GABRIELLE WAS INDEED MARRIED THIS DAY.

The ceremony was performed in front of the hearth in the great hall. There wasn't any pomp or splendor befitting a princess from St. Biel and a powerful laird from the Highlands. It was done quickly and quietly. Even though it was nearly impossible for anyone to see into the hall from outside, Gabrielle insisted that the tapestries be pulled down to cover the windows that faced the courtyard below and those that overlooked the back garden and the lake beyond. She wasn't taking any chances that the envoy or the bishop or that horrid woman, Joan, might see what was happening.

Since Brodick was her only relative in attendance, it became his duty to give her to Colm and grant permission for the marriage to take place when asked to do so by Father Gelroy. Liam and Gabrielle's royal guards were witnesses.

Gabrielle didn't think she was nervous, but apparently she was, for when she was told to place her hand in Colm's, she trembled as though she had just suffered a terrible fright. The priest began his prayer, and the impact of what she was doing suddenly overwhelmed her. Her knees went weak and she could barely breathe. A vise was crushing her chest. She was becoming Colm's wife, now and forever.

In a daze, she watched as Colm placed a length of his plaid over their joined hands. He tilted her face up and looked into her eyes as he spoke his vows, and for the life of her, she couldn't comprehend a word he said. She had forgotten any Gaelic she ever knew. Then it was her turn. She whispered her vows in her mother's language. Father Gelroy stopped her and asked her to start over.

"I don't understand what you're saying, Princess Gabrielle," he explained.

Neither did she. She knew she had promised Colm something. She just couldn't remember what it was. Had she said that she would love and cherish him? Or had she thought that she should? And had she told him that she would be faithful and true? She hoped she had, but she couldn't be certain. For all she knew, she had promised to clean his stables for the rest of her days.

Bewildered, she looked at the priest. He didn't have an appalled look on his face, which she took as a good sign.

Now and forever, until death do they part.

The prayers were finished, and the blessing was given. She was as stiff as a board as Colm gathered her into his arms, but once he lowered his head and kissed her, she came alive again. His warmth stopped her trembling, and the tenderness in his kiss melted her fears.

"You are now man and wife." Father Gelroy was beaming his approval as he made the announcement.

Congratulations weren't shouted but given in hushed voices. The guards each made a low bow to their princess and her new husband and then, at Gabrielle's insistence, went down to the courtyard to join the clan's celebration. Colm allowed Liam to kiss Gabrielle's hand, but that was all he would permit, and Brodick snatched her away from Colm long enough to hug her.

"We must toast this marriage," Liam said.

"What a lovely suggestion," she blurted out. "Another time perhaps?"

She grabbed the priest's arm and pulled him toward the stairs as she gave him instructions on what he should say to the envoy. "You will please tell the envoy that yes, you did marry us, but you won't—"

Colm stopped her. Throwing his arm around her and anchoring her to his side, he said, "I will take care of this matter. There is no need to rush."

She didn't agree. She had told the envoy that she would bring him proof of her marriage. Surely he would be suspicious if she made him wait long.

She bowed her head. "As you say."

Liam burst into laughter, and when Brodick asked what was so amusing, Liam was happy to explain.

"To Gabrielle, 'as you say' means that she doesn't agree and will do the complete opposite. She thinks to placate Colm with those words, but we have all caught on to her real meaning."

Brodick nodded. " 'Yes' means 'no,' and 'no' means 'yes'?" He pounded Colm on the shoulder. "At least she tried to placate you. My wife doesn't pay *any* attention to what I say."

Brodick didn't seem to be bothered by his wife's willfulness. In fact, he looked pleased by it.

"Laird MacHugh, do you want me to go outside and have a word with the envoy?" Gelroy asked.

"You will stay here," Colm ordered.

"But when I do face him, will you tell me what I am to say?"

"You will tell the truth," Colm said, "but you won't mention when the ceremony took place."

The laird's frown still had the power to make Gelroy shake in his boots. He tried not to let it show as he waited for his next instruction.

Liam insisted upon a toast. He ran to the buttery and returned with a jug of wine. Pouring each of them a full goblet, he wished the couple a long and happy life.

"And as you say, Gabrielle, to a perfect marriage," he teased.

Gabrielle was puzzled. A perfect marriage? Had she said something about their marriage being perfect?

"Colm, did I promise that when I spoke my vows?" she asked. "If I did, I am very sorry. Our marriage will not be perfect, and I cannot promise there will be no trouble. Look at the deception I have caused on this our wedding day. I didn't lie to the envoy, but I did mislead him. And I corrupted your clan as well, for I made them complicit in my deception. Do you not wonder what I will do tomorrow?"

Had she expected Colm to be sympathetic to her distress, she was mistaken. He thought her guilt amusing.

"Deceit? Trouble? You have already become a MacHugh," he laughed.

He kissed her again and then grew serious. "You will tell me now what wedding gifts you want from me. On this your wedding day, I will refuse you nothing."

She didn't have to think about it long. "I would like you to build Father Gelroy his chapel and pledge to have it finished by this time next year. He will need it to have a fine altar and sturdy benches."

Gelroy was overwhelmed by her thoughtfulness and generosity. Colm didn't seem at all surprised. "It will be done. What else would you like?"

Again there was no hesitation. "Tradition is important to me," she said. "And so I would like you to give me the same gift my father gave my mother."

He waited for her to tell him what it was, but she didn't say another word.

"When am I to know what this gift is?" he urged.

"Eventually."

The envoy was waiting with the bishop for Gabrielle to return. His face whitened when he saw Colm striding toward him.

"Lady MacHugh has told me you require proof that she is my wife. She did tell you we were married, did she not?"

"Yes, Laird . . . that is, Laird, another did suggest the possibility that perhaps—"

"Do you know how fortunate you are to still be standing? You should be dead, for you have insinuated that my wife lied to you. Is that so?"

"No, no, I didn't think so. Another did perhaps think that—"

"My wife does not lie." His voice had turned deadly.

"Yes, Laird. She speaks only the truth."

Gabrielle moved closer to Colm. She stared at the envoy and no one else. She didn't know if Joan was still in the crowd watching, but she hoped she had left and wouldn't cause any more trouble.

Father Gelroy stepped forward. "I know for a fact that Laird MacHugh and Lady MacHugh are married. I am the priest who administered the holy sacrament. I heard them speak their vows to each other, and I blessed their union." With a dramatic gesture to the sky, he said, "May a bolt of lightning strike me down this very second if I am lying."

He raised his eyes to heaven and waited, then nodding said, "God knows I am telling the truth, and so should you."

The bishop wanted to get back to the abbey before nightfall so he could sleep in his own bed instead of the hard ground. "I will testify that Father Gelroy speaks the truth. This issue should now be settled to everyone's satisfaction."

The envoy was convinced. "I am satisfied. Because of this marriage, you now have Finney's Flat, Laird MacHugh."

"Our laird also has the treasure of St. Biel," Gelroy said, smiling with relief at Gabrielle. The priest did not think he needed to explain his meaning. Everyone who looked at Gabrielle could see what a treasure she was.

Gabrielle blushed at the priest's compliment. "I think not, Father. My husband will have to be content with the land, for he will not get a treasure."

"As soon as possible," said the envoy, "I will have heralds sent to each clan to announce that Princess Gabrielle has been proven innocent of the accusations made against her, that your marriage is valid, and that Finney's Flat is now yours."

"You have the power to proclaim this?" Gelroy asked.

"I do."

A few minutes later the envoy and the bishop took their leave, and Gabrielle was never so happy to see anyone go. Now she could relax. Or so she thought.

One worry left, and another arrived. This was her wedding night.

The MacHugh clan was slow to disperse. They had much to celebrate. Their laird had returned victorious over their enemies, the MacKennas; their holdings now included Finney's Flat; and their beloved laird had taken a wife. As Father Gelroy reminded them, they were truly blessed. With dusk approaching, the festivities began to die down. The tables and benches were returned to the castle, and the people made their way to their cottages weary, but happy.

Liam and Colm walked with Brodick to the stables, as it was time that Brodick headed home as well.

"You are not through with the MacKennas," Brodick warned. "For every one you have killed, another will step forward. They multiply like rats. They'll soon have a new laird, and I wager he will be as much a bastard as Owen was. I hope he did not die well."

"No, he did not," Colm said quietly.

"You are our ally, Brodick," Liam reminded him. "They will come after you, too."

"I look forward to it," he said.

The stable boy lead Brodick's horse to him. "Your debt is paid," he told Colm, "but now I think you owe another one."

"What would that debt be?"

"I gave you Gabrielle."

"You forced her on me," Colm said drily. "And I am grateful."

"There is an easy way to repay me."

"What might that be?"

"Give one of your daughters to one of my sons in marriage."

"The church will not allow it," Liam said. "You are related to Gabrielle."

"Only by marriage. My wife's uncle is not a blood relative. The arranged union would be valid, and your daughter would come to my son with a fat dowry."

Colm laughed. "Let me guess. Finney's Flat."

"Aye, Finney's Flat."

"Your plan is contingent upon my wife giving me daughters and your wife giving you sons."

"It will come to pass," Brodick said. "Though I will be ahead of you, for my Gillian is already with child, and you can't bed Gabrielle for what? Five months?"

"I had thought to wait that long, but—"

"Thought to? What of her reputation?"

"Word will spread of her innocence, and if the Englishman was telling the truth, a proclamation will be made."

"And you think that will happen quickly?" Brodick asked. "Colm, you did give her six months."

Resignedly, Colm answered, "If that is what Gabrielle wants, I will acquiesce."

Brodick and Liam laughed.

"You think you can last that long? She is nearly as pretty as my wife," Brodick said.

"Of course I can wait. I have more discipline than either of you."

Colm headed back to the castle. Liam and Brodick watched him walk away.

"What do you think?" Brodick asked.

"My brother is strong-willed and disciplined. I'd give him at least one night before he changes his mind."

"I'd give him one hour."

FORTY-SIX

THE WAIT WAS AGONIZING. IT SEEMED TO Gabrielle that half the night had already passed since she had bathed and washed her hair. The tub had been removed from her room, the covers on her bed had been turned back, and two more logs had been added to the fire.

Every minute felt like an hour, but her hair was still dripping wet so she knew it couldn't have been all that long since she had washed it. Still, it seemed an eternity.

Gabrielle wore her white sleeping gown— a fine gossamer fabric adorned with gold and silver threads sewn into the neckline. She had wanted to wear her blue gown, but there were too many wrinkles in it from the packing. She smoothed a crease from the gown and sat in front of the hearth to brush her hair by the fire. The room was warm and cozy, and after such a long and frantic day, she should have been exhausted. But she wasn't. She was wide awake and in a near panic.

Where was he?

He had said he couldn't wait to have her. True, the wedding had happened sooner than he had expected, but they were married now. He hadn't changed his mind, had he?

Every sound made her stomach flutter in anticipation and fear. As she continued brushing her hair, she tried to think about less worrisome things. The weather had been nice today, and the meat pie she ate for dinner was quite flavorful.

What was taking him so long? Were the demands of the clan so much more important than her, even now on this, their wedding night?

Oh, how she wanted to get this over and done with. She had been told enough about the physical act between a man and a woman to be both curious and frightened.

She decided to compare it to her dislo-
cated finger. When she was nine years old,
Gabrielle had fallen from a stone wall she'd
been climbing. Her little finger made an odd
popping sound and was bent in a bizarre
direction. It hurt like it had been stung by a
nest of hornets, but her father had known
just what to do. While Stephen held her still,
her father popped the finger back into
place, and the hurt immediately went away.
She had known what was going to happen
and had dreaded it, but once it was finished, she didn't have to worry about it any
longer.

As far as she was concerned, the marriage act was much like that: dread, pain,
forgotten.

When her arm began to ache, she put her
brush down. The curl was back in her hair,
and the long strands were just a little damp
now. She stared at the floor and tried to concentrate on something pleasant. Some of
the water from her bath had spilled over the
tub. She had helped mop it up, but there
were still damp spots on the floor. She
stared at them as they slowly faded away.

Had Colm forgotten her?

Think only pleasant thoughts, she

reminded herself. There was absolutely no need to get worked up.

Colm had been pleased with her gift of salt, and surprised. Gabrielle suddenly realized she had forgotten to tell him that more would be coming, and by next year he would have more than enough to last his clan a good long time. He'd have extra, too, that could be bartered for seed or anything else the clan needed.

Was she so unimportant to him?

Gabrielle felt herself becoming emotional. Maybe Colm was only being kind when he'd told her he wanted her. And she had just thrown herself at him. But no, he wouldn't have done that, she decided. Colm was blunt and brutally honest. He wouldn't lie just to be kind. He didn't take much time to think about a woman's feelings. She doubted he'd ever given them a thought.

Tears came into her eyes, and she knew that if she didn't do something about them, she would soon break down. Gabrielle rarely cried, but when she did, it took a long time for her to stop. She would drag out every last pain and heartache she had ever endured and weep over each one. Since leaving Wellingshire, her list of heartaches had grown considerably, and she estimated she would have to cry for a good week to get through them all.

Concentrating on pleasant matters wasn't working. She needed to get angry.

How dare Colm treat her this way. She sighed then because it wasn't working. The man had given her his name and his protection, and he had asked for nothing in return. No, she couldn't summon up much anger at all. Granted, it was rude of him to make her wait, but not cruel.

She moved on to the king's envoy. He had put her through Purgatory with his scroll and his suspicion. Still, he was only doing King John's bidding, and, in truth, he was an affable fellow. She couldn't blame the messenger or despise him for repeating the words he had been given.

Joan. What a shrew that woman was! She had such a contemptuous look on her face when she had challenged Gabrielle. Did she think that all she had to do was announce that she was going to marry Colm, and it would come to pass? Had she expected Gabrielle to wilt in front of her? Or cower? How dare she! Aye, she was a shrew and a hateful troublemaker as well.

There weren't any tears in Gabrielle's eyes now. If Joan were to walk into her room this minute, Gabrielle just might pick up her brush and pummel her with it. Picturing this made Gabrielle smile.

There. She was feeling ever so much better.

Footsteps sounded in the hall.

Colm. Oh God, he was finally coming to her.

She jumped up, then sat down, and jumped up again. Should she stand by the fire, or should she sit on the side of the bed? Did he expect her to be under the covers?

She decided to wait by the hearth. She also decided that it was important for her to remember to breathe. She was getting dizzy holding her breath.

Dread . . . pain . . . forgotten.

Colm knocked on the door, waited a second, then opened it and walked inside. He went completely still when he saw her.

She was a vision. The soft light from the embers behind her had turned her gown translucent. He could see the perfect shape of her body. Every curve was cast in a golden hue: her full breasts, her narrow waist, her shapely hips, her long legs. She was perfection, and more enticing to him than if she had been standing there wearing nothing at all.

He wasn't going to be leaving her this night or any other.

Gabrielle's hands were at her sides, and she stared into his eyes.

She knew this man.

Why was she so afraid? He would never hurt her. Dread drifted away. Aye, she knew him well.

A width of Colm's plaid was thrown over his bare chest. In this light and in this small chamber he seemed so much taller and more muscular. She noticed everything about him. His hair was wet, and there were still drops of water on his chest indicating he had gone to the lake to wash, as did many of the other clansmen. The color of his eyes . . . the firm line of his jaw . . . his wide shoulders . . .

She wanted this man.

She stepped toward him. "Know you how handsome you are?" she whispered softly.

His reply was raspy. "I do not think about such things. When you know me better . . ."

She took another step toward him, eyes locked on his. He couldn't remember what he was saying. She brought the light scent of flowers with her as she moved closer, and all he could think of was touching her. She aroused him as no other woman could.

"I know you, Colm."

With her fingertips she traced the scar that began at the tip of his shoulder and followed it down his arm. "Your body tells your history."

He did not move as she slowly circled him, touching, caressing. "You are a warrior," she whispered as her fingers brushed across his shoulders. His muscles flexed and his skin felt warm to her touch. "You are a protector."

She gently stroked the side of his neck, and when she was again standing in front of him and just a breath away, she whispered again, "I know you."

Colm's eyes did not leave hers as he slowly removed her gown. Her cheeks became flushed, but she didn't shy away from him or shield her body. He pulled her into his arms and kissed her fiercely. Her body was so wonderfully soft, her skin silky and warm. His lips gently brushed across hers and then he wanted more. He made love to her with his kisses until passion engulfed him.

He carried her to the bed. She wasn't given time to pull the covers over herself. He quickly removed his plaid and covered her with his body. She gasped when his bare skin pressed intimately against hers.

Colm wanted to know every inch of her. He lingered over her mouth, then kissed the side of her neck, inhaled the sweet scent. He felt her heart beating under his, and when he kissed the base of her neck, she trembled. He lowered his head to caress her breasts and kiss the valley between. His hands slid down her back, the curve of her spine.

Gabrielle loved the feel of him against her. She wrapped her arms around his neck as their kisses grew more demanding.

With each touch, Colm's need increased. His fingers slipped between her thighs. He felt her tense in reaction, but he would not be denied. She began to move restlessly against him.

The way he was stroking her was driving Gabrielle wild. He made her want more. He wouldn't let her deny him as he moved lower and lower to kiss every part of her. The sweet torment soon became unbearable. Her nails raked his shoulders as she demanded release.

Her wild response made Colm burn to have her, and his own restraint vanished. He roughly pushed her legs apart and, kneeling between her thighs, he thrust inside her.

She cried out in pain and arched against him, but he soothed her with sweet words and touches. The pain was soon forgotten, and as he moved inside her, slowly at first, her hips pushed against his, and she moaned with pleasure. His thrusts became more powerful, less controlled. And suddenly she felt a rush of ecstasy. She screamed his name as she climaxed, and she squeezed him tight as he found his own release and poured his seed into her.

For long moments neither of them moved, their harsh breathing the only sound. Gabrielle thought her heart would explode. Loving Colm was the most terrifyingly wonderful experience she had ever had.

She knew she had pleased him. Though he didn't give her the words, his touch was enough. When at last he found the strength, he rolled to his side and gathered her into his arms. He kissed the top of her head and lay back. She rested her cheek on his shoulder and put her hand over his heart.

She loved this man.

FORTY-SEVEN

GABRIELLE HAD NOT KNOWN SUCH EXQUISITE pleasure was possible.

Content to stay in his arms, her hand still rested on his chest over his heart as she stared across the room at the dying embers. She thought he was asleep and tried to pull the covers up, but Colm tightened his hold on her. She snuggled closer, sighed, and closed her eyes.

"Colm?"

He yawned. "Yes?"

"Why did you hit Liam? Do you remember hitting him?"

"I remember. He couldn't walk any farther,

and he would have felt disgraced if he were carried."

"Knocking your poor brother senseless was an act of kindness then."

"You could think so."

Her mind floated from one thought to another. She was quiet for several minutes and then asked, "Did you love Joan when you were betrothed to her?"

"No."

He obviously didn't feel any further explanation was necessary.

Another minute passed and then she whispered, "More salt is coming. I forgot to tell you, but you will have enough to fill your storeroom when the last trunks are brought."

"It is a good gift," he said. "Salt has more value than gold here."

She jumped to another question almost immediately. "Those two men who were caught sneaking into the abbey to kill Liam ... were they also sent by MacKenna?"

"Yes. Evidently they were new recruits. MacKenna appears to have hired every degenerate character he came across."

"I am not sorry my guards killed them."

He smiled in the darkness. She sounded

fierce. "Go to sleep, Gabrielle. You need your rest."

"Will you tell me what happened to the men who beat Liam?"

"No."

"Just one last question, if you please. My mother's statue of St. Biel will be moved from the courtyard at Wellingshire and brought here. It's a tradition. Will you mind? It's quite large."

"I will not mind unless you plan to put a statue in our bed. Now sleep."

"Shouldn't I kiss you good night?" she teased.

"Do you realize how you tempt me? You are tender now. You should sleep."

Even as he was telling her what she should do, he was rolling her onto her back and kissing the side of her neck. He was not gentle with her this second time. Already discovering what she liked, his lovemaking was less restrained. She wrapped her legs around him as he drove deep inside her. He groaned, and when he began to move his hips, she cried out in blissful rapture. She found fulfillment first and his release followed. It was even better this second time.

Exhausted and sated, she closed her eyes. Colm lifted up on his elbows and looked down at her. "Now you will sleep," he commanded. He rolled onto his side and pulled her up against him so that her back was pressed against his chest.

She was of a mind to obey.

FORTY-EIGHT

EVER SINCE THE REVELATIONS AT NEWELL CASTLE, Coswold's life had been miserable.

The baron was sick and tired of pretending humility with the king, but he knew he was on shaky ground. John was still furious that Coswold and the others had believed Isla, that lying bitch. When Coswold dared to point out that it was Percy who had duped Isla into telling the lies about Lady Gabrielle, the king reminded him that Isla was Coswold's own niece, and he was therefore responsible for her actions. Besides, John had already taken his displeasure out on Percy. The scoundrel had been stripped of his title and his small estate and was sent to a dungeon where he could ponder his transgressions. And just to make sure that Isla learned her lesson as well, the king thought it appropriate that she accompany Percy. Perhaps the two of them would think better of conspiring against the king's wishes if they were forced to spend all their time together.

Coswold knew it was imperative to get John to forgive him. The king had a terrible temper and would assuredly blame Coswold for any trouble that might follow. He did everything in his power to please the king. Coswold followed John wherever he went and was at his beck and call day and night. He would have rolled over like a dog if he'd been told to. As a result of these exhausting efforts, John was softening his attitude. He liked having a confidant he could regale with stories about the barons' wives he had slept with.

As humiliating as it was to grovel, Coswold's newfound closeness to the king certainly had its benefits. He was present when a messenger arrived to give the king the good news. The rumor had been verified: Lady Gabrielle had been found. She had been taken in by the MacHugh clan and was living among the Highlanders in their mountain stronghold. John was elated. Now he could set about making amends with the lady and perhaps head off some of the animosity from Baron Geoffrey and the other barons.

Before John dispatched his envoy to the MacHugh holding to make his announcement to Gabrielle, he called the man to him to give specific instructions. Coswold stood by and listened. The king informed Coswold that he had chosen this particular herald because he had a flawless memory and could repeat any message to the exact word. After expressing his admiration for the king's good judgment, Coswold reminded him that he had just returned from that part of the Highlands. Perhaps he could offer some advice.

"The way to the MacHugh clan is dangerous. The Highlanders are sometimes hostile to outsiders," Coswold said. "May I suggest that your herald stop at Arbane Abbey and get an escort to accompany him the rest of the way? The monks will be accommodating if there is a reward."

He saw that the king was angered at this suggestion and Coswold hastily added, "And I, to show my goodwill, shall be happy to supply whatever you feel is needed."

"You will supply me with double your tax, Coswold, and then I will be appeased," the king said. "Give the monks whatever you want. I don't care about them, but I do want my herald to have safe passage."

Coswold filled a cart with a dozen casks of the finest wine he could buy and sent it to the abbey ahead of the envoy. He then requested that the king allow him to return to his home to get an accounting of the crop that had just been harvested. The king gave his approval.

As quickly as possible, Coswold gathered his men and headed to Arbane Abbey. Having selected only well-trained soldiers to accompany him, he was surrounded by a small but capable army. He wasn't about to take any chances. Men frequently disappeared in the wilds of the Highlands and were never seen again. Coswold was still waiting to hear from the men he had sent to verify Gabrielle's whereabouts. He had suspicions that they had stolen the trunks for themselves and hadn't gone to the MacHugh holding at all.

THE MONKS of Arbane Abbey had just settled in for their evening prayers when a loud pounding noise at the front gate interrupted them. The abbot hurriedly genuflected in the chapel and rushed across the courtyard to the gate, irritated by the inconvenience.

It was too soon for the monks who had traveled to the MacHugh holding to be returning. Their journey home would take longer than usual because of the bishop. He had been visiting the abbey when the envoy from England arrived, and hearing about the message that was being delivered to Lady Gabrielle, the bishop had insisted on accompanying the group, explaining that he seldom had the opportunity to be present when good news arrived from the English king. The monks were to take an alternate route home to deposit the bishop at his residence, which added an additional two hours to their journey. It was impossible for them to have traveled so swiftly that they would have arrived already.

The abbot slid the bolt back and opened

the gate a crack. Seeing who it was, he swung the gate wide. "What brings you back to Arbane Abbey?" he asked in surprise.

Baron Coswold walked past the abbot and entered the courtyard, followed by one of his subordinates, Cyril. He turned to him and gave orders that his troops were to make camp outside the monastery walls. Only then did Coswold address the perplexed abbot. "I come on behalf of King John," he announced.

"For what purpose?" the abbot asked.

Coswold had his explanation ready. "The king has sent one of his heralds as an envoy to deliver a message to the MacHugh holding. I have received word from travelers that there is great turmoil in the Highlands," he lied, "and fearing for the envoy's life, and knowing how important his mission is to the king, I have taken it upon myself to gather my army to assure the king's envoy safe passage."

Coswold did not realize the truth of his statement about turmoil, for he had yet to hear of MacKenna's demise.

The abbot showed the baron into the hall. "I am certain the envoy will return safely, Baron, but you are welcome to wait here and see for yourself. I will have the cook bring you food and drink. If there is anything else I can do to make you comfortable, I am your humble servant."

The abbot hurried off to make arrangements for the unexpected guest.

When the travel-weary group returned to the abbey after nightfall, Coswold was waiting to greet them.

The envoy was surprised to see the baron. "Did the king send you here with further instructions for me?" he asked.

"No," Coswold answered. He pulled a chair from the table and offered it to the envoy. "The king relies on you and knows as I do how important your duties are. Your safety is important to him . . . and since there is nothing I care about more than the king's contentment, I felt it my obligation to see to your well-being."

With an ingratiating smile, he pointed to the chair. "Sit with me and we will drink some wine and eat some cheese, and you can tell me all about your adventure. Are the MacHughs as savage and ill-tempered as I have heard? And what of Lady Gabrielle? Is she as beautiful as I remember?"

The envoy was flattered by the baron's

attention and eager to share his experience. After a second goblet of wine, he was completely relaxed and the words flowed freely.

"Do you want me to tell you word for word what each said?"

"No, no, not at all," Coswold said. "Save your report for the king. I'm only interested to know what those people are like."

"I will not be giving the king each word I heard. He only wants to know if Lady Gabrielle accepted his forgiveness and his offer of Finney's Flat."

He took a gulp of wine while Coswold waited impatiently.

"Now to answer your question, it is true. Lady MacHugh is a beauty," he said. "She seems content as well. Her new clan was happy to hear that Finney's Flat now belongs to their laird. They are—"

Coswold interrupted. "Lady MacHugh? You mean to say Lady Gabrielle?"

"She is Lady MacHugh now, for she is married to Laird MacHugh. I must tell you, I was quaking in my boots when he turned his gaze on me. He is a fierce warrior."

The envoy accepted more wine and continued to talk about his impressions of the

MacHugh laird. He didn't notice Coswold's distress.

While he chatted amicably about the wedded couple, Coswold stared straight ahead, gripping his goblet so tightly the rim began to bend from the pressure. His throat burned with the bile rising from his stomach. It took all his control not to scream his fury. Too late. It was too late. Gabrielle had once again eluded his grasp. Was the treasure lost to him as well?

Whenever the envoy paused, Coswold nodded encouragement and refilled his goblet. After so much wine, the envoy's words began to slur, and his eyelids grew heavy. "I am sleepy," he said and started to rise.

Coswold hurriedly offered him more cheese and bread. "You will sleep better on a full stomach," he said, smiling broadly when the envoy reached for the food.

"What other news did you hear?" Coswold asked. "The MacHughs are such a curious group of people. I find them fascinating," he added so that the envoy would not discern a deeper motive. By morning, he doubted the drunken man would remember anything he'd said.

"While I was waiting for Lady MacHugh to

come back outside, I ate a variety of inter-esting foods. There was a sweetbread I much enjoyed . . ."

Coswold let him ramble, hoping he would hear something of interest.

"They were celebrating," the envoy said, yawning. A piece of cheese was stuck between his teeth, and Coswold looked away. The drunkard's behavior was becom-ing more and more disgusting.

"Celebrating what?" he asked, unable to keep the irritation out of his voice.

"Finney's . . ." He seemed to have lost his train of thought.

"They were celebrating the news that Finney's Flat is now theirs?" Coswold prod-ded.

"Yes, yes. It belongs to them."

"Was there mention of anything else their laird would receive?"

The envoy blinked several times, trying to focus. "What?"

"Gold," Coswold muttered. "Was there mention of gold?"

The envoy scratched his chin. "No, no gold."

Despair was drowning Coswold, and he

slumped into the chair and buried his face in his hand. "Lost," he whispered.

He thought the envoy had fallen asleep, but he was mistaken.

"Treasure."

"What say you?" Coswold asked sharply.

"St. Biel. There is treasure."

"They know about the treasure?" he demanded. He shook the envoy to get him alert enough to continue.

"The priest . . . he said they will get the treasure . . ." he mumbled.

Coswold leaned closer to the man so that he could hear each word. "Did anyone say where this treasure is?"

"No . . . Lady MacHugh . . . Lady MacHugh said . . ."

Coswold grabbed the man's shoulders. "What did Lady MacHugh say about the treasure?"

The man's head rolled to the side. "She said the laird gets the land . . . but he will not have the treasure."

Coswold dropped the man's shoulders and stood back. Perhaps it was not too late after all.

FORTY-NINE

COLM WAS A POSSESSIVE MAN. HE KEPT A WATCH-ful eye on Gabrielle and found that he didn't like any man standing too close to her or staring overly long.

In the days since their marriage, he hadn't relaxed his guard. One evening after supper, Liam and Colm were alone in the great hall. While Willa and Maurna cleared the table, Liam decided to bring up his brother's intense watchfulness.

"Come and stand by the fire, Colm, so that I may speak to you in private."

Liam knelt on one knee and tossed a fat

log into the fire, then pulled a chair closer to the heat and sat down.

Colm leaned against the hearth and waited to hear what his brother had to say.

"Do you have reason to distrust Gabrielle?" Liam asked.

The question offended Colm, but he knew Liam wasn't trying to insult him or Gabrielle. "Of course not," he muttered.

Liam nodded. "You are right to trust her. She would never be untrue to you. I see where her heart belongs."

"And where might that be?"

His brother laughed. "You cannot be that blind. You know she loves you."

Colm didn't acknowledge Liam's words. Love was for women to talk about, not warriors.

"Why did you ask me if I distrusted her when you already held the answer?"

"Because of the way you act. You behave like a jealous man."

"I am not jealous. I guard what is mine. Gabrielle deserves as much protection as any other member of my clan."

"She is your wife, Colm."

"And I will guard her well."

Gabrielle caught their attention when she appeared on the stairs. She stepped to the side and waited while two of Colm's men carried up her trunk.

"Gabrielle, why are you taking salt to your room?"

As the men passed her she told them, "Put it across the hearth in my chamber, please."

"I'll show them where it should go," Maurna called out as she hurried to help. "But milady, why is it you want a trunk of salt in your room?"

"It isn't salt," she explained to Maurna. And then to Colm and Liam she said, "If you'll remember, Colm, I told you that all but one of the trunks were filled with salt. It took forever to find the right trunk, and as luck would have it, it was on the bottom of the stack."

"You will wear the MacHugh colors. You have no need of English clothes," he answered.

"I may not need them, but I'm still going to keep them. There are other things in the trunk as well, reminders and memories of Wellingshire and St. Biel."

"Good God, Gabrielle, you've got enough

reminders of St. Biel," Liam said. "Colm, did you see the size of the statue the abbot sent? It's in the storage room until you build Gelroy a chapel. Then it will go inside the church."

"No, Liam," Gabrielle said. "It doesn't go inside. It stays outside by the door so that all will see it as they go in. It is tradition."

"None of the statues in St. Biel are inside churches?"

"Of course not. We pray to God, not to statues."

Liam had stood when she entered the room, but once she was seated, he returned to his chair.

"Is it true that another statue is coming from your father?"

"Yes. It belonged to my mother, and now that I am married it will come to me. It's tradition."

"Any others on their way here?" Colm drawled.

"Just a dozen or so," she teased.

She was laughing at their reaction when her guards requested to speak to her. She took one look at her faithful guards' serious faces and knew immediately what they were going to tell her: they were going home.

Gabrielle took a deep breath and desperately tried to hold back the tears. It would be
wrong for her to cry. She glanced at Colm
and could tell from his expression that the
guards had already spoken to him. She
slowly walked over to them and folded her
hands as though in prayer.

"You're going home."

She looked at Stephen as she made the
statement.

"It is time, Princess. We are now convinced that your laird will keep you safe."

She took his hand in hers and said, "You
have been my truest friend, Stephen. I do
not know how I will ever go on without you."

He bowed to her and stepped back.
Gabrielle clasped Lucien's hand next. "We
have had many misadventures together,
have we not? I think you will be happy to be
rid of me."

"Nay, I will not, Princess. I will miss you,
but I will always carry you in my heart."

Faust was next in line. She took his hand
and said, "Can you believe it, Faust? You will
soon see St. Biel's mountains."

"I shall miss you, Princess."

Christien was last. She touched his hand
and said, "You have saved me from death

too many times to count. I owe you my life, Christien, and I will miss you."

"You will not have to miss me long, Princess. I will be back. I will know when it is time."

They bowed low and took their leave. A single tear trickled down her cheek. Without a word, Gabrielle left the hall and went up to her room.

Colm knew she needed to be alone. He waited as long as he could, and then he went to her chamber. She was curled up on the bed, weeping. He gathered her in his arms and comforted her the only way he knew. He let her cry.

FIFTY

FATHER GELROY HELPED HER DEAL WITH HER loss by making her feel guilty.

"Of course you miss your guards. They've been like older brothers to you all these years, but you've got to think about them finding their own path. St. Biel is their home, and you should have joy in your heart that they can now return to their lives there."

Gabrielle knew the holy man was right, but it was still difficult for her to find joy when she missed them so much. Fortunately, she was kept busy and had little time to mope.

The clan made it easy for her to settle into their way of life. Gabrielle had won them over when they heard that she had killed a man to keep Liam safe. She earned their love and respect when she married their laird and gave him Finney's Flat. Standing up to Lady Joan and putting her in her place showed them that she had a temper, which they considered a fine trait.

Everyone took turns instructing her. Maurna and Willa helped her learn how to be mistress in her home. It was up to Gabrielle to decide the menu for each meal, when the rushes needed to be changed and the bedding aired out, and a thousand other things that made the castle run smoothly.

Neither the housekeeper nor the cook ever said "no" to her or came right out and told her she was wrong about anything. They had a more subtle way to let her know when they felt she'd made a mistake.

"We shall have meat pies for dinner tonight," Gabrielle told Willa.

The cook shook her head ever so slightly. Gabrielle tried again. "We will have chicken?"

Another quick shake of the head followed that order. Gabrielle sighed. "Mutton then."

A nod of approval. "Yes, Lady MacHugh. Mutton it will be."

The stonecutter and the candlemaker instructed her in the goings on with the various clans. They felt it was imperative that their mistress understand all the feuds.

Gabrielle wasn't even sure where all the clans lived.

"Why is it important for me to know about the feuds?" she asked.

The candlemaker looked astonished that she would ask such a question. He answered with one of his own. "If you don't know who's fighting, how will you know who to speak to and who to curse?"

She didn't have a ready answer for him.

That evening as she prepared for bed, she asked Colm about the clans. "There are so many of them in the Highlands, I cannot keep them straight."

"Tomorrow I will draw you a map and show you where each clan lives."

"Will you draw this map before or after you take me to the Buchanans?"

She stepped out of the light while she removed her undergarments and put on her nightgown. Her shyness amused Colm. He was already in bed. He lay on his side and, leaning on his elbow, propped his head up and lazily watched her.

Gabrielle moved back to the fire to warm herself while she brushed the tangles from her hair.

"Why do you put that gown on?" Colm asked. "I'm only going to take it off as soon as you come to bed."

She put the brush down and turned to him. "I must pay a visit to the Buchanans. Will you take me tomorrow?"

"No."

"Lady Gillian is my dearest cousin."

"You've never even met the woman."

"She is still dear to me."

"I have duties tomorrow. I cannot."

"Could someone else take me to the Buchanans?"

"No."

"The day after tomorrow?"

"No. Come to bed."

She stared at him a long minute. "No."

He didn't seem fazed by her refusal. She was disappointed, for she hoped to make him angry. She would have stormed out of the room, but she didn't have anywhere to go. Besides, she couldn't storm anywhere unless she got dressed. Gabrielle decided there was too much effort required just to irritate him.

t only took a few more seconds for her to admit to herself that she was going to have to get into bed or she would freeze to death. She crossed the room to the side of the bed.

"Just so you understand. I'm not coming to you. I'm coming to bed."

She started to climb over him to her side of the bed, but with one movement he pulled her gown over her head and she landed hard on his chest. He pushed her legs down, trapping them with his, and then rolled over so that she was pinned beneath him.

He nibbled her neck as he said, "Just so *you* understand. I'm going to make love to you."

He had the last word.

GABRIELLE WAS WALKING to the lake with Braeden's wife, Lily, who was large with their first child. She wasn't so much timid as shy, and she spoke in a voice barely above a whisper. She was a sweet-tempered woman, and Gabrielle enjoyed her companionship.

"Is this the lake the men swim in?" Gabrielle asked.

"On the far side where we can't see them. They wouldn't mind," Lily said, "but they know we would."

"Isn't it a beautiful day? The air is so crisp." Gabrielle stretched her arms out and let the sun warm her face.

"Wait until you see the lake. It's clear water," Lily said. "Freezing to the touch, though. Even in the summer months the water never warms. Just dangling your feet in it will cause your teeth to chatter. I do not know how the men stand it."

"Thank you for warning me. I will be certain never to test it."

Gabrielle sat under a tree enjoying this peaceful time of day. The noon meal was finished, but there were still a few hours before supper.

Lily talked about the preparations she was making for the baby, and Gabrielle was about to ask her a question when Ethan and Tom came charging through the trees. Tom was chasing Ethan.

"They should not be here alone," Lily said.

Gabrielle agreed. She called to the boys. Ethan was trying to outrun Tom, but he couldn't change direction in time. She watched him trip over his own feet and propel himself into the water.

Lily shouted for help as Gabrielle kicked off her shoes and ran in after the child. The er was so cold she feared her heart uld stop. With Tom on the bank wailing, she fished Ethan to the surface and carried him to dry land sputtering and coughing.

"It's cold," he told Tom when he could get his breath.

"Lady Gabrielle, could I try—" Tom began.

She knew where he was heading. "No, you may not try the water. Both of you, come with me."

Lily wrapped her shawl around Ethan. "You'll be sneezing tonight," she predicted.

Gabrielle's teeth chattered. "Snow isn't as cold as that water," she said.

Lily nodded. "The boys' aunt lives just two cottages away from mine. I will see them home. You should go change your clothes before you start sneezing."

Fortunately, neither Colm nor Liam were inside the castle, and she was able to get to her room without being noticed. Unfortunately, little Ethan and Tom told everyone they saw about Lady MacHugh jumping into the water. By the time Gabrielle had changed her clothes and warmed herself by the fire, the entire clan knew she'd gone swimming in the lake.

Willa and Maurna pounded on her door. "Are you wanting more blankets, milady?"

"I'm fine," she assured them. "But I do want directions to the twins' home. I would like to talk to their aunt."

Willa showed her the way. When the door was answered, Gabrielle understood why the boys were allowed to run wild. The aunt was quite elderly and looked in need of a yearlong nap.

Gabrielle was invited inside. Ethan was looking no worse for wear. Both he and Tom sat at the table eating what appeared to be the same vile paste Willa was always trying to get Gabrielle to eat. The boys seemed to like it, though.

"They'll be staying inside until tomorrow," the aunt promised. "Ethan, remember your manners. Thank Lady MacHugh for saving you from death. Apologize to her for her trouble."

The apology was given and accepted. The aunt ushered Gabrielle outside and closed the door so the boys wouldn't hear.

"I'm sorry, milady. Ethan and Tom are good boys. I've had them since their parents died. It hasn't been easy. I've tried my best,

everyone in the clan has helped out, but
y need more than I can give them."

Gabrielle took the old woman's hand in
hers. "I'll speak to the laird," she promised.
"I'm sure he'll think of something."

On her return to the castle, Gabrielle felt
pangs of guilt. After her complaints to Colm
about taking on too much responsibility and
never delegating, here she was giving him
yet another problem to solve.

She was waiting at the table when Colm
and Liam walked into the great hall. From
Colm's frown and Liam's grin, she assumed
they had already heard about the incident at
the lake.

"Did you enjoy your swim?" Liam asked.

She wasn't in the mood for merriment.
Glaring at Colm, she said, "Did you forget to
ban them from the lake?"

"I thought I had," he said. "Are you all right?"

His concern calmed her down. "That boy
nearly drowned. Something has to be done."
She went to him and kissed his cheek. "You
will take them in hand? They will not live to
be six if you don't."

Willa carried supper to the table. Gabrielle
had already eaten, but she sat by Colm
while he and Liam ate.

"Do you know that after I fished Ethan out, Tom wanted to take a turn?"

Liam choked on the drink of water he had just taken. Gabrielle waited until he stopped coughing and then asked him how old he thought the aunt was.

"I don't mean to be unkind, but she looked to be at least eighty," she said.

"Actually, she's about your age," Liam said. "That's what three years with those boys will do."

She scowled at him. "That's not amusing."

Gabrielle turned back to Colm. "She loves those boys, but they're too much for her. They have too many people telling them what to do, and so they don't listen to anyone."

Colm nodded. "I'll talk to the woman."

Gabrielle was content knowing he would do what was necessary.

Two days later Gabrielle walked into the great hall carrying a basket of herbs and saw Ethan and Tom running up the stairs. Maurna, standing on the bottom step, watched with apprehension.

"Where are they going?" Gabrielle asked.

"To your chamber," Maurna answered.

Somewhat alarmed, Gabrielle was cautious to ask, "And why is that?"

"All of your things have been moved to the laird's chamber. The boys will be living here."

Maurna turned toward Gabrielle with a smile that showed she was resigned but also a little frantic.

"What about their aunt?" Gabrielle said.

"She will stay in her cottage. She is quite happy about this and said it is best for the boys. They will see her often."

Gabrielle was about to ask how the boys felt about their new living arrangements, but she heard squeals of laughter from upstairs. She had her answer.

FIFTY-ONE

IT WAS A GLORIOUS DAY. COLM HAD SURPRISED Gabrielle and taken her riding. They made their way to the spot overlook-ing the beauti-ful glen and slowed their horses to an easy walk.

Colm had never before left his duties to spend idle time with her, and Gabrielle was deeply suspicious of his motives.

"I have no other motive, Gabrielle," he told her. "I knew you wanted to ride Rogue, and so I decided to accommodate you."

"Faust would usually ride with me . . ." Her eyes widened in surprise. "You are being *thoughtful*!"

"Do you want to spend our time talking about why we are riding together, or would you prefer to actually ride?"

It was lovely having her husband all to herself, but the time slipped away too quickly.

He talked to her about Ethan and Tom. "They will be given chores that they can handle, and they may play when the chores are completed."

"Who will give them these chores and see that they are completed?"

He nudged his horse close so that he was beside her. Reaching over, he pulled her to him. "The mistress of my home."

He kissed her before she could argue. When he lifted his head, he said, "You did suggest that I delegate."

"Yes, but—"

"It's time that we get back," he said.

He'd sounded reluctant, she thought, and that pleased her. Perhaps he liked spending time alone with her as much as she did with him.

They were nearing the drawbridge when a soldier intercepted them.

"Laird, there is a messenger who says he comes from your wife's father."

"My father?" Gabrielle cried out.

Colm reached over and grabbed her reins so that she couldn't go racing off without him.

"Where is this messenger?"

"At the base of our mountain. The guards know not to let him come farther without first gaining your permission."

"Have him stay there. I will go to him to hear this message."

"Aye, Laird," he replied.

"Gabrielle, you will wait inside."

"I would prefer to go with you, husband."

"You will go inside."

She was through being diplomatic. "Perhaps I should explain a different way. I'm going with you. Before you deny me again, I will mention that I know my father's servants, and I could tell you if this messenger is from Wellingshire or not. Besides," she rushed on before he could interrupt, "I will still be on your land. You've let me ride to the overlook with my guards many times."

It was a sound argument, and he decided to change his mind.

She stayed behind him and slowed when she reached the sharp turn in the trail just above the dividing line between Finney's Flat and the mountain.

"Colm, what if he brings bad news?"

"Then we will hear it together."

She didn't have time to fret over that possibility, for once she had rounded the tight bend in the trail, she could see the messenger.

"It's Nigel!" she exclaimed. "He is one of my father's most loyal servants, and I have known him for years."

Gabrielle nudged Rogue to go faster as she called out a greeting to her father's steward. Nigel didn't wait for her to dismount, immediately handing her the scroll in his hands. She knew the missive to be genuine because it bore her father's seal. She was so excited she could barely contain herself as she read it.

"My father comes to see me . . . see us," she corrected, "and will be here by the end of the week. This is wonderful news, and I thank you, Nigel, for bringing it to me."

She looked up at Colm. "He will wish to refresh himself. May I offer him your hospitality?"

"You may." He motioned to one of his guards. "Take him to the kitchens."

As soon as Nigel was out of sight, she opened the message and read it to Colm.

"Daughter, I shall arrive at your new home

by week's end to see for myself that you are safe and well cared for. I have been told that you are married and that you are content. I shall judge for myself once I have met your husband and looked into your eyes.

"When I was told what you had endured at the abbey, I was enraged. I frantically searched for you. Word came from Laird Buchanan that you were safe and protected. My relief was great, Daughter, but my rage remained. I called up my vassals to prepare for war. Other barons joined me. The king has tried to make right the wrong Coswold and Percy have done, but I will not rest until both have paid for their sins."

There were tears of joy in Gabrielle's eyes when she looked at Colm. "My father is coming. This is happy news."

Colm lifted her onto Rogue's back. "If it makes you smile like that, then yes, it is happy news."

He handed her the reins and swung onto his mount.

"Oh, wait," Gabrielle said, unrolling the scroll again. "There's more to read." She studied the paper.

"What is it?" he asked.

"I will see you soon," she read. "And

please take my daughter to visit her dearest cousin at the Buchanans with all possible haste."

She didn't turn back to see his reaction as she rode away from him.

Colm followed, his laugh echoing across the valley.

ON MONDAY Braeden rode with Gabrielle to the bottom of the mountain to see if her father had started across Finney's Flat.

"Didn't the messenger give you the news just yesterday?" he asked.

"Yes, he did, Braeden."

"And didn't your father say he would be here at the end of the week?"

"Yes, he did, but my father often misjudges the time it takes to travel. He could be riding very fast," she explained.

Braeden could see her excitement. He didn't want to disillusion her with practicality, and so he said nothing more about the matter as they made the trip down the mountain.

Tuesday morning Colm left to attend a meeting. Laird Ramsey Sinclair had called on all the lairds to gather at his holding to discuss the recent events in the Highlands. There had been much unrest among the clans since the murder of Laird Monroe and the hostility provoked by Laird MacKenna. The Monroes were now undergoing a power struggle between two of the laird's nephews, and the MacKennas were left with no leader at all. Before things got out of hand, the lairds would meet at this summit and decide on a common course of action.

Colm could not say how long he would be away, but he assured Gabrielle that he would return in plenty of time to meet her father.

"Why must I always have an escort to look at the flats?" she asked. "I'm staying on our land. I'm perfectly safe."

"You'll be perfectly safe with an escort."

Tuesday afternoon she nagged Michael into riding with her. She came back two hours later.

Wednesday she coerced James. She returned in one hour.

Thursday Philip escorted her. It was raining, and she didn't get back for three hours.

Friday Michael rode with her again.

She didn't come back at all.

GABRIELLE HAD VANISHED. It happened at the sharp turn near the base of the mountain. Michael was riding ahead of her, and for no more than fifteen or twenty seconds Gabrielle was alone. But that was all the time they needed.

Michael thought she was right behind him. He could hear Rogue's hooves clipping over the stones. He knew his mistress had slowed the horse as was her habit just before she reached the turn. On one side was a drop with loose rocks. Rogue could lose his footing if he stepped too close. On the other was a cliff. Thorny scrub trees grew from it at perpendicular angles, like crooked tentacles reaching over the path. The thicket was so dense it muffled sound.

Gabrielle and the guard had been chatting amicably.

"I think the laird is going to widen this trail," he told her, "so you won't have to worry about your horse slipping."

Expecting a reply, he casually glanced over his shoulder. Rogue was still behind him, but Gabrielle was gone. He shouted to her and leaped from his mount. "Lady MacHugh?"

No answer. Thinking she had fallen, he shouted again as he ran back to the turn. "Are you hurt? Lady MacHugh, where are you?"

And still there was no answer. Michael bellowed to the sentry on the far ridge. "Did you see her? Our mistress . . ."

The soldier couldn't hear him, but the two sentries patrolling on the hill behind him did hear and sounded the alarm. The shouting spooked Rogue, and the skittish animal turned and bolted up the hill.

Frantic, Michael slid down the drop a ways to see if his mistress had taken a tumble. She wasn't there. Climbing back up, he then used his sword to hack some of the brush away, clinging to the hope that his mistress had somehow gotten stuck in the thorns and would soon be calling to him for help.

"She's not here. She's not here," he screamed, panic making his voice crack.

Within minutes the area was swarming with MacHugh soldiers, all searching for Gabrielle. Liam and Braeden, expert trackers, each took a section of the trail to look for footprints.

Michael had trampled most of the trail and cut through a great deal of the brush, so there was little evidence of where and how someone had gotten to Gabrielle. Liam walked farther down the slope where the trail leveled. He veered off the beaten path to the left where the ground was more dirt than rock. He walked a good distance. When he looked back, he could no longer see the trail.

"Braeden!" he bellowed.

Braeden, who had been searching the other side of the drop, came running.

"I'd say at least fifteen men," Liam estimated. He looked down at the soft ground that had been trampled by footprints and horseprints.

"I think more," Braeden said.

Liam walked back. Footprints angled off toward the thicket that reached all the way to the cliff. "It looks like a couple of them split off here."

Braeden followed him as he traced the broken and cut branches. When they reached the cliff overlooking the turn in the path, Liam stopped. "This is where they hid," he said. "They were waiting for her to pass beneath them."

"Look," Braeden said as he reached down and pulled something from a thorny twig. He raised a shred of green fabric in his fingertips. "Lady Gabrielle was wearing a green dress today." He looked bleakly at Liam. "I'll organize the men to search for these bastards. You take two soldiers and ride hard to Laird Sinclair's holding to give Colm this grim news."

Liam nodded. It was a duty he dreaded more than death.

FIFTY-TWO

GABRIELLE AWOKE WITH A POUNDING HEADACHE. She opened her eyes and tried to understand what was happening to her. She looked around a room that was unfamiliar, as was the bed she rested on. The ceiling was low, close enough for her to touch if she sat up. She was in some sort of loft. The smell in the air was musty and stale. Whatever this building was, it had not been used in a good long while. Sticks of straw poked her back, and the cover someone had thrown on her was rough against her face. She felt a sting on her cheek and reached up to touch it. When she lowered her hand, there was a trace of blood on her fingers. She then saw the scratches on her arm.

The fog slowly cleared from her mind. Rogue. She had been riding Rogue. And there was an animal. No, no. She *thought* the noise she heard was an animal foraging for food. There was a rustling sound. Then came a blinding pain.

Below, a door squeaked open, and she heard the shuffle of people filing inside. Gabrielle was suddenly wide awake. She wanted to crawl to the edge of the loft and look over, but was afraid she would be seen or heard.

She couldn't tell how many were underneath her until she heard their voices.

"You better hope she wakes up, Leod, 'cause if she don't, he's goin' to kill you and bury you on top of her. I ain't never seen anyone act like that. Did you see the crazed gleam in his eyes? It was like the devil was starin' out at me."

"I only did what I was told to do," Leod protested. "You heard what he said. Put her down quick before she can scream and then hand her off to you so you can carry her, and that's what I did, Kenny. I put her down. I don't care how mad he gets, we got stuck doin' all the work. While the rest of them are waitin' off to the east, we're crawlin' up the side of the cliff, tryin' not to make a sound while we push through that thicket. Waitin' on our bellies for hours and hours without movin' at all. The skin's torn off my hands and arms from the thorns. My legs are crampin', too. He shouldn't be yellin' at me or you 'cause we did the work."

"I know we did, but you shouldn't have used your sling to get her."

"It's what I use to get my birds."

"A woman ain't the same as a bird, Leod. Besides, you break your birds' necks."

"It's the only way I know to kill them and keep the fat on them for cookin'."

"You could have broken her neck."

"I used a small stone so I wouldn't."

"I sure hope she wakes up. Does my face look bloody?"

"It does. We should've had more help," he whined.

"We had Andrew right behind us."

"What good was he? He's so small and scrawny, he looks like he's ten, and he can't lift anything heavier than a bucket. He should have sent another man with us, not a boy."

"His looks are deceiving. He's near as old

as we are. He just looks young and puny, but I hear he's killed more than his share, and I'm meanin' people, not birds. He uses his knife on them. Strolls up lookin' so innocent and *bam!* in slides his blade."

"Did you ever see him do it?"

"No, but I heard others talkin' about it. I'd run fast if Andrew comes smilin' at me. You best go on up the ladder now and see if she's breathin'."

Gabrielle heard the sound of the ladder being dragged across the floor. The top slammed against the loft.

"I don't think this can hold me," Leod balked. "Get that kid. Make him do it."

"I told you. Andrew ain't no kid, and if he goes up, he'll diddle with her before he comes down."

Gabrielle closed her eyes, trying to still her pounding heart. She heard boots on the rungs of the ladder, and she lay perfectly still as the man came near her. He smelled foul.

He bumped his head on the sloped ceiling. The straw mattress shifted when he leaned over her. He put his hand on her chest, and while she pretended to be unconscious, his fingers moved across her breasts. She wanted to kill him.

He jerked his hand away when Kenny yelled at him. "Is she breathing or not?"

"She is, but she's still sleepin'." He shook her. "She won't open her eyes."

"Then get down here. I hear him comin'."

Leod muttered a curse as he climbed down.

"Leave the ladder where it is. He'll want to see her."

The door opened again, and the person they were waiting for entered. She didn't need to see his face to know who he was. As soon as he opened his mouth, she knew: Baron Coswold.

Gabrielle went from stunned disbelief to rage in less than a heartbeat. Why was Coswold here? What did he want from her now? But there was no time to try and understand his motives. Instead, she needed to find a way to escape.

"You're certain she sleeps?" Coswold demanded, and before Leod or Kenny could answer, he said, "How long have you been here? Were you talking? Did you say anything she might have heard?"

"We just came inside, didn't we, Kenny?" Leod said. "We didn't have time to talk. I walked in, got the ladder, and climbed to see if she was breathin' and if her eyes were open."

"She's alive," Kenny said.

"But she ain't awake."

"Bring her down here," Coswold ordered.

"But she ain't awake yet," Kenny reminded.

Gabrielle heard a scuffle, then "I'm gettin' her. I'm gettin' her for you."

The man climbed into the loft again and lifted Gabrielle off the bed. He carried her to the edge and dropped her limp body into waiting arms.

"Pull the chair out and put her there. Leod, get rope and tie her."

Gabrielle continued to feign sleep while she was pushed and prodded. Her head hung down, and her hair covered her face. She knew Coswold stood over her. She felt his beady eyes on her, heard his panting, and breathed in his sickeningly sweet per- fumed oils.

Leod wrapped a rope around her waist and pulled the ends tight behind the chair. Then he wound another rope around her wrists and tied it in a double knot.

"She's good and tied," he said. He sounded proud of his handiwork. "She can't get loose."

She felt the knots between her fingers and thought it might be a trick. Surely he knew that she would be able to undo the knots. Was he trying to prove she was awake? Or was he that stupid? She had her answer when he walked away.

"Get me a cup of water," Coswold commanded.

When he had the water in his hand, he said, "Get out. Both of you."

Kenny snickered. "He's wanting to be alone with her."

"What's he going to do with her tied to the chair?"

"Get out and stay out until I call you!" Coswold shouted.

As soon as the door closed behind the men, Coswold grabbed Gabrielle's hair and jerked her head back. He threw the water in her face.

She moaned and slowly opened her eyes. His horrible face was in front of hers.

"Wake up, Gabrielle. Wake up."

He deliberately hurt her, using the heel of his hand against her forehead to shove her head against the back of the chair. Then in contradiction he knelt down in front of her and very gently brushed her hair away from

her face, stroking her cheek with the backs
of his fingers.

His touch repulsed her.

He dragged a chair over and sat down
facing her. Bracing his hands on his knees,
he studied her curiously.

"I mean you no harm, Gabrielle."

She didn't respond. She saw the maniacal
look in his eyes.

"I want to ask you a question. That's all," he
said pleasantly. "When you have given me a
satisfactory answer, you may go home. Just
one question and one answer. You will coop-
erate, won't you?"

She didn't answer. He tilted his head and
studied her, waiting. Then suddenly he
lashed out and slapped her with the back of
his hand.

"Are you ready to hear my question?"

She refused to answer. He struck her
again. "Where is the gold?"

Before she had time to react, he said, "I
want the treasure of St. Biel. Where is it?"

She braced herself for another attack and
said, "There is no treasure."

He didn't hit her. "Yes, there is. I went to
St. Biel and became a believer. The king did
not send all the gold to the pope. He hid it."

"If that is true, he took the secret to his grave."

Coswold wagged his finger at her. "No, no. The secret has been passed down. Your mother knew, didn't she? And she told you."

"No, she couldn't tell me, because there is no treasure."

"The priest confirmed it. That's right. The envoy reported that when the priest brought it up, you said you wouldn't give it to the MacHughs. So you do know where it is."

"No, he did not mean gold."

He struck her again, cutting the corner of her lip. "I don't think you fully grasp my situation, Gabrielle. The treasure will free me from the king. I have been his pawn for the last time. Even if I could get away from him, I would have no allies. The barons see me as the royal lackey now. If the barons rebel, they will take me down with the king. So you see, I have nothing to lose."

She thought he wanted her to feel sorry for him. He was demented.

"I thought it would be so easy. I would ask for your hand and I would have you. I had heard the tales about hidden trea-sure, but I didn't believe them until the king sent me to St. Biel to make certain his steward wasn't cheating him. I looked at that magnificent palace and saw for myself several gold coins. I was told they were kept as reminders, but that the rest was sent to the pope."

Grinning, he tapped his head with his fingers. "But no one could say how much was there to begin with. The more people I asked, the more I was convinced that the king saved most of it for himself. And then I met an old man who had seen it . . . the gold . . . stacks and stacks of it. And it just disappeared. Where did it go, Gabrielle?"

"Greed has made you unreasonable. I speak the truth. There is no gold," she said.

He sighed dramatically. "Yes, there is. After all I've done . . . yes, there is."

"I cannot tell you, for I do not know where it is."

"Then you admit that it exists." He acted as though he had just tricked her into a confession.

She shook her head. "No."

He sat back, crossed one leg over the other and began to lazily swing his foot back and forth.

A long minute passed in silence. Then her fear turned to terror.

"Do you love your father?" he asked.

She gave a sharp cry. "Where is he? What have you done?"

"What have I done? Nothing yet. Your father doesn't travel with many men to protect him from ambush. He made it easy for me. I have watched him make his way toward the MacHugh holding. I knew exactly where to attack. Don't worry. He's still alive, though his condition is deteriorating. Tell me where the gold is and I will let him live."

When she didn't immediately answer him, Coswold said, "Do you think I might be lying? How did I know Baron Geoffrey was on his way here? It will be easy enough to get proof. I will send some of my men to him. If they cut off his hand and bring it to you, you will see for yourself the ring with his seal still on his finger."

"No!" she screamed. "You would not dare kill a baron."

"I wouldn't? Why wouldn't I? I've already killed a laird."

"Monroe? You killed Laird Monroe?"

He shrugged. "I couldn't let him have you. I needed to be able to talk to you about the gold. MacKenna didn't care what I did with you as long as he got Finney's Flat. Of course, he knew nothing about the treasure. I doubt he would have been so agreeable then. He proved useless to me alive, but now that he is dead, he has been helpful, for we sit inside a crofter's cottage tucked away on his land. His clan is in such disarray, they have no idea we're here."

"My husband will come for me."

"He will have to find you first, and I made certain my men went in every direction to cover their tracks. Are you willing to lose your father *and* your husband?"

"No."

"Then tell me where the gold is and be quick about it. We cannot sit here for days on end. Your husband would indeed find us then, and I would have to kill him."

"I will tell you."

His gasp sounded like a snarl. "Yes, yes, tell me."

"It's in Wellingshire," she lied. "And well-hidden."

He laughed. "Gold at Wellingshire and your father—"

"Mother could not tell him. I am the only one who knows. It belongs to the royal family of St. Biel."

"You will have to tell me exactly where it

is, for Wellingshire is nearly the size of a small country. Is it hidden in the castle?"

"No, it's buried."

"Where?" he demanded. A wild expression contorted his face, so great was his obsession.

"I must show you. It's the only way. As you said, the estate is vast."

"Then we will go to Wellingshire."

"If my husband finds out, he will follow us, and I will not let you kill him. You must send him in the opposite direction."

"How will I send word?"

"My husband can read and write."

"But how—"

"I could write a message telling him that I escaped and now am safe with my father. I would ask him to come for me."

"The MacKennas," he said, nodding. "You will tell your husband they are the ones who took you."

By the time Coswold finished telling her what to say, he believed the idea for the message was his. He called to Leod to find something to write with, and it took an hour before the man returned with ink and a piece of parchment.

Gabrielle wrote exactly what had been decided, but before she signed her name, she looked up at Coswold. "I do not want the messenger killed before he has a chance to give my husband the message. Is there a boy you could send? Not so young that he couldn't ride and not so old he would be thought a man. My husband would not kill a boy."

"Yes," Coswold said. "I will get a boy to take the parchment. Now, finish. It is growing dark, but at the first morning light we will be gone."

While Coswold paced about the cottage, Gabrielle added her final words to the message: "Please come quickly and I will forever do as you say."

BY THE TIME Liam got to the Sinclair holding, Colm was on his way home, having taken another route. Liam turned around and headed back, this time on the northern road. He caught up with Colm as he was about to cross Finney's Flat.

Colm saw him coming. A sense of dread gripped him.

"Gabrielle," Liam shouted, "she is gone! She's been taken."

"Who? Who took her?"

"I don't know," he said. "Maybe by the time you reach Braeden he will know something."

Colm's rage could not be contained. It blurred his thoughts. "If any harm comes to her . . ."

"Do not think it," Liam ordered.

But that was all Colm could think about on the frantic ride home. He could not lose her.

Night had fallen as he rode up the trail to his holding. He prayed that she had been found and was waiting to greet him. He would tell her then—shout it to the sky—that he loved her. She should have heard the words before. It could not be too late.

At the ridge one of his sentries shouted to him. "There . . . coming across the flat. One rider."

Colm and Liam turned to see a shadow approaching. In the full moon, they could make out the figure of a man on horseback. They rode to meet him, reaching him before he had time to dismount.

"I bring a message for the laird," the man said, his voice trembling. He put his hand in his shirt and pulled out the scrolled parchment.

"Who are you?" Liam asked.

"My name is Andrew."

"Who asked you to bring this to the laird?"

"He was a MacKenna. I am from the Dunbar clan. I was on my way home from hunting when the man stopped and asked me to bring this to you. He said it was most urgent. I do not know what it says, for I cannot read."

Colm grabbed the message from him and read. He handed it to Liam and pointed to the last words. "As you say" was underlined.

He ripped the man from the saddle and held him by the neck. His voice was deadly when he said, "What my wife tells me is that everything I have just read is a lie. And that means you are lying, too."

"I am just the messen—"

Colm cut off his air, squeezing his neck. He didn't let up until Andrew's eyes were bulging out of their sockets. In only minutes, Andrew had told him everything he wanted to know.

Colm gave Liam the order. "Tie him to his horse and bring him. If he lies again, he will pray for death."

ANDREW LED THEM to the cottage.

Colm knew Gabrielle was inside. He had to be cautious. The light from a single candle glowed through the window and he could smell smoke from the chimney. Coswold's soldiers were bedded down for the night around a campfire south of the cottage, where the grass was soft. Their fire burned low.

Braeden made his way through the dark to count the number and then returned to Colm. Slowly the MacHugh soldiers circled until the men and the cottage were surrounded. When they were in position, they moved forward. Colm crept up behind the guard in front of the door and killed him before he could make a sound. He lowered the man to the ground, then tested the door. It was bolted against him. He raised his hand to give the signal, and then he kicked the door open and charged inside.

Coswold had been sleeping in a chair and bolted to his feet at the sound of the door crashing in. He fumbled at his belt for his dagger, but it was too late. He knew he was going to die.

Leod had been sitting on the edge of the loft with his legs dangling down as Gabrielle sat on the straw mattress behind him.

"Kill her!" Coswold shouted.

The words weren't out of his mouth before Gabrielle, using every ounce of strength she had, thrust her whole body at Leod's back and sent him flying headfirst to the floor. He landed on his face, his neck broken.

Colm made the kill quickly. He cut Coswold's throat and tossed the bloody blade to the floor.

He shouted for his wife and ran to the ladder to reach for her. She fell against him sobbing.

"I knew you would come."

He held her tight and tried to calm his heart. "I would not lose you, Gabrielle."

She pulled back. "Colm, my father," she cried. "Coswold's army will kill him. They have . . ."

Colm stopped her. "Your father is with the Buchanans this night."

"You are certain?" she asked incredulously.

"Yes, Brodick was informed at the summit that your father had arrived. He was too weary to come any farther. You will see him tomorrow."

He lifted her into his arms.

She laid her head on his shoulder. "Take me home."

FIFTY-THREE

GABRIELLE'S FATHER DIDN'T TAKE TO COLM RIGHT away. Nor did Colm particularly like the baron. They were polite, but wary of each other.

Her father softened his attitude when he saw how Colm treated Gabrielle. It was clear to him that the laird loved her and would cherish her. Colm softened his attitude toward the baron when he saw how much he loved his daughter and how she loved him.

Willa made a special dinner of roasted pheasant and so many other dishes that Gabrielle lost count. Each time Willa carried a platter to the table, she smiled at Gabrielle.

Liam strolled in and was introduced to the baron. He said, "Did Gabrielle tell you how she saved my life?"

"I must hear this story," the baron said.

"Milady, if I could borrow you for a moment?" Maurna interrupted.

Gabrielle excused herself and followed Maurna up the stairs.

"I let Mary go home early tonight," Maurna said. "She's a good help with these two boys, and I thank you for adding her to your household. I thought the twins were down for the night. I came up to look in on them and caught them coming out of the laird's chamber."

Standing at the top of the stairs, Ethan and Tom waited with their heads down.

"I'm sorry, milady," Ethan said.

"Me, too," Tom said.

"Tell your mistress what you did," Maurna said. She was trying to be stern, but Gabrielle heard the tenderness in her voice. She knew the boys could, too.

"We just wanted to look in the trunk," Tom said without lifting his eyes.

"My trunk?" Gabrielle asked. "Why would you want to look in there?"

Ethan lifted his shoulders. "I don't know, but we did."

Tom nodded. "I found a statue in there."

"I found one, too," Ethan admitted.

"But I didn't break mine. You broke yours."

"Boys, the statues don't belong to either of you," Maurna said.

Tom took Gabrielle's hand. "Ethan's sorry."

"I'll leave them to you, Lady Gabrielle, while I go to your room and see to the damage."

"I'll take care of it, Maurna. You may go downstairs."

Gabrielle took the twins into their room and tucked them into bed. She talked to them about respecting privacy and made them promise not to go into their laird's room again without permission. Then she kissed them good night and closed the door.

On the way down the corridor, she thought to ask Colm to permanently remove the lid from the trunk. If the boys were to climb in it and the heavy lid were to close, they could be seriously hurt.

A fire warmed the chamber. The trunk lid was propped open against the wall, and one statue of St. Biel lay half in and half out, hanging dangerously on the edge. The other was on the floor and missing a head.

She picked up both pieces and moved

close to the fire to see if the stone could be repaired. Holding the body at an angle, she noticed something that caught the light. She tipped the statue and examined it more closely. She froze. Gold. The core of the stone piece had been hollowed out and filled with gold. She couldn't believe what she was seeing. She looked again. The gold was there.

Gabrielle had to sit down. She went to the bed and put the pieces in her lap.

The myth wasn't a myth? King Grenier had really hidden gold? She was dumbfounded. Then she thought, if the gold was in one statue, could it be in another? She had to find out. She gently placed the broken pieces on the bed and ran to the trunk to get the other one. She winced as she banged it against the stone hearth. It took three tries before the head broke off.

"Sorry, St. Biel," she whispered.

And there it was. Gold. The second statue was filled with gold, too.

She had to sit down again. It was all too much to take in. The statue in the storeroom had to be filled with gold as well. There was no need to break it.

Another statue was coming from

Wellingshire. The statue her mother brought with her when she married. Did her mother know the secret of St. Biel?

One thought led to another and another, and soon her mind was spinning. Was the giant statue overlooking the harbor in St. Biel filled with gold? She began to laugh. Of course it was. Oh, what a clever man King Grenier had been.

She sat on the bed a long time as she thought about the story her mother had helped her memorize. Once upon a time in the year of . . . The hints were there, but had her mother figured it out? And if she had, did she tell her husband?

Gabrielle didn't know how long she sat in a daze. She put the broken pieces back in the trunk and closed it.

When she returned to the hall, her father appeared to be more relaxed. Colm looked relieved to see her. He kissed her quickly, and said, "I will leave you to talk with your father." In a lower voice he added, "Come to bed soon."

Liam also took his leave so that she and her father could have a private conversation. Gabrielle sat close to him in front of the fire.

Before he could ask, she blurted, "I love him, Father."

He nodded. "I can see that you do."

She spent the next ten minutes telling him about Colm's many virtues.

"Do you think you will ever marry again, Father? I would be pleased if you did. I do not like to think of you being lonely."

"Perhaps."

"If you aren't too weary, I have questions to ask you . . . about St. Biel."

GABRIELLE LAY beside her husband and whispered sweet words to him. They had just made love, and she was still breathless. They had spoken briefly about Coswold, but now in the darkness she told him how frightened she had been.

"I was afraid I would not see you again."

"I could not bear to lose you," he whispered. His voice shook. "I will say this now. I love you, Gabrielle."

Tears welled up in her eyes. "You love me," she whispered. She leaned up and kissed his chin. "You have just given me the gift my father gave to my mother."

"Love was his gift?"

"It was. And it was a long time coming, I

think. For my mother anyway. She did not like Father much when they were wed. He took her from her home in St. Biel. I thought it would take you much longer to give me the words. You were forever leaving me."

He laughed. "I will admit this only once. You worried me. You had this power over me. I would lose my thoughts when I was with you. But no more will I leave you. Liam and Braeden will be given much more responsibility so I will have time with you."

They stayed quiet for a few minutes, and then she whispered, "Do you like my father?"

"I do not know him well enough to like him. He is a gruff man. He was not pleased to see the scratches on your arms and face, but when he heard Coswold was responsible, he could no longer blame me."

"The boys got into my trunk today."

He laughed. "They came in here . . ."

"They were curious. You will have to remove the lid. I fear one of them will get trapped inside."

"We'll go to the Buchanans in a few days' time so that you may meet your dearest cousin," he teased. "I think perhaps we will take Ethan and Tom with us and forget to bring them home."

"You will not leave them. They are content here. Ethan broke one of my statues."

He yawned. "He did?"

"It was filled with gold."

"It was *what*?"

"Gold," she whispered. "The statue was filled with it. I broke another one just to see, and there was gold inside it as well."

His reaction was much like hers. He was astounded. "There really is a treasure."

Gabrielle repeated the story her mother had taught her. When she was finished, she said, "Now that I know there is gold inside each statue, I realize how clever King Grenier was. The Crusaders were going to kill his loyal subjects because he made them pay a toll to pass over his mountains. They believed the country was filled with heathens, so what did the king do? He dedicated the country to a saint and changed its name, then sent a token amount of the gold to the pope. The Crusaders wouldn't dare harm any of his people. An attack on them would be an attack on the pope."

"Why would the king keep the gold hidden all that time?"

"My mother told my father that the king was a wise man. He knew that great wealth can also provoke great greed. His countrymen were content."

"And greed would corrupt their way of life."

"Yes."

Colm smiled. "Aye, he was clever to use his favorite saint to help save his country."

"There is more to tell. I asked my father, and he told me my suspicions were true." She stretched up to whisper in his ear. "There is no St. Biel."

A long silence followed, and then Colm said, "He made up the saint . . ."

"He saved his people the only way he knew how," she defended. "I wonder, though, what the church leaders would think if they knew. I cannot tell them."

"No, you cannot."

"King John rules St. Biel now, and he will not get the treasure. I will keep it safe, and one day my daughters and sons will hear the story, and it will become their duty to protect it."

Colm laughed again. "No wonder the statues are never placed inside the churches."

"It is tradition."

"Started by a king who knew it would be blasphemous."

"I will let our children and their children worry about the church."

"But you must pass the secret on," he said as he gently pushed her onto her back. "And I will do my part, love, to make certain you have sons and daughters."

ABOUT THE AUTHOR

JULIE GARWOOD is the author of numerous *New York Times* bestsellers, including *Shadow Dance, Slow Burn, Murder List, Killjoy, Mercy, Heartbreaker, Ransom,* and *Come the Spring.* There are more than thirty-two million copies of her books in print.